The Background:

England in 2066, is bizarre mix of backwards ideology and innovative technology. 'The Rulers' were voted into power in 2043. Their party, The True Order, used the slogan, 'Enough is enough.' They promised to re-establish law and order, end handouts to those who wouldn't work and bring back 'good old fashioned values.' The regime seemed tough but people wanted it.

The Rulers gradually turn the country into a dictatorship, abolishing the voting system. They bring back public hangings, which are televised. They reintroduce workhouses, for those who can't work. Poverty spreads, as does disease. The New Plague, a mysterious disease that seems mainly to afflict the poor, becomes rife. People are dying in their thousands, but The Rulers do nothing to stop it.

People mainly live in Tech-Cities, where they are protected from vigilante groups who won't conform. The roads are quiet, only the rich can afford magnetised cars. International trade is limited, as travel between countries has mainly broken down in the effort to reduce carbon emissions and keep out terrorism. Everyone is forced to call their children names that teach what The Rulers consider to be valuable qualities; names such as Chastity, Benevolence and Silence.

Breaking Up

Breaking Up

First published 2019 in Great Britain by GoApe Books.
An imprint of:

Monkey Island Publishing
Hurgill Road
Richmond
North Yorkshire
DL10 4SZ

Text copyright © 2019 Karen Langtree
Design and typography by Gill McLean
1st Edition published 2019
The moral rights of Karen Langtree have been asserted

ISBN 978-0-9930636-6-4

To Anne.

Part III

Enjoy the finale!

Part III

1

They stood, huddled together, around three gaping holes.

Only ten people had dared to gather, to pay their respects. Fear and grief mingled in a deadly concoction, twisting their tendrils around the group.

No one spoke.

At first glance, the group could have been mistaken for a circle of standing stones, silhouetted against the breaking dawn.

The rising sun mocked the sombre mood, shooting spokes of dazzling light across the sky. Refracted by the clouds, they burst into a backdrop of glorious amber, rose and yellow. But the darkness, in the hearts of the mourners, was too deep to be moved by the beauty of the sky.

Kate glanced upwards and wished it was raining. Raining so hard that her grief might be drowned by a volley of water lashing her face. Instead, she stood nestled into Nick, his arm tightly around her, squinting against the brightness of the new day.

A few years ago, Pastor Rowley had consecrated this makeshift burial ground on the wasteland, near the building they called Church. The church was merely a disused office block on a derelict trading estate in Newcastle. Other members of The Way were buried here; their graves arranged in an unsystematic fashion, so that it didn't look like a graveyard. Each was marked by a small fish symbol carved into a stone. The sign used by persecuted Christians, in the first century, to secretly communicate their allegiance to Christ.

Kate shivered, despite the warmth of the sun seeping through her jacket. Nick had moved to help the other men, as they lifted the three shrouded bodies out of the estate car. There were no coffins. There hadn't been time. It was only three days since Si had returned to them, unwittingly carrying a more deadly and infectious strain of plague than the one they had already encountered. He thought he had escaped from the Rulers, but it didn't take long to realise that it had all been staged for the purpose of carrying this new virus into the heart of the rebellion. He had begun to show signs of fever within a couple of hours of being reunited with his mother. She had acted fast, but not before several people had hugged him and spent time with him.

And now, here they were. Three bodies already, and several very sick, in isolation, in the church behind them; including Honour and Ethan.

As soon as she realised what was happening, Kate had isolated Si and anyone who had been near him, since his return. Quickly, most of them fell sick with abdominal pains, fever, chills and vomiting. The symptoms came on so fast that, before she knew it, the first person was dead. Panic had spread like wildfire amongst the followers, and many left, despite Kate and Nick's protests that they should stay here and not risk carrying the plague to others. But they were afraid. They wouldn't listen.

She and Nick were working desperately to find a cure. The current NMBs were not having the desired effect, leading her to believe that this wasn't the same as the previous strain of plague. She suspected that the only reason she and Nick had not succumbed, was because they had both been infected with the previous virus in order to trial the Nanomedibots, and this had somehow protected them. If so, she didn't understand why Si had succumbed to the new plague, when he had also taken part in the trials in Amsterdam. Her only guess was that the Rulers had injected him directly with a massive dose of the new strain.

All she had thought about and done for the last seventy-two hours, was search for a way to modify the NMBs, in order to combat this virus. She had not slept at all, despite Nick's attempts to persuade her to have an hour here and there. He had been just as busy, supervising the care of the sick, and trying to prevent more people from being infected.

Now, standing here, at the side of these gaping graves, Kate wrenched her mind away from all that. Just for these few minutes, she was here for the dead; the ones she had not been able to save. Her stomach clenched, and she choked back a sob, as they lowered the first body into the grave. Muffled sorrow from the group turned into louder individual sobs and crying.

The second body was lowered into its grave. Tears were now running down her face. She turned her eyes to the third shroud and held her breath, as it was lifted out of the car. The men fixed the straps around it to lower it into the hole.

A woman next to Kate hissed, 'This is your fault!' Then she spat on her and walked away from the mourners.

Kate's legs buckled, and she sank to the ground. Her breath burst from her body and she couldn't hold back the choking sobs. Several of the women began to wail loudly, despite being urged to quieten down, for fear of being discovered by law-keepers. Nick looked over to Kate, desperately wanting to go to her, but he was holding one of the straps around the body, helping to steady its descent into the grave.

'Rebecca!' The woman's husband shouted at the retreating figure. Then he knelt on the ground beside Kate. 'I'm sorry about that. She's very upset. Of course, you are too, and... Here.' He took out a packet of tissues and handed one to her. She took it, thinking it wouldn't do much good. Her face was covered in snot and tears.

When the bodies were in the graves, Nick returned to Kate. He looked disdainfully at the man whose wife had mistreated her. Then, he helped her to her feet and held her close, stroking her hair and murmuring what comfort he could think of.

'Ssh! You're doing everything you can. You couldn't have saved him. You couldn't have saved any of these. But, there's a chance with the others. Ssh! Come on now.'

She couldn't speak, but buried her head into his shoulder, as someone began to sing quietly.

The Lord's my Shepherd, I'll not want.

He makes me down to lie
In pastures green. He leadeth me,
The quiet waters by.'

Others joined in, barely above a whisper.

'Yea though I walk in death's dark vale,
Yet will I fear no ill,
For thou art with me, and thy rod
And staff, me comfort still.'

As the hymn faded, Nick moved to help shovel earth into the graves.

'Wait!' said a woman. 'Someone should say something; a blessing or a prayer. The Pastor would have done it, if...' she choked on her words and looked pointedly at Kate.

Rebecca's husband stepped forward. A hush fell. 'O Lord, we commend these souls into your safe-keeping. Take care of our dear brothers and sister; your precious children. May they have life everlasting. Amen.' He stepped back, next to Kate and squeezed her arm, in gentle reassurance.

Nick, and the other men, filled in the graves and two women laid out the stones with fish symbols on them. People began to walk away, but Nick and Kate stood for a few more minutes, looking at the three mounds, neither of them able to say anything to the other.

Finally, Kate looked up at the make-shift isolation ward behind her. She blew her nose, wiped her eyes and took a deep breath. 'Time for the dead is over. We have to fight for the living now.'

2

With Pastor Rowley dead, the sheep had lost their shepherd. Those who blamed her, left The Way, in fear and disgust. Those who stayed, did all they could to help Kate, in love for their Pastor and loyalty to the cause.

Si was still seriously ill. His vital signs were not good. He had a raging temperature, and his breathing was fast and shallow. Fits of delirium and hallucinations kept overtaking him. Kate had injected him immediately with an NMB, but it seemed to be having little effect, except that he was still alive.

Since then, she had managed to make alterations to the NMBs in a make-shift lab in the church building, but she was very uncertain as to their safety. Because Si and the others were showing no signs of improvement, she was forced to inject the modified NMBs. She had no idea what effect they would have and could only hope and pray that they would cure the virus. She was sure that several people would die in the next 24 hours, including Honour and Si, if this didn't work.

Exhausted, Nick had forced her to lie down on one of the camp beds they had been sleeping on, in another room. He reassured her that the patients were being monitored closely and that he would wake her at the first sign of improvement in any of them.

Peter came into the kitchen area as Nick was grabbing a quick coffee. Fortunately, Peter had been away from the Pastor's house, when Si had arrived back, talking to contacts he had, about finding a better place for them to work from. When Si started to show signs of being very ill, they had warned him to stay away, but since they felt sure they had contained the infectious people now, he had returned for the funeral of Pastor Rowley and the other two people.

'Any news?' he asked.

Nick told him about the new NMBs as he handed Peter a cup of coffee and they sat down. 'I only have a few minutes. I must get back to the isolation ward and keep an eye on what's going on. Thanks for sending us the decontamination suits, it's meant a few more people can help out on the ward.'

Peter nodded. 'I've found us a place to set up a headquarters for the rebellion.'

'Great. Where?'

'You know the Angel of the North?'

'Of course,' Nick said.

The Angel of the North was a steel sculpture erected at the end of the 20th Century. It was located just south of Gateshead and had become an iconic symbol of the North East of England. It towered 20 metres above the ground, stretching out it's plane-like wingspan of 54 metres, protectively, across the hillside.

'Most people know what it looks like above ground but not below. It's anchored to rock, 21 metres below the surface by 600 tonnes of concrete.'

Nick's forehead creased, wondering what this had to do with anything. 'And?'

'This is top secret, but the previous government created a substantial underground bunker beside the Angel, long before the days of The Rulers. It's never been used but I've managed to get access to it.'

Nick nodded. 'Wow! You certainly know some top people!'

Peter smiled. 'Yes. It's very secure. The entrance is through a camouflaged door in the hillside, leading to a tunnel. This leads down into the earth to the blast doors. They weigh a hefty one and a half tonnes, and they're going to keep out any unwanted visitors.'

'Don't the Rulers have access to it?'

'They may have access to the outside tunnel, but once those blast doors are locked from the inside, no one on the outside can open them.'

'And you have access to it?'

'I do now.'

Peter produced, from around his neck, a large key, used in the 21st century to open padlocks.

'That's it?' Nick asked, incredulously. 'Just a padlock?'

Peter laughed. 'Just a padlock. Pretty weighty, but nothing more. Remember, no one knows the place exists.'

'Hard to believe,' Nick said. 'People have visited that site for over half a century. What's it like inside? Have you been down there?'

'Not yet,' Peter replied. 'I hoped you and Kate might come with me to see if you think it would be a suitable HQ.'

Nick frowned. 'You know we're frantically trying to save the victims of this new plague. We're flat out here. I'm just grabbing a coffee and then back to work. Until we can be sure we've conquered it, we can't really think about anything else.'

Peter stood up and peered out of the dirty window, overlooking the industrial estate. 'I understand, but the Rulers are going to find you here before long. Rumours of the new plague are already spreading. How long before Zephyr rounds us all up?' He turned back to Nick. 'Maybe you and I could go. Do you think she could move the patients?'

Nick blew out his cheeks and sighed. 'They're in quarantine. It would be difficult without attracting attention and risking more infection. I'll talk to her. I'll arrange to come and look over the place with you.'

Peter nodded. 'Good. You, me, Kate; we're all on the wanted list. We need to move fast.'

'Are you feeling okay?' Nick added. 'Any symptoms?'

'I'm fine.'

'Good. I persuaded Kate to lie down finally, so I need to get back to the patients. Speak later?'

Peter smiled wearily. 'I'm heading back to Pastor Rowley's house. I'll see you later.'

On the make-shift ward, Nick spoke to the volunteer carers and checked the patients. It was only a few hours since Kate had injected them with the modified NMBs. Honour's father, Ethan, was not responding to anything. He appeared to have lapsed into a coma. His vital signs were not good; only a faint pulse and shallow breathing.

Nick checked the others. Si's temperature had reduced. A good sign. Honour's also. They were less feverish and lay more peacefully. Other patients were in varying states. But there were some good signs.

Someone tapped him on the shoulder. It was hard to see who it was at first with the contamination suits on, but as he turned, he recognised Kate.

He felt annoyance rising, but fought it back. 'What are you doing here? You can't have had more than half an hour's sleep.'

She touched his arm. 'Power nap. It'll help, but I couldn't stay away. How are they?'

'Some good signs,' Nick said. 'But I don't like the look of Ethan and a couple of the others.'

He took her over to their beds and she also examined them. Death was hovering in the wings here and it didn't seem like the new NMBs had made any difference.

She went over to Si's bed. 'He looks slightly better.'

'Yeah. Temperature receding.'

She stayed with him for a moment, taking his hand and talking to him, then saying a whispered prayer for his recovery, as she did all the time.

'We should see more signs of improvement in the next couple of hours if these new NMBs are having a positive effect,' she said, as Nick came across to her.

Nick squeezed her shoulder. 'I need to talk to you about something Peter's just told me. Is there anything else you need to do here now, or can you spare a few minutes?'

She nodded. They were heading out of the ward when someone shouted, 'Doctor Reece! He's not breathing!'

Kate's heart missed a beat. They turned and ran towards the volunteer who was calling them. She was standing over Ethan.

Nick went into action. 'Get the...'

'Already got it, Doctor.'

Nick checked for pulse and breathing. Finding neither, he placed the defibrillator pads on the chest and hit a button. A long beep rang out in the silence. "Stand clear!" Nick ordered, pressing the button again.

Ethan's body shuddered as electricity coursed through his heart. Nick looked at the screen.

'Anything?' Kate asked, hopefully.

Nick put his fingers to Ethan's neck to feel for a pulse, but shook his head.

'I'll start compressions,' Kate said.

After a few interminable seconds there was still no sign of life. Nick pressed the button on the defibrillator again.

'Stand clear!'

Ethan's body jerked and they looked at the screen, ever hopeful that his heart would start again, but there was still no sign of life. They had limited resources here and Nick was angry, knowing that if they could get to a hospital there might be more that could be done. He began compressions again, but nothing was changing. They kept trying to resuscitate him, but eventually Kate laid her hand on Nick's arm and he turned to her, knowing that it was time to give up. Ethan was gone.

They instinctively looked across to Honour. Her father had helped them so much. Please God, let Honour survive, Kate thought. It would be bad enough having to break the news to Sarah that her husband was dead.

They helped move the body to a temporary morgue, set up at the other end of the room, hidden by a screen. Then, as the volunteers prepared Ethan's body, they left the quarantine ward and took off their suits.

'Are you alright?' Nick asked, taking her by the arms and looking into her face.

She shook her head. She was crying again. Nick wiped the tears from her cheeks. She sniffed. 'I'll be fine. Just got to carry on and pray that the NMBs are going to work for the others. Ethan was already too far gone for the NMBs to be effective.'

Nick pulled her to him and held her. She was fighting back more tears, knowing that if she gave in to them, she might cry for a long time. She pushed him away and took a deep breath. 'Thanks, but I need to hold it together, and hugs just make me want to let go.'

Nick led her to the kitchen and made her sit down.

'Tell me about Peter's news,' she said, as Nick boiled the kettle.

He told her about the bunker.

She sighed. 'I think it would be impossible to move the sick right now without contaminating a whole load of new people. We only have a limited number of suits. I'm still working on an NMB that injects a preventative against this new strain of plague. Our immunity surprised me, especially since Si succumbed to it. But if I use the knowledge I'm gaining, I hope to be able to inoculate against it soon. I could continue my work at the bunker though. I imagine it'll have a medical facility. It might even be better than what we are making do with here.'

Nick pulled his hands through his hair. 'Peter wants me to go with him, as soon as possible to check it out.'

Kate shook her head. 'You can't go anywhere until we know if the NMBs are making any difference.'

*

It was early evening. Kate was in her make-shift lab, working on the NMBs, when one of the volunteers came hurrying in to find her.

'Kate! Doctor Reece said to tell you to come, quick! It's your son!'

Kate threw down her instruments and followed as the woman ran from the room. 'Is he worse?' she asked, frantically pulling on the contamination suit. 'Is he still alive?'

'I don't know,' said the woman, as she pulled her suit back on. 'Doctor Reece just said to hurry and get you.'

The worst-case scenario was playing in her head. She tried to calm her breathing but prepared herself to look on the lifeless body of her son. Tears were already threatening. No! She wouldn't allow herself to believe it yet. Her heart was pounding as she fumbled with the fastenings on the suit. Please God, don't let him be dead already! Please, please, please! She repeated the mantra as she rushed into the ward.

Nick was standing by Si's bed.

She hardly dared to look down at the bed. 'What is it?'

'Look,' Nick said.

Si's eyes were open, and he smiled, weakly. 'Hi Mum.'

His voice was hoarse, his skin pale and his eyes sunken, but he had spoken for the first time since the fever had taken hold. There was hope.

She wanted to tear off the contamination suit and hug him. Instead, she knelt beside him, putting her gloved hand over his. 'How are you feeling?'

His voice was barely above a whisper. 'I don't know. Better than I have been, probably.'

Nick's smile was optimistic. 'His temperature is lower. His pulse is strong. BP is almost normal.'

'I've got a sore throat and I'm really thirsty,' Si rasped.

The volunteer, who was staring wide-eyed at Si, reached for a glass and held it to his mouth. 'Just sip.'

'This is a really good sign,' Kate said, squeezing his hand.

'Definitely,' Nick said. 'I think you might have done it, Kate.'

She looked around the ward. 'Anyone else improving?'

'Yes. Less fever. Vital signs steadying, apart from the ones we already thought were beyond help,' Nick said. 'I've isolated them further.'

Si tried to sit up, but he couldn't move more than his head.

'Don't try to move,' Kate said. 'Just rest.'

He turned his head, seeing the other patients around him, for the first time. 'What happened here?'

'I'll tell you the full story soon, but for now you need to rest. Keep getting stronger. We want you out of here.' Kate smiled properly for the first time since he had begun to show signs of the plague.

'I need to get back to the Citadel,' he said. 'We have to get Chas out of there.'

'You're not going anywhere 'til you're better,' Nick said, firmly. He and the volunteer walked away, giving Kate a few minutes alone with her son.

She attempted to hold back tears, but they slid down her cheeks.

'Hey. Don't cry, Mum. I'm going to be okay.'

She smiled. 'I'm just thankful. I think you really have come through. Feels like a miracle. I couldn't bear to lose you as well.'

'What was wrong with me?'

'They infected you with a different strain of plague and sent you back to us. You didn't escape, Si. It was a deliberate attempt to kill you and the rest of us.'

Anger welled in his chest, like a geyser about to burst. He struggled to sit, but Kate laid a hand on his chest. 'Keep still, you're not out of danger yet.'

'I knew there was something odd going on when they drove me away from the Citadel.' Si swore; not something he did often.

Kate looked at him in surprise. 'Keep calm, son. I shouldn't have told you yet.'

'Yes, you should. Anger is a force for good. Maybe that's as good for me as rest, to motivate me to get better.' As he finished his sentence he began to cough violently. Kate gave him the water and made him sip it, until the fit stopped.

'Lie still now. Save your thoughts of vengeance until you're up and well. Just concentrate on getting better.'

He closed his eyes as Kate stroked his hair like she used

to when he was a child. The anger and coughing had made him feel much weaker again, but he was determined to recover and fight back. He thought of Chas as he drifted back to sleep. *I'm coming. Hold on.*

3

It was a couple of weeks since Chas had watched Si being driven from the Citadel, on CCTV. She had surrendered the scalpel, with which she had threatened to kill herself, and given in to her fate. Premier Zephyr had promised that Si would be released, in order to appease her. And, as if to reinforce what she had seen on the CCTV, every time she was allowed to watch some news, she heard that Silence Hunter had escaped. There was a price on his head, which meant that she had been partially deceived. They had let him go, but they were hunting him down. She was angry, of course, with herself as much as with Zephyr, for being stupid enough to trust him. And the next time Zephyr came to see her she would tell him what she thought of him.

It was mid-afternoon and Chas was walking in the rooftop garden of the Complex where she was being held captive. Despite being a prisoner in the Fortress, she felt an incongruous sense of peace in this garden. There was something about it that helped her to feel calm and centred. It might be the closeness to the sky or the sense of being outdoors, surrounded by trees and plants, despite the dome separating her from fresh air.

It was still sinking in that she was carrying two human

lives inside her. The thought made her feel nauseous. Or was it just morning sickness? She had been told that she wouldn't experience this for a few weeks. Maybe it was fear making her feel like this. Yet, even though the pregnancy had been forced upon her, she felt a tug of curiosity. What would these children look and act like? Would they react to things in exactly the same ways she and Si did? Would they have the same personalities? She assumed they would look identical to her and Si when they were children. What did the Rulers intend to do with them? And how much did they expect her to be involved with them?

Grace, the girl she had first met in the hospital, when she had been taken there with the gunshot wound, was now her carer. When Chas said that she was going to walk in the garden, Grace had stayed in Chas's room, making the excuse of 'doing a few things.' In reality, she knew Chas needed some time to herself, otherwise she became very argumentative and stubborn.

Chas was walking down a path lined on either side by enormous palm trees, having refocused her thoughts on another life, as far removed from this as possible. She'd been having dreams of a rough path through a wood of silver birches and wet ferns. She pictured herself there now, walking towards a village where she and Si lived, happy and free, outdoors; hunting, fishing, surrounded by like-minded friends. But this wasn't the path she was on now and as she came back to reality, she saw Grace coming towards her, followed by Zephyr. Her lip curled as she thought of what she wanted to say, or even do to him. Fire ignited in her belly.

Zephyr was wearing his public smile and Grace looked pleadingly at Chas, as if begging her to behave herself. Chas did not. Zephyr opened his mouth to utter some pleasantry, but before more than a vague sound emerged, Chas launched into a verbal attack on him.

'You promised! You said, 'you keep your word and I'll keep mine.' Liar! You never had any intention of truly letting him go!' It was all she could do to stop herself from lashing out at the Premier.

Grace began to apologise for her.

'Go away, Grace!' Chas snapped. 'This is not your concern!'

Grace looked at the Premier.

He nodded to her. 'You may go. Chastity and I need a few minutes alone.' He turned to Chas. 'Let's walk.' He set off back up the palm tree path and she followed, not yet having finished her diatribe.

'You think you can get away with whatever you want. You have no morals, no integrity, but I knew that anyway. I must be so stupid. I should have just ended it when I had that scalpel!'

Zephyr didn't reply straight away. He kept walking, his hands linked behind his back.

This infuriated Chas. 'Don't you have anything to say? Did you come here to rub it in?'

He stopped. 'I came to see how you are and ask if there is anything you need.'

She laughed, bitterly. 'Yeah! Here's a few things I need: my freedom, my body back, my friends safe. That imposter I thought was my brother; dead. There's a list for you. Think you can do any of that for me? Today would be good.'

Zephyr smiled and began to walk again. She stood still. When she didn't follow, he stopped and turned back. 'Firstly, I did keep my promise. I told you I would release him, and I did. I did not tell you I would find him and all his followers and wipe them out. No. That I did not tell you.'

'You lied.'

'No. I didn't tell you the whole story, that's all.' He picked at a palm leaf and wiped a fine sheen of dust from it. 'You're an intelligent woman, Chastity. I thought you might have worked it out.'

'At least I heard on the news that you haven't caught them yet.'

'Yet,' Zephyr said, flicking the 't' off his tongue as if flicking away an insect.

'He's smarter than you think,' Chas said.

'Really?' Zephyr gave her a condescending look. 'Is that why he came to 'rescue' you from the noose?'

She swore at the Premier and walked away.

He called after her. 'Just so you're clear about it, he won't be coming to rescue you this time!'

'Good!' Chas said, over her shoulder.

'He's dead.'

She stopped but didn't turn. Why would he say that? Didn't he want her to behave herself?

Zephyr began walking towards her. 'You see, we injected him with a new, more deadly and infectious strain of plague, to take as a... gift to Kate and the others. I expect there aren't many of them left now.' He paused.

She stood frozen to the spot. He took her gently by the

shoulders and turned her to face him. 'So there really is no better option for you than to see this through. You are alone, except for the clones, of course.' He reached out as if to touch her stomach.

She recoiled, despite wanting to beat her fists into his chest, then gouge his eyes from their sockets and slap the smile off his stupid arrogant face. Anger raged through every pore in her body. But it wasn't completely at Zephyr. It was more at herself for believing that he would have ever given in to her demands, if there wasn't a catch.

Without looking back, she ran from the garden.

*

Capability and Temp were sitting in the kitchen of Esme's house, listening to everything that had happened since Si had been left in Durham.

After they heard of his escape, Esme and Ben had gone back to her house, in case Si might have headed there. The law-keepers had ransacked the place, when they came searching for Mish and the others, but Esme felt reasonably safe here with her dogs, Brigitta and Kurt, to guard her. Ben loved being with the dogs, but was anxious to get back to Newcastle, having heard the news about Si and Honour being gravely ill. He had been told to stay away but every day he asked for news of them.

Temp and Capability had arrived this morning, having escaped from the Citadel, in the invisibility suits that Capability had managed to retrieve on his mission into the Fortress. He knew there was no way he could get to Chas, but had heard enough to be able to relay what was happening back to Temp. It wasn't safe for them here, but even if this house was being watched, no one would have seen them arrive.

'You can't stay long,' Esme said. 'They're bound to come back looking for you.'

'I know,' Temp said. 'We should go to Newcastle and see what we can do. Peter's there isn't he?'

Esme nodded.

'But what about the plague?' Ben asked. 'They won't let me go back.'

'I'll speak to Kate and find out what's best,' Esme said.

'Ask how Si and Honour are,' Ben said.

Capability sipped his coffee, grateful of its warmth. 'I've got contacts I know I can trust, if we need to go somewhere else temporarily.'

Esme went into another room to call Kate. Peter had managed to get all their Wearables encrypted so they could communicate without being tracked.

Temp laid a hand on Ben's arm. 'I'm sorry to hear about Ethan.'

Ben had been devastated to hear of Ethan's death. Ethan had been a father to him ever since his own parents had died and he had gone back to Seahouses to live. He tried to hold back his emotions. 'I can't believe he's gone. Sarah doesn't even know yet. And Honour's really ill. And Si...' His voice wavered and he buried his face in Brigitta's fur.

Capability looked at Temp. 'I hope Kate can do something. It's likely to be spreading through the city right now if others have caught it from Si.'

Esme came back into the room. 'Some good news. Si is

awake. Fever's gone. He's sitting up and talking. She thinks the NMBs have killed off the infection.'

Ben's face brightened. 'That's great! And Honour?'

'Same. She's not as good as Si, but it looks like she's on the mend, and most of the others too.'

'Fantastic!' Temp said. 'What did Kate say about us?'

'She said come. The contamination risk is low and she's still working on a vaccine with the NMBs.'

'Can I go?' Ben said, jumping up. Brigitta barked at him.

Esme smiled. 'Yes, you can. But you'll have to leave my dogs here.'

'I don't mind. When can we go?'

Temp and Capability looked at Esme. She would have to provide transport. 'You can take the car. It's the one you provided anyway.'

'We should go as soon as possible,' Temp said. 'Let's make it look like Ben and Esme are going somewhere and we'll get in the back in the suits. Drive us a little way Esme, then I'll take over and you can walk home.'

A few hours later Temp, Capability and Ben were at Pastor Rowley's house in Newcastle, having left the car outside the city and used the invisibility suits to get through the checkpoint.

It was an emotional reunion and Ben was eager to see Honour and Si. Kate agreed to let him put on a contamination suit, despite it being far too big for him. She wasn't yet sure that the patients were still infectious. She was giving them another few days in isolation.

Ben wanted to see Si first, because he knew the meeting with Honour would be most painful. Si was able to talk. He and Ben hadn't seen each other since Chas had almost been executed. Si was pale and weak, but pleased to see Ben who had lots of questions for him about Chas.

Kate wouldn't let him ask too many yet. 'We mustn't tire him out.'

'I'm fine, Mum,' Si said.

But Kate shook her head. 'I know best right now. Come on Ben, time to move on. I'll take you to Honour.'

Ben said goodbye and promised to come and see Si again tomorrow. He was nervous about seeing Honour. She had been told of her father's death, because as soon as she was able to speak, she had asked for him, and Nick couldn't lie to her. Ben knew she would be even more heart-broken than he had been.

When she saw Ben coming towards her bed, her eyes immediately filled with tears. He sat down beside her and held her hand. 'Oh Honour, I'm so sorry.'

She burst into tears and Ben did his best to hug her through the suit. Kate left them alone, knowing that this shared moment of grief should be private.

Honour wiped her face. 'Mum doesn't even know yet. Don't know what I'll say to her. I have to go back and tell her myself.'

Ben sat up but kept hold of her hand. 'I'll come with you. Can we take his body?'

'No.' She choked back another sob. 'Nick says it's already been buried here because of contamination and discovery by the law-keepers.'

'That'll be hard for Sarah,' Ben said.

'I can't bear to think about Mum finding out that Dad's

gone. She's going to be devastated and she's not going to want to let us come back here.' Honour sniffed and bit her lip hard, trying to stop more tears. 'But we're coming. We have to be part of this. We have to stop the Rulers before they destroy everyone and everything!'

Kate came back. She could see that Honour was getting more and more agitated. 'Time to go, Ben. He can come back tomorrow. Try and get some sleep.'

Ben gave her a massive brother-hug and followed Kate out of the ward.

As they walked back to the Pastor's house, Ben asked, 'She is going to be okay, isn't she?'

Kate smiled sympathetically. 'She is. I promise you that. All her vital signs are just about normal now. We've got this.'

Relieved, Ben blew out his breath, slowly.

'You go and get some rest now. I've got to talk to the others.' Kate left Ben in the care of some of the followers of The Way and went to find Nick.

In the kitchen, coffee was ready. Temp and Capability told their story of what had happened to them in the Citadel. All of them were now high on the wanted list and knew the law-keepers would be on the look-out for them. They had to be careful of their movements and needed to get out of the tech-city as soon as possible. They had three invisibility suits with them. Peter would be able to send for more, but his supply was limited. He hadn't made that many yet and he would need to get word to Harmony who was still living at his house near Durham. He knew the place would be under surveillance now that he was on the run from the Priory. It was only a matter of time before the law-keepers discovered them here at Pastor Rowley's house. They needed to move as soon as possible.

*

Once the NMBs had delivered the cure for the plague and Kate saw that it was working, it wasn't long before she was happy to let Si, Honour and a few others out of the isolation ward, knowing that they were no longer infectious. They were still weak but gaining strength gradually, from food and the buoyant company of Ben, Temp and other visitors.

Honour and Ben were making plans to go to Seahouses to break the horrible news to Sarah. They refused offers from any of the adults to go with them, but accepted a lift from one of the followers of The Way.

Ben and Si hugged properly for the first time since Si had escaped. 'Stay safe, little brother,' Si said. 'And come back soon.'

He turned to Honour and hugged her. 'You too. We'll keep in touch by phone, ' he said to Ben. Peter has encrypted both of them.'

Once they had gone, the others sat down in the kitchen at the Pastor's house to talk about plans for the bunker. Nick had managed to make time to go and see it, with Peter, once the patients had stabilized.

He and Peter told the others more about it. 'We'd like you to come and see it,' Nick said. 'How soon could we move everyone across there?'

Kate shook her head. 'They could go soon. We just need to find a way to get them safely out of the city. And I'm not sure everyone will want to come. Since Pastor Rowley died there's been less enthusiasm for bringing down the Rulers. You know what people are like, they'd rather stick with the status quo than bring any worse trouble on their heads.'

'So, we have to rally them again,' Si said. 'And we need to get more people on board. We have to be a force to be reckoned with to infiltrate the Citadel, and capture the Rulers and their clones.'

Peter raised his eyebrows. 'Steady on. One move at a time. First, the Angel of the North. Let's see if it can give us some inspiration as to how we might achieve all that.'

Si shifted uneasily, anxious to get into the Citadel and bring Chas back as soon as possible. He had told his mum about the clones they had implanted in Chas's womb and asked her if there was anything that could be done to prevent their birth.

'Only an abortion,' Kate had replied.

He knew that his mother didn't like the thought of abortion, but she wasn't judgmental, and he knew she would listen.

'What about Chas's mental health? And what about those clones? Two children engineered for evil purposes. What would we tell them? How would that affect their lives?'

'But they're still human beings,' Kate had said. 'They didn't choose this anymore than Chas but they're already alive. It's really tough. We need to talk to Chas.'

The conversation hadn't really got much further than that. Si had walked away, frustrated by not being able to go and do precisely that. Chas must think he had abandoned her and he hated that thought.

He was jolted back to the present conversation when the others stood up. 'Where are you going?'

'You're coming too,' Kate said. 'I thought you weren't listening. You and I are going with Peter to the Angel.'

'There are only three invisibility suits so we'll have to report back to Temp and Capability,' Peter said. 'And we'll have to walk. It's too risky to drive. Too many cameras.'

'Is it far?' Si asked.

'About 5 miles. We'll stay there overnight, as your mum thinks a 10-mile walk in one day would be too much for you.'

Si was grateful for his mum's advice. Even a 5-mile walk seemed daunting right now, but he wasn't going to admit to it.

They had put the suits on and set off by mid-morning. Si still marvelled at the feeling of invisibility. They walked through the streets of Newcastle, careful not to touch anyone, so no one was aware of them. Peter had shown them on a map how to get to the Angel and had given them certain landmarks to look out for along the way. They planned to make their own way there and meet at the feet of the Angel.

Si passed easily through the checkpoint, remembering all those times they had had to crash through the barriers or confront the guards. He was glad he could pass through unnoticed this time. Walking over the Tyne Bridge, seeing places he remembered from his childhood, was enjoyable. The sun was glinting on the River Tyne, and this, coupled with his memories, made him feel strangely peaceful. This road was a bizarre mixture of high-tech magnetised vehicles and horses pulling carts, from a bygone era. The cars moved silently in their own lanes, while those who couldn't afford them went more noisily past on the pavements. Si had to watch his step to avoid the horse manure.

He noticed that a lot of people were wearing scarves or masks over their faces. They had always been afraid of the plague, but clearly rumours of this new plague were spreading. He wondered if any were already infected.

It took Si two and a half hours to get there, having had to stop several times to rest and have a drink. Retrieving his water carrier from inside his suit was not an easy task and required somewhere inconspicuous to do it.

The others were waiting for him. There was no one about and each of them was able to reveal their feet to show that they were there.

'Don't take your suit off,' Peter said. 'Just follow the feet!'

Despite the circumstances it felt very surreal following bodyless feet and it made Si smile to himself. Peter led them to some trees, to the right of the Angel, that sloped downwards towards a dual carriageway, where magnetised cars sped silently by. In the wooded area it was more difficult to follow the feet.

'Can we strip off a bit more Peter?' Si asked. 'I'm struggling to keep you in view.'

'Yes. Should be safe now. It's not far though.'

They rolled the suits down to their waists. Having only thin clothing on underneath, it was considerably colder without the protection of the suit, cleverly designed to keep a person warm in cold conditions, but to deflect heat in hotter ones.

The entrance to the bunker was large but completely concealed within the wood. Unless someone knew where it was, they would be lucky to stumble upon it by accident. Peter unlocked the metal doors. They gave a protesting screech as he pulled them open.

He laughed. 'Hinges need oiling!'

He flicked on the lights, powered by a generator, and led them along a polytunnel, which sloped downwards for a long way, before arriving at the even wider blast doors. These were not locked, but also groaned as Peter opened them and led the way inside.

Si began filming their visit on his Wearable, to send to Temp and Capability.

'These doors weigh one and a half tonnes,' Peter explained. 'Once bolted from the inside, no one can get in from the outside.' He closed and bolted them with the long steel bolts.

It was like being in a big warehouse. Peter led them past generators, air filters and cooling systems. 'You'd think it would be cold down here, but if the number of people they were anticipating had come, it would've got really hot. So, it actually needed a cooling system.'

Si filmed the huge machines and network of pipes spreading like veins through the bunker.

'The walls are made of concrete over three metres thick,' Peter continued. 'So, a good defence against attack from the Rulers.'

There was a large office space, where operators would have worked at computers. 'This room was set up for 450 people to work in.'

'That would've been tight,' Si said, looking around.

'Indeed. Around the edge you can see individual offices for the government ministers.' Peter led them to one. Inside was a desk, a set of drawers, wash basin and a bed. Very basic.

'Can we communicate with the outside world from down here?' Kate asked.

Peter nodded. 'By the time this was created, people were using mobile phones, so they made sure they could get a signal by running a mast up through the Angel.'

'The Angel is hollow?' Si asked.

'Not hollow. They just built the mast into it.'

'Impressive.' Si said.

They went into the next room. On the walls were maps of England and the world. There were mobile phones and charging units alongside large computer screens. 'This was their Ops room and we can use it for that too.' He smiled, seeing their faces as they gawped at the old technology. 'Don't worry, we can use our own stuff, it won't be a problem.'

They followed Peter down to the next floor, passing the toilet blocks. 'They had to be careful with water supplies, so these toilets are on eco flush. We shouldn't have a problem getting fresh water.'

'Unless, we're under siege,' Si said.

'Let's hope it doesn't come to that,' Peter replied. 'But of course, if it does, these toilets are perfect. They were designed for being cut off from the outside world.'

On the next floor were lots of dormitories with bunks squeezed into small spaces. 'The people who came here would share bunks. They'd be on shifts, so one in, one out.'

Si screwed up his face and Peter laughed. 'They had their own pillow-cases.'

'Oh, that's okay then!' Si said, sarcastically.

'At least it would've always been warm,' Kate laughed. 'I've slept in worse.'

'Yeah, me too,' Si agreed.

There was also a sick bay, with a consulting room, waiting area, operating room and locked store. Peter had the key. Kate spent some time rifling through supplies and checking out equipment. As he panned around with his Wearable, Si noticed the flimsy cardboard coffins propped up in the storeroom, just off the operating room.

'What did they do with the dead?'

'Well, the place was never used of course, but they would have had to get them outside the blast doors quickly. So, people would have put on the radiation suits and gone to bury them outside.'

Kate came to join them. 'I'm impressed that all this is still in good working order. The supplies are good too. We'll just need to top them up with some modern drugs and implements and we should be good to go.'

'Good, Peter said. 'We've seen most of it now. There's a back door, same as the front, just down the corridor there, but let's go back upstairs to the canteen and get a cup of coffee. I brought some supplies. We'll need to stock the place with food.'

The canteen was large and empty, and their voices seemed too loud, bouncing off the walls and echoing around the space. The lighting was stark and bright, but there were dark corners where they hadn't switched on all the lights.

'It feels eerie down here, doesn't it,' Kate said, shivering a little.

Si was thinking the same thing. 'Yeah. I feel like we're being watched by ghosts.'

Peter laughed. 'No one died down here, because no one ever used it in the end. But we can make great use of it.'

'How many people could we potentially fit in here?' Kate asked.

'It was built to house around 1000 people, but that would be very crowded. I'd say 500 would be more comfortable.'

Si stopped filming. 'Shall I send the video to Temp?'

Peter showed him how to do it via the encrypted channel.

It was late afternoon and they were all tired, especially Si. Peter suggested they find a bunk and rest for a while, then supper. After that, they could risk a walk outside for some fresh air before going to bed for the night.

It was certainly a strange place to be. Despite being a large space, the smaller rooms could feel claustrophobic, with no natural light and the thought of being locked in by those big blast doors. Of course, they could come and go as they pleased, and Si didn't feel trapped. He thought of Chas, who was trapped in the big light airy Complex in the Fortress. It felt like there was no escape for her, especially from the two clones she was carrying. He went to sleep thinking of her and woke, in a sweat, having dreamed of her giving birth to two babies with lined and haggard faces, which Si recognised as himself and Chas in old age.

4

Chas drew her head back from the toilet bowl and wiped the saliva from the corners of her mouth. She sat on the floor of her bathroom and rested her head on the towel rail. Her mouth felt like a sewer and her body like a wilted flower. Every morning, for weeks now, she had thrown up as soon as she got out of bed and carried the nauseous feeling around with her most of the day. They had tried various remedies to help the sickness, none of which had done any good.

Grace arrived in the bedroom; her cheery tones grating on Chas in an instant. 'Chas? Hi, I'm here. How are you this morning? Any better?'

From behind the bathroom door Chas scowled at her. 'No!'

It wouldn't be so bad if she had chosen to have children. She could perhaps have put up with the sickness more graciously. But to have this thrust upon her by force made the sickness even more unbearable.

Grace had been coming in early as soon as she realised that morning sickness was kicking in. Despite Chas's often surly attitude and fierceness, Grace was drawn to her. She felt she could see beyond the outward appearance and had a soft spot for the person she saw lurking underneath. The feistiness and courage were admirable, but Grace also saw loyalty and need. Her mission was to care for Chas as much as she would let her. And even when Chas wasn't in cooperative mood, Grace was persistent.

Chas often felt a strange mixture of annoyance and gratitude towards Grace, who was slightly older than her. They seemed to have little in common, but Chas was glad of her company most of the time, even if she didn't admit it.

'I'm going to bring you some breakfast,' Grace said.

'Don't bother!'

Grace chuckled. 'Ah, you always say that, but you know if you can get something down, it settles the sickness a bit.'

This statement was greeted by the sound of Chas retching again.

When Chas came out of the bathroom, Grace persuaded her to eat half an orange and some porridge. The throwing up seemed to have abated and settled into the usual daily nausea.

'You've got an appointment with Doctor Nelson this morning,' Grace said. 'It's your eight-week check. It's gone so quickly.' Grace fussed around the room tidying and rearranging things.

'Has it?' Every day was an endless drag to Chas. When she first came to the Complex, after having the clones implanted, she had spent many hours each day trying to think of ways to escape. But she had little energy now and it took her all her time just to get through the daily routine. Grace had thrust pregnancy books at her and tried to encourage her to read about what was happening to her body, but this was the last thing Chas wanted to face.

She walked in the garden every day and spent some time in the gym, trying to keep her fitness up, but even this was a struggle. Her thoughts often turned to Si and the others. Was he really dead? Who was still alive? Was Ben dead? Kate? Something was clearly wrong if Si hadn't attempted to come for her in all this time. She had been having weird dreams about him. In one dream that kept recurring, he walked through the wall of her room, smiling, and told her to touch his hands, to prove that he was real. He had once told her about Jesus doing that when he rose from the dead. He'd asked Thomas, a disciple who doubted, to put his fingers in the holes in his hands where the crucifixion nails had been. She had laughed, of course, and told him she didn't believe in ghosts. Then he had told her that Jesus had eaten with his followers and stayed with them for a long time. She had shrugged it off as nonsense. But it had clearly affected her. In her dream about Si walking through the wall, he brought food and they ate together, then they silently walked through all the walls of the Complex and out into the sunshine. She sighed and put the dream from her mind. Maybe it meant that he was dead after all.

Grace thrust some jeans, top and underwear at her. 'Come on Chas, stop daydreaming. The guards will be here in ten minutes to take you to the doctor's clinic. You don't want them to drag you there in your pyjamas.'

Chas rolled her eyes.

Grace lived up to her name and smiled cheerfully back. 'You know you love me, really!'

Chas pulled a sarcastic face at her.

They arrived at Doctor Nelson's clinic for 10.30a.m. There was no one else there. This was a private consultation.

'Good morning Chastity. Have a seat. How are you feeling? It's a few weeks since I last saw you.'

The doctor had implanted the embryos into Chas's womb, but even though she worked for the Rulers, she had been kind to Chas.

'I feel sick all the time,' she said.

'Yes. That's normal. I sent up some ginger supplements last week. Any difference?'

'Not really.'

'It usually passes by twelve to eighteen weeks,' the doctor said, sympathetically.

'Great! Only another four to ten weeks of this to put up with then!'

The doctor smiled. 'I need to check a few things this morning. Can you get on the scales please? Then I'll do height and calculate your BMI.'

'Are you managing to eat properly?' She looked doubtfully at Chas who was looking thinner and pale. 'Are you taking the folic acid and the vitamin supplements?'

'Yes, Doctor,' Chas said, dutifully.

'Okay, blood pressure now, and then I need a urine sample from you.' She took her blood pressure then handed her a container to pee into. 'Toilet's through there.'

When Chas came back, the doctor talked to her about some tests that they were going to run to ascertain the health of the babies. 'We're going to test for sickle cell, thalassemia and Downs Syndrome. It's a simple blood test at this stage.'

Chas surrendered her arm to the blood test. 'Will you tell me the results?'

'I'm only supposed to report them to Zephyr, but I don't see the point of keeping you in the dark. You'll be less stressed if you know what's going on.'

'Thank you.'

Next, they talked about the importance of good nutrition and having a manageable fitness regime. Doctor Nelson was pleased that Chas was trying to take care of her health, because she had wondered what the psychological effects of this whole scenario would be. She questioned Chas for some time, trying to ascertain the state of her mental health.

'Zephyr told me Si is dead,' she said. 'Do you know if this is true.'

The doctor shook her head. 'They don't tell me things like that. I just do as I'm told.'

Chas looked disappointed.

Doctor Nelson hesitated. 'I'll see what I can find out. If I get any information, I'll let you know.' She looked down at her desk. 'I have to be careful. No one's safe here. If you betray them...'

She couldn't finish the sentence and Chas saw real fear in her eyes when she looked up. 'I know what happens if you cross them.'

The doctor nodded, putting her professional face back on. 'Of course you do, I'm sorry. Now, let's keep focused. At twelve weeks we'll be doing a dating scan and you'll be able to see the babies for the first time.'

'Whoopee!' Chas said, in mock excitement.

Doctor Nelson smiled warmly at her sarcasm this time. Chas knew she genuinely liked her, and it made her sorry that they had had to meet under such circumstances.

'I think that's all we need to do today, Chas,' she said, standing up. Chas noticed that she used her preferred name, for the first time. 'But if there's anything you're unsure of at any time, just ask to see me.' She put her hand on Chas's arm. 'Anything.'

Chas got up to leave. As she was about to open the door to the waiting guards, she turned. 'Have you ever betrayed them?'

Doctor Nelson hesitated. Her lips quivered, almost imperceptibly, then she said. 'Goodbye Chastity.'

*

The day dragged on, with Grace never leaving Chas's side, talking incessantly about what she was up to and her latest boyfriend. Chas managed to zone out at times, but she didn't really mind Grace's prattle. It distracted her.

'I'm going to the gym,' she announced in the late afternoon. 'What time does your shift finish?'

Grace looked at her Wearable. 'Hmmm. It finished half an hour ago.'

'Well get going then,' Chas said. 'You really don't have to stay later. I'm just a job, Grace. Go home and enjoy yourself.'

'Aw, you care about me!' Grace said, in mock surprise.

Chas rolled her eyes. 'No! Of course not! You've just annoyed me enough for one day.'

Grace looked hurt.

Chas shook her head. 'I'm only joking! But seriously, go on. You have a life outside of this place.'

Chas headed up to the gym, breathing a sigh of relief as silence cosseted her ears. The gym was up a floor and she was looking forward to a gentle workout, before going to the canteen for food. She enjoyed seeing the younger children at mealtimes, but she sat at the far end of the room and pretended not to take any notice of them. They were a lively bunch and their guardians were not overly strict. She liked watching them joke and mess about, and it made her long for a memory of her own childhood that didn't actually exist. She tried to imagine these children becoming the evil dictators that they had been bred to become, but that was hard to picture, when they were chattering, laughing and flicking food at each other. Sometimes they would look at her and wave or even come to speak to her. She secretly liked it when they did. It reminded her of being part of the commune.

It often made her think of Ben too; wondering what had happened to him since she had seen him in the crowd at the hanging. Would she ever see him again?

When she got to the gym there was someone else there. Young Zephyr was always working out at this time. They had only said a few necessary words to each other over the last few weeks, but he always acknowledged her with a nod as she entered.

He was doing weights and Chas jumped on the treadmill. Both had headphones in. Chas had been allowed a device to play music, but with no access to the outside world. She threw him the odd surreptitious glance and he did the same to her. Once or twice their eyes met for a moment before each looked hastily away. He was an exact but younger replica of the Premier. She was trying to figure out if he had the same traits and personality, but it was virtually impossible without interaction. She wondered if he was interested in why she was here and what he thought about it.

Today, she decided she would attempt to talk to him. She walked over to the weights machine opposite him and began to figure out what to do with it. She had never been in a gym before this one and she knew he was watching her as she read the instructions. Hoping that he might offer to help her, she made out that she was struggling to understand what to do. He didn't say anything.

Chas glanced at him. How to approach it? Just be matter-of-fact. 'Hi. I'm new to weights. Can you show me how to work this?'

He hesitated, then shrugged. 'Sure.' He came over. 'Sit there.' She sat. 'Make sure it's the right height for you, with this lever.' He pointed down and she adjusted the lever. 'Put this pin in where you can manage the weight. Test it out. You don't want to be straining.' He looked at her belly. 'Especially in your...' She saw a moment of boyish awkwardness and tried not to smile. 'You know...'

She gave him a sarcastic look.

'That's about it, really.' He retreated to his machine.

Chas selected a weight level that she thought would look impressive and hoped she could lift it.

They continued in silence. Zephyr moved on to another machine. The weight was too heavy for her, but she didn't want to admit it. Feeling frustrated that her body wasn't performing like she wanted it to, she lifted for only a short time, then moved on to some rowing. It surprised her just how much being pregnant was affecting her already.

'Thanks for the help,' she said, as she was leaving. 'See you tomorrow, probably.'

He stopped what he was doing. 'Yeah. Maybe.'

*

The Premier was in a meeting with his closest advisors, Ambition and Zealous, trying to figure out a strategy for bringing down the rebels. Resolution was there too, as head of operations. It was two months since Si had been released and they had struggled to get any news of him or the others. There were adverts out on HTV for information leading to Si's capture. The same for Kate, Nick, Temp, Capability and Peter. Substantial rewards were on offer and propaganda was being spread that the rebels were a threat to the security of the country. But still, all the leads that they had followed had been false. It was like the rebels had disappeared. Doctors in the plague camps were interrogated, but even in Resolution's hands, none had been able to tell them anything they didn't already know.

The plague camps had recently become successful because of Kate's NMBs and the Rulers had decided to use this as propaganda in their favour, claiming that they had found the cure. They hoped it would get the people on-side and more willing to hunt down the rebels. Later, when the rebels had been caught and executed, they would send out more of the modified plague into the workhouses and poorest areas of the tech-cities.

'There's a strong possibility that they're dead,' said Ambition. 'That's what we wanted, and maybe it's what happened.'

Zephyr was becoming more and more impatient. 'That would be good, but we need evidence. We need to know who's dead and who's still alive. We need bodies or witnesses. No one's saying anything. Someone must know something.'

'I've had law-keepers questioning people in the tech-cities near where we dropped Hunter,' Resolution said, 'but no one seems to know anything. And now, with the state of emergency declared in Newcastle, the whole city is in quarantine. No one in, no one out. He must have been there.'

'The people are afraid,' Zealous said. 'Before now, the plague was contained to the workhouse scum mainly, but this has got out of hand.'

Zephyr glowered at Zealous. He didn't need it pointing out that his plan to infect the rebels with the new strain of plague had somewhat backfired. 'Somehow we will use this to our advantage. By quarantining the infected tech-city it still looks like we're doing what we can to prevent it spreading. They don't know we started it. We're having provisions delivered and we've told them we're working on a cure.'

'But, Premier, the rebellion is still going on, because some of the rebels have been putting out their own propaganda again on HTV, telling people that we are responsible for the plague.' Zealous was becoming more frustrated. 'Why can't we jam or trace their communications? Surely we have the technology...'

Zephyr slammed his fist on the table. 'Shut up, Zealous! Don't you think I know this? Yes, we should be able to stop them, but Peter Marsden is clearly still alive, and the man is a technological genius. We've always known that.'

'We are doing everything we can to interrupt their broadcasts,' Ambition said, trying to calm the atmosphere.

'Do you want me to be more heavy-handed, Sir?' Resolution said, going back to the subject of questioning people.

Ambition spoke up. 'We have to. It's been two months now and still no trace of them.'

'But if we go around blatantly torturing people, that's going to send them into the arms of the rebels,' said Zealous.

'If they're still alive,' Ambition said.

'Some of them must be,' Zephyr said. 'We have to find them, or what's left of them. And this time when we take Marsden, he is a dead man. We make a spectacle of it.'

Ambition spoke. 'We know Kate Hunter is clever. She may have found a way to cure this latest strain, like she did with the last one.'

'How could she find a cure in such a short space of time? And she clearly didn't share it around. Look at what's happening in Newcastle. There's no way she could have saved Silence,' Zephyr said.

'No, but that might have made her more determined to get back at us. So, where are they?' Zealous said.

Zephyr swore, narrowed his eyes and growled at Zealous.

'That's what we're trying to ascertain, isn't it!'

Zealous and Ambition glanced at each other. They were worried about Zephyr's outbursts. He was becoming harder to influence and keep under their control. Between them recently, they had been discussing whether it would be a good time to replace him with Young Zephyr, who was now eighteen. But quashing the rebellion had to come first.

Resolution stepped between Zephyr and the other two. 'I have sent people to question anyone associated with Peter Marsden, Capability, Temperance, Doctor Reece – all of them. But I haven't been hard on them yet, Premier, as you requested,' he said, obsequiously. Ambition rolled his eyes at Zealous. 'I sent men to the commune where Chastity's friend Submission came from. But, not surprisingly, there was no trace of them. We searched the area for a week. Perhaps I should turn up the pressure.'

Ambition spoke up in favour of Resolution's idea and Zephyr agreed. 'We need to know what they're up to. If Hunter were still alive, I can't believe he wouldn't have made another attempt to rescue Chastity. Commander, you have permission to question individuals who may know something, and you can be as persuasive as you like.'

'I still have some people in custody, in the Priory and the Bastille. Some are from an underground sect called The Way and others were arrested at demonstrations across the North. I'll take Excellence and get started.'

'Have you questioned him about his father?' Zephyr asked.

Resolution smiled ironically. 'Excellence is loyal to you, Premier. He is ashamed that his father is a traitor. He knows nothing about Capability's whereabouts. I have already asked him if he knows any places his father might have gone. He has sisters, but he hasn't seen them for years and says his father sent them abroad. He doesn't know where.'

Zephyr stood up. 'Question him further. Make him think harder about what he knows. Why would he not know where his sisters were? Capability and Temperance may have tried to get abroad if that's where Capability's family are.'

Resolution didn't want to get heavy-handed with Excellence. He was proving to be a good right-hand man, learning quickly like a good dog. He was intelligent and keen. Very keen. 'I will question him some more, Premier.'

'Keep me informed, Commander. Meanwhile, Ambition, Zealous, keep working on anti-rebel propaganda to ensure nothing escalates. Substantial rewards for information leading to capture of rebels. Severe punishment for those caught supporting rebellion. Start executing them publicly.'

'I could start with the ones at the Priory, after questioning them, Premier,' Resolution offered.

'Good,' Zephyr said.

Resolution went to find Excellence. 'Get your things together. We're going to the Priory. We leave in one hour. We're going to try harder to find out what Marsden's housekeeper and associates know of his whereabouts.'

He also intended to interrogate Excellence about his father, on the way to the Priory. He was almost certain he didn't know anything, otherwise he was sure he would have told him. His loyalty to Resolution gave the Commander the ego boost that he was always looking for.

*

Ambition left the meeting with other things on his mind. He walked towards the elevator with Zealous.

'I'm glad Zephyr's finally suggested we crack down on these protestors.' Zealous said. 'But I still think he's losing it.'

'He does what we want him to,' Ambition said.

'Not always,' Zealous replied. 'His outbursts are occurring more often. He's not as malleable as he once was. I think we might have to replace him sooner rather than later. Don't you think so?'

Ambition nodded. 'We need to gather the other Rulers. Without the Premier. Discuss it.'

'I'll set that up,' Zealous said. 'Meanwhile we should get on with quashing as many of the uprisings as possible. Shall we have a word with Resolution before he goes off to the Priory?'

'I've got to do something first,' Ambition answered. 'You go ahead. I'll be there in an hour.'

Zealous raised his eyebrows and shrugged. 'Okay. See you there.'

Ambition headed out of the Fortress to the hospital. He had been meaning to tackle this particular concern for a while. But with all that had been going on with the rebellion, he had let his guard down, and something told him that he should be more vigilant.

Doctor Nelson was busy in her office. In what should

have been her lunch break, she was absent-mindedly eating a sandwich whilst wading through a backlog of admin. Technology was supposed to make this easier, but it never seemed to reduce her workload.

She jumped when Ambition burst through the door, without knocking. The sight of him always made her heart rate increase considerably; partly from fear and partly from some half-buried desire that was aroused every time she saw him. He was almost twenty years older than her, but he was still a good-looking man.

She tried to look unperturbed by his entrance but knew her cheeks had flushed. 'Yes? Do you want something?'

He didn't come very often, and it was never a social visit, so she was always on her guard when he appeared. He didn't speak, just sat down in the consulting chair opposite. His eyes were cold and hard, but she was used to that, after all these years of working for the Rulers. As he silently stared at her, she felt her insides twist a little harder and made an effort to control her breathing.

'I've got work to do here, Ambition. You can see that. Get on with what you want to say so I can get on with what I need to do. I have a clinic at one-thirty.'

Ambition still said nothing. She felt desperate to leave the room, but she held his stare, folding her arms and sighing impatiently. 'Well?'

He spoke slowly, threateningly. 'I know you know where it is. I just want to remind you, Anya, that I watch every move you make, every person you speak to.'

The doctor rolled her eyes. She wanted to make him think she didn't believe him, but she was never quite sure.

'You've told me this, many times over the years. Why do you need to keep telling me? And I keep telling you that 'it' is dead! My father dealt with everything and he's also dead. You made sure of that, when he wouldn't talk! So, you can rest easy, can't you?'

He narrowed his eyes. Her defiant attitude always annoyed him and yet he found it arousing at the same time. It was one of the things that had first attracted him to her all those years ago, when she was a student at the University.

'I never understood why you didn't just have me killed too,' she said. 'Then you wouldn't have to waste time worrying about it, would you?'

Ambition felt his anger rising. He should have got rid of her, but his conflicting feelings had got in the way. He came around the desk and stood beside her. She didn't look at him. Suddenly, he swung her chair towards him and pulled her up out of it. Hauling her towards the wall, he smashed her up against it. She was winded and cried out, but he had his hand over her mouth to stifle the sound.

'Damn right I should have!' he hissed in her face. Tears sprung into her eyes. He had never been violent with her before. Seeing her fear, he released his grip a little and took his hand from her mouth. 'But you've been useful over the years, here in the hospital.' He let her go and sat down again at the desk, to calm his own breathing. 'You're an excellent doctor, Anya. That has been your salvation. And, you know when to keep your mouth shut.'

She did. She knew so much more than she had ever let on and, fortunately for her, Ambition still had some stirrings of desire that had prevented him from harming her. She leaned into the wall and put her hands to her neck, swallowing hard. His outburst had shocked her. His need to keep things secret kept him from letting Resolution loose on her. But she was afraid that this may be about to change.

'If anyone ever finds out about 'it' or us, you will die, along with your mother and sisters and their children.'

Yes, and so will you, she thought, but she kept that comment to herself.

There was a knock at the door. Anya went back to her desk, straightened her clothing, glared at Ambition and took a deep breath. 'Come in.'

'Doctor, I have those ...' The man saw Ambition. 'Oh, I'm sorry, I didn't realise you were in a meeting.'

Doctor Nelson held out her hand for the equipment the junior doctor was carrying. 'Thank you.'

The junior doctor left.

'Are we finished here?' she said to Ambition.

He got up and leaned over the desk towards her. 'We're never finished, Anya,' he said, and left the room.

5

Excellence was driving. He loved accompanying the Commander on any mission out of the Citadel. He had spent most of his life in the city, studying to become a politician, like his father. The drive to the Priory was easy, with very pleasant scenery. He loved the sea in particular; the vastness and power of it. He felt invigorated by it.

The Commander was his usual silent self, which gave Excellence time to wonder about his father and where he was. Why hadn't he realised that he was a traitor? He didn't understand how a man of such high position, who had everything, could throw it all away. But then, his father had always kept things from him. He was sure Capability knew where his sisters were. The Commander had asked him lots of probing questions about his father and Excellence had wondered if he was about to be tortured. But Resolution had backed off, which was unusual, and Excellence had taken this as a sure sign of the Commander's trust in him. He was flattered and was going to make sure he didn't let Resolution down.

As they crossed the causeway to the tidal island of Lindisfarne, home to the Priory, Resolution came to life and began reminding Excellence about what they were going to do and what his role was going to be.

'We will round up all the prisoners from recent demonstrations, focusing particularly on those from the Newcastle area. We will interrogate them and select some for execution, as an example of what happens to those who threaten our national security.'

Excellence nodded, always keen to show Resolution how much he respected his judgements. 'Is there anything specific you want me to do, Commander?'

'Back me up at all times and do as I instruct you,' Resolution said as they passed through the checkpoint.

'Of course.'

'The first person I want to question is Marsden's housekeeper. I've been informed that she's here.'

'Do you want me in on that?' Excellence asked.

'Yes. It will be more intimidating if we're both there. You can also question her. Put as much pressure on as you can.'

Excellence was flattered. The Commander usually kept the pleasure of torturing prisoners to himself.

They drove onto the island that had once been a tranquil village community, earning its living from fishing and tourism. There was nothing left of that now. The people had been driven away when the Priory was built.

They pulled up to the main entrance and were admitted by Doctor Redman, the new chief. He was an efficient man, chosen very carefully since the last two chiefs had been arrested themselves.

'Welcome Commander. Do you require refreshment after your journey?'

'No, thank you, Doctor. We would like to begin our business.'

'Certainly. Follow me. I have the prisoners you asked for. They're being held in a meeting room.'

Resolution and Excellence followed the Chief. Thirty-four people awaited their arrival. Some were crying, others were cowed and fearful, but some stood defiantly, staring hard at Resolution and Excellence as they entered.

'Why are there children here?' Excellence asked, seeing some younger people.

'We're not used to holding children here,' Doctor Redman explained. 'but I was told to take anyone sent to me from the demonstrations.'

Excellence felt a shudder go through him at the thought of the Commander torturing children, but he shook it off. If he was going to keep his status as the Commander's right-hand man, he needed to toughen up.

Resolution spoke to them. 'You are being held here for crimes against the Rulers. Each one of you will be questioned and given a chance to change your allegiances. If you give us any information about the whereabouts and capture of the rebel leaders, you will be freed. If not, you will be held here until the date is set for your execution.'

A woman began to cry. A man shouted. 'Let the children go! They're innocent.'

'No one is innocent!' Resolution answered. 'Each one of you chose to take a stand against the Rulers or chose to take children with you. Each person is responsible for their own actions and their consequences.'

Another woman came forward. She knelt at Resolution's

feet. 'Please, have mercy and let them go.'

The Commander smirked. Asking for 'mercy' was akin to lighting the fuse on his sadism. He kicked the woman away. 'No one leaves here alive unless they help us.' He grabbed a young teenage boy nearby, looked him squarely in the face, then threw him across the room. 'No one!'

The boy skidded over the floor and smashed into a table. People gasped and some whimpered. A girl ran to pick him up.

Excellence spoke. 'The Commander shows no mercy. Find some useful information in the depths of your little brains, if you want to get out of here. And don't think it'll work to make up lies, we check out every lead. Only useful information and sworn allegiance to the Rulers buys you a ticket out of here.'

Resolution and Excellence swept out of the room, followed by Doctor Redman. 'Let them stew together for a while,' Resolution said. 'They will stoke each other's fears, then most will be ready to talk.'

'Won't we get a lot of desperate made-up stories?' Excellence said.

'Of course,' Resolution answered. 'But some of them will be true. The law-keepers will follow up each one. The rebels can't have just disappeared. Someone knows where they are.' He turned to the Chief of the Priory. 'I want to talk to Marsden's housekeeper first. I saw her in there. Bring her out for me. Her name is Harmony.'

'Certainly, Commander. Do you want her taken back to her room?'

'Yes' Resolution said.

Redman indicated to the guards to go back in and remove her. 'Are you sure you don't want refreshments first? I have some very good food prepared for you.'

Excellence was keen to say yes, but Resolution shook his head. 'Have iced water brought to her room for us. We are here to work, not feast!'

'Whatever you wish, Commander,' the Chief said, feeling insulted. Excellence felt the desire to apologise rising in his throat, but he swallowed it down, knowing that Resolution would be furious with him.

Resolution was pleased at his authority here. The Chief seemed to respect him in the chain of command, not like that fool at the Bastille.

Redman led them to a locked room, where the woman was already sitting on the bed. She drew up her knees and cowered into the corner.

Resolution waved the Chief away. 'You can leave us now. We will call when we need to be let out.'

'Very well, Commander.' Redman left the room and it locked behind him.

Resolution fixed Harmony with his cold stare. 'You know who I am, don't you?'

She nodded and Resolution saw pure fear in her eyes. That gave him pleasure. He smiled. 'And you are Harmony. You worked for Peter Marsden. Am I correct?'

She nodded again.

'This is Captain North, my second-in-command.'

Excellence had never heard Resolution refer to him like this before. He stood taller and glared harder at the woman.

'We will be questioning you about your employer's involvement with the rebels. If you answer each question truthfully, you have nothing to fear. If you don't help us, you have everything to fear.' Resolution's smile grew more derisive as a silent tear slid down Harmony's cheek.

'Put her in that chair,' he commanded Excellence. 'Secure her wrists and bind her feet together.'

Excellence dragged Harmony from the bed. She began to whimper but didn't say anything. The Commander unpacked some implements from the bag he was carrying. He held up a small hammer and examined it. Then a scalpel. Excellence watched him with fascination, knowing he was already enjoying himself.

'He handed the scalpel to Excellence. 'Make sure this is sharp. Test it.'

Excellence took the implement. He wasn't quite sure if the Commander meant him to cut Harmony. He moved towards her.

'No! Test it on yourself. Let her see.'

He was taken aback by the command but didn't falter. Resolution turned away and pretended to busy himself with other implements. His revulsion for blood was still his worst enemy. Excellence held his hand above Harmony's face and ran the blade of the scalpel across his finger. Bright red blood seeped up and dripped down over Harmony's face. He didn't flinch, even though it stung like hell, and it had the desired effect on Harmony. She whimpered and began to beg.

'Please, Sir. Please don't do this. I know nothing about Mr. Marsden's dealings with the rebels. Please!'

Resolution ignored her. 'Go clean yourself up,' he said to Excellence, not looking at the wound. 'And make sure she's clean too.'

Once Excellence had cleaned her face, Resolution turned and smiled callously. 'Let's begin.'

*

The prisoners in the Priory were just ordinary citizens who had been drawn to protest against the Rulers, by the propaganda videos from the rebels. They agreed that the Rulers were mistreating them and felt it was time to say so. That was all. They didn't want to die for their views.

Some of the prisoners were crying, others were talking quietly about what they should say, in order to get out of there alive. Most of them didn't know any of the rebels personally and hadn't a clue what they could tell the Commander. There were some, however, who had been at Pastor Rowley's house when Kate and Nick were there and had fled when Si returned.

'I know where they are,' one man whispered to his wife. 'We have to keep it to ourselves though. We need to be the ones to give that information to the Commander if we want to get out of here alive.'

'How do you know?' she asked.

'I overheard it in the market one day, not long before we got involved in the protest march.'

'So, he said where they were?'

'He said he thought they must have found sanctuary in the Old Cathedral.'

'Was he certain?'

'Sounded like it. Said he'd seen strange goings on up there.'

'You never told me,' she hissed.

'Well, I'm telling you now!' he barked back, then looked around furtively. 'You must keep it to yourself and back me up when I tell the Commander I know where they are.'

She tutted. 'I'm not stupid!'

At that moment, an arm came around the man's neck and the boy who had been thrown across the floor held him in a strangle hold. He had overheard the last words of the conversation. The man's wife cried out and grabbed the boy, but she was pushed aside by a girl. The man was struggling to free himself.

'Don't even think about betraying them!' the boy growled in the man's ear. 'If you do, I'll kill you before the Commander gets a chance to.'

The man was stronger than the boy and managed to pull him off. There was a skirmish until several people came to pull them apart.

'He knows where the rebels are!' the boy declared. 'And he's going to buy his freedom by keeping it from all of you so that you die, and he doesn't.'

There were shocked mutterings and murmurs all around the room.

'Give us all the chance to free ourselves!' a woman burst out. 'Don't be so selfish!'

'Good for you, is what I say,' said a man. 'I'd keep it to myself too if I knew anything.'

'Don't you see?' the boy said, glaring angrily around the room. 'They're not going to let any of us go. The Commander cares nothing about you. He has no mercy. He'll take your information and use it to quash the rebellion, then he'll probably kill you anyway! The Rulers will go on oppressing and killing people with plague. The rebels are our only hope of true freedom.'

'What do you know?' spat the man, wiping blood from his nose, where the boy had punched him.

'We're all dead, unless we find a way to get ourselves out of here,' the boy said.

'And how do you propose we do that?' asked another woman, sarcastically.

'We stick together and fight back,' said the girl.

'Yeah, 'cos we can overpower the guards and get out of this prison easily,' the man's wife said.

'We have a chance if we agree to stick together.' The boy, though young, spoke with authority and people began to quieten down and listen. 'I know Silence Hunter. He's my friend. I won't let any of you betray what he and the others are working for. We should stick together and fight our way out of here. And if this guy here really knows where the rebels are, we join them.'

There was more muttering around the room.

'Who's with me? Believe me, I've seen the Commander at work before. You're dead if you try to do this his way.'

'What do we have to lose?' A woman said. 'I think the boy's right.'

'We can't break out of here,' the injured man said. 'Don't be idiots.'

'What's your name, son?' A man asked.

'My name's Ben.' He reached out for his companion's hand and she stood defiantly next to him. 'And this is Honour.'

*

Resolution was done with Harmony. She was either a very devoted employee or truly knew nothing of significance. She sat slumped in the chair, her eyes closed, barely conscious from Resolution's torture wand and some more traditional beatings from Excellence.

'We will be back tomorrow,' Resolution said. 'Think harder about what you know.'

'Shall I untie her, Sir?' Excellence asked.

'No, leave her there,' Resolution replied. 'Maybe it will help her to think straight.' He called to be let out of the room.

Excellence wanted to put a glass of water to her lips, but he didn't dare. To show even a touch of compassion would be utter weakness, and he remembered that Resolution had called him Captain North.

'Let's eat, Commander.'

Resolution took one last look at Harmony. There was some blood on her face, spoiling his handiwork. He looked quickly away and shut the door behind them. He felt the need to draw out his work here, savouring the pleasure he would get from torturing people for answers he knew most of them didn't have. 'Yes. I've worked up an appetite now. We will deal with the other imbeciles after we've eaten.'

*

The prisoners were feeling the strain of not knowing what was going to happen to them. Ben and Honour had attracted a small group of people to them as they told some of their story, in the hope that it might make people feel strong enough to fight back. They had been discussing ideas of how they might break free from the Priory if they all acted together. Ben knew very well that some of them would unquestionably die in the struggle, but he didn't voice this to anyone. He must inspire them. He thought of all the times he had been inspired by Chas and Si to keep going, especially recalling how they had first saved him from the slaver-traders and supported him through grief for his brother and parents. They had given him hope and that was what he had to do here.

'You're a brave lad,' one man said. 'They gave you the wrong name, eh? You should have been named Courage.' The man smiled at him. Ben was surprised at how many were willing to listen to someone of his age. But they were desperate, and any glimmer of hope was worth listening to. Of course, there were some who thought Ben's idea was ridiculous and wanted nothing to do with it.

It was late when Resolution and Excellence entered the room with the Chief of the Priory.

The people were hungry and thirsty. No sustenance had been provided since the morning. Now, water was brought to them and when they had finished every last drop, Resolution spoke.

'This is your opportunity to talk. To tell us what you know of the rebels and their whereabouts. If your information leads us to them, you will be freed in due course.'

'Not true,' Honour whispered.

'Do you have something to say already?' Resolution said to her.

'No, she doesn't,' Ben said, digging her in the ribs.

Resolution looked around the room at the array of emotions on display. He sensed a new defiance in some of the faces and turned to Honour. 'We will start with you.'

Excellence took her by the arm.

'No!' Ben protested. 'You won't take her. You won't take any of us.'

Resolution stared at him. 'Take him as well.'

Excellence grabbed his arm. Ben and Honour began to wrestle against Excellence, kicking and punching him. He was well built and strong, but he was struggling to hold both of them.

'Now!' Ben shouted. 'Now! We fight back. Come on!'

A few people moved towards Excellence and the Commander. Resolution was surprised but not disconcerted.

The Chief called for guards, who rushed in within seconds, apprehending those who had made the feeble effort to fight back.

'Don't be foolish!' Resolution said, once all those who had attempted to fight were on the floor on their knees. 'I have told you the only way to get out of here alive.'

Some people were crying again.

'Take all the children first,' Resolution commanded.

There were three other children, younger than Ben and Honour.

'Wait!' shouted the man, who had fought with Ben

earlier. 'I know things about the rebels. I'll talk for my own freedom and for my wife's.' Then, he pointed at Ben and Honour. 'These two are friends of Silence Hunter. They could be useful to you. Free the other children in exchange for them.'

Resolution looked at Ben and Honour on the floor, then at the man who had spoken. 'Take him and his wife for questioning,' he ordered Excellence.

He kicked Ben in the ribs. 'Do you know Silence Hunter? And Chastity Komchenski?'

There was no point in denying it. Half the room knew it was true and Ben suddenly felt annoyed with himself for being so open about his identity.

'Yes!' he shouted. 'But you won't get anything out of me! I don't know where they are now.'

'Unlikely,' Resolution said. 'And if you're important to them you could be just the enticement we need, to draw them out of hiding.' He spoke to the guards. 'Take these two to a separate cell. The rest of you have until morning to think about what you know.'

6

The rebels had been in the bunker for some weeks now and their numbers were increasing, to the extent that the bunker felt crowded and often stifling.

The authorities in Newcastle had declared the city in quarantine, just a few weeks after Si and the others had got safely out to the bunker. No trade was allowed in or out. Kate had finally found a way to inoculate those in the bunker against the new plague. Anyone who came to join them was quarantined and inoculated before being allowed any contact with the others.

Their propaganda videos had provoked lots of protest marches across northern tech-cities. Scouts from the bunker were going out to the nearby tech-cities regularly, bringing recruits back. Once Newcastle had been quarantined, the fear of plague and the rumours that there was protection against it, for those who joined the rebels, was a strong incentive. Some people came back to the bunker, keen to be fully involved. Others pledged their support.

There was a wariness towards the new people at first. What if they were spies? But they agreed not to leave the bunker, once they came, so that they couldn't give anything away.

Temp was looking through the periscope that gave them a 360° view of the Angel of the North and surrounding countryside. Someone was always on duty, keeping watch for signs of law-keepers. He saw a group of young people gathering at the feet of the statue. They arrived over the course of an hour, in two's and three's, looking dishevelled and unsure.

Temp summoned Si and Capability to take a look. 'What do you make of that?'

Capability looked through the periscope. 'Tourists?'

People came to the Angel of the North all the time, but usually in small groups.

Si took the periscope. 'They look like they're listening to a talk,' Si said.

Temp looked again, then he stepped back. 'That guy giving the talk... I know who he is.'

'Who?' Si looked again.

'It's Mish!' Temp said.

Capability raised his eyebrows. 'Didn't think we'd see him again. Looks like he's brought some more supporters.'

'He's the guy who Chas lived with, in the commune in Northumberland, isn't he?' Si remembered how jealous he'd felt when she told him about those months without him and this guy who'd helped her find Resolution. He swept that feeling aside. 'How did he find us here?'

'Good question and one I intend to find the answer to,' Temp said. 'Coming?'

Si and Temp headed outside. 'Mish also helped Ben and Honour after you were taken and drove them to Newcastle. Then he went back to find his commune. The

Rulers kidnapped him, as bait, to get Chas to lure you to the Citadel, and beat up his father.'

'Makes you wonder why he'd come back,' Si said. 'Did he and Chas have a... you know... were they...'

'In a relationship?' Temp asked, smiling a little. 'I don't know. He certainly cared about her though.'

Si wasn't sure he wanted Mish around. He wanted to rescue Chas. They were meant to be together. What if she preferred this guy? Si had been pushing to go back to the Citadel for weeks now, but they wouldn't let him. They kept saying they weren't ready. But he was ready. He was desperate to get her out of there.

Mish saw them approaching from the trees. He stopped talking and gradually, all the heads turned their way. Temp smiled as they approached and walked straight up to Mish, greeting him with a man-hug. 'Mish. How are you?'

'Aye, good, good,' he said smiling back. 'We've come to join ye.' He waved his arm across the group.

Temp looked at them. They were all aged between fifteen and twenty-five, he guessed. 'You're all welcome. Thank you for coming.' He turned back to Mish. 'This is Si.'

Mish held out his hand to shake. 'Good to meet ye at last.'

Si was surprised by Mish's strong Scottish accent. There was only a moment's hesitation before Si offered his hand. 'You too.'

Mish spoke to the group. 'Everyone, this is Silence Hunter!'

They began to clap and whoop! Si was taken aback.

'Let's keep it down guys,' Temp said. 'We don't want to

attract attention.'

'Ach, sorry. They've been hoping they'd meet ye, Si. We're with ye all the way. We want to see an end to the Rulers' power.' There was more cheering from the crowd again, but Mish quietened them. 'And I want t' help ye get Chas out o' there.'

Si tried to hide his conflicted feelings with a smile.

'Come inside and tell us how you found us,' Temp said. 'We thought no one knew we were here.'

Inside the bunker, Temp introduced Mish to the other leaders of the rebellion. Kate was keen to quarantine them, but Mish assured her that they had not had any contact with anyone from a town for over three weeks. Knowing that they would have had symptoms immediately, Kate felt assured that they weren't contaminated. Each person was assigned a mentor and taken off to be given a tour of the bunker and shown where they would sleep. They were told to come to the canteen in an hour where there would be a briefing.'

'You come with us, Mish,' Temp said. 'We need to talk.'

Temp led him to the Ops room, where the others had assembled. Nick made drinks and they sat down to talk. Mish told them that he had been in Durham a few weeks ago and overheard someone talking about the rebels and how no one was going to Newcastle because of the latest outbreak of plague. He had asked about the rebels. The man was wary, but Mish had told him his story, which seemed to convince the man that Mish was a rebel himself. The man said that he belonged to The Way and had been at Pastor Rowley's house, where he'd heard that the rebels were using the Angel of the North as a symbol of the rebellion.

'That was all he told me. I don't think he knew about the bunker. So, I went home, gathered those who wanted to come and set off to find you.'

'And were you just going to camp at the feet of the Angel 'til we showed up?' Si asked.

Mish grinned. 'You got it! Didn't expect to see ye so soon, but then I didn't know ye were right here under our feet!'

'It's worrying that rumours are spreading about the Angel,' Peter said. 'The Rulers know about the bunker.'

Temp shrugged. 'At least they if they come, they can't get to us easily. That was the point of coming here wasn't it?'

'Yes, we could barricade ourselves in and last for a long time with the supplies we have here,' Peter said.

'But we need to be on the offensive,' Si added. 'We don't want to be stuck here waiting to be starved out. Our purpose is to end the tyranny.' He had been restless for weeks now. 'We've sat here for too long doing nothing. We need a definite plan of attack.' He glanced at Mish. 'And I need to get Chas out of there before we do anything that could endanger her.'

'I'm with ye on that, Si,' Mish said.

Si wasn't sure whether he meant the bit about Chas or the whole attack idea.

'Si's right,' Temp said. 'We do need to make our move.'

Capability nodded. 'We've sown doubt into their minds about where we are and whether they wiped us out or not, by keeping quiet all this time. But we need to be proactive now, especially if word gets out that we may be here.'

'Maybe it's time for me to make a new propaganda video,'

Si said. 'No one really knows that I'm still alive, apart from the people here. If they see me, it could stir up anger and hope; a good mix when directed towards the right things.'

'It's time for them to know that you're still alive and kicking,' Mish said.

Peter nodded. 'I can get holo-images of Si in every public place and on every HTV screen across the country.'

'And what if we could really scare the Rulers by making sure they know what we're capable of?' Si suggested.

Everyone looked expectantly at him.

'What's your idea?' Kate asked.

'We use the invisibility suits, gain access to the Citadel and the Fortress. Video me in there; in the heart of the Ruler's stronghold. They know we have the suits, but they still think they can protect themselves from us.'

There was more silence as they imagined the scene Si had painted. Temp nodded. 'I like the idea.'

'It's too risky,' Capability said.

'I agree,' Kate added, looking anxiously at her son.

'You did it in an invisibility suit,' Temp said.

'True, but I know my way around the place, and I have security clearance to places and know how to get access to others.'

'Exactly,' Si said. 'That's why you should come with me.'

Capability's features betrayed his fear.

'It's a thought,' Temp said.

'It's possible,' Peter said.

'And I could find Chas,' Si said, trying not to look at Mish.

'That would be virtually impossible,' Capability said. 'She's being held in the Complex with all the young clones. Heavy security. That's one place I don't have access to.'

'We'd find a way,' Si said.

'Listen to Capability,' Kate said. 'He knows what he's talking about.'

'I could come with ye,' Mish said. 'No offence to the older people, but he could do wi' someone his own age; able to move fast and think quickly.'

Temp raised an eyebrow. 'We'll try not to be offended by that!'

'No, I didna mean...'

Nick and Kate looked at each other. Nick knew she was torn between her maternal feelings and wanting to push forward with the rebellion.

Si shook his head. 'No offence, Mish, but I'd rather Capability came. He knows the place. Or maybe Temp. You must remember a lot about it too.'

Kate spoke up. 'Let's come back to this. We need to meet the others in the canteen. There's a briefing and it's nearly meal-time.'

As they walked to the canteen Mish took Si aside. 'I'd like to come. I want to help you get Chas back. I couldn'a rest easy since I went back to the commune, knowing she's still there. I just hope she's still alive.'

'You don't know what they did to her, do you?'

'All I know is that she was saved from the noose by you. Is she okay? I mean, probably not okay, but... what've they done?'

'I've got a lot of explaining to do. I'll tell you more

over dinner.'

Si was uncomfortable. What did Mish know of his relationship with Chas? And what were Mish's feeling for her? He couldn't ask the guy. Mish was rugged and good-looking. Si thought he looked more Chas's 'type.' But what would Mish do when he found out about the clone babies, and that they were replicas of Chas and Si? What were they going to do about the clones anyway? There was so much to unravel and a lot of it seemed an impossible task. Two things Si did know though: He was going to get to Chas very soon. And he was not taking Mish with him.

'Where's Ben?' Mish asked, breaking into Si's thoughts.

'You helped him, didn't you?' Si said.

'Aye. I saved his ass at the hanging. That's how I got involved.'

'Yeah, he did tell me. Ben's gone back to Seahouses with Honour.'

'Oh aye, the feisty lass.'

Si chuckled. 'Yes, that's her. Chas will like her. Honour reminds me of her. Yeah. Her dad died of the new plague that they infected me with, when they let me loose. She survived it, like me. My mum managed to modify the NMBs to combat it, just in time to save some of us. Anyway, Ben went with her to break the news to her mum, in Seahouses. All I've heard since, is that Sarah wanted them to stay.'

'Poor things. Terrible to lose your dad. I thought I'd lost mine to the Rulers when they beat him up.'

'Yeah, I heard about your dad. They killed mine too. The Rulers have a lot to answer for. Ben says Honour needs time to recover. Well, that's Sarah's excuse for keeping them there so long. They're both itching to get back.'

'Aye I can imagine.'

They arrived at the canteen. After the briefing for the new people, Mish sat down next to Si and began to eat. 'Mmm. This is good,' he said with his mouth full. 'So, tell me what's happened to Chas.'

*

Every time Chas went to the gym now, Young Zephyr acknowledged her and they talked a little more. A couple of sentences about working out and healthy eating, had turned into a fifteen-minute conversation yesterday. Chas was starting to think that what she had at first mistaken for surliness was probably shyness. She realised that he spent a lot of time alone and not much time with anyone his own age of the opposite sex.

He was uncertain about approaching her and she had started each conversation. His answers had been short and to the point at first, but as the days went on, they expanded, and he relaxed more.

She had discovered that working out was one of his favourite things to do and he spent many of his free hours at the gym. His favourite subject was not, as she had imagined, politics, but art, and he spent many of his remaining hours sculpting. Wood was his favourite medium. He also told her that he was being forced to study for a degree in Politics, via the internet and tutors specifically selected by The Rulers.

Chas was surprised and stored all this information about him away. As well as the serious stuff, he told her that his favourite food was peanut butter and jam sandwiches, at which she screwed up her face. He laughed at her and asked her for her favourite food, which she told him was cabbage. This made him laugh even more.

Today, when she arrived at the gym, he was cycling, near the door.

She couldn't help smiling. 'Are you waiting for me?'

If he hadn't already been hot from exertion, she could have sworn that he blushed. 'Well, kind of. I mean, I'm here and you usually come at this time, so...'

Chas put her towel on the bench and filled her water bottle from the fountain. Her energy levels had been increasing recently as the sickness was finally abating. She hopped up onto the treadmill and gradually increased the speed to 10K per hour. They didn't speak for thirty minutes, but she was aware of Zephyr's eyes on her from time to time.

'You haven't told me much about you?' he said, suddenly, stepping off the bike and grabbing his towel from the bench.

'What?' she said, removing an earphone.

'You haven't told me much about you,' he repeated, coming to stand by the treadmill.

'I expect you know everything interesting there is to know about me anyway,' she said, continuing to run.

He shrugged. 'I know the political stuff, yeah. Zephyr and Ambition told me all that before you arrived.'

'Well then,' she said, keeping her eyes on the screen in front of her.

He stood awkwardly for a moment, contemplating whether to leave it at that. 'But what about the stuff that makes you tick? You know, the stuff they don't care about, but it makes you...you.'

She slowed the treadmill down to a walk. 'Well, you know I love cabbage,' she said.

He smiled. 'Yeah. I know that. But what about... well, I told you I like sculpting. Calms me down. What do you do to calm down? You must have something, especially since you're in this hell-hole!'

'I wouldn't call this a hell-hole. It's more comfortable than anywhere I've ever lived before. Although, you could argue that lack of freedom constitutes being in hell, so maybe you're right.' Stopping the treadmill, she got off and wiped her face with the towel.

'You're evading my real question,' Zephyr said, with a hint of a smile.

Chas screwed up her mouth, thinking. 'I don't do calming down. I need other people to get me there.' She thought of Si and the numerous times he'd had to step in before she did something stupid, and the many times when he'd been too late. 'Grace is good at it.'

'Grace?'

'Yeah. The girl who looks after me. She's like my bodyguard and nanny rolled into one.'

'Right.'

'She's cute. You'd like her. I should get her to come to the gym sometime.'

He blushed again.

'Why don't you eat in the canteen?' she asked.

'Why would I? I have a private apartment. I'm waited on like royalty.'

'You are royalty. You're next in line to the 'throne' when they're fed up of Old Zephyr.'

'Yeah, great!' he said, sarcastically, taking a long drink from his water bottle.

She paused, noting his reaction. She would have to find a way to ascertain exactly how he felt about the Rulers. What if he was as much a prisoner here as she was?

'Do you think of Zephyr as a father?'

He nearly choked, spraying water everywhere, then looked at her as if she was stupid. 'He's not my father, is he? I don't have a father or mother. I'm a freak!' He turned away and walked off to the other end of the gym, where he stuck in his headphones and began lifting weights.

Chas cursed to herself for blowing it and resumed her running. It clearly riled him; being a 'freak,' as he put it. She would have to watch what she asked him about. She hoped she might find out something that might help her escape. And besides, she had been enjoying his company lately. What to do? Should she try to apologise or just leave it for today? He had that surly look back on his face. She recognised it as a retreat into himself, because it was how she often felt.

At the end of her session, as she gathered her things to leave, she walked over to him. 'Hey.' He had his back to her and earphones in. He either didn't hear or was ignoring her. 'Hey.' She said again, touching him on the arm.

He turned and took out one earbud.

'For what it's worth, I'm sorry. I didn't mean to offend you.'

He shrugged and replaced the earbud. Chas walked

towards the door. There was nothing more she could say. Besides, she needed a shower and food. Grace would be gone, so she'd have some peace.

'Do you want to have dinner with me?'

She turned, not quite believing what she had just heard. What should she say? Her heart began to race a little. What was she getting into? She didn't want him to get the wrong idea but there again, she did want to try anything that might get her out of here.

'Yeah okay.'

'Tomorrow,' he said. 'After your gym session. You can shower in my apartments.'

'You sure that will be okay with... them?'

Zephyr gave her a conspiratorial smile. 'I doubt it, but they won't know, so it doesn't matter.'

7

At dinner, Si told Mish what had happened to him and Chas after the execution had been stopped. Mish was finding it hard to take it all in and asked lots of questions about cloning.

'So, she's pregnant with twins?'

Si nodded for what seemed like the hundredth time, as Mish incredulously repeated himself.

'What are ye gonna do about that?'

Si rolled his eyes. 'What can I do, except get her out of there.'

'Aye. That's true.'

'What's the plan?' Mish leaned over the table. 'Ye know I just want to help. I know she's your girlfriend. I'm not tryin' to take her from you. But I do care about her.'

Si blushed and shook his head. 'I'm not sure what's going on between us. You never know with her. You can think she wants you one minute then feel totally rejected another.'

Mish grinned. 'Aye, aye, I know that. I have to admit, I did want there to be something between us, but she didn'a want anything of the sort. We had some good times though, before we went hunting for her brother.'

'And it turns out he's not really her brother after all.' Si said. 'I don't understand that.'

'Aye. Ye said they did a DNA test though. Mebbe he got to it and swapped it.'

'He didn't know about it until afterwards.'

'Maybe a mix up or bad test, then.'

'I don't know,' Si said.

'Let me help ye, Si.'

Si hesitated. Maybe it was just foolish pride that was making him want to be the one that rescued Chas. If he stuck stubbornly to that plan and it failed, he wouldn't be able to forgive himself. Maybe Mish would be useful, and he had explained that he didn't want Chas as a girlfriend. But what if she wanted Mish? Stupid, stupid, irrelevant questions anyway! Chas was her own person. She didn't belong to anyone and she would make her own decisions, no matter who went to rescue her. And that was all that mattered. He should only be thinking of getting her out of there.

'Well?' Mish said.

'Sorry. Yes. Okay. If the old folks don't have any objections.'

They took the plan to the others after dinner. After much discussion, it was decided that Temp, Si and Mish would go to the Citadel and, using the invisibility suits, gain access to the Fortress. Capability would give all the access codes to Temp. He was also going to go through a detailed layout of the Fortress with them before they left.

'I really don't think you should try to get to Chas. It could ruin everything if you got caught,' Capability said. 'And you're much more likely to make a mistake if you go after her at this stage. Just get in, do the video, get out.'

Kate spoke up. 'I have to agree with him, Si. We're planning an attack on the Citadel. Wouldn't it be better to get her out then, amidst all the confusion?'

'No!' Si insisted. 'She could get hurt. She's in no condition to be fighting her way out of a battle zone, is she?'

'Let's just do the propaganda thing first. We can always go back for her once we have them scared,' Peter said. 'They're not going to hurt her. She's their experiment.'

Si shook his head. 'But then they'll be more guarded against us using the invisibility suits. They might have worked out a way to detect us.'

'They'd be stupid if they hadn't already done that. They know we have invisibility technology,' Peter said.

Mish backed Si's plan. 'So, it makes sense to do it now.'

'What if they already have a detection system for invisibility suits?' Nick asked.

There was a pause as everyone tried to think of what to say. 'Look,' Temp said, 'We haven't designated an overall leader up 'til now, but maybe we need someone who has the final decision on strategic matters. And we all pledge to abide by their final decision.' He looked pointedly at Si.

'And who would be leader?' Si said.

'We should put it to a vote amongst everyone in the bunker.'

The others agreed that a vote would be organised for the next day. Si was irritated; certain that the new leader would forbid him from going after Chas. But he agreed that whoever was chosen would have the final say. Capability and Nick didn't want to be put forward as candidates, so it was between Kate, Temp, Peter and Si.

Si tried to reign in his impatience. He just wanted to get to Chas. Too many weeks had gone by and he was afraid she would think they had forgotten her, or worse, think that they were dead. Hope was powerful, and he wanted her to still have some.

The next day, when the vote for a leader was announced, there was a buzz around the place, as people gathered in huddles to discuss this new development. The idea of a leader made them feel that something significant was about to happen and many thought it was definitely a good idea to have someone in overall command. They were told the four candidates and given a few hours to mull it over. The vote was to be at midday. Si and the other candidates were staying in their quarters until the election was over, so that they couldn't influence anyone.

Mish knocked on Si's door.

'Hey. D'ye mind some company?'

Si waved him in. He was feeling restless, and being cooped up in the tiny room was only making it worse.

'It's interesting listening to everyone talking,' Mish said.

'You probably shouldn't tell me anything,' Si replied.

'Och, no, mebbe not. How are ye? Ye look fed up.'

'It's doing my head in, being stuck in here. If they vote for anyone else but me, I know they'll stop us from rescuing Chas straightaway. But on the other hand, I don't think I'm cut out to lead this thing. I mean, I'm okay with being the symbol of rebellion. But the real leader? Making those important decisions about people's lives... I don't want that responsibility.'

'Ye wouldn't have to make the decisions on your own y' know,' Mish said.

'Maybe not, but I'd hate to have the final say on whether we risk loads of lives to storm the Citadel or whatever the plan will be.'

'Aye, I understand.'

There was silence between them for a few moments. Then Si said, 'I think we should go, now. You and me. We'll do the video and find Chas before anyone can stop us.'

'You want us to go maverick?'

'Yeah. I don't think we should wait any longer to get her out of there. I've been having dreams about her being experimented on and awful things happening to those babies.' He shuddered, recalling some of the dreams about Chas giving birth to hideously deformed children.

'Count me in. Whatever you need me to do.'

Si looked at him. He hardly knew Mish, but he was already beginning to like and trust him. 'Thanks.'

Mish looked thoughtful. 'They beat up my dad really badly when they took me to the Citadel. I know what they're capable of. Chas's ex-brother, Resolution, he's in charge of all that, isn't he?'

'Yeah, he is. And he's capable of a lot worse than beating.'

'Aye, I know. He tortured me when he was trying to get information.'

'I've been there too. He's a psycho.'

'Well at least we won't feel guilty when we kill him,' Mish said.

'I think Chas'd like the pleasure of that!' Si got up and

bundled some things into a bag. 'Okay, I know where the invisibility suits are. Can you grab us some sandwiches and water from the canteen? I'll meet you at the front blast doors in 10 minutes, with the key to Peter's car. I know where the car's hidden.'

'Okay.'

Si shook his head. 'I hope they don't elect me as leader. I don't deserve it.'

'Ach, dinna fash! You're a good guy!'

No one noticed them leaving the bunker. As they emerged onto the grassy bank below the Angel of the North, Mish looked up at the towering monument. 'Bring us luck, lady!'

Si shook his head. 'It's not female!'

'Aye, she is,' Mish said. 'Look at her curves!'

Si laughed.

They turned away from the Angel and headed towards the road. 'The car's hidden about half a mile from here. We should be well on the way before they miss us. There's another hour 'til the election, so they'll still be in their rooms.'

Si felt guilty taking Peter's car. He hoped the others would forgive him, when he came back with Chas and the propaganda video. It would have been better if they could have consulted Capability about security at the Fortress, but they would just have to manage without insider knowledge.

Mish drove. 'Goodbye Lady-luck!' he said, as they left the Angel behind.

'I don't believe in luck,' Si said. 'I'm kind of into praying these days.'

'Aye?' Mish looked at him, questioningly.

'My mum and quite a few of the others are members of The Way. Have you heard of it?'

Mish shook his head.

'It's a faith group. I see how praying helps them get through the tough stuff. And they really believe in the power of prayer.'

Mish shrugged. 'D'you?'

Si nodded. 'I think so. Never used to, but whenever I call for help, I feel more able to cope; even if there isn't a big bolt of lightning from the sky to strike down the bad guys!'

Mish laughed. 'Aye, well, say one for us now. We need all the help we can get.'

They drove in silence for a long time, lost in their own thoughts.

'Should we call in on Esme? Leave the car there?' Mish asked.

'I don't think so,' Si said. 'The others are bound to contact her.' He had turned off his Wearable deliberately, but he turned it back on now. Just as he suspected, he had missed calls from his mum and Peter. He didn't listen to the messages; just turned it straight off again. He could predict what they might have to say, and he didn't want to hear it. He had to stay focused on the task they had come to do.

They left the car a few miles from one of the gates to the Citadel. 'When we get in there, we need a sign so we know where the other is,' Si said.

They thought for a while. 'How about...' Mish suggested, 'if it's safe, we reveal part of an arm or something, so we know exactly where the other one is.'

'I can't think of anything else,' Si said. 'Let's go with that. We'll meet by the Lion statue outside the Fortress. I'd say, 'see you there,' but hopefully I won't actually see you.'

Mish smiled.

'If there are people around, whoever gets there first, throws stones at the lion's feet every 10 minutes, so when the other arrives they know what to look for.'

'Okay,' Mish said. 'Good luck!'

'You too,' Si said.

'Thought you didn't believe in luck.'

Si grinned, they pulled the suits over their heads and disappeared.

It was easy enough to get through security at the gate, wearing the invisibility suits. Si climbed onto the back of a van as it moved slowly through the checkpoint, then jumped off before it drove away. The Citadel was bustling with people and he had to be careful not to bump into anyone. He hated it here. Despite the huge impressive buildings, he felt hemmed in and trapped. Even though the people here lived privileged lives, with all the latest gadgets, he wouldn't want to be part of it. He couldn't wait to get out again. He had a third invisibility suit tucked inside his own suit, for Chas. They would make the propaganda video in Zephyr's office first, then go and find her.

It took him quite a while to get to find his way through this vast city, but eventually, he saw the Fortress looming behind the buildings to his right, and within five minutes he was walking towards the statue in the square. Remembering the last time he had been here, when Chas was nearly executed, sent a chill down his spine.

There were quite a few people about, and security guards, with guns, patrolled the pathways around the building. A metal fence surrounded the Fortress, enclosing some gardens, but there was no one in them. He walked towards the Lion. There were people milling around in the square, so it wasn't safe to reveal any part of his body. He wondered if Mish was there. He looked for the stones being thrown, but when he didn't see any, he threw some himself.

Then he felt an invisible body bump against him. 'I'm here,' Mish whispered.

'Yep! Hold on to me,' Si whispered.

He led Mish to an alley where there was no one about. 'Have you been there long?'

'About fifteen minutes,' Mish said. 'Took me ages to find my way.'

'Me too,' Si agreed. 'So many people here. It's hard to dodge them all.'

'Are ye ready to get in there?' Mish asked.

'Definitely,' Si said. 'If we get separated once we're inside, the next meeting place is Zephyr's office. It might take some time to find it, since we have no idea how to get there. I've been in the cabinet meeting room, so it might be near there.'

'Could ye find it again?' Mish asked. 'Maybe we should shoot the video there.'

'Not sure. It's a maze of corridors and security doors. But Zephyr's office would make more impact. It's more intimate, like we've managed to get to the heart of the place, if we get right into his office.'

'Seems to me that just by getting inside the Fortress we've

done well.'

'We agreed on the office with the others, so let's go for it. It'll give Zephyr more of a jolt.'

'Aye, sure,' Mish said. 'You're the boss.'

'We'll try to stay together. Hold onto me. I'll go slowly.'

'If we get separated, how long do we wait for each other?' Mish asked. 'If one of us waits an hour with no sign of the other, should we try and get out again?'

Si hesitated. He didn't want to give up at all, but he realised that this could go horribly wrong. 'No. Make it two hours. Let's give each other plenty of time.'

'Aye, okay.'

'Ready?'

'See that couple approaching the gates?' Si said.

'Aye.'

'Let's follow them in.'

They moved in behind the man and woman as the guard opened the gate and asked for their ID. While he was checking the information from their Wearable on his, Si and Mish slipped past.

They waited. 'We might as well follow them,' Si whispered. 'If they're heading inside.'

The man and woman entered another security check at the door. Both were admitted instantly, and Si and Mish squeezed in behind them.

*

Kate had been furious with Si when she discovered that he and Mish had taken Peter's car. The election votes were being counted and the three candidates stood together in the strategic planning room with Nick and Capability.

'It doesn't surprise me,' Temp said. 'He was desperate to get to Chas.'

'If he wins this vote, he doesn't deserve to be leader, if he can't stay in control,' Capability said. 'We can't afford to have someone in charge who just acts on a feeling.'

'I agree,' Kate said. 'We shouldn't have put him into the equation. I'm sorry. I know how much he cares about Chas, but I never thought he'd go off-piste like this.'

'Well, you know what he did to find you,' Nick said. 'When he's passionate about something there's no stopping him. It's one of his strengths.'

'Not in this situation,' Peter said. 'He's going to jeopardize everything. Did he leave a note?'

Kate shook her head. 'And I've tried calling him lots of times, but he has his phone switched off.'

'I called Esme,' Peter said. 'She hasn't seen them.'

'There's nothing we can do,' Temp said, pragmatically. 'We just have to trust them to be careful.'

'We need to pray,' Kate said.

Peter looked at his Wearable. 'The winner of the election will be announced in twenty minutes. We should get to the canteen.'

'And what if it's Si? What do we tell them about his absence?' Kate asked.

'We tell them the truth. We owe them that. Then, if they've voted him leader, we ask them whether they want to stick with their decision or not,' Peter said.

'I'm so annoyed with him, Nick,' Kate said, as they made their way to the canteen.

Nick, hearing fear, more than anger, in her voice, put a hand on her arm. 'He'll be alright. He's survived a lot so far.'

Kate shook her head. 'He's let us down.'

Nick took her hand. 'He's doing what he thinks is right. Be proud of him for that.'

In the canteen, Nick took charge of the election announcement. People murmured about Si's absence. 'The votes are now in,' Nick said. 'Our candidates are Kate Hunter, Peter Marsden, Temperance Alliston and Silence Hunter.'

The three candidates present stood up.

'Where's Si?' shouted a voice from the crowd.

Nick glanced at Peter, then spoke calmly. 'We apologise that Si can't be here. He's been called away on a task that couldn't wait.'

There was a little more murmuring at that, but Nick pressed on. 'I have the result in my hand.' He opened the envelope and the noise quietened down. 'You have voted that Kate be the leader of the rebellion and take us forward to defeat the Rulers. She will be supported by all of us, but Kate has the final decision on what we do. Kate is a good choice. She's level-headed, smart, passionate and will do the right thing.' He smiled at her. 'Together we will restore justice and peace!'

The people began clapping as Kate stepped forward. She realised that she had been holding her breath, waiting for the outcome. The enormity of responsibility landed abruptly on her shoulders, like a heavy weight and she had to take a moment before she could speak. 'I'm honoured to be chosen as leader. I will make decisions that I believe are the best for us all and for this country. I will not be making them alone, but in consultation with Temp, Peter, Nick, Si and Capability. Every single one of you is important to the success of our mission; to bring an end to this despotic regime and put forward leaders to guide us in democracy, community and justice for all.'

The crowd rallied to Kate's speech and began to clap and cheer again.

'It won't be long before we are ready to move on the Citadel. We will be asking each of you to train in an area where you think you can be most useful. Think of your strengths. Each of you is like a body-part, having a different purpose. Let's create one powerful body, working together, moving in union with each other.'

More clapping.

As the meeting dispersed, the others on the platform congratulated Kate.

'I think they chose the right person,' Temp said. 'You're wise, Kate. You'll keep us on the right track.'

'Thank you Temp, but I need you all. This terrifies me.'

'It terrifies me too,' Capability said.

'Together we're strong.' Temp added.

'Sounds like the title of a song!' Kate said and they all laughed. 'I need a bit of space just now, if you don't mind. To think.'

Back in her room, Kate wanted to think about the mission, but she couldn't help thinking about Si. She was the one who would have to discipline him and Mish when they got back. She wasn't looking forward to it, but Si had to work together with the rest of them. He had jeopardised everything by going off on a tangent. She laughed ironically as she remembered his anger at Chas doing this very thing, almost a year ago, when she left Amsterdam.

'Just come back to me, son,' she whispered. 'Please God, bring him back alive.'

There was an urgent-sounding knock on the door. Nick opened it. 'Kate. Sorry. I know you wanted some time, but you have to come and see this.'

Nick led her to the Ops room, where the others were gathered around the screen. Kate put her hand over her mouth as she watched a group of men, women and children kneeling in the sea.

'It's the Priory,' Peter said.

The camera panned along the frightened faces and then onto Resolution, with Excellence and the Priory Chief at his side. There were guards, with guns, scattered along the beach.

'You know what's going to happen here,' Temp said. 'And we can't do a thing to stop it.'

The Commander began to speak into the camera. 'This is what happens to those who take the law into their own hands. Those who oppose the Rulers threaten our society and will be executed. The Premier wants you to know that he is protecting you from these rebels.' Excellence waded into the sea and, with another guard, dragged out a weeping woman and cowering man. 'These two have helped us with information about the rebels' whereabouts. They will be spared, as long as the information is useful. For now, a reprieve.' The man and woman were thrown onto the sand.

'Anyone who has information that leads to the capture of the rebel leaders, will be rewarded.'

He turned to the guards. 'Begin.'

In the Ops room, they watched in horror as the guards waded knee-deep into the water.

'No!' Kate shouted as the first shot was fired and the first body fell face down into the sea. Tears seeped down her face. Could they really defeat these terrible people, or was their mission to usurp the Rulers just a futile waste of human life? 'God help them!' she whispered.

Another person was shot, and another. There was hysteria amongst the captives now. Someone tried to run out of the water. Another tried to swim away. They were both shot. The sea lapping the shore was awash with blood.

'Hold them,' Resolution commanded, averting his eyes from the bloody sea.

More guards waded in and held each person that was still alive.

Then Resolution called for two young people who were not in the sea to be brought forward. They hadn't been featured until now and another gasp rippled around the Ops room, as everyone recognised Ben and Honour. He made them kneel before him on the sand.

'Is Silence Hunter still alive?' he asked Ben, as Excellence held him.

Ben said nothing.

A guard pointed a gun at the back of Honour's head.

'Is Hunter alive?' Resolution asked again. Ben began to visibly shake. He glanced at Honour, who whimpered as she tried desperately to control her emotions.

Resolution indicated the two people he had spared. 'They cooperated and have been allowed to live. Cooperate and your friend will live. I will ask you once more and that is all. You have 5 seconds to answer truthfully. If you don't, she will die.'

Honour was shaking and looking at the floor. Everyone in the Ops room held their breath.

'Oh please, please, no!' Kate muttered. 'No, no, no!'

'Is... Silence... Hunter... still... alive?' Resolution spaced out the words as if talking to a naughty child. 'One... two... three...'

Ben swallowed hard. 'No!' he shouted. 'The Rulers...' he hesitated and rephrased. 'He died of plague.'

'And his mother and the other rebel leaders? Are any of them alive?' There was a pause. 'I will resume counting. Four...'

'I think so,' Ben yelled.

'Who?'

'All of them,' he said quietly.

Peter asked urgently. 'Does he know where we are?'

'I don't know,' Kate said. 'I don't know what Si told him.'

'We need to get out of here, fast, if he does,' Capability said.

Resolution didn't ask this. 'You did the right thing. You have saved your friend's life. For now.' He turned to Excellence. 'Take them away. They are coming with us.'

'Why didn't he ask?' Temp said.

As if hearing Temp's question, Resolution addressed the camera. 'I have information on where the rebels are hiding. If it proves to be true, there will soon be no more need for alarm. The country will be safe again. You can all go back to leading peaceable lives.' He turned to the guards. 'Bring all the children out of the sea. They have been saved by the cooperation of these people.'

Guards dragged the few frightened, crying children to the shore.

'And now, let us finish this.'

More people were executed until it got to the final woman in the line-up. She was dragged up off her knees, whimpering and shaking. 'Bring her to me,' Resolution shouted. As the woman knelt before him, he spoke to the camera again. 'Look, Peter Marsden. If you are watching. Look what you've done.'

Peter gasped, and his face crumpled as he recognised Harmony. 'Oh God, no!' he groaned.

'Stop what you are doing. Give yourselves up and this will stop.' He nodded to the guard and walked away. There was a shot and Harmony fell face down in the sand, blood pooling around her head.

The screen went blank and shock held the Ops room in a paralysing grip. Kate had buried her face in Nick's jumper. Peter wept.

After a while, Kate raised her head and wiped her face. 'Now,' she said. 'Now is the time to attack the Citadel. It's time for a final battle. He thinks he's sown fear, but all he's done is sow rage!' In her voice there was a fury they had never heard before. 'He just made a very wrong move and we're going to take advantage of it.'

Briefly, she thought of her son, but there was no time to wait for Si to return. They had to act now.

8

Zephyr and the Rulers had been watching the executions together.

'Do you believe that Hunter is dead?' Ambition asked.

Zephyr shrugged. 'It's likely, but we have to know for certain. Meanwhile, Kate Hunter and Marsden are almost certainly alive and stirring up the masses. What is this information the Commander has about their location?'

Ambition addressed the whole cabinet. 'The man questioned told him he had heard that the rebels have taken refuge in the old Cathedral at Durham.'

Zealous spoke up. 'And has this been checked out?'

'The Commander is taking some law-keepers there on his way back from the Priory,' the Premier said.

'Let's hope we find them,' Ambition said. 'We need to finish this.'

'I don't believe that boy knows nothing,' Zealous added.

Zephyr shook his head. 'No. But if we find them at the Cathedral it won't matter, and if we don't, Resolution will get more out of him.'

*

Chas had made the mistake of telling Grace about her

dinner invitation with Zephyr.

'Ooh, a date!' Grace squealed. 'You need something nice to wear. I'll get you something, because you sure as hell can't go in one of the outfits in your wardrobe. Eugh!'

Chas's wardrobe consisted of sweatpants and sweatshirts. Grace eyed them all with distaste, then, banging the wardrobe shut, she looked Chas up and down, appraisingly.

'Oh, for goodness sake!' Chas exclaimed. 'It's not a date. And he's only ever seen me in gym gear anyway. I don't suppose he cares.'

'That may well be. But I care. I'm not having you turn up to a date...'

Chas scowled at her.

Grace continued. 'Okay, not a date. A meeting with the future Premier, looking like a vagrant.'

'I hardly look like that!'

'Well, no. Okay, that was a bit harsh.'

Chas sighed. Despite how different they were, she liked Grace, and sometimes indulged her whims. 'Go on then, if it keeps you happy. No dresses though!'

'I know, I know. Right. I'm going out to find you something.' Grace picked up her coat, ready to go. 'I'll be back soon for a try-on session!' She grinned happily at Chas, who rolled her eyes.

'Just don't tell anyone about it. Young Zephyr doesn't want anyone to know.'

A fleeting look of worry passed over Grace's face, but she brushed it aside. 'Okay. See you later.'

Chas wondered why Young Zephyr wanted to have dinner

with her. She was nervous and that put her on her guard. He certainly wouldn't be taking advantage of her. She could still defend herself, babies or not. She wondered if he had been primed to try and get more information out of her about Si or the others. But surely the Rulers knew by now that she didn't know anything significant. She was hoping to get something out of this meeting herself; anything she could learn about the Complex and the Fortress that might help her escape. She would have to ask her questions carefully, without arousing suspicion. Maybe it would take more than this one meal to gain his trust and cause him to let his guard down a little.

There was a knock on her door. Not Grace, she would just come in.

'Yes?'

Doctor Nelson opened the door.

Chas was surprised that she felt vaguely pleased to see her. 'Hi. What's up? I'm not due another body invasion until next week.'

The doctor raised her eyebrows at Chas's view of a check-up. 'It's not that. May I sit down?'

Her face was grave. 'You asked me to find out what I could about Si.'

'Yes. And?' Chas braced herself for bad news.

'Well, I tried searching databases and asking a few subtle questions, but found nothing. No one seemed to know for sure if he's dead or not.'

'Okay,' Chas said. 'At least there's no definite information that he is dead.'

Doctor Nelson looked down at her hands.

'What?' Chas sat down, feeling the panic swirling around her insides.

'I just saw a news broadcast... It's Resolution... he brutally executed some prisoners, live on HTV, at the Priory.'

'What? No! Was Si there?' Chas stood up.

Doctor Nelson stood up and took her arm. 'No, but he had a boy and girl and he threatened to kill the girl if the boy didn't tell him whether Si was dead or alive.'

Chas had to sit down again suddenly, as black dots began to swim across her vision.

'Are you alright?'

'I think so. Did they look like young teenagers?'

'Yes.'

It could be Ben.

'The boy told him Si was dead. Killed by the plague,' the doctor said.

Chas swore and put her head down between her legs. Doctor Nelson sat down beside her and put her hand gently on her back. 'Take deep breaths.'

'What did Resolution do?'

'He didn't kill them.'

Chas's head throbbed. Resolution had Ben. Si was dead. Was he really dead? Could Ben be lying? Why would he lie when Honour's life was at stake?

'I can stay with you for a while, if you like,' Doctor Nelson offered. She stood up and went to get some water. Chas sipped it until the pounding in her head began to subside.

'You don't need to stay. I'll be okay.'

'I was worried about the effect it would have, but you had asked me for information. I'm sorry it's not what you wanted to hear.'

'I'm grateful you told me.'

'Don't let on that I told you,' Doctor Nelson said.

Chas shook her head. 'I won't. Grace tells me stuff too. I never betray my friends.' She glanced at the doctor, who smiled sadly and took Chas's hand in hers. 'Thank you. I'll do everything I can to help you, Chas. I'll leave you now, but I'll come back in the morning to see how you are.'

'Thanks.'

Chas lay on her bed, thinking over all the possibilities about Si; and Ben and Honour at the Priory. This thought worried her more than Si being dead.

Grace was only gone a few hours, before she waltzed back into the room, looking very pleased with herself. Chas was still lying on the bed.

'I've got a few things of mine here for you to try.' Chas sat up slowly and Grace spread various tops and trousers over the bed. 'There's some really nice things that I just know will suit you...'

Chas pushed aside her news. She couldn't face sharing it with Grace right now. She needed to think it through. She wasn't paying attention though and Grace suddenly stopped babbling.

'Are you okay?' Grace said.

'I'm fine. Let's just get on with this.'

Grace looked at her suspiciously but knew Chas would tell her what was bothering her when she was ready. Chas looked at the clothes in amazement. She hadn't worn anything like this since that awful experience on the catwalk when she, Si and Ben were sold as slaves to Kahn.

Ben. She tried not to think of him for now, but she would find a way to help him.

'Let's start with these.' Grace held up a pair of black flared trousers and a red top with lace sleeves and a one-sided off the shoulder look. Chas grimaced.

'Just put it on, Chas,' Grace said, impatiently. 'Come on. Get those disgusting sweatpants off.'

Chas gave her a sarcastic look and pulled off her clothes. She slipped easily into the outfit, which was slightly too big. Despite being well into the first trimester of the pregnancy, she was not showing at all.

'There! Look!' Grace said, drawing Chas in front of the full-length mirror on the inside of the wardrobe door. 'You look great! Red really suits you.'

Chas stared at the image of a girl she didn't recognise. She rarely looked in a mirror if she could avoid it. She preferred life in open spaces, where she didn't have to think about such things. Suddenly, she was hit by a pang of longing for that life. For Dis and Emmy and the life she had known before Si had stumbled across her path and set off the explosive events that had led her here. It was so powerful that it brought tears to her eyes and she had to stifle a sob.

Grace saw it. 'What's wrong?' She took Chas gently by the hand and made her sit down on the bed. 'Are you feeling unwell? Shall I call for Doctor Nelson?'

Chas hated Grace's fussing. 'I'm fine. Honestly, I'm fine. I just...'

Grace ignored the brush-off and took Chas's hand in hers. She squeezed it tight. 'It must be very hard, what you're going through. I'm here for you. You can talk to me about anything.'

Chas shook her head.

'I'm just here if you need to. Okay?'

Chas looked at her. She was kind, and despite everything Chas projected on the outside, she needed kindness, especially now. She nodded and squeezed Grace's hand.

'Now,' Grace said, standing up. 'What do you think of that outfit?'

Chas also stood up and took a deep breath. 'I hate it, but I'll wear it.'

Grace looked disappointed.

'What?' Chas said, feeling slightly exasperated.

'Well, I've got lots of other things for you to try on.'

'This is fine!' Chas insisted.

Petulantly, Grace said, 'Well, at least let me decide what to do with your hair and make-up.' She came behind Chas and began to fiddle with her hair, pulling it into different styles and looking in the mirror.

'Enough!' Chas pulled away from her. 'I'm meeting him in the gym. I'm going straight from there. So, I'll have to take these clothes in my holdall and change at his apartment. I'll be showering there. I'll sort my hair out and I won't be wearing make-up!'

Grace was about to object, but Chas silenced her with a look.

'Okay, okay. At least let me give you some shoes to go with those trousers. You just can't wear trainers!'

'Fine,' Chas said, taking a pair of black, strappy court shoes, with a modest heel. She looked doubtfully at them, but stuffed them into her bag, along with the clothes she took off. Grace took them out again and folded them carefully, giving Chas a look of disapproval.

Chas put her gym gear on.

'Enjoy it,' Grace said. 'He'll be so happy when he sees you looking glam.'

'Hmmm,' was all Chas said as she headed out of the door.

Zephyr was already working out when she arrived, as usual. They said hi, a little more shyly than before and worked out in silence for most of the session.

As they finished, Chas felt awkward. Zephyr hadn't mentioned the meal and she wondered if he had forgotten or changed his mind.

'My apartment's on the top floor. Looks out onto the garden,' he said, grabbing his things.

'Lucky you!' Chas replied, not really knowing what she should say to that.

She followed him up the stairs. 'I hope you're hungry. I've ordered my favourites.' He grinned at her.

'And they are?'

'Spicy tiger-prawn skewers, followed by steak and chips with salad. I'm not really much of a dessert guy but I've ordered a selection of mini desserts, in case you like them.'

'Right. Er... thanks.' Chas had always just eaten whatever appeared in front of her, or whatever she had caught or foraged, which was often very basic.

Zephyr led her through the garden to a secluded corner that she hadn't noticed before. He unlocked a gate, hidden in an ivy clad wall, and they entered another private garden, leading to his apartment.

He led her in through French doors, to his lounge/dining space. It was open plan, with a kitchen area to the side, and immaculately clean and tidy. Zephyr threw his holdall on a chair.

'The en suite shower is through my bedroom and there's a changing room leading off it. The food will arrive in thirty minutes. I have a chef assigned just to me. He's really good.'

'Thanks,' Chas said, pushing open the door to a huge, king-sized bedroom with French windows, overlooking the garden. She hesitated at the door. 'Erm...'

'Don't worry, Chastity. I'm staying out here. I promise.'

'No, it's not that. And please, do NOT call me that. Call me Chas, if we're going to be...'

He waited.

'If we're going to be friends?'

She nodded.

He smiled. 'Sure. Then you have to call me Zeph. But not in public. Okay?'

'Yeah. I was going to ask if you're changing into something...' she felt stupid, 'Smarter.'

He looked amused.

She sighed and rolled her eyes. 'It's just that Grace has made me bring an 'outfit.' She refused to let me have dinner with you in sweats.'

Zephyr burst out laughing, which put Chas at ease, and she laughed too.

'I can't wait to see it. Yeah, sure, I can do smart. You have the first shower. There's a hairdryer, toiletries and stuff. Use whatever you need.'

There was no lock on the en suite door, which made Chas slightly nervous, but as the warm water ran over her, she relaxed. How could this Zephyr be the next Premier; about to step into the role of despotic leader, when his clone was put aside? He seemed too... ordinary. But this thought made her remember her old instincts not to trust anyone too readily.

Reluctantly, she put on the outfit Grace had given her. It felt alien and she was incredibly tempted to put her gym gear back on, if it hadn't been so pungent. She emerged from the bedroom, feeling like a stranger.

Zeph was taken aback. 'Wow! You look... different.'

Chas smiled, sarcastically.

'I mean, you look... amazing! It's just that I've never seen you looking so... elegant.'

'Not really me!' she said.

'It suits you.' Zephyr moved towards her, but she backed away, and picked up a glass of prosecco from the table.

'This for me?'

'Yeah,' he said, switching direction and heading towards the bedroom door. 'Just make yourself at home while I shower and change. You can give voice commands to the HTV if you want to change the channel.'

She sat down on the huge sofa in front of the equally huge HTV screen. Zeph had switched it on, and a band was playing soft rock music in the corner of the lounge. The prosecco tasted good and she pulled a face as the bubbles went up her nose. She flicked through the four channels they were restricted to. Another control feature of the Rulers. There was a comedy show, a nature programme, a political debate and the news. She flicked back to the music channel, not wanting to linger on the news. Getting emotional was the last thing she needed.

The view across the garden was beautiful and peaceful, pulling her away from the HTV. It was always warm and light under the dome of the Complex and Zeph had left the French doors open. Chas could hear birdsong. She picked up her glass, along with the other one that Zeph had poured for himself, and wandered outside. Small birds hovered around a feeding station, and somewhere she could hear water; a garden fountain perhaps. She went looking for it and found a large, marble, bowl-shaped water feature, with water trickling over the rim. It rested on a bed of pure white pebbles and was lit by underwater lighting. She stopped to take it in.

'Peaceful, isn't it?' Zeph said, having approached silently from behind.

A surge of fear sparked through her like an electric current. She hadn't heard him approach and this worried her. Was she losing her instinctive hunter skills from being stuck here for so long?

'It's beautiful,' she said, as the fear subsided.

'Shall we sit here for a while?' There was a decking area with comfortable seats. 'Thanks for bringing the drinks out.' He took them and put them on a table, then offered her the sofa, but she took a single seat, not wanting him to sit next to her.

He had changed into a white T-shirt and jeans. His skin

was tanned, and he was wearing a very nice eau de cologne. She had to admit to herself that he was very attractive.

'This place is idyllic,' she said.

He nodded, smiling, but the discontentment didn't go unnoticed.

'You're treated like a prince here. I've never seen this kind of luxury before.'

He looked around. 'I've never known anything else and I've come to take it for granted, I'm afraid.'

'You should try living in the real world.'

He nodded. 'Maybe I should. Maybe I would if I was allowed. I see plenty of it on HTV. And I've been told plenty about it by my tutors, and Ambition and the Premier.'

'Have you never been outside this Complex?' Chas asked, incredulously. 'Surely you must have been?'

'I've been into the Citadel, under supervision. But, no. Never been outside the city.'

Chas raised her eyebrows, incredulously, and they stared at the fountain for a while. 'So, you're a prisoner too, then?'

'Of course,' Zeph laughed.

'But, don't you want to be Premier? Have all that power?'

'I've got no choice. That's what they bred me to be. That's what they've drummed into me since I was a child. That's what they think I want, because that's what's safest for me to have them believe. And, in the end, I have to do it, don't I?'

'No. You don't,' Chas said, emphatically.

'Just like you don't have to have those babies?' Zeph said,

pointing to her virtually flat stomach.

Chas stood up. He had pushed the wrong button. A flash of anger and frustration shot across her face.

He knew immediately that he had said the wrong thing. He stood up too and went to take her arm. 'Sorry. I didn't mean to...'

She shook him off. 'You're nothing like me and your situation is worlds apart from mine.'

'I know. I'm... I say stupid things sometimes.'

'I should go. This was a bad idea,' she said, starting to walk back to the apartment.

He followed. 'Chas. Wait. The food will be here any minute.'

'You eat it, then. Or find someone else to share it. I'm sure one of your Ruler friends will come over.'

At this, Zeph's temper also flared. He grabbed her arm and pulled her to a stop. 'Are you blind? Stop being a petulant little girl for a moment. Stop feeling sorry for poor little you and only you!' He let go of her arm. She stood in silence, shocked by his outburst, but not afraid of him. 'I have no 'Ruler friends.' I have no friends, full stop. My life here isn't my own. I'm just their puppet waiting in the box for my strings to be tied on. They think they've trained me to be just what they want. They hope that my genes have prepared me to be a hideous leader, like the current Premier. But that is NOT who I am!'

Chas waited a moment, her face set in stone, staring into his angry features. She saw sincerity and it shocked her. It confused her. Did this mean she should trust him? Trust the next Premier? Trust the man whose gene pool was a mix of past dictators and sociopaths?

Slowly, she said, 'Then why are you still here?'

He turned away from her, fumbling for the right words. Chas waited. Seeing his distress, she began to feel some sympathy for him, despite her natural inclination to be wary. He turned towards her but couldn't look her in the eyes. His face was flushed but he finally spoke with clarity. 'I'm a coward, I guess. I thought there was no real chance of me getting away from them.'

'Didn't you even try?'

'No. I didn't know where I could go, even if I managed to escape.'

'You don't know anything 'til you try. You make it up as you go along sometimes.'

'Is that what you do?'

'Yeah.'

He shrugged, still not able to look at her. 'Like I said, I'm a coward.'

'You wouldn't have invited me here if you were a coward. But you should've at least tried to get out of here, if you really don't want to be what they're forcing you to be.'

He sighed. 'I knew they'd hunt me down and bring me back. The Commander's reputation goes before him.'

'They wouldn't let him loose on you. You're too important.'

Zephyr shrugged. 'They might. To scare me. And he's a psychopath. I've met him and heard the rumours.'

Chas nodded. 'They're true.'

Zeph looked at her then. Her eyes had taken on a steely quality and her face told him the answer to his question before he asked it. 'You've encountered him then?'

'Long story,' Chas said.

Just then, the Virtual Assistant announced that someone was at the apartment door.

'I want to hear it,' Zeph said. 'Wait here please, while I get the food. I don't want anyone to know you're here.'

Chas was glad of a moment alone to take in some of what he had just revealed to her. She had hoped to gain some information from him, to use him in some way to get out of here. Now it seemed that she might be trying to take him with her. Another complication.

She heard voices. One was Zeph's and the other was familiar too. It didn't sound like a conversation with the delivery boy about food. They were heading back towards the lounge and suddenly she knew the voice. The Premier. Quickly, she looked around for somewhere to hide. Fortunately, the garden was well endowed with bushes and she crouched behind the nearest one.

The two Zephyrs came into view; she could just see them through the leaves. Young Zephyr was clearly agitated but trying to stay calm. Old Zephyr placed a takeaway bag on the kitchen work surface.

'I've already told you, I'm really hungry. I haven't been eating well for a few days and with my workouts, I got really hungry, that's all.'

Old Zephyr looked at the prosecco glass and bottle on the table. 'Are you drinking alone?'

'Yes. Is that a crime?'

The Premier picked up the glass. 'You've been forbidden to drink alcohol except on social occasions.'

'So, I break the rules sometimes,' Young Zephyr said.

The Premier slammed the bottle on the table and growled. 'Well don't! And don't lie to me. Where is she?'

'Who?'

'Chastity. Who else would you be entertaining? A few of the children? Treating them to prosecco and a share of your takeaway. Or one of the carers?' He snorted. 'Somewhat beneath you.'

'You're way off the mark and out of line old man,' Young Zephyr barked back.

The Premier laughed. 'Who opened your cage, puppy! This has all the hallmarks of association with Chastity Komchenski. I know you've seen her at the gym.'

'Of course, but we barely talk.'

'But you have talked?'

'A few words.' Young Zephyr tried to hold the Premier's stare.

Zephyr looked around the apartment and walked towards the open French doors, looking, it seemed, directly at Chas in the bush. Her heart was racing.

'If I find you associating with her there will be consequences for both of you.'

Young Zephyr came towards his older counterpart. Chas could see the stark reflection in their features. Apart from the signs of age on the older man, they were truly identical.

'Why would I associate with her? I know what she is, what she's done and what you're using her for. She's pregnant. I want nothing to do with her. She's invading my space in the gym, that's all.'

'She's a woman. She's clever and maybe you find her attractive.'

'Why are you making up this ridiculous story? Are you trying to find something to punish me for?'

The Premier looked him up and down. 'I've got guards waiting outside. I'm going to have them search your apartment.' He looked out of the French doors again. 'And the garden.'

Both Chas and Zeph thought the same expletive at the same time. Chas looked around for a way to get out of there. Then she remembered her gym clothes. They were in the bedroom.

'This is outrageous! I forbid this absurd intrusion of my privacy,' Zeph shouted.

'You forbid it, do you?' The Premier laughed, coming closer to Zeph, almost spitting in his face. 'You forbid nothing! The power is mine, until they give it to you, and that is not yet!'

Chas saw her chance, as the two locked in eye-to-eye combat. She bolted towards the bedroom side of the apartment. She had to get those clothes back. Zephyr was ordering the guards to come. How long did she have? Minutes? Seconds?

The window was ajar, thankfully, and she climbed in. She had not lost her ability for stealth. The clothes had been neatly folded and placed on the back of a chair on the other side of the room. But the door was slightly open to the lounge and she could hear Zeph still arguing with the Premier. She swept past the gap in the door, glimpsing them both for an instant. The prosecco glass was still in her hand and she poured the remaining liquid away down the shower plughole. She grabbed the clothes but where was her bag? Valuable seconds ticked by as she hunted and finally found it, in a cupboard. Wow, he really was a tidiness freak! She put the glass into the bag and whisked the heeled shoes from her feet, throwing on her trainers.

The sound of other voices in the apartment reached her ears. Maybe two guards?

'Search everywhere,' the Premier commanded.

Chas threw herself out of the window and crouched as she tried to decide how to get out of the garden.

'Wait!' Young Zephyr said. 'Okay, I admit I am waiting for someone.'

Chas thought another expletive.

'It's not her though. I've been watching that girl who looks after her. I got talking to her. She's called Grace and I've invited her here for dinner.'

Talk about making it up as you go along, Chas thought. Now what?

'A carer? Really!' the Premier scoffed. 'You are desperate then! You know we could pay for women for you if you need them. We've told you that.'

Zephyr banged his hands down on the table, causing the prosecco glass to topple and smash on the wooden floor. 'I don't want prostitutes! It's not about sex. I may be just a clone, but I'm still human! I want...' He stopped, knowing that he was revealing too much.

The Premier looked disdainfully at him. 'You want love? Is that it? You're weak. You need better training.'

'Conditioning, you mean.'

The Premier shook his head. 'This discussion is for another time. What time are you expecting this girl?'

'In about half an hour. If she turns up.'

'Oh?' The Premier said. 'Is there some doubt?'

Zeph shrugged. 'I hope not, but I sensed some nervousness when I asked her to come. She was a bit... awestruck.'

The Premier laughed. 'Of course she was! Then she'll come, won't she! I'll wait. Continue the search.'

Chas didn't hear any more. She crept around the front of the apartment, thinking that there must be a gate to the garden that wasn't in view of the French doors. She was right, but there was no way to get to it without running across the open lawn and if anyone looked out of the front windows, they would see her. She estimated it would take about five seconds to reach it.

She heard a crunch on the gravel around the back of the apartment and knew she had to go for it. She reached the gate, but it was locked. Panic fluttered in her stomach. The wall around the garden was too high to climb over. At that moment, the gate sprung open. How? She glanced behind her to see Zeph looking out of the window. She nodded and slipped out.

She had to find Grace. Glancing at her Wearable for the time, she hoped Grace's curiosity to know how the night had gone meant that she hadn't gone home yet. They had to swap clothes and Grace had to go to Zephyr's apartment. Now! Chas felt panic rising. Could she persuade her? Even if she was still here, Grace was going to freak out!

She found her lounging on the bed, watching HTV and eating popcorn.

'Good! You're here. Get up and get into these clothes!'

Grace nearly choked on her popcorn, spewing some of it over the side of the bed. When she could talk, she said, 'What? Why? What are you doing back so early? Did it not go well?'

'You could say that! Come on. Get changed into these.' Chas began stripping off the clothes Grace had brought her.

'Why?'

'Because you're going instead of me!'

Grace laughed. 'Er... no, I'm not!'

'Yes! You are. The Premier turned up. He was suspicious about Zeph ordering enough food for two. They must monitor his web interaction or something. I was hiding in the garden. Old Zephyr told him that if he was seeing me there'd be consequences... whatever that means. So Zeph made up a story that he had been talking to you and he was waiting for you. Now the Premier is hanging around to see if you turn up!'

Grace blanched. 'I can't do it, Chas. I'm a rubbish actor.'

Chas was already stripped to her underwear and thrusting the clothes at Grace, who was frozen to the spot. 'Come on, Grace. Get into them. Now!'

'Don't shout at me, Chas. I can't do it. I'll... I'll mess it up. I know I will. Then we'll all be in trouble.' Tears sprang into her eyes.

Chas wanted to slap her, but something stopped her. A voice in her head, that sounded like Si, said, take it easy on her. Persuade her gently.

Chas sat down on the bed and grabbed Grace's hand,

pulling her down beside her. She sighed. 'Look, Grace. We need you. Remember how incredibly brave you were last time you helped me. I was amazed by your courage. And you bluffed your way through all that questioning afterwards. You're a pro. Just believe in yourself. I think Zeph is going to be an ally. He doesn't want all this crap of being a tyrant. We could help him, and he could ultimately help us bring down this evil regime.' She could see Grace blinking hard to stop the tears falling. 'You can do it. You won't have to stay long. Just 'til the Premier goes away. I'm sure Zeph will carry the thing off. You won't have to say much, if anything.'

A tear trickled down Grace's cheek and she quickly swiped it away. Chas waited. She didn't do this kind of emotion well. If Grace still said no, she might just revert to bullying her anyway. Time was ticking away, and her adrenalin was pumping.

Grace stood up and began to take off her clothes.

Relief washed through Chas. 'Thank you.' She gathered the clothes and helped her get into them. 'Hey, you look so much better in them than I did.' She smiled, trying to make Grace smile too. 'Do you know where his apartment is in the Complex?'

Grace nodded.

'Okay. You'll be fine. Go on. Hurry. It won't take long. You'll be back in an hour, I'm sure, and you can tell me how great you were.'

Grace looked at herself in the mirror and adjusted her composure. To calm herself she took a deep breath, then left.

Chas waited on the bed, checking the time frequently. Waiting was so much harder than action. An hour passed and Grace did not return. Her stomach churned as she tried to think of what she could do to help, if things had gone wrong. She tossed and turned, walked around the room, tried to sleep. Nothing made the time move faster and her anxiety for Grace grew with each tedious second.

Suddenly, the door opened.

Chas sat up. 'Thank goodness! I was wondering what...'

It wasn't Grace, it was Resolution.

9

A few hours before this, Mish and Si had entered the Fortress. It looked like a castle on the outside, but on the inside, it was a maze of modern corridors and chambers, with security doors to pass through. Si and Mish found themselves loitering by these doors frequently, waiting for someone to come along and open them. Some of the corridors were not particularly wide, so it was difficult to make sure that no one brushed against them. Both felt the adrenalin coursing through their bodies at being effectively trapped in this building, with the enemies who were seeking to hunt them down and destroy them. It always felt surreal to wear invisibility suits, even though they had both worn them before. The fact that you could see everyone, walk among them, stand right next to them, meant that it was almost impossible to grasp that they could not see you. The way people looked right through you was disconcerting, because it always felt like they were staring directly at you. The clench in Si's stomach was constant and tight. His heart rate was fast, and he suspected Mish felt the same.

Each door they passed through led them to yet another seemingly endless corridor. Everywhere looked the same to Si. He would have liked some signage on the walls, at junctions, to tell you where different rooms were, but there was none. They wandered around for ages, listening to people talking, to try and find out where Zephyr's office was situated. After an hour, Si sat down on a bench in an atrium, and felt Mish sit down next to him. People were coming and going but no one was very close to them.

'This feels hopeless,' Si whispered.

'We'll find it somehow. We just have to keep going,' Mish replied.

'Optimist. I like that.'

Mish laughed, quietly. 'Let's sit here for a while and see if we hear anything useful.'

They observed the comings and goings for a while. The volume of people was thinning out, as it was getting later in the day. Suddenly, a man was coming towards them clearly intending to sit on the bench. They managed to jump out of the way just in time, but lost touch with each other.

Si walked in the direction he thought Mish might be, but, aside from bumping into each other, there was no way to tell where the other was. Then Si caught sight of someone he recognised. Resolution. What should he do? If he followed him, he might just find a place he recognised. If Mish had seen him, maybe he would think the same. He had to take the chance. Resolution was walking quickly, leaving the Atrium. Si dodged a couple of people about to walk into him, when he had been concentrating on Resolution. He followed, as quickly as possible, hoping that Mish was following too.

Resolution headed away from the main corridors towards the elevators. Si panicked. Being in an elevator could be impossible if there were lots of people in it and tricky, even if there were just the two of them. Surely Resolution would sense another presence?

There was no one else in the elevator and Resolution got in. Si had a split second to choose whether to follow him or not. He didn't see that he had much choice and slipped across the threshold as the doors closed.

It was made of glass, which to Si was a relief as he didn't feel quite so closed in. Resolution stared out of the window as they sped upwards. Si almost held his breath. He wanted to feel around the elevator to see if Mish was there too, but he didn't dare move, in case he made a noise or did anything that might alert Resolution to his presence.

He watched Resolution. He had never had the chance to observe the man, relatively calmly, at such close quarters. What was going through his psychopathic mind? Si had a strong urge to ask him. He didn't see any family resemblance to Chas, now that he had the opportunity to study his features. If they weren't really family, what did that mean for her? She had clearly grown up with him until she was sent away. He longed to get to her and resented having to find Zephyr's office first. But he had to do something for the rebellion, to justify to himself going maverick. It may give him some leeway, as well, with the others when he got back. If he got back. Where was Mish when he needed his optimism?

The doors of the elevator opened at the top floor and Resolution stepped out. Si recognised where they were. This was the entrance to the Complex, where all the clones were kept. Where Chas was being held. Should he follow

Resolution inside? He was supposed to be finding his way to the Premier's office first. Mish might be there already. They had agreed to wait only two hours for the other to arrive.

He didn't have long to make his mind up. Resolution was already going through the DNA scan to enter. Si couldn't resist the force drawing him towards Chas, even if it was only to see her. He didn't know how long Resolution was going to be there, or how he would get out again, but he had to follow.

He slipped in, so close to Resolution that he was almost touching him. He had to hold his nerve and keep repeating to himself that he was invisible. The Commander began walking, then suddenly turned and looked straight at him. Si froze; his heart in his mouth. Resolution frowned. Every fibre in Si's body wanted to run, but that would be a mistake. Resolution began walking towards him. Si managed to persuade his feet to move and he swept to one side. Resolution walked past him, back to the door, turned, frowned again and looked around. Si was sure he was on to him. He kept still, barely breathing, feeling the sweat trickle down his spine. He was totally trapped here if the Commander discovered him. But Resolution shook his head and continued walking. Si let out the breath he had been holding, very slowly and quietly, then followed at a distance. As he suspected, he was not the only one looking for Chas's room. Resolution found it and entered without knocking.

Si heard Chas swear as the door closed. He felt like banging his fists on the wall like a frustrated child. He couldn't get in there now, with Resolution in the room. He reigned in his feelings and put an ear to the door.

'What do you want?' Chas said, facing Resolution, arms folded. She wanted so much to demand to know what he had done with Ben and Honour, and her head pounded with the knowledge that he had probably killed Si. Instead she forced herself to say, 'Why do you keep coming here?'

Resolution sat down in a chair. 'To see how you are.'

'I don't need your regular visits, thanks. I know you just come to torment me.' She thought he looked at her like a hungry wolf. 'You can't hurt me anymore. The Premier would kill you. At least, I suppose, I should be grateful for that.'

'I don't want to hurt you. You are an agent of the Rulers now. You are helping the cause. I'm proud of you, sister.'

Si could hear the conversation and knew Chas was getting riled.

She got off the bed. 'Cut the crap. You're not my brother, are you? No wonder you destroyed our family. You weren't even really part of it.'

Resolution smirked. 'I don't know why our DNA doesn't match but I assure you, your parents were my parents.'

'They couldn't have been, could they? I don't know why, but you're lying.'

'I wish they weren't my parents, believe me. I could do without being the son of illegal immigrants. The amount of lying I've had to do to cover that up. Then you come along...'

Chas looked at the door. She was anxious that Grace might come back any second. 'Oh, just go away. Leave me alone. You've won, haven't you? You killed Si! Now you're

Mister Important again and I'm a prisoner of the State. Just go away.'

Si was taken aback. She thought he was dead. He hadn't grasped that.

Resolution didn't move. 'How are the babies coming along? Cooking nicely, are they?'

She involuntarily put her hand to her stomach and gave him the coldest stare she could muster. But she said nothing. All she wanted to do was scream at him and attack him, but it would only make him happier if she did. She had tried it on some of his other visits. He always got the better of her. And he enjoyed it.

She lay down again, on her side and turned away from him. 'Talk all you like. I'm going to sleep.' She closed her eyes.

He watched her for a few minutes. She hadn't been much fun this time. No real rising to his taunting. He was bored and frustrated that he couldn't do anything to her. He bent over and whispered in her ear. 'Goodbye, dear sister. Don't worry, I will come back to visit soon.'

The smell of his breath made her feel nauseous, but she didn't flinch.

Si backed away from the door as the handle turned and Resolution came out; a scowl on his face. The door remained ajar and Si could slip in now, give her the invisibility suit; rescue her. After all, that was his main reason for being here. But Resolution was heading back to the entrance of the Complex. If Si didn't follow him, he might not get out for hours and he had another task to do before getting Chas out. Mish could be waiting for him right now at the Premier's office, and if he didn't turn up soon, he might leave.

Si looked briefly into the room. Chas was turned away from the door, but he could see her. She was okay. He desperately wanted to say her name out loud; to touch her; to let her know he was there. But that would start something that there wasn't time for now. He wanted to scream. Reluctantly, he turned away and hurried after the Commander, reaching the entrance just as Resolution was leaving. He just made it through, halting abruptly, hoping he had not caused enough noise or air movement to alert Resolution. He had to get back in the elevator with him. Following him was his best chance of finding places he recognised in the Fortress. Nearly an hour had passed since he had begun trailing him.

Inside the elevator, Resolution was locked in his own thoughts, which, by the look on his face, were not pleasant ones. Si felt himself trembling a little from all sorts of emotions. He thought about all the things he would like to do to this man if circumstances were different.

The Commander got out at another floor and headed along the corridor. Si followed, realising that he recognised this floor. Resolution was heading to his own office and Si shuddered at memories of being interrogated there.

Resolution went inside but Si didn't follow. This was as useful as the Commander was going to be. Time was ticking by. The place was virtually empty now, as most people had gone home for the evening. Si had to find the Premier's office before Mish gave up on him. There was a good chance that it was on this floor. He searched around. None of the rooms were secure entry so he opened every door and realised he didn't know what the Premier's office looked like. How would he tell if this was it? He berated himself for not thinking of this before and for being stupid enough to think that this would be so easy. How was Mish going to find it?

He reached a section of the corridor with a reception desk and waiting area. On the desk was a name stand which said: Serendipity Raines: Premier's PA. Behind the desk was another door. Si said a silent prayer of thanks. This must be it. There was no one about, but as he tried the handle he found, to his frustration, that this door was locked. He sat down on one of the waiting room chairs, head in hands.

'Si?'

His heart missed a beat. The voice came from nowhere.

'Mish?'

Of course it's Mish, you idiot!

A head revealed itself two seats away. The floating head made Si laugh, in spite of how he was feeling. He also took off his headgear.

'Ye made it,' Mish said. 'I was beginning to worry.'

'Yeah, I bumped into Resolution.'

'Not literally I hope,' Mish said, grinning.

Si shook his head. 'Have you been here long?'

'About half an hour. How are we going to get in?'

'I don't know. The place is virtually empty now. I guess we have to wait 'til someone comes, which is probably going to be tomorrow.'

'Ach, that's a shame. I just want to do this and get to Chas. And I'm starving.'

Si smiled. 'I saw her.'

'You saw Chas?'

'Yep.' He told Mish about his encounter with Resolution.

'So, she's okay?'

'Well, she's unharmed. We should be able to get her out.'

'That's great.'

'I guess all we can do now is try and get some sleep here. Shall we take it in turns?' Si looked at the uncomfortable options. Number one; spread over the chairs or, number two; lie on the floor. But they were both used to roughing it.

'Aye. Ye go first,' Mish offered.

'You sure?'

'Aye. I'm fine.'

They pulled the suits back over their heads and Si lay down on the floor, near Mish's feet. 'Don't stand on me.'

'Dinna fash, I won't,' Mish said.

Si had been dozing for half an hour when he heard voices approaching. Mish nudged him with his foot.

'Someone's coming!' he whispered urgently.

They both stood up, reassured that they couldn't see each other, as Premier Zephyr came into view.

Si pulled on Mish's arm, indicating that they follow him.

Zephyr opened his office with his Wearable and went in, but it was impossible for Si and Mish to follow, he was too quick.

'Now what?' Mish said.

Si wanted to punch the door in frustration. 'Maybe we should just knock!'

'Are ye serious?' Mish asked, incredulously.

'No, of course not!' Si said, realising that they didn't know each other very well if Mish had thought he was serious. 'Maybe when he comes out there'll be an opportunity to get in.'

'Aye, mebbe.'

They could hear Zephyr moving around in his office, making a phone call, but they couldn't hear what he was saying.

Just then, Ambition arrived in the waiting area. Si and Mish had to hastily step away from the door. Ambition knocked and the Premier opened the door.

'Good. Come in. Resolution is on his way.'

The door was held open slightly longer and Si managed to slide in behind Ambition, hoping that his presence was not felt. He doubted if Mish had got in, but if Resolution was on his way, Mish might get in with him.

They would have to wait until this meeting was over to do the filming. But, that was okay. They were here, in the Premier's office, with the Premier, and he didn't have a clue. Peter's invisibility technology never ceased to amaze him.

'Sorry to call you here at this time of night,' Zephyr was saying. 'I won't keep you long, but I had to talk to you while this is still fresh in my mind. I want Resolution's input too. Drink?'

Zephyr held up the whisky decanter.

'Yes. Thanks. Don't worry, Premier. I had nothing better to do this evening.'

Zephyr detected a hint of sarcasm in his tone. There was another knock at the door. 'Let him in, will you?'

Ambition opened the door to Resolution. 'Commander. Come in.'

As he stepped inside, Mish squeezed carefully through behind him. The last thing they needed now was him bumping into Si and making a noise.

'Drink, Commander?'

'No, thank you Premier.'

'Sit down, both of you.' Zephyr gestured to the sofas at one end of his office.

'What's this all about then?' Ambition asked.

'Did you bring the boy and girl from the Priory, Commander?' Zephyr asked.

'Yes, Premier. They're in the cells. I'll question them in the morning. They know Silence and Chastity. The boy is called Ben and has been with them for some time.'

Zephyr nodded. 'Good, they should have some information and we may be able to use them to draw Hunter out of hiding, if he is still alive. If not, they may work as bargaining tools with the rebels.'

Si began to breathe hard. They had Ben and Honour. Here. This threw the whole rescue mission into chaos. How could he leave without them, knowing what Resolution would be planning to do to them, tomorrow. Could he and Mish get them out before that and rescue Chas?

Zephyr continued. 'Good work, Commander. The executions were a stark warning to any other would-be rebels.'

Resolution nodded; a look of satisfaction on his face. Si had to close his eyes to stop himself running at the man and mashing his stupid face into a bloody pulp.

'That's not why I brought you here though,' the Premier said. 'I'm concerned about Young Zephyr. I think he might be... attracted to Chastity.'

Si gulped back an involuntary noise that almost escaped.

'What makes you think that, Premier?' Resolution asked.

Zephyr explained about the mysterious takeaway for two, his search of the apartment and the arrival of Grace to have dinner with Young Zephyr.

'Unusual, I admit,' Ambition said.

Zephyr sipped his whisky. 'It doesn't add up. Why order a takeaway half an hour before the girl was supposed to get there? And why would he be associating with a carer all of a sudden? He knows we would forbid it and he's never bothered with anyone before.'

'Maybe there's been no one of his age in the Complex before. Should we reassign this girl?' Ambition asked.

Zephyr shook his head. 'I don't think this is about her.'

'Maybe he's being rebellious,' Resolution said.

'That's what I'm afraid of,' Zephyr replied. 'And his manner was insolent when I challenged him. I've not seen that before.'

'You think this is Chastity's influence?' Resolution proposed.

Zephyr nodded. 'I do. And I'm sure she had been there. I think the other girl was just a decoy. He was very nervous, aggressive towards me even. He did not want us to search the apartment, that was clear.'

'And when you searched it, you didn't find Chastity, I presume,' Resolution said, thinking that he would have done a more thorough job.

'No. But Zephyr had been drinking prosecco.'

'He's not supposed to drink alcohol unless we allow it,' Ambition offered.

'Yes, I know that!' Zephyr said, impatiently, 'But, prosecco is not the kind of drink I'd expect him to be breaking the rules with.'

'Maybe he'd opened it in anticipation of the girl's arrival,' Ambition speculated.

Zephyr shook his head. 'There was only one glass.'

'Well, if Chastity was there, surely there'd be two,' Ambition said.

'She's very good at becoming invisible,' Resolution said. 'And maybe they hid the other glass.'

Ambition's eyes widened. 'You don't think she's got an invisibility suit?'

Resolution shook his head. 'She couldn't have.' But then he remembered that sense he had felt as he entered the Complex, as if he were being followed. When he had seen her, in her room, she didn't look like she had just arrived, but that didn't mean she couldn't have been at Young Zephyr's apartment earlier. He wasn't going to admit that he had been to her room though.

'We don't want him mixing with her,' Resolution said. 'She's dangerous company for our future leader.'

'That's what I thought too,' Zephyr said. 'I'm worried that he's going soft. I think we should remove him from her influence for a while, and from the luxury he's accustomed to. He needs to remember why he's here. He has a purpose and he must not stray from it.'

'I agree,' Ambition said.

'So do I,' Resolution added. 'I could... 'retrain' him, Premier.'

Zephyr raised his eyebrows. 'We'll see. I'm not sure we should let you loose on him yet.' He looked at Ambition, who shook his head.

Zephyr poured more whisky for himself and offered it to Ambition, who accepted.

'I was thinking,' Ambition began, taking a sip of his whisky. 'We could use his connection with Chastity. Once we're sure he has conformed to our way of thinking again, he could work on her... win her over. Then she wouldn't be any danger to the clones, and we could use her as a visible sign to the people that we kept our promise and didn't execute her. When the time comes for Young Zephyr to take over as Premier, she could become his wife.'

Si only just resisted shouting. He felt like a caged lion. His fists were clenched but he didn't dare move. There was no way he was going to allow this ridiculous plan to happen.

Resolution was outraged. There was no way that bitch was becoming the Premier's wife.

'It's certainly worth thinking about,' Zephyr said.

Resolution stood up. 'No!'

This was probably the one and only time Si would ever agree with him.

The others looked at him in surprise. Realising that he was overstepping the mark, he sat down again. 'With all due respect; the Premier has never taken a wife. Wouldn't it be a distraction from his duties? I'm sure the Rulers decided at the beginning not to give the Premier a wife.'

Zephyr banged his glass on the table, spilling whisky over the sides. 'Maybe, it's not just their decision. I am a person too! Don't I get a say?'

'Of course, Premier,' Ambition said. 'But I didn't think you wanted a wife.'

Zephyr picked up his glass, wiping away the spilled liquid with a serviette. 'I don't. But perhaps Young Zephyr needs one to keep him... happy, and on side.' Ambition nodded. 'If we give him Chastity, it could cement his loyalties to us even more. I'm sure she would satisfy his needs and the clones could become their children. Imagine the authenticity of that!'

Resolution fumed. There was no way he was going to let Chastity rise to the position of Premier's wife. 'Except that one of the clones will look identical to Silence Hunter, not Zephyr; what message would that send out?'

Zephyr stood up. 'Let's sleep on it. The plan may need a few tweaks, but it could be advantageous. We'll meet again in the morning with the whole cabinet.'

As they left the room, Resolution was silently plotting how he was going to prevent this ridiculous idea, whilst Ambition was feeling smug that he had suggested it.

Zephyr cleaned the glasses and adjusted a few things on his desk. He didn't like anything out of place. 'Lights out,' he said to the VA, and closed the door behind him.

Si whispered into the darkness. 'That is one hundred per cent NOT going to happen!'

10

Chas was still waiting for Grace to return. Resolution's visit had annoyed her and made her even more anxious to know if Grace was okay. She was tossing restlessly on the bed, wondering how long she should resist the urge to go back to Zeph's apartment. Just after eleven o'clock the door to her room opened and Grace tiptoed in.

Chas sprang up. 'Where the hell have you been?'

'I'm sorry,' Grace whispered. 'I didn't know if you'd be asleep. I thought I'd just check.'

'Asleep?' Chas looked at her incredulously. 'I was worried sick about you when you didn't come back straight away.'

Grace began to giggle.

'What's so funny?'

Grace tried to stop giggling, seeing how angry Chas was.

'Are you drunk?' Chas said.

Grace threw herself down on the bed and keeled over. 'I did drink a lot of prosecco!'

Chas stood over her, hands on hips. 'All this time I've been worrying, and you've just been enjoying yourself with Zeph.'

'He's so lovely,' Grace said, closing her eyes.

Chas marched into the bathroom, filled a glass with water

and came back. Grace had her eyes closed; a big stupid grin on her face. Chas threw the water over it.

Grace coughed and sat up suddenly. 'Hey! Why'd you do that?'

Chas had gone back to the bathroom for another glass. 'Drink this one.' She handed it to Grace, with a towel. 'Tell me what happened when you got there. Was the Premier still there?'

Grace gulped the water down and wiped her face, which was now streaked with mascara. She looked like she was about to cry.

'Sorry,' Chas said.

Grace made a discontented noise.

'Was he there?' Chas asked again.

'Yes. He was sitting at the table with Zeph. He looked surprised to see me. They both did, but Zeph covered it instantly, pretending he was expecting me.'

'What did Old Zephyr do?' Chas prompted.

'He asked me some questions about how I'd become friendly with Zeph. That was the hard bit because I didn't know how I was supposed to have got this invite to dinner. I looked at Zeph in a bit of a panic and tried to be quite vague about it. Zeph took over the talking. The Premier was pleasant with me, but I sensed he knew this was all a bit of a con. He left, telling us to have a pleasant evening, in a really sarcastic voice, and made Zeph walk to the door with him. I heard him talking to Zeph in the hallway, but I couldn't make out what he said.'

Chas sighed. 'And then what?'

'Zeph came back and thanked me for coming. He asked

me if I'd like a drink and would I like to walk in the garden with him. I was really nervous in case I'd get into big trouble, but he stopped me before I said too much and indicated for me to follow. So, he poured me a glass of prosecco and took me outside. He walked me to the most open part of the garden, then indicated for me to say nothing. Then he checked himself for listening devices and indicated that he wanted me to do the same. Neither of us had anything on us, so he asked if you were okay. Then he asked me if I would mind staying for dinner, in case the apartment was bugged, or they were watching it. So I said yes, and we had food and he asked me loads about my life (which seems pretty trivial compared to his). And it was great.' She sighed. 'I really like him Chas. He was so nice to me and he's so fit.'

Chas rolled her eyes. 'D'you want to sleep here for the night? You're not fit to get home.'

'I can get a taxi,' Grace said, yawning. 'It might look suspicious if I stay with you. I'll see you in the morning.'

'Okay,' Chas said. 'Just be careful. They may be watching you now.'

Grace looked anxious.

Chas suddenly felt guilty for involving her. 'You'll be fine. They probably just think you're some bimbo that Zeph has taken a fancy to, and looking at the state of you, they're probably right.'

Grace looked upset, then began giggling again.

Chas tutted, shook her head, then smiled. 'Go home, bimbo!' she said, affectionately. 'Thank you for doing that. I am grateful. I know how much courage it took.'

Grace surprised Chas by hugging her. 'I don't think I had

much choice but I'm glad I did it. See you tomorrow.'

Moments after Grace had closed the door, Chas gasped as a gripping pain in her abdomen made her double up. She breathed heavily as it began to subside. The stress of the evening's events was taking its toll. For a moment she wanted to call Grace back, but she quickly pushed that aside as she began to feel okay again. Grace had done enough, she deserved to go home. Chas wanted to talk to Zeph now, but that too would be dangerous. She would wait until they were at the gym together tomorrow.

*

Si and Mish watched the video back on Si's phone. They had waited an hour before they dared turn on the lights and start making the video. Si realised that he hadn't really prepared what he would say. His thoughts had been consumed with rescuing Chas.

It was hard to sound confident and defiant when your legs felt as weak as saplings in a gale, and your heart was beating so fast you thought it might burst out of your chest.

This was the third take that they were watching. 'What do you think?' Si asked.

'It's good now,' Mish said. 'Ye sound like the leader of a rebellion; like you're ready to take the Rulers on single-handedly for the sake of the people.'

Si gave a quiet, ironic laugh. 'Well, that's not true. I'm peeing my pants here in case someone comes back.'

Mish also laughed.

'Do you think it'll inspire people to join us?' Si asked. 'You heard them talking about those executions.'

'I know. But once they see you're still alive and you've penetrated the Premier's inner sanctum they can't fail to be impressed. People must be realising by now that the Rulers are oppressing them. They have to fight back.'

'I hope so. And thank you. I couldn't have done this without you.'

Mish shrugged. 'Hey, I only held the camera.'

'No. I needed to tap into your courage.'

'Feeling's mutual,' Mish said.

Si began to put the invisibility suit back on. 'Let's get up to the Complex and find Chas. And what are we going to do about Ben and Honour?'

Mish also began to pull his suit back up. 'I don't know what we should do. How could we get them out of there? We both know how guarded the cells are.'

'If we don't, I hate to think of what Resolution will do to them tomorrow.' They were ready to pull the hoods over their heads. 'Let's get to Chas first. Maybe she can think of something.'

'Okay,' Mish said. 'It's nearly midnight. How will we get in? I doubt there'll be much coming and going at this time.'

'True. But if we go up there, at least we'll be ready when there is some movement. And the sooner we can get out of here the sooner we can get this uploaded.'

'And face the music when we get back to the Angel,' Mish added.

Si grimaced. 'Don't want to think about my mum's reaction.'

They pulled the hoods over, becoming completely

invisible once more. Si activated the emergency override to allow them to exit the office, before heading back along the corridor, to find the elevator to the Complex.

Just as they came to the door, a girl was coming out. She looked curiously at the empty elevator, whose doors were just opening. Si and Mish ran past her and through the doors of the Complex just as they were closing.

Grace felt the air move either side of her and shivered. Then she shook her head, attributing the weird sensation to being drunk, and got in the elevator.

'I can't believe our luck!' Mish whispered.

'Not luck. Providence,' Si whispered back.

'Oh, the Angel,' Mish said.

'No. That's just a hunk of metal cemented in the ground. I told you that.'

'Oh, ye mean y'r prayer,' Mish said.

'Yeah. Come on, let's find her and get out of here.'

The Complex was dimly lit by night lights and there was no one about. It was peaceful here, but Si and Mish were not in the mood to benefit from it. Mish held on to Si to make sure he didn't get lost. They encountered one member of the night staff on the way, but she was totally unaware of them.

When they reached Chas's door, Si opened it, cautiously. The room was dark, but Si could see her form curled up on top of the duvet. He thought it best to take off some of the invisibility suit so that she wouldn't be totally freaked out when he spoke. He peeled it down to his navel.

'Chas.' He spoke gently.

She sat bolt upright and turned. Her eyes widened. He

was only a shadow, but she knew his voice.

'Si?' Was this just another dream, where Si came into her room and tried to get her to leave, then all hell broke loose, and she would wake up in a cold sweat? He'd never been a floating torso in her dreams before.

'Lamp,' she said to the VA. The bedside lamp switched on and she could see more clearly. Not only was Si there, but Mish's torso on the other side of the bed.

'It's not usually both of you who come,' she said.

Si and Mish looked at her quizzically.

She shook her head. 'I've never seen you both together in my dreams of being rescued. It's usually only one of you.' It was actually only ever Si, but, just in case they were real, she didn't want to offend Mish.

Si sat on the bed, which was also weird as he didn't have a bottom half yet, but the bed sank down next to her. 'We're real this time Chas. Feel me. You're going to get out of here tonight.'

Before she could stop herself, her eyes filled with tears. She blinked them away. Since the pregnancy she had been more emotional. 'You're not dead then?'

'No,' he smiled. 'I'm not.'

'Well, you took your time coming.'

'I know. I'm sorry,' Si said. 'There's a lot to explain, but maybe not now.' He handed Chas a package that had been stuffed inside his invisibility suit. 'Here. This is your ticket out of here.'

She got off the bed and winced as a sharp pain stabbed at her pelvis.

'Are ye okay?' Mish said.

'Yeah, I'm fine. How did you two come to be together?'

'I joined the rebels when I left here. Again, long story for another time,' Mish said. He couldn't help himself grinning, overwhelmed by how pleased he was to see her.

She looked from one to the other, still not quite believing they were real. It was very strange having them in the same space.

Si wanted to tell her so many things, but most of all he wanted to pull her to him and just hold her. He wished, for the first time, that Mish wasn't here. But there was no telling how she would react to a hug anyway. She could be unpredictable at the best of times and this wasn't the best of times.

'How did you get in?' Chas asked.

'A woman was coming out as the elevator arrived, 'Mish said. 'We legged it in just as the door was closing.'

'Grace,' Chas said.

'You know her?'

'Yes. She's my... carer. And she's the one who tried to help me escape from the hospital.'

'Oh, I remember you telling me about her,' Si said.

'Was she drunk?' Mish asked.

Chas smiled. 'Yes. We all have some long stories to tell and she's part of mine.' She unfurled the suit, so that the visible part all but disappeared. 'If we're going to get out of here, we have to take Zeph with us.'

Si's hackles rose, remembering the conversation in the Premier's office.

Mish spoke. 'You're joking, right?'

Chas shook her head. 'You know I don't joke, Mish. He

could be an asset to the rebellion. He's not like them. He doesn't want to be Premier. But if he joined us, he could be a powerful ally.'

'He's not going to join us, is he?' Si said. 'He's a clone: Engineered, born and bred to take over from the current Zephyr when they get rid of him. He's programmed to be a despot.'

'No! He's not. That's my point. It doesn't work like that and he doesn't want it.'

'How do you know?' Si said, hearing the jealousy in his voice, hating it and not being able to control it.

'We do gym at the same time. We got talking and he invited me to his apartment tonight.'

'You went to his apartment?' Si felt his annoyance rising.

Chas looked at him as if he had just accused her of betraying him. 'Yes, I did. And he's a nice guy. He's quite shy. We had a good time, until we were rudely interrupted by the Premier and a couple of guards.'

'Did he mind the two of ye being together?' Mish asked.

'He didn't catch us. I was in the garden when he came in. I managed to hide and get away. Zeph told him that Grace was coming for dinner, so we had to substitute her for me as quickly as we could. Hopefully we convinced Old Zephyr.'

'You didn't,' Si said.

'What do you mean?'

'We've been in his office tonight.'

'You were in there with him in the suits?'

'Aye,' Mish said. 'He had a meeting with Ambition and Resolution. They think Young Zephyr's hot on you.'

Si felt himself flush with anger and got up to cover it. 'I

need the bathroom.' He went in and closed the door.

Chas shook her head. 'What's up with him?'

Mish laughed. 'He's jealous, can't ye see that? He's in love with ye, Chas.'

This time it was her turn to blush. 'Don't be ridiculous.'

Mish pursed his lips. 'Ah, come on. Ye know it. Y'have feelings for him too, right?'

This was awkward. Very awkward. This was the last conversation she had been expecting to have tonight. She shrugged. What should she say? She didn't really know how she felt about Si right now. She had thought about him almost every day since she had last seen him, having dreamed all sorts of crazy dreams about him. She had thought about the clones as if they were their children, at times. Then she had also thought angry thoughts about him. Where was he? Why had he left her here all this time without even a message? And here he was being all irritated and jealous.

Yes, here he was.

Finally.

Si came back before she answered Mish's question.

'I'm not leaving without Zeph,' she insisted. 'If they think he's got feelings for me, they'll be on to him before long. They'll realise he's not who they want him to be.'

'Too late,' Si said. 'They already think that.'

'They said so?'

'Aye,' Mish said. 'In their meeting. They're going to retrain him, whatever that means. Then they've got plans to...'

'It means Resolution is getting involved,' Si interrupted. He didn't want her to know about the marriage idea.

'That's not happening,' Chas said. 'We have to take him

with us, Si.'

Mish appealed to Si. 'I think she's right. He could be an amazing asset to the rebellion. Imagine their faces when they see we have the next clone Premier on our side.'

'They want rid of clones,' Si said. 'They don't trust them. They don't think they're... human.'

'Is that what you think?' Chas exploded. 'Because I've got two of them growing inside me, remember, and they look like you and me. Are we going to treat them as sub-human?'

'No, it's not what I think,' Si said. He looked at her belly, not knowing what they were going to do with the babies. 'Other people think that way. There are all sorts of rumours.'

'Like what?' Chas asked.

'That the clones are being bred for evil. That they're genetically programmed to obey the Rulers unequivocally. That they're going to replace ordinary people when the plague has taken its course.'

Chas tutted. 'Stupid gossip, and we have to change that. These are people, just like you and me. Not born in the same way, but they still feel and think all the things we do. There are children here. You've seen them. They deserve the chance at a normal life, even if they are identical physical copies of the Rulers. They aren't identical in their thoughts and feelings. They're independent beings.'

'He's really got to you, hasn't he?' Si said, bitterly.

Chas was using all her self-control to keep her voice down. 'None of this is Zeph's doing. I've been in here for months. I've worked this out for myself. I am capable of that, you know! I've watched the kids and talked to Zeph. I've drawn my own conclusions.'

Mish stepped in. 'Come on, you two. Stop arguing. You've just been reunited after months of wishing that would happen. Let's calm down and figure out a way to get Zephyr out with us.'

'We only have three invisibility suits,' Si said. 'It would be impossible to get him out with us.'

'Unless he has the freedom to go wherever he chooses,' Mish said. 'He is the next Premier, after all.'

'They keep him on a tight leash,' Chas said. 'He's only ever been outside the Fortress a few times into the Citadel, but even then, accompanied by bodyguards. And he's never been outside the city.'

'And now they'll be watching him even more closely, I guess,' Mish said.

Chas sat down on the bed again, taking some deep breaths.

Si sat down beside her. 'Are you alright? You don't look well.'

She shook her head. 'I'm fine. It's just been a stressful night. Resolution was here earlier too.'

'I know,' Si said. 'I followed him in here.'

'You were in here with him?'

'No. I couldn't get in, but I heard a lot of what he said. I had to leave with him.'

Mish explained further. 'We had a job to do before coming for you.'

'He comes regularly to torment me,' Chas said.

'Nice,' Si put a hand over hers. 'Come on Chas, let's just get you out of here.' They looked at each other then and it was as if they were alone. Chas wanted so much to go back to a simple life in a commune with Si. But it seemed like that was never going to happen.

She inhaled deeply. 'You two get Zeph out first. When Zeph is safely out of the Citadel, come back for me.'

Si's frustration welled up again. 'I'm not leaving without you. He won't come with us anyway. He doesn't know us.'

'He knows who you are, Si. He's seen plenty of pictures on HTV.'

Si shook his head. 'What if something goes wrong and they're on to us? Let's get you out first. We can come back for him.'

'I'm not going without him,' Chas snapped, standing up again.

'Och! You two! Had yer wheesht! You're like two wee bairns!' Mish said.

They stopped arguing, wondering what on earth Mish had just said.

'How about this?' he continued. I'll stay here and hide. Si, you get Zephyr and Chas out, then come back for me.'

'That's risky,' Chas said. 'Better if they find me here, not you, if Zeph goes missing.'

'No. They'll question you. Resolution will question you. Not having that,' Si insisted.

'They won't let him touch me,' Chas said. 'That's why he comes here. He's frustrated.' She laughed.

'Si's right, though,' Mish said. 'They'll question ye and you've got enough to deal with. Please, let me stay. I can keep hidden 'til Si comes back.'

'That'll be virtually impossible without the suit,'

Chas said.

'I can do it,' Mish insisted. 'Remember our days out hunting? Good training for keeping a low profile.'

'That was out in the open,' Chas said.

There was a pause as they all thought for a moment. 'Let's go with Mish's plan,' Si said.

Chas shook her head. 'Okay, okay. You know if they find you, they won't hesitate to set that sadist on you.'

Mish shrugged. 'Dinna fash! They won't find me.'

'There's Grace, though. She'll be here in the morning. She might find you.'

'Can I trust her?' Mish asked.

'Yes,' Chas said, 'But she'll be scared.'

'I'll stop her from raising any alarm when she finds ye gone. We need to get ye as far away as possible before they know you're gone.'

'Okay. Be gentle with her. She's quite timid.'

Chas went into the bathroom to put on the invisibility suit. She pulled the close-fitting garment over her body. From the outside there was still no evidence of the children she was carrying. But the pain that kept coming at her was turning into a nagging ache. She brushed it aside. Soon she would be out of here and then Kate and Nick would know what to do... she hoped.

'Let's not tell her about Ben and Honour,' Si said. 'I want her out of here. She'll never go if she knows they're prisoners here.'

'Agreed,' Mish said.

11

Premier Zephyr couldn't sleep. He finally got up and went back to his office. His mind was in turmoil about Young Zephyr, and his own tenuous position as Premier. He kept wondering how much longer he had left in this position. He could see the Rulers getting irritated with him and the looks that passed between them. Young Zephyr was not going to be a teenager much longer. And what would they do with him once they replaced him with this younger model?

The Rulers pretended to suck up to him, but he knew it was only a front. Once he was no longer of any use to them, they would get rid of him. He didn't trust any of them. No one was his friend. The only person he had ever trusted was Temp, way back when he was young, and Temp had been assigned to mentor him. He'd always liked Temp, until he had betrayed the Rulers. Zephyr had always taken it as a personal betrayal.

He wondered if he could get rid of Young Zephyr. Of course, there was another, younger clone waiting in the Complex too. He thought of the little boy who had always treated him with such affection; almost like a father. He would think of what to do about him another time. He wasn't an imminent threat. But Young Zephyr was. He sat at the desk, flicking his pen back and forth.

Then he noticed it. Such a small thing, but the picture of Kim Il Sung, on his desk, was out of place. Zephyr was a very meticulous man. When he left the office, he always made sure everything was in order. No one could have got in here after him. Even the Rulers didn't have access to this office. How could the picture be out of place?

What did it mean? His thoughts went back to the meeting with Resolution and Ambition. They had talked about invisibility technology. It was something the Rulers had been keen to acquire, but had not had the chance to develop fully, once Peter Marsden had defected to the rebels. They should have defended the Fortress against it, but they had become complacent. Could someone have been in here without his knowing? Could they be here now? He felt his hackles rise. Was he being watched at this very moment? He tried not to give any indication that he might be aware of it. But if they were in the Fortress, how many were here and where else had they got into? Invisibility was a threat the Rulers should have guarded against years ago, with body-heat detecting equipment. It wasn't like they didn't have it. It was old technology now. They were fools for not already putting it in place.

Then he had an idea. He could smuggle Young Zephyr out of the Fortress to a secret location and blame it on the rebels, citing invisibility technology. He could get rid of his younger rival without arousing suspicion.

He walked out of the office, leaving no gap behind him for anyone to follow. It took all his willpower to leave the photograph in the wrong place, as 'evidence' of his theory that the rebels had got in. He had to take Young Zephyr immediately, and he knew exactly where he could keep him hidden, until he decided what to do with him. Could he murder someone who looked so like himself? He had been ruthless all his life. He couldn't afford any weakness now.

It may not be wise for him to go to the Complex himself to kidnap Young Zephyr. He thought of Resolution. Could he involve him? Resolution had always been keen to rise to the top and keep in with Zephyr, even though Zephyr couldn't stand the man. But he had to admit he might be the best man for this job. He would offer him more power and status if he did this favour for him and kept his mouth shut. And if anything went wrong, he could bluff his way out of it and blame it on the Commander.

He called Resolution.

*

Chas felt nervous about leaving Mish behind, but she knew that getting Zeph out was important. 'Don't get caught. Stay hidden and trust Grace. But try not to frighten her.'

Mish smiled. 'I'll do my best.'

'Thank you for doing this,' Si said, giving Mish a man-hug. He wasn't convinced about taking Young Zephyr with them, (he would rather have had Mish by his side) but he knew this was the only way to get Chas to come with him.

'Let's go,' she said, pulling the suit over her head.

Mish felt an invisible kiss brush his cheek, then the door opened, and they were gone.

It was hard to tell what time it was inside the Complex, but the corridors were still deserted. Chas led the way, holding Si's hand. They emerged in the garden. The night sky, visible through the dome, was still black. An owl hooted nearby and made Si jump.

'That's weird!' he said.

'They have all kinds of birds in here,' Chas explained. 'I've not been up here at night, but I'm not surprised there are owls.'

'Dare we take the hoods down?' Si asked.

'No point. We're nearly there. There's a garden entrance to Zeph's private garden and apartment. It's hidden, but he showed me where it was. He told me he'd leave it unlocked in case I ever wanted to 'drop in'. Well, now's as good a time as any.'

She led Si to an ivy clad wall, behind a grove of trees. 'Feel along here. It's in this wall somewhere.'

They split up, feeling along the wall, beneath the ivy for anything that would indicate a gate. 'Here,' Chas said.

Si followed the sound of her voice. She had opened the gate a fraction and he felt for her arm to establish where she was.

'Hold on to me,' she said. 'I expect he's sleeping and he's going to get a hell of a shock. When we get there, I'll take off my hood, so he's not too freaked out. You grab his arms, I'll put my hand over his mouth. The last thing we need is him calling the VA for help.'

'I reckon he'll be even more freaked out by a floating head above his bed,' Si said.

'You think we should stay invisible then?' Chas asked.

Si was surprised that she didn't just overrule his idea. 'Maybe, at first. He'll recognise your voice and you can explain to him to get into the suit. Might be less freaky than the floating head.'

'Alright, let's do that. Ready?'

'Aye, aye captain,' Si said.

She kicked him in the shins and led the way.

There were security lights in the garden, but they didn't sense the bodies, being movement rather than body-heat sensors. They could only see because there was a lamp on in the bedroom. One thing they hadn't discussed was how they would get into the apartment. Si presumed it would be locked. But he was wrong. The French doors were unlocked.

'Rubbish security,' he whispered.

'I guess he feels totally safe here,' she said. 'You have to get through so much security to get into the Complex in the first place.'

'True,' Si whispered. 'And yet, here we are.'

'Shhh! We're going in.'

The door slid silently open. All was still. Si wondered if Zephyr was awake in the bedroom with the light being on. He might see the door open, and panic.

Chas had obviously thought the same thing. She called out as she opened the door a crack. 'Zeph, it's me, Chas.'

There was no reply, so they moved into the room. Zephyr was asleep with a holo-book still projecting above him.

Si let go of Chas and went to stand on the other side of the bed. 'Ready?' she whispered. 'On three. 1... 2... 3!'

Si grasped his wrists; Chas covered his mouth. 'Zeph.

Wake up! It's me, Chas.'

As soon as they touched him, he woke with a start.

'Don't panic. It's Chas.'

His eyes were wide, looking around, not seeing anyone.

'I'm wearing an invisibility suit.'

Si let go of his wrists as Zeph sat up. 'What the...? How did you get one of those in here?'

'Si is here,' she said.

Zephyr swore with the shock. 'Silence Hunter!' He turned to Chas. 'How did he get in here?' Then he laughed. 'Stupid question.'

Si didn't know what to say, so just kept quiet.

'We're getting out of here and you're coming with us,' Chas said. 'Here, put this on.' She pulled out the third suit.

'I can't come, Chas' Zeph said. 'If I do, they'll be on to you in no time.'

'They'll be on to us anyway when they discover I'm gone. Grace will keep it from them for as long as possible.'

'You've got to get out of here,' Si said. 'They're planning to 're-educate' you, whatever that entails. They're suspicious of your involvement with Chas.'

'What? How do you know all this?'

'I was in your...' (he nearly said 'father's', the resemblance between the two men was so perfect.) 'I was in the Premier's office earlier. I overheard his conversation with Ambition and Resolution. They think you have ... they think you and Chas are... involved.'

'Come on Zeph, we should move now,' Chas said.

Zeph got out of bed. 'Let me get dressed and grab a few

158

things.'

'There's no room for 'things' in here,' Si said, indicating the suit, even though Zeph couldn't see his arm.

'Oh, right. Let me get dressed then.'

'Thin clothing is best,' Si said. 'Nothing loose.'

Zeph went into the bathroom. 'Okay. I won't be long.'

Suddenly the VA spoke. 'Visitors at the door.'

'Zeph,' Chas said. 'Who would it be at this time of night?'

Zeph came out of the bathroom and looked at his Wearable, where he could see who was there. He swore. 'It's the Commander with Excellence and a couple more guards.'

Chas and Si looked at each other in panic. 'Come on!' Chas urged. 'We have to leave, now! Get that suit on!'

'Visitors at the door,' the VA said again. 'Will you answer it, Sir?'

Zeph spoke to the VA. 'No.'

'Shall I give them a message, Sir?'

'Sleeping message,' Zeph said.

'Certainly, Sir.'

Chas unravelled the invisibility suit. 'Come on. I'll help you.'

They could hear the sound of the door being broken in.

Zeph swore. 'Get out of here! It's too late to take me. Go! I'll stall them.'

'He's right, Chas,' Si said, pulling the invisibility hood back over his head.

'Go!' Zeph said. 'I can handle this.' He thrust the suit back at her.

'You should keep it,' she said.

'No, Chas!' Si grabbed the suit, stuffing it inside his. We can get Mish out. Come on.' He turned to Zeph. 'I'm sorry.'

'Don't be. Hurry!'

They could hear people in the living area. Zeph was half dressed.

'We'll come back,' Chas said, pulling the hood over her face. She found his hand and squeezed it.

'I know,' Zeph said. 'Thank you both. Go through the window.' He opened it, then barged into the living area. Si and Chas heard him shout, 'What the hell do you think you're doing?'

There was a scuffle as Resolution ordered the guards to take him. They heard a lot of grunting and shouting. Punches were being thrown and something smashed onto the floor. Then it went quiet. Chas wanted to rush in and help him, but Si urged her on. They were already out of the window and in the garden. 'Come on, Chas!' he whispered, urgently. 'I haven't come all this way just to get caught or leave you behind. He wants you to escape.'

Si held her hand tightly, as much to keep her from going back as anything. 'You lead and find that gate.'

They picked their way through the shrubs and across a lawn. They could see back into the lounge, through the French doors. Zeph was slumped in a chair, not moving and the guards were handcuffing him. Chas stopped.

'Keep going!' Si said, pushing her on.

'Okay!' she hissed.

They found the gate and made it into the public garden

of the Complex. Chas stopped suddenly again, making Si crash into her.

'What's up?'

She was doubled over. The pain in her abdomen was getting worse; stabbing now, as well as aching like the worst stomach cramp. She slowly stood up and waited a moment to get her breath.

'Chas, what's wrong? Is it the babies?'

'I think it might be. Come on we've got to get back to Mish.'

She began to move again. He wished he could see how she looked. If she collapsed whilst invisible, it would be hard to get her back.

'Tell me if you're going to keel over,' he said.

'I'm not. I'll be fine.' Despite the bravado, she was getting more and more anxious. She felt something trickle down the inside of her leg. This was not what she needed right now.

'If we get back to Mish quickly, we can give him the suit and get out behind Resolution and the guards,' Si said.

'Don't be ridiculous,' Chas said. 'There's no point in taking that risk. We should wait 'til someone comes on duty. Looking at the light, it won't be long. An hour maybe.'

Si felt the sting of her abruptness, but he agreed with her. And besides, an hour's rest would probably do her good.

They opened the door to her room to find it empty. 'Mish,' Si called.

He emerged from the bathroom. 'What are ye doing back here?'

Si and Chas took off their hoods. 'Resolution and some

guards came for Zephyr. They took him. We couldn't stop them,' Si explained.

'One of us should follow them to see where they're taking him,' Chas said.

'You just said it would be too risky to follow them,' Si said.

'Yes, for all three of us, but if we want to know where they're taking him...'

Si wasn't sure. He would have to leave it up to Mish to get her out and he didn't want to do that. He wanted to go with her. But she was right, it would be useful to know where they were taking Zeph so that they could attempt to come back for him.

'I'll go. Mish, you get her out of here as soon as you can. I'll meet you at the car. If I don't come by tonight, get back to the Angel.'

'Will do,' Mish said.

'She's not well, so take it slowly,' Si added.

'I'm fine,' Chas said to Mish. 'Si worries too much.' She turned to Si. 'Be careful. Keep a safe distance from Res.'

'*You* worry too much,' Si said, glad that she cared.

'I need the bathroom,' she said, suddenly. 'Get going.' She shut the door of the en suite, abruptly.

Si shrugged. 'Doesn't do goodbyes.'

Mish smiled. 'Be careful.'

Si nodded and began pulling the hood back over his head. 'I'll see you...'

He was interrupted by a horrible groan coming from the bathroom.

'Chas?' He tried to open the door, but it was locked.

There was another groan.

'Chas, let us in,' Mish said.

'No. I'm on the loo.'

'Are ye alright?' Mish asked.

'That's one hundred percent no!' came the reply, followed by another groan.

'What's happening?' Si asked.

'Bleeding,' Chas said, through gritted teeth. 'Pain.'

'Is it a miscarriage?' Mish asked.

'Probably.'

'Open the door,' Si said., rattling the handle. 'What can we do to help?'

Pulling herself off the toilet, she saw a lot of bright red blood in the bowl along with some clots of dark blood, floating on the surface. She heaved herself to the door, but she was weak, and as she tried to stand up, a wave of nausea swept over her, and everything started to go black. She sat down with her head between her knees. The blood was still coming. She swore and reached for the door handle.

'Find Doctor Nelson,' she said to Si, as the door opened.

'Don't you have a way of calling her?' Mish asked, looking around the room.

Chas shook her head. 'There's an emergency call code I can give to the VA, but it'll just go through to the paramedics. I don't want them. I want her.'

'Maybe we should call it, Chas. This looks like an emergency to me,' Mish said.

She shook her head. 'Si, do you remember where she works in the hospital?'

Si shook his head. 'Vaguely.'

He and Mish lifted her off the floor and laid her on the bed. Mish grabbed towels and put them under her. She was shaking and shivering.

'I'm going,' Si said. This was serious. She looked like she was dying. Her face was ashen. She had pulled the invisibility suit off in the bathroom and was wearing only a thin T shirt and pants, that were fast becoming soaked in blood.

'Chas, hold on.' He kissed her forehead, which was damp with sweat. Her eyes were closed, and she curled into a tight ball, clasping her stomach as another wave of pain pulsed through her.

Mish pulled the duvet over her. 'I've got this, Si. I won't let her go. If I think it's more urgent and you haven't brought the doctor, I'll call the paramedics. Hurry!'

Si pulled the hood over himself once again. The door opened and closed, and he was gone.

12

He had no clue how he was going to get out, and began to pray. As he approached the door of the Complex, Resolution and his guards were bundling Zephyr through. He thanked God that he had reached the door in time and managed to slide through behind them. The guards held Young Zephyr up.

He was conscious but groggy. 'Where are you taking me?'

Resolution called the elevator. 'The Premier has accommodation for you.'

'He's behind this? Why?'

The elevator arrived. Si wondered if he could get in there with them without being detected. He decided against it. It would be a tight squeeze, and someone was bound to feel his presence. He would have to wait until they were gone. Even though it might help to know where they were taking Young Zephyr, this was not his priority right now.

It was getting light outside as he went down in the elevator. There was no sign of Resolution and the others when he reached the exit floor. He was able to exit the Fortress in the wake of one or two very early risers coming in.

The hospital was not far. He ran most of the way, terrified for Chas. He didn't care if the doctor would be able to save the babies or not, just as long as she could save Chas.

The hospital was busy at all times of the day. He prayed that Doctor Nelson came to work early and would be in her office. If she wasn't there, he would have to get some other help for Chas. He couldn't wait for her.

The hospital was a maze of corridors, but he read the signs on the wall and followed a route that he hoped led to the doctor's department, vaguely remembering some of it.

When he got to the right department, he looked for her name on a door. Finally, he found it: Dr. A. Nelson. Should he knock? Just go in? He hadn't thought about how he was going to tell her about Chas. He would have to take off his hood and hope that she didn't scream. Hope that he could trust her not to give him away.

He waited until the corridor was clear, and knocked. There was no answer. He knocked again, but still no answer. Damn! She wasn't there. He tried the door and it opened. The office was empty. This was the worst scenario. He would have to call for paramedics somehow and potentially give himself away. He could try getting back into Chas's room and get her to do it, but how long would that take, getting through security?

He found a pen and paper and quickly scribbled down a note for the doctor to find.

CHAS IN DANGER. MISCARRIAGE. COME QUICKLY.

He was about to head out of the room when the door

opened. It was her. Si felt a wave of relief flood through him and he said a silent prayer of thanks. It occurred to him that she might just read the note and he wouldn't have to blow his invisibility.

She was carrying a briefcase in one hand and a cup of coffee in the other. She yawned and put the briefcase on top of the note Si had left on her desk, then took a swig of her coffee and yawned again.

No! Si thought, frantically. Put your briefcase on the floor.

She spoke to the VA to ask for her patient list for the day. A projection of names and appointment times came into view above her desk. She began to touch each name and look at details of the patients.

Please! Si prayed. Make her see the note.

She continued to analyse her patient list. There was no other way for it. Si prayed one more prayer: Please don't scream.

'Doctor Nelson.' His voice came out of nowhere and she jumped, spilling hot coffee on her hand.

'Who's there?' she said, looking around the room, nervously.

'Don't be alarmed,' Si said, speaking softly. 'It's Silence Hunter. I'm going to take off the hood of the invisibility suit I'm wearing. I need your help.'

Doctor Nelson remained calm as Si revealed his head. Her eyes widened, but she didn't flinch.

'I've no time to tell you how I got here, but you have to come quickly. Chas is in danger. I think she's having a miscarriage.'

'What?' The doctor grabbed some things. 'Where? Why didn't she call the emergency line?'

'She wants you. She trusts you.'

'Where is she?'

'In her room. There's another boy with her. We were going to get her out of here.'

Si felt his insides tighten as he revealed all this to the doctor. She worked for the Rulers and he was giving her all the information she needed to have them arrested.

'Chas trusts that you'll help and not give us away.'

Doctor Nelson was throwing things into a big bag. 'I won't give you away. Let's get to Chas. Put your hood back on and follow me.'

She led Si back through the hospital corridors, but not out of the entrance. They went down several floors in an elevator, to get to a corridor that needed DNA security clearance. It was long and dimly lit, leading to another elevator.

'This is a secure entrance to the Fortress and leads directly to the Complex,' she explained, as they stepped into the elevator. 'It's so that we can get to any of the clones quickly if they need medical help. Like now.'

'What can you do for her?' Si asked. 'Could she die? She looked in a bad way.'

Doctor Nelson didn't want to think about that. 'I'm sure she won't die. Miscarriages are common, but I might need to transfer her to the hospital. I need to see her to know what to do.'

But this pregnancy was not normal. The doctor knew that. There had been several host deaths before, when clones had been implanted, and none of them had been carrying two clones.

'Just save her, please,' Si said.

'She won't die,' Doctor Nelson replied. 'I won't let her.'

They arrived at the Complex, but in a different place to the entrance Si had used. Again, a DNA security check was needed, as the elevator opened straight into the Complex.

They hurried from the elevator. There were a few people up and about now, including some of the carers of the young clones.

'Doctor Nelson? Is something wrong?' asked one woman.

'Yes,' the doctor replied. 'It's Chastity. But don't worry. I'll send for back-up if needed.'

'Can I be of assistance?'

'No, it's fine, thank you,' the doctor called over her shoulder, as she kept walking. 'You have your duties. I'll call if I need anyone.'

'I think Grace is probably with her by now,' the woman called. 'She's usually here early.'

Si wondered what Grace would make of it all. Another person they would have to trust.

They got to the room and found Chas almost unconscious. She had lost a lot of blood. Mish was holding her hand and Grace was wiping her brow. She looked like she had been crying.

'She's here, Chas,' Grace said.

Chas stirred and tried to move. Mish moved out of the way to let the doctor in.

'Everybody out, please. I need to examine her, and I

don't suppose she wants you all watching.'

'Too right,' Chas whispered.

Mish retreated to the bathroom, because he wasn't wearing his invisibility suit. Grace and Si went out of the room.

'Am I dying?' Chas asked.

'You're not,' Doctor Nelson assured her, whilst examining her. 'But you're haemorrhaging. And you've probably lost the babies. I'll have to get you to the hospital. You may need a D&C and a blood transfusion.'

'I want Si and Mish with me.'

'One of them can come, if they keep covered up and out of the way.'

Chas gripped her hand. 'You won't betray them, will you?'

Doctor Nelson stroked back the hair from Chas's matted brow. 'I promise you, I won't.'

She called for the paramedic team. Then she called the others back in and told them what was happening.

'You should go with her,' Mish said to Si.

'Thank you,' Si replied, knowing full well that he would have fought Mish if he had wanted to go with her.

'Can I come with you?' Grace asked.

'You can't do anything,' the doctor said. 'Why don't you stay here and get this place cleaned up ready for her to return?'

'Is that what you want?' she asked Chas. 'Do you need some company down there?'

'I'll be fine,' Chas said. 'Si will be there.'

Grace looked at the floating torso beside her. 'But you

won't be able to see him.'

'It's okay,' Chas said. 'You stay here.' Her voice was barely audible, and her face was a mask of pain.

'No more talking,' Doctor Nelson said. 'The paramedics will be here soon. You two need to disappear. Si, I think it will be safer if you stay here for now. I'll come back for you as soon as she's settled and stable.'

Si bent down and kissed Chas, holding her hand. 'You're going to be alright. I know it. I'm praying to the Big Guy and he's going with you.'

She smiled at him and gripped his hand as he kissed her clammy forehead, then pulled the hood up and disappeared, along with Mish. 'Come soon,' she said, as Si and Mish moved into the bathroom out of the way.

Within a few minutes the paramedic team arrived, and Chas was quickly hooked up to a drip. Then, with Doctor Nelson leading the way, they were gone.

'You can come back now or appear or whatever you call it,' Grace said.

Si and Mish peeled back the invisibility suits.

Grace stood shaking her head. 'I just have to say, that is really freaky!'

'Sorry about that,' Mish replied.

Grace was biting the skin at the side of her thumb. 'I hope Chas will be okay. All that blood. It looks awful.' She stared at the mess on the bed.

'She's in good hands,' Mish said. 'The doctor looked like she knew what she was doing.'

'I just hope she keeps quiet about us,' Si said. 'But I think she will. If Chas trusts her, that's a good sign. Chas has good intuition about these things.'

Grace began to remove the blood-stained towels and bedding. 'I need to get this place cleaned up.'

'Here, let me help,' Mish said.

Si was too anxious to think about anything but Chas and what they should do next. 'Do you mind if I take a walk in the garden. I feel a bit sick and I need to think.'

'Aye. Nay problem,' Mish said. 'We've got this.' He smiled at Grace.

Si pulled the suit up again and disappeared out of the door. His head was swimming with conflicting thoughts about what on earth they were going to do next. He needed to think, but also, he wanted to pray, to ask for guidance. More and more he found himself turning to the 'Big Guy in the sky' as he often referred to God. His mum's faith always seemed like a rock to her, even in the hardest times. In Amsterdam, when he was trying to come to terms with his father's death, she had told him that she sometimes felt that her sufferings enabled her to help others. He hadn't understood this. The pain was too much, but he recognised that his mother had come through such pain and probably more. She told him that he needed to hate before he could forgive, but that he should come to a place where he might leave hatred behind, because hate was what would keep him from being free.

It all felt too much at the moment. But he turned to the Big Guy anyway, to ask for some wisdom on what to do now.

*

At the Angel, everyone was reeling from the shock of what they had witnessed at the Priory. Peter was very quiet. Harmony had been a good friend, not just his housekeeper, and to watch her die in that way had shaken him to the core. But it also made him more determined that they had to stop this tyranny.

The rebels were getting restless and demanding that action be taken right now! Kate tried to reassure them that they would be rising up against the Rulers, very soon. She tried to sound confident and rousing, like she had seen Si do on the propaganda videos, but inside she felt afraid. How many more would lose their lives, and would it actually achieve what they hoped?

She confided her worries to Nick.

'It's a risk, Kate, but we have to take it. We've come this far. You've done amazing things with the NMBs and now we need to complete this and set the people free once and for all.'

'But say we do manage to defeat the Rulers, what will we put in their place? Who will run the country? And what will we do with them? And the clones?'

Nick rubbed his hand over his face. These questions had been going around his head too, but he wanted to reassure her. 'We may have to step in and run things until we find some suitable leaders to take over. As for what to do with the Rulers and their clones... I don't know.'

'Killing them seems wrong, despite what they've done, but what else would we do? Can they be rehabilitated?'

'I don't know,' Nick said. 'We'll have to cross that bridge when we come to it.'

Kate shook her head.

'What about Si?' Nick asked. 'Have you heard anything from him?'

'No. That keeps going around my head too. Where is he, Nick?' Tears sprang into her eyes. 'I'm so angry with him for going off like that, and yet I understand his dedication to Chas. She'd better appreciate it, and I just want him back.'

Nick gave her a hug. 'Come on. We have a meeting with the others. I hope Peter's up to it.'

They gathered in the Ops room and discussed what to do next. After listening to Kate, Temp spoke up. 'We have to attack the Citadel. If Si, Mish and Chas are still there, we'll find them.'

'How are we going to attack? What weapons can we get our hands on?' Capability asked.

'I've got access to drone weaponry,' Peter said.

'Explain more,' Nick said.

'It's something that's been in development for over fifty years. The Rulers haven't used these drones yet because they wanted to appear benevolent,' Peter explained.

'I know they have them,' Capability added. 'We've used them in covert operations, but like you say, Peter, they've avoided using them as weapons against the people so far.'

'They prefer more subtle ways, like the plague,' Kate said, sarcastically.

Peter nodded. 'Now that we've exposed what they've been doing with the plague, I wouldn't be surprised if this weaponry comes out. I can get us some drones and if we use them in the assault on the Citadel before they realize we're coming, we may have an advantage.'

'How would drones help us?' Temp asked.

'We could send an initial cohort of people into the Citadel in invisibility suits. The drones will fly over the Citadel, also using invisibility technology, controlled from here by me. Once they're inside, and near the Fortress, I will activate the drones to begin targeting the Fortress, dropping small explosives in strategic places. As chaos ensues, the rest of us can enter the Citadel, with RIPs. I can't get enough invisibility suits for the number of people we have, so we'll have to go in as we are.'

'What are RIPs?' Kate asked.

'They're a type of bullet called a frangible. RIP stands for Radically Invasive Projectile.'

'It sounds hideous,' she said.

'It is,' Peter agreed. 'But it's effective. It breaks apart inside the body on impact, causing a lot of damage and certainly death.'

Kate hated the idea of starting a war in which innocent people might get killed, but it seemed the only way to end the tyranny. She thought of The Teacher and how he had taught 'love your enemy,' 'pray for those who persecute you,' and she had tried to do this. But masses of people were going to die at the hands of the Rulers, if they didn't stop them. 'How can we make sure innocent people don't die?'

Peter shook his head. 'We can't be completely sure because there's always room for human error, but these guns also have targeting technology that makes it almost certain that you will hit the target you are aiming for.

Bullets can literally change course in mid-air.'

'Can you get some of these?' Temp asked.

Peter nodded. 'I've got contacts in ATD - Arms Technology Development.'

'Someone sympathetic to our cause?' Nick asked. 'You're a highly wanted man, remember.'

'How could I forget?' Peter said, smiling. 'Yes. I've known Sam for years. He's been a good friend and he always loved Harmony's cooking.' His smile faded, to be replaced by anger. 'He won't give us away. In fact, once he hears about Harmony, he may join us.'

'What about if we want to take prisoners, alive?' Temp asked.

'I can modify the Wearables to include an App that emits a high-pitched sonic beam, targeting the victim,' Peter said. 'It will incapacitate them for enough time to secure them.'

'Wow! You are a useful person to know,' Temp said.

Kate was beginning to hate being in charge of all this, but they were all looking at her, as leader, for a final decision. 'Okay. How soon can we implement the attack?' she asked.

'We could be ready in a few days,' Peter said.

'We should get this place organised for bringing back wounded,' Nick said.

Temp nodded. 'Good idea. I think you and Kate should stay here, ready to receive anyone. And if there's anyone among the rebels who is medically trained, keep some of them here. We'll need some too.'

Kate was torn. 'They elected me leader. Won't they think

I should be there on the frontline?'

'Not if we explain it to them,' Peter said. 'Temp can lead the attack. You okay with that, Temp?'

'Of course. What about vehicles? What can we get?'

Capability spoke up. 'Leave that one with me. I'll find some magnetized law- keeping transporter vehicles. They hold up to 10 people.'

Everyone looked at him, surprised.

'I won't ask how, but great, thanks,' Temp said.

Kate took a moment to think. 'We should take the Rulers alive, where possible, and especially the Premier. We need to show the people that we have them, before deciding what to do with them.'

The others agreed. 'Capability, you should go with Temp. You know who they are. Can we give the rebels any idea of who to look for? Are there any pictures of them online?'

'Probably not anything easy to find. But I'll have a look. I know their names from before they joined the party. The pictures might be old, but it'll give people some idea,' Capability said.

Kate summed up their planning. 'Good, thanks. So... Peter, to organise the weapons. Capability, to organise transport and find pictures of the Rulers. Temp, to organise everyone into cohorts and lead the attack. Nick, to organise this place into more of a hospital. Me? Help Nick, but first I need to make the initial announcements about our plans and hopefully get everyone fired up.' She looked across at Nick. He knew what she was feeling.

'And you will succeed,' he said. 'You were elected as leader by over 70% of them, because they have confidence in you to make good decisions. They trust you.'

She smiled nervously and nodded.

'It's true, Kate,' Temp added. 'We trust you. You were elected for a reason.'

'We're a team,' she said. 'That's what counts. Let's tell them today. I'll call a meeting in the canteen at four.'

The men headed off to do what they needed to do.

Kate remained in the Ops room, thinking. Her faith in God had always been strong since she met Morgan. Before they married, he had taken her to a meeting of The Way, in Durham. She had thought it exciting to be going to a meeting of a forbidden group. Over the course of several meetings she began to believe what they believed. She wanted to follow the ways of The Teacher. He had been a radical leader in his time, standing up against hypocrisy, corruption and oppression. They believed he still lived on, in another dimension people called Heaven, and his Spirit was in each one of them. It gave them strength, courage and hope that enabled them to face all sorts of trials in his name. It was a dangerous life to lead, but Kate had decided to become a follower.

The Way was generally a way of peace; trying to live a good life and change things that were not good, by love and kindness. Starting a war did not seem like following that path. Was there justification for doing this for the greater good? What would The Teacher advise? She asked for an answer as she wrestled with her conscience. Strength, courage and hope were present; now she wanted certainty.

Young Zephyr had been taken to a location outside the Fortress, but still in the Citadel. He was locked in an apartment he had never been in before, with a couple of guards that Resolution had left. He knew it was on a high floor, because when he looked out of the window, he could see over the rooftops of many buildings and the Fortress was visible just over the river. He was angry but he had given up questioning the guards about anything. They were saying nothing, and he thought they probably knew nothing except to carry out their orders. Resolution had left without telling him what was going on; just telling him to get some sleep. Well, that was out of the question! His head and body ached from the battering they had taken in his struggle.

Zeph knew, from Chas and Si, that the Premier had sanctioned this move. He just didn't understand why Resolution had come for him in the night and been so secretive. If the Rulers' only motive was to keep him away from Chas and 'retrain' him, then why the need for this clandestine kidnapping?

The apartment was luxurious and well stocked with food. There was an HTV, but Zephyr was too wound up to watch anything. He made coffee and stood looking out of the window until dawn, trying to figure it all out and hoping that someone would come soon to tell him what was going on. Thoughts about Chas occupied his mind and he hoped that Si had got her out of the Fortress by now. He was going to miss her, but he wanted her to be free from the Rulers' grasp. He wondered if he would ever see her again.

By 9 a.m. he couldn't stay awake any longer and finally fell asleep on the sofa.

It was mid-morning when he was woken by a firm hand shaking him. He looked up to see the Premier in front of him. At first, still groggy from sleep, he thought he was dreaming; seeing an image of himself floating above him.

'Here.' The Premier thrust a cup of coffee into his hand.

Zeph sat up, yawning. 'Are you going to tell me what's going on then?'

The Premier gave him a hard look. 'You've been moved from the Complex for a while to continue your education as the next Premier.'

Zephyr took a sip of the hot coffee and put it down on the table. The Premier quickly placed a coaster underneath it. 'Where am I?'

'You are in my private apartment,' the Premier said. 'You will stay here for a while.'

'A while? How long is that? And why the cloak-and-dagger stuff; kidnapping me in the night?'

The Premier didn't answer the question. 'What were you doing with Chastity Komchenski last night?'

Zeph shook his head. 'I told you, I wasn't with her. It was her carer; Grace. You saw her.'

'A smoke-screen. It didn't add up. Are you romantically involved with her?'

'Grace? Not yet.'

'No!' The Premier banged his hands flat on the table. 'Don't lie to me, Zephyr. Are you in a relationship with Chastity? How long has it been going on?'

Zephyr stood up. 'I'm not in a relationship with her.'

'What has she told you about the rebels? Does she know if Silence Hunter is still alive?'

Zeph almost laughed. 'She hasn't talked to me about anything like that. She's not stupid! I've had a few words with her at the gym. We mainly talk about which machine to use and banal things like that.'

The Premier stood up and sighed in frustration. 'You have everything you need here. I'll be back later.'

'Who is going to 're-educate' me then?' Zeph shot at him as he was about to leave. 'Ambition? You know you're just his puppet, don't you? He's too scared to put his face out there to the people.'

The Premier grabbed him by the front of his shirt. 'I am not their puppet! I make my own decisions and they follow.'

Zeph did laugh then. 'You think so?'

The Premier grabbed hold of him. Zeph could have knocked him down but he knew it was pointless. The Premier flung him backwards and he fell into the sofa, still laughing.

'You think you're so smart,' the Premier said. 'But I'm going to save you the trouble of ever having to rule this country!' Right now, he thought he could kill the boy with his own hands, but he had to be wise about it.

'Good!' Zeph said. 'I don't want it. You can keep it!'

The Premier didn't answer, but left, slamming the door behind him.

13

Chas lay in a hospital bed, drugged up with painkillers. Her arm ached as the blood transfused into her veins. She was barely awake, but she felt strangely calm and comfortable. Nurses fussed around her from time to time, checking that she was doing well.

She had undergone a surgical procedure to make sure the miscarriage had been complete. Doctor Nelson had performed this, wanting to be sure she knew exactly what was happening. There had been no chance of saving the babies.

Chas drifted in and out of sleep. Sometimes she dreamed of invisible babies appearing out of nowhere in the room. Sometimes she dreamed of Si lifting her out of the bed and carrying her home, down a winding path of silver birch, to a log-cabin in the forest. She knew that the babies were gone, and she felt a strange mix of relief and sadness. She had cried when Doctor Nelson had told her that they hadn't survived.

'Chas?'

She opened her eyes to see Doctor Nelson standing by the bed, smiling gently at her.

'How are you feeling?'

'The best!' Chas whispered, with ever present sarcasm. She couldn't make her voice any louder than that.

'Are you comfortable?'

'Not bad,' Chas said. 'Except for this thing in my arm. How much longer does it have to go?'

'Maybe a couple of hours.'

Chas closed her eyes. 'Can you get Si in here?'

The doctor shut the door to Chas's private room and sat down. 'Not yet. I'll have to tell Zephyr what's happened. He's going to find out anyway and if it doesn't come from me, he's going to wonder why.'

'What's he going to do with me now? I'm probably as good as dead,' Chas said. 'Unless you get me out of here.'

'You're not going anywhere until I'm sure you're strong enough.'

'How long will that be? How are we going to stop them from finding Mish and Si? They won't leave without me.'

The doctor shook her head. 'I don't know what to do. All I know is that you're my priority. I'm going to keep you safe.'

Chas opened her eyes and looked at her. Worry lined her face. 'You're a good doctor. You shouldn't be working for this lot.'

'No, I shouldn't. I wish I didn't have to.'

'What have they got over you? Why don't you just leave; find another job?'

'I can't. And it's... complicated.'

'Try me. I won't tell.'

The doctor shook her head. 'No. You have enough to concern you.'

The door opened and a nurse came in. 'Oh, sorry Doctor. Do you want me to come back later?'

'No. It's okay. I'll leave you to sleep now. I'll be back later.'

Chas watched her leave. There was something she was hiding. Some reason she was trapped here. She closed her eyes, resolving to find out. Maybe she could persuade her to come with them when they got out of the Citadel.

*

Mish and Si were discussing what to do next. It felt like weeks since they had left the Angel of the North, and yet it was only just over 24 hours. Grace was keeping watch to make sure that no one came into the room, at the same time as trying to find out how Chas was.

'We need to get the footage of me in Zephyr's office, out of here so we can upload it. And we need to communicate with mum and the others.'

Mish knew that Si wouldn't leave without Chas. 'Ye want me to take it?'

'Will you?'

'Of course.'

'Thank you. Go back to the Angel and tell them what's happened. Tell them what Chas said about Young Zephyr too. See what they think.'

'Your mum is going to be stottin' mad that I've left you here.'

'Probably. But she knows I'm stubborn. She won't blame you. Don't worry about her.'

'Aye. I think they're all gonna be mad wi' me.'

'I'm sorry you'll have to face that on your own,' Si said.

'Ach, dinna fash! I've faced a lot worse,' Mish said, smiling.

Grace came back into the room. 'I've got some news on Chas.'

They looked expectantly at her.

'She's okay. She's having a blood transfusion.' She paused and looked down at her feet. 'But she's lost the babies.'

'As long as she's okay,' Si said. 'Thanks for finding out.'

Grace smiled.

'I want to go and see her,' Si said.

'We could head out together,' Mish suggested. 'I'll get this out there.' He pointed to his Wearable. 'You get into the hospital.'

'There's a secret entrance from here,' Si said, 'But you need DNA clearance. Do you have it?' He turned to Grace.

She laughed. 'No. I'm a nobody. I only have clearance to come in the main entrance here.'

'Okay. We'll go the front way.'

'Do you know what's happened to Zeph?' Grace asked.

Si shook his head. 'I just know that the Commander took him. Who knows where he is now? I don't think Zephyr will allow the Commander to torture him though.'

Grace shivered and hugged her arms around herself.

Mish stood up and put his arm around her. 'Hey, we'll protect you.'

'You can't, can you? You're going. And you can't protect Zeph.'

'We could get you out of here. You could just leave as normal and meet me outside the Citadel.'

Grace shrugged. 'What will I do then? My whole life has been here in the Citadel. I know nothing else. I don't know if I could live outside the city walls. And besides, I need to stay for Chas, and maybe Zeph too, when he comes back.'

'Aye, well. If you're sure,' Mish said.

She smiled at him. 'Thanks for thinking of me, but yes I'm sure.'

'You're braver than ye think,' Mish said.

'Or just stupid,' she laughed.

Si stood up and reached for his invisibility suit. 'Okay. Let's get going.'

They put their suits back on. Mish hugged Grace and she giggled. 'I've never had a hug from an invisible man before.'

'Stay safe,' Si said, and they were gone.

*

The Premier was feeling nervous. He had effectively kidnapped Young Zephyr, but he could probably keep it from the other Rulers for some time if he planned it carefully. He had called a security meeting this morning and was briefing Resolution and the Rulers about updating security on the entrances to the Fortress. He told them about his hunch that someone using invisibility technology had been in his office.

'I want it implemented as soon as possible,' he said to Resolution. 'Get it organised today.'

'I'll get security onto it right away, Premier. Meanwhile, I will question the boy and girl I brought back from the Priory.'

'Good,' Zephyr said. 'Find out what you can, but don't kill them, Commander. Let's keep them alive for now, in case they have some value to the rebels.'

'Of course,' Resolution said.

Just then, a call came in from the hospital. Zephyr answered it and a holo-image of Doctor Nelson appeared in the room.

'Hello Doctor. What can I do for you? I'm in a meeting. Is it important?'

From the chair in her office, Anya could see the other Rulers gathered in the meeting room. She saw Ambition there and hesitated. 'I... would you be able to come over here when your meeting is finished, Premier? It is important, but it can wait 'til then.'

Zephyr nodded. 'Of course. I will speak to you later.'

Ambition was always alert when Anya had anything to say to the Premier, especially when she seemed hesitant to share it in public. 'Are we finished here?' he asked.

'Yes,' Zephyr said. 'Thank you, gentlemen. Let's meet again tomorrow. These are difficult times and we need to stay in communication.'

'Do you think the rebels will try anything, Premier?' Zealous asked.

'They would be foolish to, but we must remain vigilant. Commander, look to the security of the Citadel. Put all law-keepers on high alert.'

Resolution nodded. These tasks were delaying him from questioning his prisoners, and he was always keen to do that. However, maybe they would be more ready to talk when they had wallowed in their cell for a while.

As the others left, Ambition said to Zephyr, 'I need to talk to Doctor Nelson about something too. Shall we go over there together, Premier?'

'Yes. Why not? We can discuss what to do with Young Zephyr as we walk.'

The two men headed out of the meeting room, towards the elevator. Ambition would have to think up a reason why he was accompanying the Premier to Anya's office. He had to know what she wanted to tell him. It was unusual for her to summon Zephyr.

'I will send guards to remove him from the Complex today,' Zephyr said, bringing Ambition's thoughts back to Young Zephyr. 'Shall we put him in my private rooms in the Fortress? We can keep that secure, to make sure he stays there while we talk to him. I hoped you might be the one to do that, Ambition. He won't listen to me.'

'Yes. I'll do it,' Ambition replied. This would be the perfect opportunity to get Young Zephyr completely ready to take over. The idea of offering him Chastity as a wife may be a good one. If he was capable of love, he was open to being controlled. They would have a fresh clone to manipulate, and this Premier, who was becoming more and more difficult, could be disposed of.

*

Si and Mish were crossing the foyer of the Fortress, as Ambition and Zephyr walked in from another corridor, accompanied by two guards. Mish and Si couldn't speak to each other but realised that they were all heading in the same direction; to the main entrance. They fell into step a little way behind them.

Zephyr and Ambition were talking about security. 'We should have installed body-heat detecting equipment years ago. We knew Marsden had people working on individual invisibility.'

'Well, we're doing it now. Hopefully not too late,' Ambition said. 'At least the rest of our security is excellent.'

Zephyr nodded.

Si gripped Mish's arm. They had to get out right now, with Zephyr and Ambition. Mish had the same idea and moved to follow them. Si's heart raced as he stood just a few feet behind the guards who were with the Premier. People were coming in and out. This wasn't a clear space. Anyone could bump into them at any moment. They kept moving to dodge people as they brushed past them. Mish felt like he was holding his breath until they emerged into the open. To Si's dismay, Zephyr, Ambition and the guards headed in the direction of the hospital. Si and Mish waited for a few minutes until they were out of view, then they moved to a spot where there weren't many people.

When they were out of earshot Si spoke. 'Damn. Maybe Doctor Nelson has told them about Chas already.'

'Aye, she might have. She couldn't very well keep it a secret,' Mish said.

She could have waited a bit longer,' Si said.

'What're ye goin' to do?'

'Follow them. I'm still going in.'

They hurried along the street and caught sight of them as they turned a corner. They were definitely headed to the hospital. Mish and Si stopped for a moment in the hospital car park, where they could talk. 'We're not going to be able to get back into the Fortress if they've already installed the heat-detectors,' Mish said.

'Not through the main doors, but there's that secret entrance through the hospital that only certain people have access to. If Doctor Nelson's willing to help Chas, then she might be willing to help us, when the time comes that we need to get back in. I need to get to the hospital and find out what Zephyr is up to. You need to go. Get that video out as soon as you get out of the Citadel.'

'Aye, I will. I'm not taking the car back to the Angel. Ye'll need it when ye get Chas out. I'll visit Esme and see if she can help me. Take care, Si.'

'And you. What will you do at the checkpoint? If they're installing new security on the Fortress, they might be doing the same there.'

'Aye. I'll have to take my chances. I canna get out any other way.'

They parted company and Si headed into the hospital, looking for the signs that would lead him to Doctor Nelson's office, whilst watching out for Zephyr and Ambition. He didn't know where they would have taken Chas, so the doctor would have to show him. He wondered how long it would be before he could get her out of there. She had looked like she was at death's door. He couldn't imagine that she was fit to go anywhere today. And how would he get her out anyway, if there was heat-detecting equipment installed at the checkpoints?

He had seen no sign of the Premier and Ambition, but he was wary. He listened at the door for voices, but heard no one, so he pushed the door open slowly and looked inside. It was empty. He sighed impatiently and sat down in the swivel chair at her desk. There were no photographs of family on the desk. In fact, the room was cold and impersonal. It surprised him, because Doctor Nelson seemed a warm-hearted person and she had been good to Chas. He wondered what had driven her to work for the Rulers.

It was only a few minutes before she came into the room. Fortunately, she was alone. He didn't want to startle her, but there was no other way to get her attention than to speak.

'Doctor. It's Si. I've come to see Chas.'

She froze for a moment, then looked around the room. 'You scared me again! I don't think I'll ever get used to that. Where are you?'

Si stood up and pulled the hood back. 'I'm here.'

She looked terrified. 'You can't be here. I'm expecting the Premier any minute. He and Ambition are talking to another senior consultant at the moment, but they're coming here next.'

Si had expected to find them already here, so he was glad of a few minutes alone with the doctor. 'Where is she? Is she okay?' Si asked, pulling the hood back over his head and face.

'Yes. She's okay. She lost a lot of blood and we've just finished giving her a blood transfusion. She lost the babies.'

'Grace told us about it.' Si felt a strange pang of regret for the babies; he hadn't expected that. 'But she'll be alright?'

'She will.'

'What will they want to do with her now? Will they want to make her do it all over again?'

Doctor Nelson sighed. 'I don't know. I'm not sure her body could take it. You have to get her out of here.'

'I intend to. Can you take me to her?'

'Yes, but I have to deal with Ambition and Zephyr first.'

'Have you told them about Chas?'

'Not yet, but I can't keep it from them. They'd be suspicious. That's why I asked the Premier here. They mustn't find you here.' There was panic in her eyes.

'They won't. They can't see me. I'll stand in that corner by the window and keep quiet 'til they're gone.'

The doctor was biting her lip. 'Okay. Just don't...'

There was a knock on the door and she hurriedly sat at her desk and flicked on her screen as if looking for something. 'Come in.'

As the two men entered, she stood up. 'Premier. Ambition. Please have a seat.' Si was impressed by how instantly calm and composed she appeared.

'What can I do for you, Doctor? You sounded like you had something important to tell me. Do you mind Ambition being here?' Zephyr gave her a disingenuous smile and she inwardly cringed. She did not want Ambition there; ever. But she had no choice.

She returned the same kind of smile. 'No, it's fine.' Avoiding eye contact with Ambition, she braced herself to deliver the bad news. 'You're not going to like this, Premier.'

He gave a small twist of his head and dropped the smile.

'Go on.'

'Chastity haemorrhaged last night, and she's lost the clones.' She paused briefly for a reaction, but they just stared at her. 'We had to do a D&C and give her a blood transfusion, but she's going to be okay.'

'Oh well, that's alright then,' Zephyr said, sarcastically. He stood up and walked towards the door. Si anticipated that any minute he might blow. And he did. He marched back to the desk, slamming his fists down on the surface. 'That's okay, then, isn't it!' he shouted, making Anya jump and recoil. 'As long as the little renegade is fine. All the luxury she's had, living in the Complex these past months and this is how she repays me.'

Anya didn't speak. There was nothing she could say. She looked at Ambition. He stood up. 'Premier, we can always try again with the experiment. I'm sure Doctor Nelson can get the girl ready to do it again.'

Zephyr was not ready to be soothed. 'What has she been up to, to cause this to happen. Has she not been closely monitored? Has she been doing too much? She's been at the gym a lot. Could that be it?'

Anya shook her head. 'We've been monitoring her progress carefully, Premier. And the gym should only have had a positive effect. I gave her strict instructions on what she was allowed and not allowed to do there.'

'But did she follow them? How do you know? Were you there with her?' His temper was mounting, and Anya was in the direct firing line. She knew that people had been imprisoned in the Priory for less. She glanced again at Ambition, sending a plea for intervention.

'Premier,' Ambition began. 'This is not the doctor's fault. These things just happen to women sometimes. There's often no logical explanation. And Chastity was carrying two clones, which is an experiment not previously tried.'

'She was with Zephyr last night. I know it. Could they have done anything to cause this?'

Si knew what he was getting at and, despite himself, he wondered this too. Were Chas and Young Zephyr having a relationship? He wanted to punch himself. What was wrong with him? First Mish, now this? He had to stop doubting her.

'No,' Anya said, firmly. 'They couldn't have caused this, even if they were having a sexual relationship.'

'Premier. Let's go and think this through rationally,' Ambition said, calmly. 'It was an experiment. She was a host. You can try again if you want to.' He turned to Anya. 'Will she be damaged by this?'

Anya looked down at her hands and spoke quietly. 'Possibly.'

Zephyr banged on the table again and swore, making them all jump.

Ambition gave Anya an exasperated look. 'You can use someone else, Premier. Surely the host is not the issue.'

'I wanted it to be her. The irony of us having clones of her and Hunter at the beginning of our master race was... supreme.'

'Come,' Ambition said, coaxingly, as if talking to a child coming down from a tantrum. 'Let's go and think about it, Premier. I'm sure we'll figure out a way to try again with the doctor's help.'

Zephyr breathed deeply. His face was still set in anger, but he was taking control of himself. 'I will be in contact, Doctor. Ambition, you wanted to speak to the doctor about something.'

Ambition waved his hand dismissively. 'It can wait, Premier. Let's go back to the Fortress and see how the modifications to security are coming along.'

Zephyr nodded and allowed Ambition to take control of the situation. Almost imperceptibly, Ambition shook his head at Anya as they left.

Si remained quietly in position for a while, watching Anya with her head in her hands, leaning on the desk. He felt like an intruder and didn't want to startle her all over again. She was clearly frightened and upset. After a good five minutes had passed, he spoke.

'Doctor Nelson, are you alright?' A pathetic thing to say, but he couldn't think of anything else.

His voice startled her. 'Oh! I'd forgotten you were there! Chas is in real danger now, whatever they decide. We have to get her out of here as soon as possible.'

'When will she be fit to travel?' Si asked.

'A few days, at the earliest.'

'I've got an invisibility suit for her, but they're modifying their security detection on the Fortress. If they do the same at the Citadel checkpoints, I can't get her out that way.'

'I'll help you get her out.'

'But you'll put yourself in danger. You know what they'll do to you if they find you helping us.'

'I know, but I can't let them do anything else to her. I should have stopped it in the first place. I'm a useless coward!' She broke into sobs.

Si was taken aback at the strength of her feelings towards Chas. They had clearly built up a very good relationship in the last few months. He felt awkward and foolish. How could he comfort her, especially in an invisibility suit?

'I'm sure there's a way we can do this without involving you.'

She shook her head. 'I'm involved already. They'll blame me if she goes missing, whether I had a direct hand in it or not. No. I owe it to her. I owe her so much more than I've ever admitted.'

Si thought this a strange thing to say. 'You've done your best for her, under the circumstances. None of us are free under this regime.'

'You're right. But now, I need to put some things straight.' She stood up and took some tissues to wipe her face, then straightened her clothes and composed herself. 'Come with me. I'll take you to her and try and arrange it so that you can take off your suit and spend a few minutes being visible with her.'

'Thank you.'

Si followed her down the corridors and into an elevator. They went up a couple of floors and emerged onto a pre- and post-natal ward. Chas was in a private room, with a window looking onto the corridor. Once inside, Anya drew the blinds. Chas was asleep. The blood transfusion was finished. She looked pale but peaceful. Si almost didn't want to wake her. All the jealousy he had felt earlier melted away and he only felt love. He knew they were meant to be together. Her hands lay limply by her side and he took one of them in his and kissed it.

All that Anya saw was a hand floating in the air, as she checked Chas's vital signs and the monitors she was hooked up to.

'Wait, Si,' she said. 'I need to make sure no one will come in for a while. I'll go and do that now. Wait for my word please.'

'Okay,' Si said, replacing Chas's hand by her side. He watched her breathing, steadily. All the tension and angst she normally carried in her face and posture was gone. If her chest hadn't been rising and falling slightly, and the monitor bleeping, he would have assumed she was dead. If only he could protect her and keep her in this cocoon of tranquillity forever. But he knew it was an illusion. She was in danger and to protect her he would have to break into her peace.

The door opened and Anya came back in. 'It's all clear for now.' She closed the door behind her. 'You can take the suit down. Probably not all the way off, in case you need to put it back on quickly. I'll keep watch, but I've given instructions not to be disturbed.'

'Okay,' Si said, beginning to remove the suit to his waist. It always felt good to peel it off. Anya peered through the cracks in the blinds.

'You can wake her,' she said. 'It'll do her good to see you.'

Si moved the hair back from Chas's forehead and stroked her cheek, speaking gently, close to her face. 'Chas.'

She didn't respond. He tried again. 'Chas. It's me: Si. Can you open your eyes?'

He touched her on her face, her arms, her hair. 'Chas, can you wake up?' He kissed her lips. She opened her eyes and he smiled at her. 'I'm here.'

Chas wondered if she was still dreaming. So many times, since she had been in captivity, she had dreamed of him kissing her. She looked around and began to wake up to where she was, as she saw Doctor Nelson standing at the window.

'How are you feeling?' she said.

'Ecstatic!' Chas croaked.

Si smiled at her ever-ready sarcasm.

'What are you doing here?' she said to Si. 'Isn't it dangerous?'

'It is, but I had to see you and know how you were.'

'Doc says I'll live,' Chas said. 'Can you pass me some water?' She shuffled up to a sitting position and took the glass from Si.

Anya turned to her and nodded. 'You're going to be fine, and, in a few days, you're going to be out of here.'

'Oh well, Grace will be pleased. She'll be fretting like mad I expect.'

'No,' Si said. 'The doctor means out of the Citadel. We're getting you out.'

Chas looked at Anya. 'You're helping? I know you won't betray us, but they'll lock you up, if not worse, for 'losing' me.'

Anya moved towards the bed and sat down. 'I'm coming with you.'

Chas and Si were both shocked by this revelation. 'But I only have two invisibility suits,' Si said. 'And they might not even get us out with the new security measures.'

'I'll think of something. We have a couple of days to prepare. Chas is not fit enough to move anywhere 'til then.'

'Why are you helping us?' Si said.

The doctor looked at Chas and took her hand. Suddenly, tears welled up in her eyes and began streaming down her cheeks. Chas felt uncomfortable at this sudden show of emotions and wanted to pull her hand away, but didn't want to make things worse.

'What's wrong?' she asked. 'You don't have to help us escape. I'm sure we could think of something that wouldn't incriminate you.'

Anya shook her head, batting away the tears. 'It's not that. I want to come with you, if you'll let me.'

'What do you mean, 'If we'll let you'? Of course we will,' Si said.

She shook her head and glanced at Chas. 'You might not want me, after I tell you the truth.'

Chas and Si were confused. 'About what?'

She wiped her face. 'Si, please keep a look out in case anyone comes.'

Si stood up and went over to the window, peering through the blinds. 'Everyone looks busy. I think we're okay.'

Anya nodded and turned to Chas, letting go of her hand. 'I need to tell you something. I can't keep it a secret any longer.'

Chas was alarmed. She had suspected that the doctor had a secret that made her wary of the Rulers and kept her working for them. 'Is it to do with betraying the Rulers?'

'Something like that, but it goes back a long way to my teenage years.'

'Both Chas and Si were intrigued. 'I don't understand what that has to do with us,' Si said.

Chas tutted and shook her head. 'Just listen, Si. It clearly has, or she wouldn't be telling us, would she? Go on, Doctor.'

'I hope you'll forgive me.'

Again, Chas didn't understand, but a knot was forming in her stomach. 'I'm sure there's nothing to forgive. Whatever it was, your motives would've been good.'

Anya closed her eyes briefly and nodded. 'I was eighteen...'

Just at that moment, Si swore. 'Sorry!' he said, grappling to pull up his suit. 'Zephyr's coming!'

The doctor jumped up. 'What?' She looked out of the window. He was talking to a nurse at the workstation. 'Hurry Si. I'll go out and see what he wants.'

She wiped her face, took two deep breaths and went out to meet Zephyr. Chas closed her eyes, annoyed at the interruption. The doctor had obviously been working up to telling her this for a while.

'Premier,' Doctor Nelson said. 'What can I do for you?'

Zephyr saw that she had been crying. 'I've come to apologise to you, doctor. Ambition thinks that I was too hard on you.'

She was taken aback. 'Thank you, Premier. I am doing my best for her. And for you,' she added quickly.

'I know you are,' Zephyr said, his voice controlled and business-like. 'I'd like to see her.'

Anya glanced back towards the room, hoping that Si was invisible again by now.

He was.

'What do you think she was trying to tell us?' he said to Chas, whilst keeping an eye on proceedings outside the room.

'How do I know?' Chas said.

'Looks like he's coming in,' Si said, moving into a corner to keep out of the way.

Chas sighed, lay back and closed her eyes.

Anya came in first. 'She's resting, Premier. Her body has had a lot to deal with in the past few hours. She'll be fine in a few days though.'

He nodded. 'Can we try the experiment again? Will she be strong enough?'

Si saw her wince. 'It would be safest to wait at least three months for her body to get fully fit again.'

Zephyr nodded. 'But after that?'

Si thought the doctor struggled to keep a composed professional face. Knowing that they were both listening to her conversation must be hard for her. 'After that... yes you could try again.'

'Good,' Zephyr said. 'When will she be ready to go back to the Complex?'

'I'd like to keep her here for at least five days for close observation.'

'Right,' Zephyr said. 'I will visit her when she is back in the Complex. Thank you, doctor.'

Zephyr left and Chas opened her eyes. 'You could have told him there was no chance of trying again.'

Anya shook her head. 'That would put you in more danger Chas. If he thinks you're useless to him he'll have no qualms about getting rid of you.'

'That's true,' Si said.

'But we're getting out of here, aren't we?' Chas asked.

'Yes. I hope so,' Anya said. 'I need to make some arrangements. We have a few days to sort things, because you're not going anywhere in that time. Si, you'll be safest at my house, I think. I'll take you there. Where's your friend? The boy who was with you in Chas's room?'

Chas had almost forgotten about Mish. 'Is he safe?' she asked.

Si peeled back the invisibility suit. 'I hope so. He was heading out of the Citadel to upload the propaganda video we made in the Premier's office. We want the people and the Rulers to know that we can infiltrate the Fortress and that I am well and truly alive. He's heading back to the Angel of the North where the rebels are gathered.'

'I hope he gets out safely,' Chas said.

'Yeah, I hope so too,' Si said.

'Will you tell Grace what's happening?' asked Chas, turning to Anya.

She shook her head. 'I think she's safer if we don't. If she doesn't know anything, they'll leave her alone.'

'Resolution might question her about Zephyr and me,' Chas said.

'Will she talk?' Si asked.

Chas glared at him. 'Of course she will, if that psycho gets his hands on her. She's brave, but torture is another thing.'

'I know,' Si said.

'Maybe we should take her with us?' Chas said.

'Mish offered, but she refused.' Si said. 'We can ask her again. I'm sure you could persuade her,' he said, turning to the doctor. 'What do you think, Doctor Nelson?'

She shook her head. 'Please, call me...' she glanced at Chas. 'Call me Anya. Doctor Nelson seems too formal, if we're going to run away together.' She smiled at them. 'I don't think it would work to take Grace. It would look suspicious. If she wants to leave of her own accord, she can, but it would mean giving her information that could potentially harm her, by making her a conspirator.'

'Give her the choice,' Chas insisted. 'We owe her that. Just tell her that we're leaving and don't tell her anything else if she wants to stay.'

Anya nodded. 'Okay. I'll talk to her.'

'And what about Zeph? Did you find out what's happened to him?' Chas asked.

Si shook his head.

'What's this?' Anya asked.

'I think Resolution's kidnapped him,' Si explained.

Anya raised her eyebrows in confusion. 'Why would he do that?'

'I know it sounds ridiculous, but we were there when they came for him in the middle of the night.'

Anya shook her head. 'I'll try to find out without asking anything suspicious.'

'We need to find him,' Chas said. 'He's on our side; I know he is. He could help us.'

Si sat down beside her. 'Chas, we have to get ourselves

out of here now. When the rebels attack the Citadel, we'll make sure he's rescued.'

'And the children,' she said.

'The clone children?' Si asked.

'Yes, they're innocent victims of all this.'

Si nodded. 'And the children.'

Anya nodded. 'Okay. That's settled. Now, Si, come with me. You're going to lay low for a few days while I sort out our escape and Chas gets her strength back.'

'Can't I come and see her?'

'No. I want you completely out of the way, so it's one less thing for me to worry about,' Anya said. 'No sneaking in here. Promise?'

Si pulled a face, but Chas agreed with Anya. 'Do as she says. I don't want you moping around here anyway, giving me ear-ache.' She gave him a playful look.

He sighed. 'Hmmm. You're clearly on the road to recovery already.'

She held out her hand to him and he squeezed it. Then, to his surprise, she pulled him towards her and kissed him on the lips.

'Let's go,' Anya said, peering through the blinds.

'Doctor... Anya,' Chas said. 'I want to hear the rest of what you were about to tell us.'

Anya bit her lip and nodded. 'Soon. I promise.'

14

Kurt and Brigitta began barking before Mish even knocked on Esme's door. Who needs heat-detecting security? Just get dogs, he thought. Getting out of the Citadel had been straightforward. Thankfully, they hadn't extended the new security measures to the gates yet.

He was still invisible when Esme answered. She looked out, perplexed at first, a shotgun in her hand. 'Who's there?'

'Dinna fash! It's me. Mish. Can I come in?'

The dogs were growling behind her. 'Quiet!' she commanded, lowering the old-fashioned shotgun. 'Yes, get inside.' She ordered the dogs to their beds, even though they kept up a low growl, confused by being able to sense Mish, but not see him. 'Get out of that suit in the other room,' Esme said. 'Otherwise, the dogs will go berserk! Then you can tell me what on earth you're doing here.'

When he came back into the kitchen a few minutes later, Kurt and Brigitta jumped up and barked again. 'Quiet you two. You know him.' With disgruntled noises they lay down again in their beds.

'They're good protection,' Mish said. 'What's with the gun?'

Esme brought a tray of scones, china cups and a teapot with her old cosy over the top of it. Mish liked her old-fashioned style. It somehow made him feel safer. 'It belonged to my father. He kept it for shooting small game for food when times were hard. I've never needed it,' she glanced at the dogs, 'but recently I've felt the need for more protection. And you're making me feel even more uneasy. Last time you came here you were being tracked.'

'Not this time,' Mish said.

Esme poured the tea. 'So, tell me what's going on.'

Mish was already tucking into the scones. He'd only had a few sandwiches, in the past thirty-six hours.

Esme raised an eyebrow. 'I've got more food if you're hungry.'

'Mm..hm. That'd be great,' he said, spraying crumbs everywhere. As he ate, he explained everything, from before they left the Angel of the North, to the present moment. 'And I've got to upload this video as soon as possible and call Kate and the others.'

Esme nodded. 'How are you going to get back there?'

'Can you help me? I want to leave the car for Si, when he gets Chas out.'

She sighed. 'Sorry, I don't have a car. You'll have to walk or hitch.'

'Okay. It's fine.' Mish finished the tea and food. 'Thanks for this. I'm going to call them now. Then can I shower? I probably stink.'

Esme laughed. 'I hadn't noticed, but yes of course.'

Mish was not looking forward to speaking to anyone at the Angel, but he had several numbers he could try. He chose Temp, hoping that he would be the most amenable. None of their numbers were traceable, but they had caller ID on each other's phones.

Temp answered straight away and a 3D image of him appeared above Mish's phone. 'Where the hell are you, you irresponsible little idiots!'

Not so amenable then, Mish thought. 'Aye. I'm okay, thanks,' he replied.

'Where are you?' Temp repeated, angrily. 'Is Si with you?'

'No. We carried out the plan. I've got the video of us in the Premier's office. I'm out of the Citadel, but Si... Si's still there, with Chas.'

'Has he been captured?'

'Not when I last saw him. We were about to get her out, but she wanted to bring Young Zephyr.'

'What? Why?'

'She's convinced he'll help us. But it went wrong. The Commander came for Zephyr in the middle of the night and it looked like he was being arrested. Then Chas had a miscarriage. Horrible. Lots of bleeding. We called the doctor and she took her to the hospital. Si followed. I came here. That's the last I know.'

Temp swore. 'So, we don't know if Si and Chas are okay or have been caught. Great!'

'Si told me to contact ye and upload the video as soon as I got out. I can be back at the Angel in a couple o' days.'

'Well, Si's not in charge. Kate was elected. I need to talk to her before you do anything with that video. We're ready to attack the Citadel. We need to think what's best to do. I'll call you back.'

The image disappeared and Mish breathed again.

*

At the Angel, Temp went to find Kate. She was with Nick and Peter in the Ops room. They were talking about the expected delivery of the weapons.

'I've got news for you and you're not going to like it,' Temp said.

Kate's face blanched. 'Go on.'

'Mish just called me.' He explained everything Mish had told him.

Kate sat down, saying nothing.

'We have to go ahead with the attack, Kate. Everything's planned,' Peter said. 'We still have an element of surprise.'

Kate nodded. 'I know. I agree.' Nick laid a hand on her shoulder.

'Shall we use the video?' Temp asked.

'I think we wait until we've attacked the Citadel,' Peter said. 'It could put them on alert. Once we're in, we could use it to rally more people to start diversions in their own cities. It could take some of the military away from the Citadel.'

'Can we see the video?' Kate asked.

'Get him to upload it to our private group,' Peter said.

'Where is he now?' Nick asked.

'Mish? He's at Esme's. He's planning to walk back here,' Temp said.

'Probably best if he stays there,' Peter said. 'We'll be ready to go in a couple of days. The drones are being delivered today, we have the RIPs and we've briefed the people who are infiltrating the Citadel first, in the suits.'

'I hate the thought of those bullets ripping people's insides to shreds,' Kate said.

'At least they'll die a quick death,' Peter said.

Temp called Mish and a holo-image appeared. He could see all of them from his end, which was daunting. 'Kate, I'm sorry about Si. He told me to leave and get the video uploaded.'

'The two of you shouldn't have gone in there without approval,' Kate said. 'You should have tried to stop him.'

'Aye, well. He would have done it anyway and I figured he needed back-up.'

They told Mish the plan and that they would contact him when they were in place to attack the Citadel. 'You have a suit,' Kate said. 'You should go in with the others, with the drones.'

'Aye, okay. They're improving security to the Fortress to detect invisibility, using body-heat sensors. They didn't have sensors on the city gates when I came out, but they might have them by the time you get here.'

'They're slow,' Peter said. 'They should have done it years ago, but they never believed I could get invisibility to the level I have. We need to be careful then. If they have got it on the gates, the attack with the drones will have to start there.'

'I'll go in first,' Mish offered. 'If I get caught, you'll know it's not safe to send the others in.'

'How will we know if you get caught?' Nick asked.

Mish shrugged. 'I won't come back.'

'What about contact between us all?' Kate asked.

'The drones will be tracked,' Peter said. 'You can keep an eye on things from here. If they've improved security at the gates, we send the drones in from outside.'

'I just don't like the idea of opening fire on the innocent people who live in the Citadel,' Kate said.

'We're not going to,' Temp said. 'The target is the Fortress. The drones will drop incendiaries on it.'

'Si and Chas are potentially in there,' Kate said. 'And we saw Resolution take Ben and Honour away. They could be there too.'

Temp grimaced. 'It's a risk we have to take, Kate. This is a war on the Rulers now. Si chose to jeopardize our plan. Do Ben and Honour know where we are?'

'Possibly.'

Temp swore. 'We need to move quickly then or we might have law-keepers descending on us.'

'We're not going to blow the Fortress up, Kate. We're just going to cause chaos and take out the entrances, so we can get in there,' Peter said.

'There'll be casualties,' Kate said.

'Of course,' Temp replied, becoming slightly impatient. 'But we have to do it. Are you up to this, Kate?'

She stood up, annoyed by Temp's challenge. 'Yes. I'm up to it.' She turned to Mish. 'Send us the video and wait for instructions.'

'Aye ma'am,' Mish said, and his image disappeared.

There was a knock on the door and a lookout entered. 'Peter, a big lorry has just arrived at the Angel.'

'Okay, thanks. I'll be at the doors in a few minutes.

Assemble some people to bring in the delivery.'

Kate addressed the others. 'I'm ready to do this. Don't doubt me. I question our actions to make sure we're thinking it through. I know there'll be casualties and fatalities. It doesn't sit well with me, but I know it has to be done to save lives in the long-run. Are we ready?'

The others agreed that they were. 'Okay,' Kate said. 'Let's go and make sure people know what's required of them.'

*

Ben and Honour were in a cell together. 'I guess this is where Chas and Si were held after the execution,' Ben said.

Honour shifted on the hard bed. Her stomach had been churning ever since they were brought here. 'Now we know how they felt.'

'I'm surprised Resolution hasn't questioned us yet,' Ben said.

'Tortured us, you mean,' Honour added.

'I didn't like to say that,' Ben replied, 'in case it worried you.'

Honour laughed. 'Oh Ben, you're funny. Don't you realise it's all I can think about?'

Ben looked around the cell. He suspected they were being watched. 'We know nothing, so at least he can't find anything out from us.'

They knew where the rebels were. Si had been in contact with Ben, and they had been planning to join them after the protest where they got arrested.

'We're strong. We can keep going.' She reached for Ben's

hand and squeezed it.

Ben pulled a face. 'I've heard stories from the others of what Resolution is like, and we saw it with our own eyes on the beach.'

Honour shuddered as the scene replayed in her mind. Her voice went quieter. 'Do you think we'll get out of here alive?'

'Of course,' Ben said, more boldly than he actually felt. 'Si and the others will come for us.'

'But they don't even know we're here,' Honour said.

'They'll find us. I know they will.' Ben held her hand tighter and she leaned into his shoulder, struggling to hold back tears.

*

Zephyr waited twenty-four hours before calling an emergency meeting of the Rulers. He had to get his story straight about Young Zephyr and be sure that Resolution was going to back him up. He called the Commander into his office before the meeting with the Rulers was scheduled.

'How are things going, Commander?'

'Very well, Premier. All the entrances to the Fortress have upgraded security now. They're doing the same for the checkpoints. It will take a bit longer, as it's more complicated.'

Zephyr shifted uneasily in his chair. 'Yes, yes, thank you for overseeing, but that's not why I called you in.'

Resolution knew what this meeting was about, but he waited for the Premier to say it, smirking inwardly at Zephyr's awkwardness.

'I want to talk about the removal of Young Zephyr and thank you for your assistance.'

'My pleasure, Premier.'

'In an hour I'm going to tell the Rulers that he has gone missing, possibly taken by rebels in invisibility suits. They know of my suspicions about a security breach, so my story will be credible.' He moved the photo frame on his desk a fraction to the right. 'I need you to back me up.'

'Of course, Premier. What do you want me to say?'

'We thought the Complex was the most secure part of the Fortress. I'll tell them that I've already sent you to investigate. I'll ask you what you've found so far. Make sure no one else gets involved.'

'Fine.'

'Good. I've been thinking about what to do with Young Zephyr,' the Premier said. 'And I've decided he has to disappear... for good.'

Resolution raised his eyebrows. 'You want him assassinated?'

'Yes, and I want you to do it.'

'It's a lot to ask of me, Premier. You're asking me to commit treason and it carries the death penalty.'

'I'm well aware of that, Resolution.'

This was the first time that Zephyr had ever called him by name.

'If we're found out, you will die and so will I. But my death was always on the cards anyway, when the next clone took over.'

'You think they'll murder you?'

Zephyr laughed, ironically. 'Of course they will.'

'What about the younger clone?' Resolution asked. 'Do you want him killed too?'

He watched the indecision pass over Zephyr's face. But it was more than that. There was some kind of attachment.

'No. It would be too suspicious if he disappeared as well. I have time to think about him.'

'He will grow up, just like the other one did,' Resolution said.

'I know that!' Zephyr snapped, standing up and walking to the window.

Resolution felt able to push his agenda here. 'You offered me a reward for helping you, Premier. I've proved that I'm loyal only to you.'

Zephyr turned. 'You have, and my gratitude will be shown to you. I've arranged for a much better apartment in the Citadel for you and money has been transferred to your account from my private account.'

This wasn't what Resolution was after. 'That's generous of you, Premier, but you promised me promotion.'

Zephyr nodded, reluctantly. He knew what Resolution wanted.

'I want to be made a Ruler.'

'I'll make it happen... when you've got rid of Young Zephyr.'

Resolution stood up. 'Fair enough.' He moved closer to Zephyr. He wasn't afraid of him anymore. The Premier had made himself vulnerable to him. 'But if you don't keep your word, Premier, I will have to tell them what you've done.'

Zephyr squared up to him. 'You wouldn't do it. You are implicated here too.'

'I'll find a way to pin it all on you.'

'Don't try to blackmail me, Resolution,' Zephyr said, pushing him away.

Resolution grabbed hold of the Premier and pinned him against the wall. He was stronger and much more used to using force to get his own way. 'Don't let me down then.' He let go. 'I'll see you in the meeting... Premier.'

As he left the office, Resolution felt good. He could easily get rid of Young Zephyr and now he had power over the Premier. He was finally going to achieve his desire to be one of the Rulers. No one would ever look down on him again. His past would be finally put to bed. All he had to do now was get rid of Chastity once and for all. A plan was forming in his head to kill two birds with one stone. He could blame that on invisible rebels too.

The meeting was about to start as Resolution walked in. 'Ah, you're just in time Commander.'

Resolution sat down at the far end of the table from Zephyr as he launched into his speech.

'I'm not going to beat about the bush. I've got bad news. I went to visit Young Zephyr this morning, to tell him that today he was being moved out of the Complex for a while and that Ambition was going to be 'tutoring' him personally. But he's gone. It looks like a struggle has taken place. I called the Commander immediately to investigate.'

Shock and fear swept through the room, like a wave breaking, and questions were fired at the Premier.

'Who can get in there? It's strict access by DNA recognition only,' said one Ruler.

'You already know that I believe we may have been

infiltrated by people using invisibility technology,' Zephyr said.

More questions and fears were voiced.

'What have you found out, Commander?' Ambition asked.

'So far, it's hard to tell. I have men up there now, picking through everything. Today, I'm going to interview everyone who works there. Someone must have seen or heard something; or possibly be involved.'

'I'll help you, Commander. We need to find him as soon as possible,' Ambition said. He had already had a covert meeting with the Rulers about replacing the clone of the Premier with Young Zephyr. The timing of this was highly suspicious and he wondered if one of the Rulers had not liked the idea. No one had given any indication of disagreement.

'I have it all under control,' Resolution said. 'I've got plenty of men on the investigation and I like to question suspects and witnesses personally.'

'Yes, leave it to the Commander, Ambition,' Zephyr said. 'The rest of us need to be vigilant. If people have come into the Fortress in invisibility suits, some of them may still be here.'

'How can we be protected from them?' another Ruler asked, in a fearful tone.

'You have tazers. I suggest you carry them at all times,' Resolution said.

'You can't really tazer someone you can't see, can you?' someone said, derisively.

Zephyr glared at him. 'The updated security is in place

now and if nothing happens in the next few days, I think we're safe inside the Fortress.'

'Just be vigilant,' Resolution repeated. 'I'm sure you have nothing to worry about. My men are on high alert.'

The meeting disbanded.

'Commander, may I have a word before you leave?' Zephyr said, as the last of the Rulers left the room.

'We need to make this look real. You are going to question everyone about his disappearance, aren't you?'

'I just said so, didn't I?' Resolution no longer felt the need to be so obsequious. 'Excellence is up there now, gathering the staff together and calling in everyone who was on duty that night.'

'Good. There's no need for too much pressure, Commander, as we know what really happened. Are you sure no one saw you take Zephyr?'

'I'm sure,' Resolution said. 'It was completely quiet.'

'Even so, make sure you weren't seen and if you were... Well, you will have to get rid of anyone who saw you. Will you interview the children?'

'Yes.'

'I want to be there when you do that,' Zephyr said.

Resolution looked at him with a faint smirk on his lips. Zephyr had his weaknesses and one of them was the younger clone of himself. 'You don't trust me, do you?'

'I've never trusted you, Resolution. All along there's been something not right about you, and I don't just mean your psychopathic ways. There's something between you and Chastity. You may not be related, but there's something.'

Resolution felt his anger beginning to rise. He struggled

to control his voice. 'There was never anything between that low-life and me. You know why she hates me. That's all there is to it. And she was in the Complex when I took Zephyr, so I will have to question her.'

'She was otherwise engaged, losing the clones,' Zephyr said, bitterly.

'She could have seen or heard something. You suspected that she was with Young Zephyr earlier in the evening, didn't you? She will have to be questioned.'

Resolution had just thought of a way to finally get rid of Chastity. If he told Zephyr that she had witnessed something, Zephyr would have to allow him to kill her, along with Young Zephyr. This could be his perfect solution to the Chasity problem.

'Fine. You can question her,' Zephyr said. 'But don't damage her. I want to try the experiment again. Her carer was with Young Zephyr that evening too. Make sure you question her thoroughly. She may have seen something and Zephyr may have said something to her about his relationship with Chastity. The girl is called Grace.'

Resolution nodded. 'I will be thorough. You can be sure of it. I will report back to you. You have to trust me now, Premier.' He spat the title at Zephyr. 'Because if I tell them what you've done, you're a dead man walking.'

As Resolution turned to go, Zephyr snarled, 'And so are you!'

Resolution didn't bite. He wanted to laugh as he walked down the corridor. Finally, he had the upper hand. Zephyr knew that if this went wrong, Resolution could plead that he was carrying out orders without questioning them, as he should. He might be able to get off the hook. But Zephyr? Ultimately, he was just a pawn in the game the Rulers were playing. If Resolution played this right, he could get rid of Chastity and Young Zephyr and receive his promotion to Ruler status.

He found Excellence already interviewing the staff of the Complex, having called in everyone who had been there the night of the kidnap. He knew nothing of the Commander's involvement and Resolution was not going to tell him anything. It was better if he knew nothing and just carried out his duties legitimately. Less pretence; less risk.

Grace cowered in line with the rest of the staff. Despite some trepidation, there was a buzz of curiosity and gossip. But she was quiet. It was all she could do to stop herself from shaking. Her stomach churned and she felt sick. How was she going to keep to herself what she knew about that night? She knew of Resolution's reputation for cruelty and persistence and he probably knew that she had been with Zephyr earlier that evening.

'Have you already questioned some of them?' Resolution asked Excellence.

'Yes, Sir. A few.'

'You haven't questioned a girl called Grace, have you?'

'No, Sir.'

'I need to question her myself. Anything so far from any of the others?'

'Nothing, Sir. Most of them weren't here and the few who were, say they were asleep in their rooms, near the children they look after. I'm sorry, Commander. I've been tough, but I genuinely think they saw nothing.'

'It's fine.'

Excellence was surprised at his easy tone.

'The Premier doesn't want us to get too heavy-handed with anyone, so just bear that in mind. Where is this girl, Grace? She was with Zephyr earlier that night. I'm going to question her and then I'm going to question Chastity at the hospital.'

Excellence called Grace forward. Her heart began beating so hard that she felt like it must be visible to everyone. She gulped and took a deep breath. She could do this. She would do it. For Chas. For herself. Then, if she survived an interview with the Commander, she would get straight out of the Citadel.

15

Si had been waiting in Anya's apartment for over twenty-four hours. She had come and gone, assuring him of Chas's safety and that she was doing well. It was one of the most frustrating twenty-four hours of his life. He couldn't do anything or contact anyone, even though he desperately wanted to speak to his mother, to find out what was happening and how angry she really was with him. He wondered how Mish was getting on and if he had made it back to the Angel.

At least the HTV provided some contact with the outside world. There were reports about rioting in some tech-cities and law-keepers arresting demonstrators. There were images of people being shot at, and bodies lying on the streets. Cars and buildings were on fire and people were running in all directions. Even though smoke filled the screen, he noticed slogans on placards, some of which were trampled and broken, while others were still being thrust high by brave protestors. 'End the Plague', 'A Plague on the Rulers' and the one which caught his attention the most, abandoned by the side of a road, 'Silence Hunter is NOT Dead!'

There was no going back now. He hoped the video of

him in the Premier's office would show the people that he certainly was not dead, and prepared to fight the Rulers to the bitter end. Did this mean he would die? It might. And he was prepared for it. A sense of conviction and purpose came over him as he waited in the apartment, and he felt a strange sense of peace. He had been talking to the God his mother followed, and he realised now, that he followed too. His conviction was not so much that they would defeat the Rulers. He knew that good did not always triumph over evil, but he knew that this Being that he believed in would be there with them in the battle. And that counted for something. How did he know? He couldn't explain it, even to himself. All he knew was that he believed it, was experiencing it, was aware of a presence. It felt strangely familiar.

Anya came back in the evening. Si had made a meal for them both.

'Thanks for this,' she said, as they sat down to eat. 'Everything is ready. We can leave in the morning.'

'Great. What's the plan?'

'We'll be going in an ambulance with two paramedics and two dead bodies. You'll both wear the invisibility suits and lie on top of the bodies.'

Si nearly choked at the thought of lying on a dead body. 'Why?'

'In case they have the body-heat detecting devices installed. I'll tell them that the bodies are not long dead, that's where the heat source is coming from. They'll actually be long dead, but the guards won't suspect anything. I doubt they know anything about corpses. If they come into

222

the ambulance to look, you and Chas will have to get under the trollies, out of the way.'

'Why would you be taking two dead bodies out of the Citadel?' Si asked.

'Good question. I've reason to believe they're plague victims. I've been ordered to destroy them away from the Citadel. That should be enough to keep them out of the ambulance. The driver and I will be kitted out in decontamination suits.'

Si nodded. 'Clever idea. Who will you get to drive? Someone in on our plan?'

'No. I can't trust anyone.'

'So, what will you do with the driver when we get away from the Citadel?'

Anya shook her head. 'They'll have to come with us. We'll have to take them to the Angel. I'm looking for someone who might be sympathetic to the cause, so that when we get there, they might be happy to join the rebellion. If not, they'll have to be kept under guard.'

They ate in silence for a while, both thinking about the scenario.

'How are you going to prevent them discovering Chas's disappearance straight away?' Si asked after a while.

'I'm going to tell them at the hospital that I'm taking her back to the Complex. It should take a while before anyone realises that she's not there. Enough time for us to make our escape, anyway.'

'Have you told her all this?'

Anya nodded. 'I told her just now, before I came back here. She's worried about Young Zephyr, but I haven't been able to find anything out about him. I know he's missing because the Commander has been questioning the staff of the Complex.'

'He's covering his tracks,' Si said. 'I don't think he's in this alone, you know. He's got no reason to kidnap Young Zephyr.'

Anya shook her head. 'It must be one of the Rulers, or even the Premier. I'm not sure why though. Are you finished with that?' Anya picked up her plate and gestured to Si's.

'Oh. Yes. Thanks.'

She took the plates to the kitchen and Si followed, carrying other things from the table.

'Chas is worried about Grace too,' she said. 'Resolution has been questioning everyone.'

'Is Grace alright? I hate to think what might have happened if Resolution got his way with her.'

'I asked some of the staff. They told me everyone was questioned, but he didn't do anything to them except ask questions. They couldn't understand it.'

'And is Grace okay?'

Anya hesitated. 'I never managed to speak to her. She was one of the last to be questioned and she hasn't been seen since.'

Si put his fork down and closed his eyes, sighing deeply. 'Does Chas know this?'

She shook her head. 'No. I lied to her. I thought she wouldn't come tomorrow if she knew.'

Si looked up. 'You're right. It was probably a good call. There's nothing we can do for Grace or Zephyr... yet.'

Anya nodded. 'So, you'll come to the hospital in your

invisibility suit with me at seven in the morning. I'll organise the ambulance. First, I'll have to take Chas back to the Complex. When we're there she'll get into the invisibility suit. You stay in her hospital room. I'll come back for you, then follow me to the ambulance. Okay?'

'Sure.'

Anya blew out a long breath and took a sip of wine. 'Let's get an early night.'

They finished up in the kitchen and Anya looked around her apartment. It was a beautiful place, but she wouldn't miss it. It was finally time to break free from the Rulers, and especially from Ambition. He had controlled her for too long.

'Can I ask you a question?' Si said.

'Yes, of course.'

'What were you going to tell Chas the other day before Zephyr interrupted?'

Anya shook her head. 'I have to tell her first. I'm sorry.'

Si was puzzled. 'And it has something to do with Chas?'

'I'm sorry. I can't tell you any more. Like I say, she has to hear it from me first.'

*

Outside the Citadel, a small army of invisible people were gathering. Temp and Mish were among them. The plan was that Mish would enter the Citadel in the morning in his invisibility suit. If he went undetected and came back to tell them, the others would follow. There were ten gates into the Citadel. Part of the invisible army was camped at each one of them. Temp would call the leaders of each group to tell them to move into the Citadel at the same time. The drones, also cloaked by Peter, would fly silently overhead, until the moment to reveal them was announced. Peter had control of them from HQ, back at the Angel of the North.

'This is it then,' Mish said to Temp as they huddled together under invisibility cloaks, using them as blankets.

Temp nodded, even though Mish couldn't see him. 'Yep. This is it. You nervous?'

'Not really,' Mish said. 'I'm just ready to take back our freedom; or die trying.'

'Me too,' Temp said. 'Get some sleep now.'

*

Premier Zephyr was pacing his office. It was after midnight, but he couldn't sleep. So much was buzzing around his head. He was paranoid that Ambition was on to him about Young Zephyr. He had seen that distrustful look on his face, more and more, recently, and he felt that Ambition was keeping things from him. He had noticed the way Zealous and the other Rulers couldn't look him straight in the eye any more, and furtive glances passed between them.

He couldn't wait any longer. He had to be decisive about Young Zephyr. If he got Resolution to kill him, there was nothing they could do about replacing him for a long time. The other clone was years away from being ready to take up the Premier's role. He laughed to himself. Yes, that was all it was; a role. He was an actor in a play, not the director. He hadn't written the script either. Ambition was the director and the other Rulers looked to him for leadership. They were a lot older than him and had created Zephyr to be their front man; to preserve their anonymity; to be the face the people saw and feared. But the Rulers had listened to him and abided by his decisions over the years. He realised now that they had allowed him power and they were soon going to take it away from him. Who would defend him? Who would leap to his side against them? He realised with irony that the only person who might possibly do this now was Resolution. And not out of loyalty, only out of selfish ambition and self-preservation.

Well, if that was all he had, that was what he would have to call on. Young Zephyr must die. It felt a bit like killing part of himself, but he wouldn't have to see it. He would just get Resolution to deal with it. Take him outside the Citadel, kill him, get rid of the body.

He called the Commander and told him to come to his office immediately. He didn't want to give this order over the phone.

It didn't take Resolution long to get there. Zephyr explained simply and quickly what he wanted. 'I want it over by morning,' the Premier said.

'And do you have a story for the Rulers?' Resolution asked.

'We've already spun it. Invisible rebels took him. He's gone. We just never find him.'

'And my promotion?' Resolution asked.

'You will have it soon. I will call a cabinet meeting tomorrow. I've been thinking about it. They haven't replaced Capability yet. I'm going to tell them that you're my choice of replacement. As I'm still Premier, they will have to accept it.'

Resolution nodded. 'I hope you succeed, because I have my own plans if you don't.'

Zephyr rose up to his full height. He was taller than Resolution and refused to be intimidated by him. 'Don't threaten me, Commander. I am the one in power here. Remember that.'

Resolution laughed derisively. 'Yes, of course, Premier. I will carry out your orders. I am, after all, your most loyal subject. Or is that your only loyal subject?'

Zephyr was seething, but controlled himself. He needed Resolution, for now.

'One more thing you should know,' Resolution said. 'I have questioned Chastity. She saw me take Zephyr. She described things she couldn't have known otherwise and she enjoyed threatening me with exposure. We have no choice but to get rid of her.'

Zephyr didn't know what to say. He wanted to use Chastity for his experiment, but he couldn't risk her being a witness. Frustrated, he nodded. 'Do what you have to.'

*

Resolution's mind was already focused on the task ahead. He would carry out the Premier's orders regarding Young Zephyr, adding Chastity to the hit list. The Premier didn't have to know that he had not really interviewed her. This was purely personal.

He relished the thought that finally he was going to get his wishes. Chastity gone and him made a Ruler. He almost didn't want to arrive at the hospital to apprehend

Chastity because savouring the idea was so good. She had plagued his life for too long, sister or not. He had to admit to himself, he would have liked to know how the DNA test had come back negative, but he knew Chastity was puzzled by it too.

In order to get her to come with him, without struggling or trying to attract attention, he had an insurance plan. He hurried down to the cells and extracted his most recent prisoner: Grace.

'You're coming with me,' Resolution said, hauling her up from the bed and securing her wrists.

'Where are you taking me?' Tears sprang up and Grace began to plead. 'I haven't done anything wrong. Please don't torture me.'

'Be quiet, girl! I'm taking you to see Chastity.'

'Why?'

'Didn't I just tell you to be quiet?'

Grace nodded.

'And wipe your face. I don't want a snivelling wreck with me.'

Grace did as she was told.

Resolution took her to his car. 'When we get to the hospital, you do as I say. I'm going to untie your hands and you are going to walk beside me. Don't say anything to anyone. If you try anything, I will kill you. Understand?'

Grace nodded.

The hospital was quiet, with night staff at their stations and minimal activity. He was a recognisable figure of authority, so there was no problem getting past security that had been placed on Chastity's room. The guard submitted to the Commander's orders.

She was sleeping on the bed when he arrived.

'Stand over there,' he ordered Grace.

He shook Chas by the shoulder. 'Get up!'

Her eyes were open in a flash and she sat bolt upright. She looked terrified. He hadn't ever seen fear on her before and he liked the idea that he had finally made her afraid.

She looked to the door and tried to back away from him, but where could she go? Then she saw Grace, standing in the corner, like a frightened child who had done something naughty.

'What's she doing here?' Chas asked.

Resolution ignored the question. 'Get dressed. You're coming with me.'

'Doctor Nelson didn't tell me anything about this. I'm staying here. She's taking me back to the Complex in a few hours.'

'No, she's not. Anything she's told you has been overruled by the Premier's orders.'

Chas's heart was pounding. She looked at Grace, taking in her terrified eyes. She cursed Resolution. In a few hours she was supposed to be getting out of here with Anya and Si and he was not going to stop her. She was going to have to get herself and Grace out of this somehow. She found some jeans and a sweatshirt and pulled them on, along with her boots. Resolution was on the other side of the bed and she tried desperately to think of how she could fight him off. She hadn't thought about her knife for some time but now she longed to feel it in her hand.

'You can't do much about it, Chastity. There is a guard

outside, and he will do what I tell him.'

'What does the Premier want with me at this time of night?'

'That's not for you to know.'

'The nurses won't let you take me. They're under Doctor Nelson's orders.'

Resolution laughed. 'Do you think they're going to argue with me?'

She knew he was right, but she wasn't going to let him take her without a fight. He was between her and the door. There was no alternative way out, but there was a bathroom with a lock on the door. She made a dash for it, but he was ahead of her and blocked her way, grabbing her by the arms and twisting them up behind her. She was bent forward, pain shooting up her arms. She kicked out at him behind her and managed to catch him in the knee. He buckled slightly but didn't lose his grip.

Grace didn't move; too terrified to try to intervene.

The guard outside the room heard the scuffle and came into the room. 'Need some help Commander?'

Between them they managed to subdue Chas, pushing her face-down onto the bed, the guard holding her legs.

'Get me a wheelchair,' Resolution demanded.

The guard was gone for a couple of minutes. From his pocket he pulled some ties and secured Chas's arms and legs together. She struggled and swore, but knew it was a lost cause. She couldn't fight them both off single-handedly, with no weapon.

Resolution grabbed Grace roughly by the arm and she whimpered. He pushed her face towards Chas, then pulled out a gun and pointed it at Grace's head. 'If you struggle or attract attention, she will die first. Do you understand?'

That's why he had brought her. Of course. Chas's pulse raced and she felt sick. This was looking less and less like it was an order from Zephyr, and she was in big trouble if Resolution was acting on his own.

'What do you want with me?' she said. 'Let her go and I won't try anything. You have my word.'

Resolution looked at the guard. 'Take her to the car park. My car is waiting.' He followed with Grace; the gun in his pocket.

The nurses on duty looked questioningly at Chas's bonds, but didn't try to stop them. Resolution had told them that the Premier had asked for Chastity to be transferred immediately from the hospital to the Complex, because of a security breach. Chas wanted to appeal to them, but she was scared that Resolution would carry out his threat.

'Where are you taking us?' she asked, once the car was moving.

Resolution said nothing, no matter what she asked him or what she said. She felt tears of frustration stinging her eyes. So close to escaping. She thought of Si and Anya and wondered what they would do in a few hours when they came for her and she was gone. Her frustration was turning to anger, which she stored, and began formulating a plan to save Grace and escape from Resolution.

Leaning in towards Grace, she tried to reassure her, but Grace was locked in her own world of terror.

The streets of the Citadel slipped slowly past them. She didn't know the city at all, so it was impossible to know where they were going. They only drove for about ten minutes through the empty streets, before pulling up outside a gated apartment block. There was a guard on the gate and Resolution spoke to him.

'I'm here for the boy.'

The guard waved him through.

The boy? Who did he have there? Si? No! Her brain ticked back to events of a few nights ago. It was possible that this was where they were keeping Zeph. In that case, maybe the Premier was involved in this after all.

Resolution drove into the parking lot beneath the block, got out and locked the car, leaving her and Grace inside. The place was deserted. Could they escape?

'I'm so sorry you're caught up in all this Grace, but you need to help me if we're going to get out of this alive. Try the doors. Get in the front. Try anything.'

Grace just sat still, crying to herself. Chas leant across to her. 'Grace! Come on! Pull yourself together. Do you want to live?'

Grace nodded.

'So, stop snivelling and do something useful. Can you get these ties off me?'

Grace fumbled with the ties. 'No. They're locked into each other.'

At least she was doing something now. That was positive.

'Okay. Never mind. Get in the front and try the locks and windows.'

She tried all the doors and windows, but the car was impenetrable. Resolution had them well and truly trapped.

Chas kicked the seats and shouted in frustration.

Grace looked scared again, so Chas stopped. 'I'm sorry. Don't be scared of me. I'm just frustrated. We can get out of this if we think and work together. Are you up for that?'

Grace made a conscious effort to hold back her fear. She took a deep, shuddering breath. 'Yes.'

Chas gave her a reassuring smile. 'Well done. I know this is hard for you, but we can do it.'

Just then, they saw Resolution returning with 'the boy.' It was Zeph. He was walking unsteadily and wasn't putting up any kind of fight. She realised why, when Resolution thrust him onto the back seat and his head landed in her lap. He was a dead weight.

Resolution went around to the front and pulled Grace out. Chas panicked. Was he going to shoot her here? She managed to heave Zeph's head off her knee, onto the seat, and he slumped forwards, as if he was about to roll onto the floor. He'd likely been drugged.

Chas tried to get out of the car, but she couldn't open the door.

Resolution was chastising Grace. 'What were you doing in the front, bitch? Did you think you could get away?'

Grace whimpered, as he tied her hands to make sure she wasn't going to try anything foolish while he was driving.

The car drove out of the parking lot and back through the gates.

'Zeph. Can you hear me? It's Chas?'

He lifted his head a little from the seat and looked hard at her, trying to focus. 'Oh, hi,' he said and slumped back down.

Great! Chas thought. No use. She wondered how long the effects of the drugs were going to take to wear off.

She kicked the back of Resolution's seat and swore at him. 'What are you doing? Does the Premier know about this?'

He didn't answer.

He stopped just before the checkpoint and turned around. 'Keep his head down on your lap. I don't want them seeing him.'

'They'll wonder why you have the next Premier tied up in the back of your car, eh?' Chas said.

Resolution suddenly pulled out his gun and pointed it at Grace again. Grace squealed and closed her eyes tightly. 'Shut up Chastity and do as I say, or she dies, and you get to watch!'

'Okay, okay!'

'Keep your filthy mouth shut, or I swear there will be more dead people than you or I would like right now.'

She closed her eyes and held on to her temper as best she could.

They passed through the checkpoint without a problem. The guards didn't question the Commander when he said he was transporting prisoners. The windows of the car were darkened glass and they could dimly see three people.

She was almost certain now that Resolution intended to kill them. And it looked like she was going to be their only hope of survival.

16

At first light Mish made his way to the checkpoint. He was wearing the invisibility suit, but he was nervous. He approached the gate behind a delivery vehicle. As the checkpoint guards questioned the driver and looked at his ID, Mish slipped past, into the Citadel. That was it. So simple. There was clearly no body-heat detecting equipment installed at this gate yet. Now he just needed to get back through and tell Temp.

Temp was waiting, anxiously, but broke into a grin when a body revealed itself right beside him. 'It still gives me the creeps when someone just appears right next to me.'

Mish grinned.

'Okay. This means we're ready to attack.'

He called the groups who were waiting near the other gates of the Citadel. Then he called Kate, back at the Angel. 'We're moving in.'

'Great,' Kate said. 'The rest of the people are on their way. You won't believe how many there are, Temp. We sent messengers into all the tech-cities nearby. So many people have joined us. They'll start to arrive in less than an hour.'

'Good.' Temp said. 'Once you see reports of chaos in the Citadel, send them in!'

'Once we hear the drones have begun their work and you're in, we're going to release the footage of Si in the Premier's office. We hope this, combined with the attacks on the Citadel, will cause a massive surge in support across the country. We'll rally people that it's time to fight back, wherever they are.'

'Should stretch the law-keepers and keep them all from converging on the Citadel,' Temp said.

'Yeah, hopefully. And I think some people will come to join you in the Citadel. With all that's been building up over the past year; the plague victims being cured and the propaganda we've been putting out, I think people are finally ready.'

'I agree. This is the right time. We must get going. Tell Peter to release the drones,' Temp said.

Peter and Nick were there in the Ops room. 'I'm on it,' Peter said.

Kate didn't relish overseeing this operation, but she was determined to be a steadfast and confident leader. However, she couldn't help a motherly word of caution. 'Be careful sounds such a stupid thing to say, but...'

He smiled at her. 'Yeah, I know. And be assured, we'll do our best to find Si and Chas.'

'I know. Thank you.'

Temp, Mish and the others in their group pulled up their suits. The drones flew overhead, also invisible.

'Let's go!' Temp said.

*

Resolution drove for over an hour, out onto the moors

surrounding the Citadel. Chas kept Zeph's head down on her knee, subconsciously stroking his hair. He appeared to be asleep. She could hear Grace, now and again snivelling and letting little sobs escape. No one spoke. Chas's mind was working overtime. She thought about pleading with Resolution again to let Grace go. Even if he threw her out of the car, here in the middle of nowhere, at least she would be alive and that would be one less person for her to worry about. But there was no point. Resolution had already made it clear that all three of them were coming with him and therefore, all three of them were going to die.

'Zeph. Can you hear me?' she whispered, getting close to his face.

Nothing.

'Zeph.' She shook him. 'Zeph, can you hear me?'

He groaned.

'Open your eyes if you understand what I'm saying.'

He opened his eyes and tried to move; but couldn't. 'My head feels... like lead.'

'You've been drugged,' she said, keeping her voice low so that Resolution couldn't hear. 'Do you know who I am?'

He tried to look up at her, but in the dark he couldn't see much. 'Where are we?'

'In a car,' Chas said. 'Resolution is driving us out of the Citadel, across the moors. He has Grace as well. I think he's going to kill us.'

'Is the Premier behind this?'

'I don't think Zephyr wants me dead,' she said. 'He still wants to use me when I'm recovered.'

'Recovered?' Zeph tried to sit up again but he couldn't

move.

'I lost the babies,' she replied.

'Oh.' There was silence for a moment.

'They're gone. I'm glad. Not for them, obviously. But for me. I...' She tailed off, feeling a lump come into her throat. She kept feeling emotional and couldn't understand why.

Zeph's eyes were closed again. Chas didn't say any more. She had to think of a way out of this mess. Her only weapon was her feet, at the moment. Perhaps when Resolution pulled her out of the car, she could use them to disable him. Then she hoped that Grace might join in the fight. She groaned. Pity help them!

Her mind flitted to Si. He would pray one of his one-liners at this point. Chas still wasn't convinced by the faith thing, despite having lived with people from The Way for a year in Amsterdam. But now was a good time to try it out. She'd try anything at this point.

'Okay, God, whoever you are. If you're there and listening and care at all about us, I need your help.'

She shrugged. Nothing felt any different. The dark, silent moors continued to slide past.

Just then, something big ran out in the road in front of the car. Resolution swore and the car swerved to avoid it, hitting a rock by the side of the moor. The car spun several times. Grace was screaming, Zeph was groaning and Chas braced herself against the back of the seat. She could do nothing for Zeph, with her hands tied. The ground on either side of the road sloped downwards, not steeply, but enough to send the car off balance, tumbling over and over.

*

Anya arrived at the hospital just after 7 a.m. Si was following her, in the invisibility suit. He was nervous, but anticipating their escape was a good feeling. They reached Chas's room and went in, to find the bed empty and the security guard gone.

Anya went to the nurse's station. 'Where is Chastity?'

'I've just come on shift, Doctor, but I was told she had been taken back to the Complex in the middle of the night.'

'What? I didn't authorize this! Who took her?'

The nurse wasn't used to Doctor Nelson raising her voice. 'I was told the Commander came for her. He said she wasn't safe here and that he had orders to return her to the Complex immediately.'

Alarm bells began to ring in both Anya and Si. 'Where's the guard who was on duty last night?'

'I don't know, Doctor. I can find out who it was, if you want me to?'

'Yes. I'll speak to him. Send him to my office. I'm going to the Complex. This shouldn't have happened without my authority.'

Anya marched off towards the secure corridor. Once inside the elevator, Si spoke.

'Do you think she'll be there? Why would Resolution come for her?'

'I don't know. Maybe she'll be there. Maybe Zephyr has ordered her back to the Complex, but why in the middle of the night, I've no idea.'

Si removed his head covering. 'Maybe the rebels have

240

attacked? Or he thinks there is more danger from people in invisibility suits. He's clearly nervous about that.'

'Let's just hope she's back in her room. I've got everything arranged and we're already running late.'

The elevator arrived at the Complex and they hurried to Chas's room, but there was no sign of her. Si removed the top half of his suit and called out in case she already had her invisibility suit on. They felt every surface and moved into every space, in case she was unconscious, but the room was empty.

He swore. 'What are we going to do now? If Resolution has her and it's not an order from Zephyr...' He tailed off unable to voice his fears.

Anya sat on the bed, trying to think. 'I might need to alert the Premier to her disappearance. He's probably our best bet to find her.'

'We know Resolution took Young Zephyr on the Premier's orders. Do you think this is part of the same plan?'

Anya shook her head. 'Could be.'

'So, if you tell him about Chas's disappearance, we could see how he reacts. Then we'd have a clue if he's involved.'

Anya nodded.

'Do you think the Rulers are involved in this? It doesn't make any sense.'

Anya was silent for a while. 'I'm going to talk to Ambition. See if he knows anything. First, I'll arrange a meeting with the Premier in my office. You should be there to observe. Then, I'll get Ambition in, separately.' She stood up. 'Let's get back to the hospital. I need to talk to the driver and call it off for now.'

Frustration coursed through Si's veins. For the first time in ages, he remembered what it had felt like when he was aware of the nanomedibot in his bloodstream. He felt physically sick. This had all started with him being pursued for that piece of life-saving technology. He remembered how his first encounter with Chas had been, when she threatened to kill him with her 'bloody big knife.' Despite himself he smiled at the memory. They had been through so much together. He couldn't lose her now and he was determined to find her. Where was all this going to end? He thought of his mum and the rebels at the Angel. He wished he had an idea of what was happening. He had so much to tell them about the clones and Young Zephyr. He felt guilty that he had probably jeopardised their plans, but he wouldn't change his decision to come for Chas. Had Mish got back to them with the video from the Premier's office? Had they put it out there?

'Si, are you alright?'

Anya was bending over him and it was only then that he realised that he was doubled over.

He stood upright and breathed deeply. 'Yeah, I'm okay. Just had one of those moments.'

She smiled sympathetically. 'Overwhelmed?'

'Something like that. I'm okay now though. Let's get back.'

As they stepped out of the secure corridor at the hospital, there was a sudden loud 'boom' then a low rumble as the building shook, like an earthquake had rocked it. People in the corridor ahead fell against the walls and each other. A man pushing an instrument trolley, toppled against it, shaking a few of the instruments onto the floor. Someone screamed. Si had never felt anything like this before. It was surreal; like being in a movie.

'What was that?' Anya asked another doctor.

'I don't know.'

Within a few seconds there was another 'boom' and the building rocked again. Bits of plaster fell from the ceiling and dust swirled around. People began to panic. Some ran to windows to see if they could see anything outside. Others crouched on the floor, whimpering. People were coughing and shouting.

'A car's on fire!' someone cried.

'And the Haines building is burning!' shouted another person.

'The Citadel is under attack!'

'Get away from the windows!' A doctor commanded.

They felt the concussive punch of another explosion and several windows shattered, bursting shards of glass everywhere. Screaming erupted. Some hid behind desks or just fell to the floor, others ran towards the stairs. Patients cried out for help from their beds.

Si didn't know what to do. He was still invisible. He whispered to Anya, 'I'm going outside to see what's happening. Stay here. Get to somewhere safe. I'll be back to find you.'

She nodded, but started to give orders. People had been hurt by the flying glass.

'Everyone, keep down!'

She then spoke to specific staff who looked less panicked than others. 'You! And you! Help me tend to the wounded.

Get the patients to safer spaces, away from the windows.'

Si left Anya doing what she did best, and raced towards the stairs, emerging from the hospital to find pandemonium on the streets. People were running and screaming. More explosions burst around him. Where were they coming from? He looked around, but he could see nothing. Suddenly, his heart missed a beat. This must be it: The start of the rebel attack! He had to find Chas!

*

In the Fortress, the Premier had called an emergency meeting of the Rulers. Those already in the Fortress had come as quickly as possible, but because of the chaos outside, some were unable to get there.

They looked frightened and couldn't understand what was happening. The Citadel had always been a place of security, away from the rabble outside its walls, where they were able to carry on their extravagant lifestyles without hindrance.

'This has to be the work of the rebels,' Ambition said. 'They're dropping small incendiary devices. The Fortress has been locked down. Security guards have been posted at every entrance and exit as an extra precaution, on top of what we already have. We're safe in here, but we need to end this as quickly as possible.'

'They must be using drones and stealth technology to cloak them,' Zephyr said. 'Marsden's work?'

'Of course,' Ambition said. 'I've ordered all guards to the gates and law-keepers on the streets. The military are coming, and they will end this. Where is the Commander?'

Zephyr's stomach lurched. 'He's... out of the Citadel... on business.'

'What business? We need him here. He should be organising the military response to this, not me! Let's get him on the phone now.'

'No need,' Zephyr said. 'I've already done it. He's on his way back, bringing reinforcements.'

Ambition nodded. 'Right. Excellence is leading the counter-attack in the Citadel, but it's virtually impossible to know if we've killed the rebels because we can't see anyone or anything.'

Another Ruler spoke up. 'There must be a way to uncloak the drones.'

'Excellence is working on it,' Ambition said. 'Have we got footage of what's going on outside?'

Zephyr called on the VA to bring up pictures from the cameras around the Citadel. 'The attacks are mainly going on around the Fortress. The rest of the city seems unaffected.'

'They're clearly trying to get in here,' Zealous said.

'They're after us!' another Ruler said, with terror in his voice.

'Of course they are!' Ambition said, disgust in his voice at the cowardice shown by some of the Rulers.

At that moment, an incendiary hit the Fortress itself. White knuckles gripped the backs of chairs and the edge of the desk.

'How protected are we from this kind of attack?' asked another Ruler.

'The Fortress is sturdy. Its walls are made to withstand

attack,' Zephyr said.

'Should we stay together in here?' Zealous asked.

'Yes. You're in the hub of the Fortress. You will be fine.' Zephyr tried to reassure them, almost experiencing satisfaction at their fear. He realised that a loathing for their smugness had been growing within him over the last months. 'I need to go back to my office. I'll be keeping an eye on things from there.'

Back in his office, Zephyr tried to call Resolution, but there was no answer. He left a message. 'Where are you? All hell is breaking loose here. Get back here as soon as possible. I presume your business is finished now?'

17

Chas was the first one to move. She realised she must have been out cold for a while, as it was getting light outside. The car had rolled but was upright. She tried to move, but the seat belt held her tightly. Her head pounded like a hammer was smashing into her eye sockets, and her face felt sticky to the touch. Blood soaked her shirt. A burnt chemical smell from the passenger airbag hit her nostrils. The driver airbag had not released. Everyone had been wearing seat belts, except Zeph, but no one else was moving.

She tried again to move, to see if Zeph was alright. He had been thrown around the car like a shoe in a washing machine. She had felt the force of him as his body hit her, but she couldn't defend herself with her arms tied. She was bruised and battered, and his body was now lying motionless; half on the floor, half on the seat.

'Zeph? Can you hear me?'

No response.

She got the same silence from Grace and didn't bother with Resolution. She hoped he was dead.

She was able to reach for a shard of glass with her fingers and began to saw at the ties holding her hands in place. It seemed to take forever, but eventually she sawed through the plastic and her hands were free. Her body felt numb. Probably shock, she thought. The only pain she could feel was in her head. She pressed the seatbelt release and it came loose easily. Cautiously, she moved to see if Zeph was still alive. Twinges of pain shot up her left arm and it suddenly felt hard to breathe. She sat still again, taking shallow but steady breaths. Then she moved again, very slowly.

'Zeph. Zeph! Can you hear me?'

She felt for a pulse in his neck. Yes, it was there, and he was breathing, but she had no idea what injuries he had. His arm was at an odd angle and she decided it was broken. He had cuts and gashes on his head, face and arms. She was scared to move him.

'Chas?' It was a weak voice from the front. 'Chas, are you okay?'

'Yes, I think so. Are you?'

'Yes. I must have blacked out. But I'm okay. Are you injured?'

'Yes, but I can manage. Can you see what's happened to Resolution? Is he dead?'

'I don't know. His airbag didn't go off. He's got blood all over his face and clothes. He could be dead. Is Zeph alright?' Grace asked.

'See if you can find a pulse,' Chas said. 'Zeph's unconscious but he's alive.'

'Oh, thank God,' Grace said, a sob escaping from her lips.

'Can you find a pulse?' Chas asked again.

'I'm scared to touch him,' Grace said.

Chas was about to swear at Grace, but she held back.

She needed Grace to keep calm if she was going to be useful. Wincing, she climbed halfway into the front and felt Resolution's neck. It was hard to tell if there was a pulse. There may have been a faint one. She couldn't be sure. If he was breathing, it was hard to detect it.

She shook her head. 'He's as good as dead. Come on! The car will have sensors that alert the emergency services. We need to get out of here.' She began to climb over the seats. Pain made her gasp and she had to sit still in the back seat for a moment.

'Wait,' Grace said. 'Don't we need their help?'

'Technically, yes, but we can't risk being found here with the Commander. They'll arrest us and we'll end up back in custody in the Citadel. We can't go back.'

Grace began to cry. 'I want to go back, Chas. I want to get checked out at a hospital. And what about Zeph?'

'I know, I know,' Chas said, trying to keep her cool. 'But we can't be found here. Resolution wasn't doing this on his own authority. It's the Premier who's trying to get rid of Zeph. We have to make our way to the nearest tech-city and find help.'

'This wasn't supposed to happen to me,' Grace sobbed.

This time Chas lost her temper. 'Hey!' she shouted. 'None of us chose this, but here we are. And you know what? This car accident might just have saved our lives.'

'What do you mean?'

'He was going to kill us, Grace. Wake up! Now, come on. Help me find a way to get Zeph out of the car. Give me your wrists. I'll cut them free.'

The door on the nearside rear opened, but Grace's door

was jammed. They had to climb over Zeph and carefully drag him out. He was heavy; a big unconscious guy, who worked out, was hard work for two young women to move, and they were terrified that they might be making his injuries worse.

They got him out onto the grass and Chas looked him over again. His pulse was steady and felt stronger. There was no bone poking through the skin of his arm, so Chas ripped some material from his shirt and made a sort of triangular bandage. Then, she carefully moved the arm to his chest, securing it with the makeshift bandage to immobilize it. The pain brought him round and he cried out.

'Zeph!' Grace cried, kneeling by his head. 'It's okay. You're alive. You're going to be alright.'

Chas wasn't so sure. She looked around. How far were they from civilization? Resolution had probably been driving them somewhere remote. What were the chances of her and Grace being able to carry Zeph a long distance? And he could have internal injuries too. He might die.

She didn't know how long they had been there, but it must have been some time. If an ambulance was coming, she thought it would have arrived by now.

'Zeph, can you speak?' Chas said.

His eyes were open, and he was trying to focus. 'Yes.'

'Where have you got pain?'

'Arm,' he said, wincing as he tried to move it.

'I know. I think it's broken. Anywhere else?'

'Everywhere,' he said.

'Can you sit?'

He tried. With the help of the girls, and several attempts,

he managed to sit up.

'How does that feel?'

'Terrible. I think I'm going to throw up.' He vomited into the grass. 'Sorry.'

'Don't worry about it,' Grace said, wiping his face with her skirt and fussing over his cuts, trying to wipe away blood with her sleeve.

'Where's the Commander?' Zeph asked.

'Dead, we hope,' Chas said. 'We need to get out of here and get some help. Are you able to stand?'

'I don't know. I'll try.'

He managed to stand, but as he tried to put weight on his left leg, it buckled and he almost went down again, crying out in pain. Chas and Grace caught him. He was breathing heavily.

'Wow! That hurt. I'm going to be sick again.'

'Sit him down,' Chas said. 'Another fracture; in the leg, maybe,' She was beginning to think their situation was hopeless. 'Listen, you two stay here. I'm going to walk to the road and try to flag down a car. I'll come back for you.'

'What if an ambulance comes from the Citadel?' Grace asked.

Chas shook her head. 'I think it would have been here by now. Maybe the car was so damaged it didn't send the distress signal. I don't know. But if it comes, you'll just have to go with it. At least Resolution can't hurt us now.'

Chas set off back to the road. She wasn't sure what she should do next. Return to the Citadel to find Si and Ahya? How would that work? Or head towards the Angel of the North, where Si had told her the rebels were? Kate and

Nick would be there, and they would be able to help. That seemed the most sensible plan.

As she reached the road, she heard a scream. What was happening? She half-ran, half-limped back as fast as she could. Every breath was painful. She could see Grace and Zeph huddled together by a rock and Resolution, lying on the ground, as if he had fallen out of the car, pointing the gun at them.

No! This couldn't be happening. He was dead.

Resolution had his back to her, so he didn't know she was approaching, but Grace and Zeph could see her.

'Where's Chastity?' she heard him ask.

'She's gone,' Zeph said.

'She'll be back,' Resolution said. 'She's hard-hearted but she wouldn't leave you two here. She has her weaknesses.'

'Give up, Commander,' Zeph said. 'It's over. You're dying.'

Resolution coughed. 'It's never over!' His hand was shaking.

Zeph pulled Grace in behind him. 'Just put the gun down.'

'No!' Resolution said. 'I've got to finish the job.' He squirmed, trying to get into a better position, and cried out as pain engulfed him. Chas moved silently towards him.

Zeph was trying to move. 'Get behind that rock,' he said, urgently to Grace. She scrabbled behind it, trying to pull Zeph with her.

Resolution was breathing heavily. 'My task was to kill you and Chastity. And you're still here, so...'

His hand was shaking badly as he pulled the trigger.

Grace screamed, and Chas ran at Resolution.

She threw herself on him and tried to wrestle the gun out of his hand. They struggled together for some moments. He tried to kick her, but pain shot up his leg and made him double up. She jumped out of his reach and rolled away. He fired the gun again, but his aim was poor. Chas threw herself on him again. She was sure her head was about to explode. She could hear Grace screaming in the background. She managed to get on top of Resolution, and, gasping for breath, she grabbed the hand holding the gun and smashed it on the ground until he let go.

'You're meant to be dead!' she screeched, scrambling to her feet and pointing the gun at him. 'Why aren't you dead?'

He gagged. He was covered in blood and the smell, sight and feel of it on himself suddenly overpowered him. He began to throw up.

When the vomiting stopped, he said, 'Why don't you just go ahead and shoot me? You've been waiting long enough.'

She held the gun shakily in two hands. He was right. She had waited for this moment for a very long time and all she needed to do now, was pull the trigger.

Grace had stopped screaming. The shot at Zeph had gone wide and she was cowering in his arms as they watched.

'Finish him!' Zeph said.

Resolution wiped his face and looked at Chas. 'Go on then, Chastity, shoot me! Get it over with.'

He looked like an injured dog, covered in blood and vomit. He was still bleeding from a severe gash across his forehead. Chas remembered when they had left him for dead before, after escaping from Lindisfarne. A voice in her head (probably Si) reminded her of the prayer she had uttered just before the car crash. She thought God could have come up with a better way to save them from Resolution. Nevertheless, here they were. He was now at her mercy.

Mercy.

The word bounced around her head to the pulse of her pounding headache.

She looked at the man she had thought was her brother. His eyes were closed now, and his breathing was shallow. She thought of all the pain he had caused her, and others, and of the desperate need she had felt to kill him and get ultimate revenge. She had dreamed of it, savoured the thought, longed for the opportunity. And now, here it was, and there was nothing to stop her pulling the trigger. How was this supposed to feel?

Anger welled up, making her eyes water. She held tightly to the gun, because her hands were shaking so much. She wiped her eyes on her sleeve.

Mercy.

This was an unfamiliar voice and she wished it would shut up. He didn't deserve it. But isn't that the point? said the voice in her head.

She moved closer and put the gun to his temple. Bending down to his face, she said, 'Goodbye brother.'

Resolution didn't open his eyes or make any movement. Grace hid her face in Zeph's shoulder. Then, Chas stood up, took her finger off the trigger, put the gun in her pocket and walked towards Zeph and Grace.

'You're not going to kill him?' Zeph asked.

She shrugged. 'He's as good as dead anyway.'

'You should make sure,' Zeph said.

Chas just shook her head. 'Let's get out of here.'

Grace had opened her eyes and extracted herself from Zeph's arms. 'How?'

'We'll get Zeph nearer the road, then I'll try again to flag down a car.'

*

Si decided to take off his invisibility suit. If the rebels were here, invisible, he needed to let them know that he was here too. It was so frustrating not being able to see where the attack was coming from. He bundled the invisibility suit up and carried it, thinking he might need it again. The cold air touched the bare skin on his arms, and he shivered. Where should he head for? Explosions were going on around him. People were running and screaming. Law-keepers were swarming everywhere, but not knowing where to aim any of their shots. Some were firing randomly and hitting innocent people. And these were real bullets, not the usual tazers.

He was close enough to a law-keeper to see him go down, his chest ripped apart by one of the RIP bullets that the rebels were using. A current of ice-cold adrenalin leapt through him, and he ran, thinking that it could so nearly have been him.

He headed towards the Fortress, which was clearly the target. The rebels would be trying to infiltrate it. Where were they? He wanted to find out if Temp or Mish were here, but he hadn't a clue how to find them. He only hoped they might recognise him and not shoot him by mistake.

*

Kate had released the footage of Si in the Premier's office as soon as they began to see reports on HTV of the attack. The others from the Angel shouldn't be far from joining the first cohort of rebels in the Citadel. They would have to fight their way in, without invisibility suits and she knew some of them would die. In tech-cities around the country, people were rising up, having been inspired by what they saw going on. She hoped Si's video would boost their confidence.

*

Ambition knocked on the door of Zephyr's office.

'Have you seen this, Premier?' he said, calling up the video that the rebels had put out.

Zephyr watched in horror as Si stood there in his office, addressing the people.

'I knew someone had been in here,' he said, touching the picture on his desk.

'And look at what's happening around the country!' Ambition waved his hand at the other holo-screen playing news images of tech-cities under siege. 'This is unprecedented.'

'I've called on all law-keepers to do whatever it takes to restore order,' Zephyr said.

'What are we using?'

'Drones and EXACTO weapons, not just tazers.'

'I agree. We have to quash this with brute force,' Ambition said. 'Shouldn't the Commander be doing this? Where is he?'

'He's been in touch,' Zephyr lied. 'He's out there with the law-keepers and Excellence is looking after matters from here. He's keeping me informed.'

Ambition nodded. 'Good. You should come back to the meeting room, Premier, and be with the others. They're anxious.'

'Of course. I'll be there soon.'

'Any word on the disappearance of Young Zephyr? It may be connected with this attack, don't you think?' Ambition asked.

The Premier shook his head. 'No word. But if the rebels have him, as we suspect, I think there will be a ransom demand before too long.'

'What do you think they'll want in exchange for his return?'

The Premier shrugged. 'I don't know. They may want Chastity and those children the Commander brought in from the Priory. But I think it's gone beyond that now. We must stop this attack. That is our priority.'

When Ambition left, Zephyr called Resolution again but there was still no answer. Something must have gone wrong with their plan. He cursed Resolution, but Ambition was right, he would have to join the rest of the Rulers now.

The Rulers were very agitated when he re-entered the meeting room. The screens were showing more rebels breaking into the Citadel through the checkpoints. Guards were shooting at them, taking some down, but they were outnumbered, and rebels were getting through. Another explosion rocked the Fortress.

'We're being blown apart,' one of the Rulers cried.

'This place is not impenetrable. They're bound to get in eventually,' shouted another.

'Stay calm! We are counter-attacking,' Zephyr said. 'This is the safest part of the Fortress.'

'What about our clones up in the Complex? They must be vulnerable.'

There were murmurs of agreement.

Zephyr shook his head, then he banged on the table. Several Rulers jumped, as if an explosion had just occurred in the room. 'What has got into you all? You're supposed to be the Rulers of this country and yet here you are, cocooned in your Fortress, like snivelling cowards!'

There were protests but Zephyr silenced them with another slam of his fists and a great roar like they had never heard from him before. 'Be quiet, all of you! Listen to me! The clones are safe. You yourselves designed the Fortress and you know that the Complex roof is covered by blast resistant glass. And even if it was shattered, no one is being allowed in that part of the Complex and all entrances to the garden are locked down. The Complex is one of the most secure areas in the Fortress.'

One of the Rulers began to speak again. 'But Premier...'

'Shut up! You are safe. The Fortress is safe. You made me your leader. You put me in charge. Now, for once in your lives, trust me!'

The Rulers looked silently from one to another. Their

looks did not go un-noticed by Zephyr. He didn't even believe his little outburst himself. He knew he was on borrowed time... if they survived this.

*

Chas found the walking more difficult than she had thought it would be. It was raining, for which she was grateful. The cold water beating against her face was helping her to keep going. The road was quiet, as she had expected at this time of the morning. She dared to ask for some more divine intervention. But please, no more crashes!

She kept thinking about Si and Anya. What would they do when they found her gone? She couldn't imagine Si leaving without her, but she couldn't go back there straight away. She had to take Zeph and Grace to the Angel of the North where they would be safe.

She didn't know how long she had been walking, when a car came towards her. She flagged it but it didn't stop. Great! Several more came in quick succession but none stopped. Some radical action was required. As the next car came towards her, she jumped into the road waving her arms and immediately regretting it as pain shot through her torso. The car slowed and pulled up.

'What's wrong?' the man said, leaning out of the window. Then he noticed her blood-streaked face and swore. 'What happened to you?'

'There's been a car accident. Can you help me and my friends?'

The man was alone; nervous and agitated. 'How many? Are they seriously hurt?'

'Three of us. I've left the others near the site of the crash. Car rolled off the road. We're all walking but need help.'

'Didn't your car put an automatic call out to emergency services?'

'Seems not. Will you help us?'

'I should call them.'

'Fine,' Chas said. 'But can you take me back to my friends first?'

The man hesitated for a moment. Chas tried to look innocent and helpless, whilst fingering the gun in her pocket.

He hesitated some more, until his conscience got the better of him. 'Okay. Get in.' He released the door lock and she got into the passenger seat.

'I've probably walked a couple of miles,' she said.

He glanced at her. 'You look awful. I'm surprised you made it.'

'Yeah.' She half laughed. 'Me too. My head is killing. You don't have any pain-killers, do you?'

'Sure. In there.' He pointed to the glove compartment.

'Here,' he said, handing her a water flask from the cup holder.

'Thanks.' She washed down the tablets, hoping they would help her to carry on.

More cars had been passing them. 'Everyone seems in a hurry all of a sudden,' Chas said. 'It was deserted 'til a few minutes ago.'

'You don't know?' He looked at her in astonishment. 'There's been an attack on the Citadel. Bombs going off, explosions near the Fortress. Loads of people are getting out if they can. It's chaos at the gates. Rebels streaming in, over-powering the guards. People clamouring to get out! Guards firing everywhere! Hideous!'

'That's awful!' Chas's mind began to race. She had to get back there as soon as possible to help the rebels and to find Si and Anya.

'These so-called rebels are animals!' the man said, clearly a resident of the Citadel.

Suddenly, she saw Zeph and Grace. 'Oh! There! That's my friends.'

The man pulled up at the side of the road, looking anxiously at Zeph and Grace. 'Look I need to get going. This road might get clogged soon. I'll call an ambulance. Then I'm off. I can't really do anything else.'

Chas drew the gun from her pocket. 'Well, actually you can. I need your car. I have to get to the Citadel.'

Panic shot across his face and he automatically lifted his hands.

'I'm sorry to do this,' Chas said. 'And I don't want to hurt you, but you need to leave the car. Call 999 when we're gone. There's a wrecked car down there and a body.'

The man blanched.

Grace and Zeph tried the car doors.

'Release the doors,' Chas said, pointing the gun directly at his head.

He was shaking now and did as he was told. Grace helped Zeph into the back seat. The man turned around. His eyes widened as he recognised Zeph. 'Isn't he the... he looks younger than on HTV.'

Chas almost laughed. 'He just looks like him. Now get

out of the car.'

Again, he did as she told him. Chas moved into the driver's seat, turned the car round and headed back to the Citadel.

'I was going to take you to the Angel of the North, where the rebel base is. But that guy just told me the Citadel's under attack.'

'What? How?' Grace asked.

'Will this be the rebels?' Zeph said.

'Yes. We have to go back straight away. I need to help them. I'm going to find Anya... Doctor Nelson. We'll have to get you some medical treatment at the hospital.'

'What will they do to the Citadel?' Grace asked.

'I don't know,' Chas replied. 'But this is it. The Rulers' reign of oppression will end here.'

'If the rebels are successful,' Grace said. 'The Rulers have a lot of power.'

Zeph winced as pain shot through his arm. 'We need to save the children. They'll be trapped. If the rebels storm the Fortress, they might kill them.'

'I know. We've got to prevent that,' Chas said. 'But you need medical attention first.'

'So do you,' Zeph said, before closing his eyes and leaning his head on Grace.

18

Si felt a hand on his shoulder. He turned sharply but saw no one.

'It's Mish,' the voice said.

'Oh, thank God!' Si said. 'I didn't know what to do for the best.'

'We're about to storm the Fortress. Others are pouring into the Citadel as we speak, but they don't have invisibility suits.'

'Where are the bombs coming from?'

'Invisible drones,' Mish said. 'They're targeting the buildings. We're not trying to destroy them, just create chaos.'

Si nodded. 'Plan working so far.'

'Come with me.'

Mish grabbed his arm and pulled him across the road, into the square. Panicked people were running in every direction. Another explosion rocked the square and flying debris caused Mish and Si to fall to the ground, covering their heads.

'Are you alright?' Si said, getting to his knees and brushing debris off his body.

'Yeah, I'm okay,' Mish said. He took hold of Si's arm and

kept going. Guns fired randomly into the crowd. A woman screamed and fell to the ground just ahead of them. They dodged her convulsing body.

Si swore. This was hideous. He hadn't imagined innocent people getting killed. How naïve he'd been. Of course, people were going to die. This was the reality of redeeming the country.

Mish pulled him into a gap between two buildings.

'Si!' Another voice spoke out of the ether. It was Temp. Si felt big invisible arms hug him. 'What are you doing here?'

'I was trying to escape with Chas and Doctor Nelson, but that went wrong. Chas has been kidnapped by Resolution, along with the oldest clone of Zephyr. I've no idea where she is. She could be dead.' He swallowed a sob before it started.

'Sorry to hear that,' Temp said, taking off the hood of his suit. 'We'll do our best to find her, but first we have to press on with our mission.'

Si nodded. 'I understand.' He said a silent prayer for her to be safe... somehow. 'I'm coming with you.'

'We don't have any spares,' Temp said, pulling out the RIP weapon from beneath his invisibility suit.

'I have a suit here,' Si said, showing him.

'Great,' Temp said. Then, he spoke to a group of invisible people that Si hadn't realised were there. 'Get to the front of the building. The drones will cut holes in the entrances and we're going in.'

From various points around the square, unseen rebels were emerging and dashing towards the Fortress, dodging random bullets and explosions. Temp's cohort headed for the main entrance. Some of the rebels went down, crying out as holes appeared in their invisibility suits, flowering with bright blood. Si, Temp and Mish ducked and dived for the shelter of anything solid; fountains, walls, statues, cars. Bullets ricocheted off the objects. Dust and debris flew around them, cutting and ripping at their suits and skin, making them more visible.

'Keep going!' Temp yelled across the square to the others. The noise was deafening. His voice was lost.

Then, there was a low rumble, different to the explosions and shooting, causing the ground to vibrate. Armoured vehicles moved into the square.

'Keep going!' Temp called out again, urging the ordinary men and women who had joined the rebels only weeks ago, to plough into battle, like men running over No Man's Land during the First World War.

Some of them made it to the entrance of the Fortress. The doors were sealed. Temp rolled back his sleeve and made a call from his Wearable.

'Target reached.' Then he shouted, 'Evacuate the area. Everyone, move!'

The drones moved into place and lasers began cutting through the doors. Then, the rebels surged towards the gaping holes, pouring through the entrances. The sensors screamed as invisible bodies were detected, but the rebels had already shot the guards who were waiting.

'More will be on their way,' Temp shouted. 'Find the Rulers. Keep in contact!'

Upstairs, in the meeting room, the Rulers were panicking.

'They're in!'

'They've breached the Fortress!'

'You said we were safe!'

Even Zephyr and Ambition were beginning to lose their nerve, but they tried not to show it.

'Shut up!' Zephyr roared.

This had little effect. 'We have to get out of here!' yelled one Ruler.

'There must be somewhere safer than this!' cried another.

'What about down in the basement, Premier, where the cells are?' Zealous suggested.

'Be quiet! All of you!' Ambition yelled.

The hubbub began to subside. 'You're making matters worse. If we leave here for the basement, we will be more vulnerable.'

'So, we just sit here and wait for them to come for us?' Zealous said, squaring up to Ambition. 'We should split up, at least. Then some of us might survive.'

'No!' Zephyr said. 'We wait here. If they get to us before they're shot down, we negotiate. They won't kill us.'

'You think so?' said one of the Rulers, sarcastically.

'We have to make ourselves seem like a useful... prize. Alive.'

'Is this the end for us?' asked another Ruler.

Zephyr smiled ironically. 'There is no end for us. We are cloned. Even if we die, our clones will live on.'

'They're just children. And who's to say the rebels won't kill them too.'

'The children are safest in the Complex. There are guards on every corridor,' Ambition said. 'They won't get to us. Just try to keep calm.'

*

Chas drove the car up to a checkpoint to get back into the Citadel. The driver had been right. A mass exodus was taking place. There were no guards left alive at the checkpoint, and chaos ensued as people tried to get ahead of others. A fight had broken out between two drivers whose cars had collided. A woman was trying to calm them down, to no effect. Others were trying to squeeze their cars around the accident. A woman and two young children had plastered themselves against a wall, trying to sidle past and keep away from the traffic chaos. The children were crying, and she was trying to protect them with her arms and body. Meanwhile, from the other direction, rebels were pouring in, pushing past the escapees. Some had guns, which they fired randomly, while others were hitting out with whatever weapons they had been able to cobble together to join the fight.

'If we try to get a car in, I can see it being attacked. We're better off leaving it here and going on foot; can you make it Zeph?' Chas said. She looked at him, knowing he was putting on a brave face.

He nodded. 'I'll be fine. Let's go.'

Chas looked at Grace. Her face was a picture of horror, as she watched the scene. 'How can this be happening to the Citadel?'

'It's about time it did,' Chas said. 'No one here lives in the real world. The cocoon has been ripped apart. You can stay here if you don't want to come back inside with us.'

Grace looked at Zeph. 'No. You need help to get him to the hospital. I'm coming.'

Chas smiled at her. 'I knew you were made of steel underneath that delicate exterior.'

They abandoned the car. Grace and Chas helped Zeph get out and supported him between them. He was heavy but they were not going to be deterred.

'I can walk,' Zeph said. 'I'm too heavy for you two.'

He tried to walk on his own, but after a few steps he stumbled and almost fell. Grace was the first one to catch him. 'You're not too heavy. We can do it. Let us help you.'

He smiled up at her and nodded.

'Are you crazy?' shouted a man as they pushed their way against the crowd. 'Get out of here. The rebels have invaded. They're destroying the place.'

They didn't respond, just continued to push on, into the city. They pressed on into the Citadel. It was hard going with Zeph almost a dead weight. They had to keep stopping to rest. Chas was anxious to get to the hospital and try to find Si and Anya. They must stop the rebels from harming the clones. Chas knew that although the rebels' motives for attack may be good, the clones would be a target. And once people were engaged in destruction, they might not worry too much about killing children. She wondered who had ordered the attack. She couldn't imagine Kate being comfortable with all this.

As they got closer to the centre of the city, they could hear more explosions and gun fire. Sirens sounded all around them, as emergency vehicles raced in all directions. Chas looked at Grace, knowing she was terrified, but her body language also spoke of determination. Chas recognised Grace's attraction to Zeph and her resolve to protect him. She had sometimes felt this towards Si, especially in the beginning. But now it was more of a relationship of equals and she had even experienced a longing for Si to protect her. And he had. Many times. She hoped, prayed even, that he was still alive and unhurt.

'Watch out for law-keepers,' Chas said. 'We need to keep out of sight as much as possible. They might recognise us.'

'Or they might randomly shoot us,' Zeph said.

'Don't say that,' Grace said.

Zeph squeezed her hand. 'I'm sorry. You're doing great. Chas is right though. We need to keep low.'

As if to reinforce the point, a bullet whizzed past very close to them. Grace screamed.

'Get down!' Chas shouted, throwing them all to the floor. Zeph cried out as pain shot through his body and especially his arm.

'Chas!' Grace shouted. 'His arm! Be careful!'

'Would you rather he got a bullet in his head?' Chas looked up. She couldn't figure out where the bullet had come from at first. Then she saw the law-keepers on the roof of the building opposite. She looked for cover.

'Sorry Zeph. Are you okay?'

He nodded, but was clearly struggling with the pain.

'We're going to run for that shop entrance,' she said, pointing across the street. 'Ready?'

Zeph and Grace braced themselves to get up.

'Now!'

They hauled Zeph up with as much help from him as he could manage. He stifled the urge to cry out.

'Come on! You can do it!' Grace urged.

Entering the thick of the fighting, they made it to the shop door. The noise from explosions, tanks and general chaos was overwhelming. There were people everywhere, some with weapons in their hands, others just trying to get to safety. Some law-keepers were trying to herd people away from the fighting and others were firing, seemingly randomly, at people.

The hospital was in sight and they moved as quickly as they could, reaching the building without being fired on again. Chas was uncertain what to do next. If they asked for help for Zeph, staff might recognise him and Chas, and it might lead to them being put under guard. But the decision was taken out of her hands.

'We need help!' Grace shouted, as soon as they entered the building. Medical staff were hurrying around, and injured people were clamouring for attention. Reception was unmanned. No one took any notice of them at first.

'Grace!' Chas urged. 'We need to find Doctor Nelson. She'll help Zeph. We could be arrested if you're not careful.'

Grace suddenly became angry. 'He needs urgent help! Look at him. I can't believe he's made it this far. What if Doctor Nelson isn't here? Or injured? Or dead?'

'She won't be,' Chas said. 'She can't be.'

Grace shook her head. 'I'm getting help for him, whatever it takes.'

Zeph was struggling to keep upright, the pain having intensified, as if it knew help was nearby. He stood hunched over but was able to speak. 'Grace, I appreciate your concern for me, but Chas is right. Let's find Doctor Nelson.'

Just then, a young doctor became free. 'Can I help you?' She took one look at Zeph and it was clear from her face that she recognised the features of the Premier. 'What are you doing with the Premier? How did this happen to him?'

With all the blood and dirt on them it was hard to tell that Zeph was much younger than his older clone.

'He's not the Premier,' Chas tried. 'He just looks like him. He's much younger. See? He needs help.'

'I can see that,' the doctor said. She called to a colleague for a trolley. 'You look like you need it too.' She looked from one girl to the other.

'I'll be fine,' Chas said. 'but take her. She needs treatment for shock too.'

The doctor looked curiously at Zeph as they loaded him onto the trolley. 'Come with me. You both need patching up. Things are in chaos here, but I'll see what I can do.'

Chas hesitated. 'Can you take me to Anya? Doctor Nelson?'

The trolley moved off and they followed, Grace holding Zeph's hand. The doctor nodded. 'Do you know her? She was on the third floor, last time I saw her: directing things there. I can get a message to her to let her know you're here. What's your name? Are you a friend?'

Chas wasn't sure what to say. 'I... yes. And a patient of hers. She's helped me a lot. I need to speak to her urgently.'

'Do I know you?' the doctor asked, looking more closely at Chas.

'I've never seen you before,' Chas said, resisting the urge to run. 'If you could get word to Anya for me, I'd appreciate it.'

They arrived at a treatment room and the medical staff around the trolley began working on Zeph.

'You two sit there. They'll get to you soon. If I see Doctor Nelson, I'll tell her you're here. What did you say your name was?'

'Just tell her the girl who lost the babies is here,' Chas said.

'Oh! I'm so sorry,' the young doctor replied, softening a little.

Chas waved her concern away, wishing she would just go and find Anya and hoping, in the meantime, that they wouldn't be recognised.

*

As this was happening, an ambulance arrived at the Accident and Emergency entrance. The paramedics rushed the trolley, carrying an unconscious man through the doors. An oxygen mask covered his face and an IV line was already in place.

'What happened to him?' asked the orderly.

'RTA out on the moors. He needs urgent attention. Heavy bleeding. Head injury. Probably fractured cheekbone there.

Possible internal injuries.'

'Leave him with us. We'll do our best.'

The orderly called for help several times, before a couple of medics came running. They wheeled him into a side room and began to examine him. His face and clothing were caked with blood, but the paramedics had managed to stop the bleeding. They began cleaning him up and assessing his wounds.

19

The rebels had spread out into different parts of the Fortress, moving carefully, since guards were everywhere. Si had picked up a weapon from one of the fallen guards. After some initial shooting and pandemonium in the entrance lobby, as more guards flooded in, it fell eerily quiet. The remaining guards were clearly alert to the fact that they had been invaded by invisible people. Orders and questions were being barked back and forth via the guards' Wearables. Now and again a shot would be fired, as one of them thought he had seen someone, or felt something touch him.

Si, Mish and Temp had decided to stay together, along with three other rebels. They were moving towards the meeting room and Zephyr's office as quickly as they could, under the circumstances, trying to keep physical contact with each other. This wasn't easy when they were held up by security doors; having to wait for guards to pass through them so that they could slip through, one by one in their wake. Once through a door, they had to guess where the others were and try to make contact again. It was tempting to use force against the guards, but this stealth method was going to be more effective in the long run.

There was no guarantee that any of the Rulers were there, but it was worth checking out. It was at the heart of the Fortress and Si had drawn the conclusion that there was a distinct possibility of Zephyr being there.

When they finally reached the right area, as they had suspected, the door of the meeting room was flanked by four guards; a sure indication that someone important was inside. At this point, Si wished they could see each other and decide what to do next. None of them really knew for certain that all of the others were even there. Si was holding on to someone, though. He pulled the person towards the end of the corridor, far enough away from the guards so that they couldn't be heard. This end of the corridor was clear of people.

'Who's here?' Si whispered, when they had moved far enough away from the guards.

'Temp.'

'Mish.'

'Deter.'

There was no other reply.

'Anyone else?' Temp asked.

'Great! Down to four of us!' Mish said.

'What's happened to the other two?' Deter asked.

'We haven't got time to worry about it,' Temp said. 'We need to get in there. Be ready to use your weapons. Each of us take out the guards, without any noise. Are you up to that?'

'Yes,' they each replied.

'Si take the furthest one. Deter, next one. Mish, nearest one. I'll go last and when I'm in position, I'll say 'now' and we do it quickly. Understood?'

They all agreed.

'Then, we take off our suits. Mish, you knock on the door and pretend to be one of the guards. Whoever answers, is about to get a gun in his temple. We break in and hold them at gunpoint. Si, if Zephyr is there, you put your gun to his head. Deter cover the rest of them. Make sure they don't send any panic signals. Then we call Kate and let her know we have them. She can advise from there.' There was a pause as they processed the instructions. 'Are you ready?'

Si's heart pounded harder as they walked back down the corridor. His mouth felt dry and he longed for water. Out of the blue, a picture of his father came into his mind, saying, 'I'm proud of you, son.' It startled him. He hadn't thought of his father for a while and the clear picture made him gasp. He took a moment to steady himself, fighting back the tears that stung his eyes. In his mind he whispered, This is for you, Dad.

As they approached the guards, Si went over, in his mind, how, back at the Angel, Temp had taught them to render someone unconscious. He'd never tried it for real before, so he was relieved when the guards went down with minimum struggle, and crumpled to the floor.

They took off their suits and left them, in a heap, by the door. 'Okay Mish,' Temp said.

Mish knocked on the door.

'Say something,' Temp said.

Mish put on a deeper voice and changed his accent. 'Message for you, Sir.'

The moment before the door opened seemed to last a

lifetime. Then it opened, just a crack. Mish kicked it wide, felling the man who had opened it. There was confusion and panic as the rebels burst in.

'No one move!' Temp ordered. 'Put your hands above your heads and sit down at the table. Keep your hands above your heads!'

In shocked silence the Rulers complied. Ambition stared at Temp. 'The wanderer finally returns!'

'Shut up, Ambition!' Temp said.

They were all sitting at the meeting table now. 'Si,' Temp said, nodding in the direction of Zephyr. Si walked towards the Premier and held his gun as steadily as he could against Zephyr's temple.

'You will cooperate with us, and you might get out of here with your lives.' Temp addressed his former boss informally. 'Zephyr, make sure your guards are called off. Tell them that if they try to get in here, we will kill you.'

Zephyr called Excellence, explaining that the rebels had him and the other Rulers hostage. 'Don't try to get in here,' Zephyr said, glaring at Temp. 'They will kill us. Cooperate until you receive further instructions.'

'You won't get out of here alive, you know,' Ambition said. 'This place is full of law-keepers and guards. You're dead men.'

'We managed to get in here,' Si replied.

'Yes,' muttered one of the Rulers. 'And they told us you'd never be able to get to us.'

Zephyr scowled at the man.

'Yes, well, you're all liars,' Temp said. 'What do you expect? You lied to the people so why wouldn't you lie to each other?'

'What do you hope to achieve, Temperance?' Zephyr asked.

It was Si who answered. 'It's time to restore justice and equality to the country. And that means the end of your reign.'

Ambition laughed. 'And you think this will achieve it do you? We're not the only corrupt ones in this country. Power can corrupt anyone.'

'Only if they let it,' Si replied. 'Good people in power will change things.'

Zealous spoke up. 'You don't think power will change you, Silence Hunter? Your friend Temperance was a Ruler. And Capability North, he's still officially one of us. Many hunger for power. And power will devour them!'

'No!' Si said. 'Temp and Capability had the courage to leave that life behind.'

'Oh, they've seen the light, have they?' Ambition laughed.

'What do you propose to do with us?' asked another Ruler, looking nervously at the gun Si was pushing into Zephyr's temple.

'You'll have to wait and see what we decide.' Temp walked behind the Rulers, looking across the table into each face. Some looked afraid, others defiant. 'When reinforcements get here, we will be transporting you all to the Bastille, which you will hand over to Peter Marsden and our forces. They're waiting to take over, once Premier Zephyr makes his speech.'

'What speech?' Zephyr asked.

'You're going to tell all law-keepers and guards to stand down. And you're going to call the Bastille and the Priory and get them to surrender to us.'

'I'll do no such thing!' Zephyr protested.

Temp smiled sardonically at him. 'Oh, I think you will, Zephyr.'

'You have big ideas,' Ambition scoffed.

'So did you,' Temp said. 'And now they have failed. A new way is opening.'

Ambition shook his head and looked contemptuously at Temp. 'You could have been great, Temperance.'

Temp ignored him and sent a message to Kate:

We have the Rulers. Locked in a room with them in Fortress. Si with me.

Si turned Zephyr to face him. 'Where are Chas and Young Zephyr?'

The Premier blanched.

Ambition looked at him. 'I'd like to know that too, Premier.'

'I know as much as you,' Zephyr said.

'I suspect you know a lot more,' Ambition said. 'Young Zephyr mysteriously disappears in the night when we were about to remove him to a safe place. And Chastity too?'

'I told you, these people have taken them, with their invisibility suits. They got into my office, didn't they?'

'Why would we be wasting our time asking you where they are if we had them?' Mish said.

'A good point,' Ambition agreed. 'And now Commander Resolution seems to be off the radar too.'

'I was in the Complex the night Young Zephyr went

missing,' Si admitted. 'I saw Resolution kidnap him from his bed!'

The Rulers began to mutter and ask questions all at once.

'We all know that the Commander has a propensity to go maverick. I suspect that is what has happened here,' Zephyr said.

'It doesn't make sense,' Ambition protested. 'Things were going well for him. Why would he risk it? I think you had something to do with it, Premier.'

There were more shocked reactions from the Rulers.

Ambition continued accusing Zephyr. 'I think you wanted rid of Young Zephyr. You're afraid we are going to get rid of you!'

Zephyr stood up, forgetting, in his rage, about Si pointing a gun at him. He was fully focused on Ambition.

'Well, aren't you?' He looked around the table at the other Rulers. 'Isn't that your plan? I'm just your puppet. I know that's what you all think, despite your feigned allegiance. When I'm no longer of use to you, you have other clones waiting in the wings. Your allegiance is really to Ambition, isn't it?'

The Rulers looked shifty. No one wanted to meet the eye of the Premier, except Ambition, who stared at him coldly.

Si, Temp and Mish watched the Rulers fight amongst themselves. They were falling apart without the help of the rebels. Si pushed Zephyr down into the chair. 'Sit down!'

Zephyr resisted at first, until the gun pressed firmly into the back of his head.

'You all need to calm down,' Temp said. 'None of that matters now. We just need to know where Young Zephyr and Chastity are.' He moved in on Zephyr, who knew he was defeated.

'I don't know where they are. Resolution took them out of the city last night. He was going to kill them and get rid of their bodies. By now it will be done.'

Si felt like he had just been punched in the stomach. In a fit of anger, he hit Zephyr across the side of the head with the butt of his gun! Zephyr reeled and nearly fell off the chair. Temp pushed Si backwards and gave him a warning look. None of the Rulers moved to help Zephyr.

At that moment, Temp's Wearable buzzed. It was Capability. Not wanting the Rulers to hear anything, Temp converted the call into a message and read it:

Get them to call off the law-keepers and security around the Fortress. They're still shooting at us. I'm coming in. Where are you?

Temp sent a message back:

Meeting room. Bring reinforcements.

'Call off the attack on our people,' Temp said, addressing his order to Ambition.

'It's your people who are attacking. We are just defending ourselves.'

'Get them to stand down,' Temp said. 'If they don't, I will kill one of you.' He looked around as if deciding who it would be. The other Rulers looked at Ambition. Would he call Temp's bluff?

He hesitated, standing up and coming towards Temp. 'Give it up, Temperance. You're not going to win this.

Surrender and we will spare you. You may even fit right back in here. You know you loved the power really, until you had that sentimental wife and runt of a child to distract you.'

This time it was Temp's turn to let anger get the better of him. He launched himself at Ambition punching him in the face. Ambition fell back onto Zealous, but recovered his balance and launched at Temp. Zealous and another Ruler stood up. Si and Mish looked at each other. They could easily lose control here.

'Stop!' Si yelled and shot his gun into the ceiling, while Mish and Deter tried to break up the fight. Zephyr tried to grab the gun from Si and in the process of wrestling with him the gun went off, shooting one of the Rulers in the arm. The man cried out, grabbing hold of his injured arm.

By now, Si had wrestled the gun out of Zephyr's grip and pushed him back into the chair, hitting him again. The gun was once again pointing at his head and Mish and Deter had pulled Ambition and Temp apart.

'Temp! What the hell!' Mish cried.

Temp swore. 'Get that scum out of my sight! Find something to silence him otherwise I'll silence him for good.'

Deter took Ambition to the other side of the room, pushed him to his knees and put his gun into the back of his head. 'Speak one more word and you're dead!' he said.

Temp turned to Zephyr. 'Now, call off the law-keepers and the security guards.'

'You can't leave us defenceless, Premier,' Zealous protested.

Zephyr shrugged. He had nothing to lose. He had decided that he stood more chance of survival in the hands of the rebels, than in the hands of the Rulers. He called Excellence and ordered a stand-down.

*

'Chas!' Anya came into the room where Chas was waiting, having been treated for her injuries. They had taken Zeph into another room, to treat his more serious injuries and Grace had insisted on going with him.

Chas stood up and before she knew what was happening, Anya embraced her, stifling a sob. Surprisingly, Chas found her touch comforting.

'I thought you were dead! They told me Resolution took you.'

'He did,' Chas explained. 'Me, Grace and Zeph. We're all fine, well... sort of. Zeph has some bad injuries, but they're looking after him now.'

'How did you get away from Resolution?'

'You could call it divine intervention,' Chas said. 'The car crashed. He's dead. At least, we left him close to it, on the moors. Where's Si?'

'I don't know. He went to find out what was going on. He hasn't come back.'

Chas's stomach lurched. 'The rebels have attacked. It's carnage out there.'

'I know,' Anya said, 'We're overrun with casualties here.'

Everything within Chas wanted to go and find Si, but her instincts told her that he would have to fend for himself.

If he was dead, she couldn't help him. If he was captured, she couldn't help him... yet. If he was okay, he would be fighting with the rebels. Stay Alive, Si.

'Can you get away? We need to get the children out of the Complex. If the rebels get in there, who knows what they'll do.'

'Surely they wouldn't hurt children?' Anya said.

'It wouldn't be in Kate's plan, but who knows what rampaging people will do? They're angry and they're tasting revenge, success maybe, right now. I know what a thirst for revenge can do to you.'

An image of Resolution's dying face appeared briefly in her mind. But oddly, that driving destructive emotion was gone. She was surprised at how different she felt, having chosen not to take that ultimate revenge.

'Let's go together,' Anya said. 'I'm not losing you again.'

Chas looked at her enquiringly. 'You're freaking me out with your over-zealous concern for my well-being. I'm okay, you know. I've coped with worse than these few cuts and bruises. And the miscarriage... honestly, I'm fine.'

Anya smiled at her. 'I know. You're a strong young woman. And...' she shook her head. 'Let's get to those children.'

Chas nodded. 'I'll tell Grace where we're going.'

She found Grace, holding Zeph's hand and talking soothingly to him. 'He's been sedated,' she whispered, as Chas came in.

'Then there's no need to whisper,' Chas whispered back. 'Is he going to be okay?'

'Yes. He has a broken humerus, tibia and some fingers.

They've looked at x-rays and scans and nothing serious internally.'

Chas was relieved. 'We need to get him out of here.'

'What? Now?' Grace cried.

'Not right now,' Chas said. 'Anya and I are going back to the Complex to get the children out. You stay here with him. We'll either come back for you or send someone to get you. Okay?'

Grace nodded.

'If anyone tries to take him away, you have to stop them,' Chas said.

'Oh right. Yeah, cos I'm good at that.'

Chas shrugged. 'You'll think of something. Stay put if you can.'

Unexpectedly, she hugged Grace, who was taken aback by this show of affection, so out of character for Chas.

'You will come back, won't you?' she said, looking almost tearful.

'Of course,' Chas said. 'I've got nine lives and only used about seven so far, I think.' She grinned and went back for Anya.

'I can get us into the Complex via the secure passageway,' Anya said, as they walked down the corridor. A doctor and a couple of nurses approached Anya to ask for her help, but she made her excuses and directed them to someone else. She was torn between her medical duty here, and helping Chas, but the thought that they could save the children spurred her on.

'Do you have anything we could use to defend ourselves?' Chas asked. 'A surgical knife maybe?'

Anya frowned, but drew her into an operating theatre further along the corridor. Then she hesitated.

'What? Where's the knife?' Chas asked, growing impatient.

She shook her head. 'It's just that these things are meant for the preservation of life, not the taking of it.'

'Just a deterrent,' Chas said. 'Only for use if absolutely necessary.'

Anya wavered.

'Come on,' Chas urged. 'I promise I'm not going to stab the first person who gets in my way.'

Anya unlocked a cabinet of surgical instruments. Chas took out a scalpel, remembering when she had threatened to slit her own throat with such an implement. 'You need something too,' she said to Anya. Anya also took a scalpel.

'I'm not sure I could use it like that,' she said.

Chas shrugged. 'No defence against guns, but better than nothing.'

At that moment, another blast shook the building. This time it was a direct hit on the hospital. People screamed in the corridor. Lights flickered and went out. They were plunged into darkness as they both hit the floor. Within seconds, emergency lighting had come on.

'Are you okay?' Chas asked. But Anya was out cold.

Chas swore.

*

In another part of the hospital, Resolution was coming round. He was lying on a trolley in the corridor several floors below. At first, he had no idea where he was. It was dark, with only emergency lighting available. He felt something over his face and realised it was an oxygen mask. He pulled it off. Medical staff were trying to keep people calm. No one in this part of the hospital had been hurt by the blast, but confusion and fear were running riot.

Resolution lifted his head and winced. That hurt. He tried to remember what had happened. At first it was all a blur. He remembered something about driving over the moors. He tried harder. He saw Chastity's face and remembered the blood all over his face and clothes. Suddenly feeling the urge to throw up, he half sat up and retched over the side of the trolley. Looking down at himself, he saw that his blood-stained clothing had been removed and replaced by hospital garments. He tentatively touched his face and then his head where the pain seemed to be radiating from. A wound had been glued up across his forehead, but his face felt clean. He realised that he was wearing a neck brace and probably shouldn't be moving.

He tried harder to remember what had happened.

Zephyr.

Premier Zephyr?

No. Young Zephyr.

It was coming back to him. The Premier had told him to get rid of Young Zephyr. That was right. And Chastity was there too. Had he killed them? There was another girl. He couldn't remember why she had been there.

He tried to move again. He had to find out what was going on. He was clearly in a hospital. In the Citadel? Maybe. Maybe not. He managed to sit, but pain coursed through him again. He reached for the mask and gulped at the oxygen for a few minutes. His neck felt stiff in the brace and his head throbbed. A shooting pain stabbed in his chest. He gasped. An orderly saw him move and rushed over to him.

'Lie down, Commander. You need to lie still.'

Resolution looked at the man. 'Where am I?'

'In hospital, Commander.'

'Yes, I can see that!' He wanted to add 'fool' to his reply, but held back. 'Which hospital?'

'In the Citadel. You were in a crash on the moors. They brought you back here. Although, with everything that's happening, how they got into the city, I don't know. It's...'

'Stop prattling!' Resolution butted in. 'Who else was brought in with me?'

'No one, Sir. You were alone. I'll see if I can find an available doctor. Please, just lie still.'

Resolution's mind raced. Maybe Chastity and Zephyr were dead, then? Had he been driving back here? He shook his head, to clear the fog, then regretted it instantly as everything from his neck upwards protested. He remembered Chas taunting him when he was injured, and he remembered pointing a gun at Zephyr and the other girl.

The orderly came back with a doctor. 'We're trying to get you a bed, Commander. We've assessed you for internal injuries and we're satisfied there is no internal bleeding, but you have a hairline fracture on your skull and severe whiplash.'

'And my chest? Why the stabbing pain?'

'You've no internal bleeding and nothing broken. I think

it's bruising and maybe the effects of the shock. The pain relief will help.' Resolution became aware of the canula in his hand and the IV drip beside him.

'What's going on outside?'

'It's the rebels, Commander. They've attacked the Citadel. And penetrated the Fortress.'

Resolution tried to move again. 'I have to get there.'

'You can't go anywhere, Commander.'

'Does the Premier know I'm here?'

'No, Sir. The Premier and most of the Rulers are being held hostage by Silence Hunter and some of the others. Apparently one of them used to be a Ruler!'

Temperance. Resolution had to do something. 'I need to contact Excellence North. He is my second in command.' He looked for his Wearable. 'Where is my phone?'

'Probably removed when you came in, Commander. I'll see if I can find it.'

The doctor hurried away, leaving Resolution trying to figure out what he should do next. One thing he was certain of was that he was not going to lie here and do nothing.

20

Anya was only unconscious for a minute or two. As she came round, the silhouette of Chas's face swam into view, peering down at her.

'Thank God! I thought you were out for the count!' Chas said. 'You've got a small gash on your temple.'

Anya sat up and put her hand up to it, wincing slightly. 'Yep. Nothing much. I'll live. What just happened?'

'I think the hospital was hit directly. Can you walk?'

Anya pulled herself up using the edge of a table, with Chas supporting her. She swayed a little. 'Woah!'

Chas held on to her. 'You okay?'

'Bit dizzy, but I'll be fine.'

'Can you keep going?'

'Yes.'

They opened the doors to a silent corridor, filled with dust and rubble. Large pieces of masonry blocked their way, and breathing in the dust made them cough a lot.

'Can we get through?' Anya asked.

'We'll have to try. We should get some wet cloths to cover our faces,' Chas said, coughing some more.

Just then, Anya doubled up.

'What is it?' Chas said, moving to support her.

'Sorry, Chas. I think I'm going to faint.'

Chas helped her back inside the theatre and laid her down, elevating her feet onto the rung of a trolley.

'You know what you're doing,' Anya said. 'I'm sorry. It's probably just shock. I'll be fine in a few minutes.'

'I'm going back into the corridor to see if I can make a way through for us,' Chas said. 'I'll come back in a few minutes to see how you are.'

'Cover your face with something,' Anya said. 'There's some strips of cloth, used for wound dressing, in that cupboard over there.'

Chas got the strips and soaked them in water. She gave one to Anya and tied the other round her face.

It was hard to see in the dimness of the emergency lighting, but the dust was beginning to settle. She managed to move some of the smaller bits of masonry and make a passage that they could climb through. Her eyes were stinging by the time she went back into the theatre.

'I've found a way through. Do you think you can move?'

Anya was sitting up. 'I'm okay now, I think.'

'Great. Let's go!'

'Chas.' Anya didn't get up.

'Here let me help you,' Chas said, crouching down beside her.

Anya shook her head. 'I need to tell you something. Just in case... you know... anything happens to us and we don't get out of here... together.'

Chas stopped. 'Is it to do with what you started to tell me the other day?'

'Yes.'

Chas was torn between wanting to get to the clones and wanting to know what Anya had to say. This could be her only chance to find out.

She sat down beside her on the floor. 'Okay. Tell me. But make it quick.'

Anya sighed and fidgeted with her uniform. 'When I was eighteen and about to go to Med-school, I had a relationship with a married man. Not just any married man; one of the Rulers. My parents are respected doctors, retired now, but working here in the Citadel at the time.

As you know, adultery is punishable by death, under the Rulers, so we were playing a dangerous game. To make matters worse, I got pregnant. You know that pregnancy outside of marriage is also forbidden. The pregnancy is terminated, the mother executed. I was terrified. And so was the Ruler I was having the affair with. He made all sorts of threats towards me and my family. Told me I had to get rid of the baby in secret.'

Chas was growing impatient, realising that this was turning into a long story. But she was intrigued and didn't interrupt.

Anya continued. 'I told my father, who was furious. Furious with me and with the man I'd been seeing. But Father knew there was nothing much he could do to him, without putting me in danger. I pleaded with him to find an alternative to getting rid of the child, and, being a doctor, my father also wanted to save the child's life, but of course his main concern was for me.'

Anya paused and glanced at Chas.

'So, you got pregnant by a Ruler and that's why you work

for them now?' Chas asked.

'Sort of.'

'It doesn't make sense, and what does it have to do with me? Is it something to do with the cloning?'

Anya shook her head. 'There was a woman who worked for us. A cleaner. She already had children but, for a huge price, she agreed to pretend to be pregnant herself and take the baby when it was born, as her own. She insisted she could fool her husband (whom she called something derogatory in her own language).

My mother and father kept me hidden away, until the baby was born, claiming I was ill, suffering from depression. Then the cleaner, who had been making it look like she had a baby growing in her belly, took my child, as one of her own.'

'Is it still alive? Do you know what happened to the baby?' Chas asked.

Anya nodded. 'The Ruler didn't know that we saved the child. It would've been too dangerous for my family, her family and the child. We made him believe I'd had an abortion, and that I'd suffered depression because of it. He kept pestering my parents to let him see me and eventually they did, after the baby had been taken away. For a while he appeared kind and supportive, and he got me a place to do my medical training at the university here. But after a while, he became more controlling and I realised he wasn't interested in me anymore, only in making sure I kept quiet. He forced me to come and work for the Rulers when I was qualified, so that he could keep me under his control and make sure his secret never came out.'

Chas shifted position, eager to go and thinking the story was finished. 'I'm sorry for you, but not sure why you're telling me all this. We really need to go now.' She got up.

'Wait,' Anya said. 'I'm not finished.'

Chas sighed and tried to hold her tongue.

Anya continued. 'I never saw my child after she was given away and I tried not to think of her. It was hard and painful, and I didn't succeed. I often imagined what she looked like, what she was doing, but I never tried to make contact. It would've been too dangerous for us all. But I know Malina kept her safe, because recently, she came back into my life.'

Chas felt sick. Malina was her mother's name. Her mother; an immigrant and cleaner for rich people who lived in the Citadel. 'What are you saying?'

A superfluous question. She knew what Anya was saying.

'It's you, Chas. You're my daughter.'

She felt physical pain, as if she had just been punched in the stomach. She clutched her belly, so recently bereft of children. She had to sit down and crumpled to the floor. All these years believing she was the child of poor immigrants. All these years believing Resolution was her brother. She couldn't speak.

'I'm sorry, Chas. I hated having to do what I did. I hope you'll forgive me and understand why I had to do it.'

Ignoring how she felt, Chas stumbled to her feet. 'I... I can't process this right now. You gave me to that family. And when Zephyr brought me to the hospital, did you know who I was?'

'Not at first. But I did some research on you and put the pieces together.'

Chas shook her head. 'And you still let them do all those things to me? How could you?'

'I didn't have much choice. That's what I thought then. I didn't know what to do for the best. I could've got us both killed if he knew who you were.'

Chas walked towards the door. 'You're a coward! There's always a choice.'

Anya scrambled to her feet. 'Yes, I'm a coward. But I loved you. I thought I was protecting you.'

Chas pulled the door open. 'I'm going to get those clones out. I don't want your help! Stay here. You can get out, there's a way through the rubble. Stay in the hospital and do what you do. I can't be around you right now.'

Anya moved towards her. 'Please, Chas. I don't want to lose you again.'

'You never had me,' Chas said, and disappeared out of the door. Anya sank down on the floor again and let the tears flow.

Chas began climbing through the rubble. Her mind was not focusing on the task in hand. She also realised that, without Anya, she couldn't get past the DNA security to get through the secret passage, into the elevator and into the Complex without being seen. Swearing, she climbed backwards again.

The door of the theatre swung open. 'How can I get into the Complex without you?'

Anya looked up and stifled a sob. 'Let me come!'

Chas felt the stab of guilt, but she couldn't do this with

Anya in tow. 'No! I don't want you with me. Is there another way?'

Anya sighed. 'There's a code that will over-ride the DNA check. Here.' She took out a pen from her top pocket and beckoned to Chas to let her write on her hand. She held onto her for a moment. 'Stay safe, please.'

Chas pulled her hand away and walked towards the door. Hesitating, she said, 'One more thing. I need to know who he is. Who is my father?'

Anya looked away.

'Tell me!' Chas shouted.

Barely audible, Anya said, 'It's Ambition.'

Chas left, slamming the door behind her.

*

Capability arrived at the meeting room with reinforcements. The guards and law-keepers had stood down, at Zephyr's request as rebels piled into the Fortress and rounded many of them up, at gunpoint.

'Traitor!' Ambition spat at Capability. 'I knew you weren't up to this. I should have acted on my suspicions and got rid of you.'

Capability walked up to Ambition. 'Well, it's too late now. I'm going to get rid of you, and it's very satisfying. Secure him,' he said to one of the rebels.

Each of the Rulers and Zephyr had their hands tied behind their backs.

'We're not finished by a long way,' Ambition said. 'Even if you kill us, we won't die.'

'You mean the clones?' Capability said. 'I'm sending

rebels to round them up. There won't be any immortality for any of you. You will all be transported to the Bastille for questioning and will remain there until we decide what your fate will be.' Some of the Rulers started to speak, but Capability silenced them. 'You'll have your chance to talk when you get to the Bastille.' He turned to the rebel he had put in charge. 'Take them down to the vehicles and get them out of here. Don't let anyone stop you.'

'What are you going to do with the clones?' Ambition shouted as they led him away.

'That's none of your business,' Capability answered.

'You can't kill them. They're only children!' Zephyr said, thinking of the boy he was fond of.

Capability turned to Zephyr, ignoring his protest. 'You will remain here for now. You're going to make a video for your forces and the people, telling them that you have willingly handed over power to us.'

'And if I refuse?' Zephyr asked.

Temp stepped in. 'We'll kill you.'

As he was being led away, Ambition turned. 'Do not cooperate with them, Premier. You mustn't concede to them on camera.'

'Get him out of here,' Temp said.

The room emptied until there was only Temp, Capability, Si and Mish left. Si took Capability aside. 'What are they going to do with the clones? Zephyr's right. We can't kill them. I'm going up there to make sure they're protected. I want to take Mish with me.'

'I've got it in hand,' Capability said.

'I'm going,' Si said. He thought of Chas and how she had

been determined to protect the children.

'No one will harm them now,' Capability said. 'I've ordered our people to bring them out when we're sure it's safe.'

'Even so,' Si insisted, 'I have to go. I... owe it to Chas.'

'I'm coming with you,' Mish said.

Capability shook his head. 'We know you'll do what you want to do, whether I forbid it or not!'

Si felt the dig.

Temp had been speaking to Zephyr, but came to join the conversation. 'Zephyr will cooperate, but he has a condition. He thinks Ambition and the others were planning to get rid of him. He wants immunity from execution, if that's what we're going to do to the Rulers.'

Capability sighed 'We haven't decided what their fates will be yet.'

'We can't give him immunity. He's done terrible things,' Si protested.

'If we want to gain power here, the most effective and least damaging way will be to have his cooperation,' Temp said.

Si bit back his anger and changed the subject. 'We want to help get the clones out.'

'Fine,' Temp said. 'We can handle Zephyr. We'll get him to make the speech on camera, and hand over the Bastille and Priory to us. Then he can be taken to the Bastille.' He turned to Si and Mish. 'Be careful. Just because he's told the guards to stand down doesn't mean everyone will obey.'

'Call us when you make contact with the clones,' Capability said. 'I'll tell my men that you're coming. They'll escort you out and there'll be transport waiting outside to take them to the Angel. Do you know how many there are?'

'Not exactly,' Si said. 'When I looked around the school there were maybe ten children.'

'Right. I'll get something sorted.'

Si turned to Mish. 'Okay, let's go.'

He thought of Chas and fought back his grief. He couldn't believe that when the end was in sight, Resolution had finally murdered her. I just hope she knows I'm doing what she wanted.

*

Chas had made it through the rubble. The covering on her face was making it easier to breath but her eyes were weeping from the dust. There were bodies in the corridor, some were dead, but others groaned in pain. Anya would find them. She wasn't the kind of person to just sit in that theatre, wallowing in self-pity for long. Despite her anger, Chas knew that Anya was a good doctor. She tried not to look at the bodies as she picked her way carefully through the debris.

'Help me!' A weak voice rasped as she passed.

She looked back to see a young orderly lying on his side. His face and chest were covered in blood and his arm had a long gash in it. She didn't really know what to do for him, but she couldn't ignore him. All she knew was that she must try to stop the bleeding.

'Hey,' she said, bending down to the man. 'What's your name?'

'Inspiration,' he croaked.

'I'm Chas. I'm going to tie this around your arm to stop the bleeding, then I'm going for help and I'll bring you water.'

She pulled the wet cloth from around her face and tied it as tightly as she could around the top of his arm. She didn't know if this would help much, but it was all she could do.

'I'm going to get help now.'

He grabbed her arm. 'I'm scared.'

'I know,' she said, prising his fingers off her. 'But I'll be back with help very soon. I promise.' She scrabbled back through the hole.

Anya was still sitting on the floor of the theatre. 'Get up!' Chas said, harshly. 'People need you. There are serious casualties in that corridor. They need medical help.'

Chas didn't look at her any longer, but went to the sink and ran the tap into a receptacle she found nearby.

'Hurry. There's a man out here bleeding to death.'

Anya got to her feet and immediately resumed her role as doctor. 'Look in that cupboard and bring that bag there, it has emergency kit in it. I'm going to see if I can contact anyone else to bring back-up.'

They clambered back through the rubble and Chas took her straight to the man. 'Here,' she said, lifting his head to drink the water. 'I've brought a doctor. You're going to be alright now.'

Anya assessed the man, then glanced tentatively at Chas. 'Well done. This tourniquet has helped already.'

'What else can I do?' Chas asked.

'Back-up is coming,' Anya said. 'See if anyone else is

alive.'

Chas wanted to get to the Complex and find the children, but she couldn't leave this scene of devastation until more help arrived.

'There are two people alive I think,' she said, coming back to Anya, just as a couple of doctors arrived.

'Thank you, Chas. Go now. We can deal with this.' She turned her attention to her patient and began to tell the other doctors what to do.

Chas looked at this strong, determined woman and saw herself for the first time. Then, she turned away quickly and headed down the corridor.

It took her a while to find the secure corridor that led to the Complex, but she used the code and got in. The elevator was still working, and she stepped out into the Complex. All was quiet. In fact, it seemed deserted. Where were they? Had they escaped? Been taken by the rebels? She assumed that the carers and teachers would have gathered all the children together, so she went to the school area first. No sign of anyone there. The play area was also deserted. As she rounded a corner, she literally bumped into a carer coming the other way.

'Chastity! Where did you come from? We thought we'd never see you again. No one knew what had happened to you.'

Chas recognised the woman, who was probably in her early fifties, and tried to recall her name. 'It's a long story.'

'Well, no time for that now,' the woman said. 'Are you here to help?'

Chas nodded, suddenly remembering her name. 'Where

are the children, Martha? We have to get them out to safety. The rebels are coming, and I don't know what they intend to do.'

'You think they might harm us?' The woman asked, looking more frightened.

'I don't know. People get aggressive in these situations. They think of these children only as 'clones.' Some don't consider them 'real' human beings.'

'But that's ridiculous!' Martha said, defensively. 'I've looked after these children since the first one was born and they're just normal kids.'

Chas doubted that, knowing how indoctrinated they were into the ways of the Rulers. 'Did you look after Zeph? I mean the Zephyr who's my age?'

Martha looked anxious. 'Yes. I'm very fond of him, but where is he? What's happened to him? He suddenly disappeared with no warning.'

'Don't worry,' Chas said. 'Another long story, but he's safe. Where are the children? We have to get out of here.'

'They're in the school.'

'But I went in there.'

'We've got them hidden.'

Chas raised her eyebrows. 'Very well hidden.'

Martha smiled. 'I know how to look after them. Come with me.' They hurried back towards the school. 'I saw on my Wearable that the rebels have got the law-keepers to stand down. They have the Premier and the Rulers as hostages.'

'Good. That means we should be able to take the children out through the Fortress. If the fighting is over, we should be safer.'

On entering the school, Martha called the children and carers out of their hiding places. The little ones thought it was a game and that they had been found. Martha and the others kept up this pretence. But the older children knew this was no game, and Chas saw the fear in their eyes, as they bravely played along for the sake of the younger ones.

'Hi everyone,' Chas said. 'Remember me?' She had not talked to them much, but they had all seen her around, frequently. Some of them nodded.

'Are you Zeph's friend?' asked the boy whom she recognised as the youngest version of Zephyr.

'I am,' Chas said. 'And you're also called Zephyr, aren't you?'

He nodded. 'He's my brother.'

Chas smiled. 'Of course.'

'Where is he?' the boy asked.

'He's safe. Don't worry about that. You'll probably be able to see him soon, but first we have to leave the Complex.'

'Why?' asked another boy.

She hesitated, trying to think of how to explain this to them without frightening them. They were all staring at her now. Martha stepped in. 'We're going on an adventure. We've been on adventures before, haven't we? Remember when we visited the museum in the Citadel and went to the big park?' Some of them nodded. 'Well, now we're going on another one.'

'Where?' asked a little one.

Chas spoke. 'To see a huge angel who's nearly as tall as

the Fortress.'

Some of their faces lit up and they began to ask more questions.

'Where exactly do you mean?' Martha asked, taking Chas aside.

'The rebel leaders have a base at the Angel of the North. Have you heard of it?'

'Yes,' Martha replied. 'But it's a long way and these children have never been outside the Citadel. Anything could happen to them outside these walls, if people find out what they are.'

'I'll find a way to speak to Kate Hunter. You've heard of her?'

Martha nodded.

'She'll make sure we're expected at the Angel. And on the way there, I'll make sure nothing happens to any of these children.'

Martha's brow furrowed. 'Single-handedly?'

'If I have to, yes. But I'll probably find people to help us. I certainly know some at the hospital. Zeph is there. And Grace and... Doctor Nelson.'

Martha turned back to the children and plastered a bright smile to her anxious features. 'Okay everyone. Stick very close to your key-worker. Are you ready for an adventure?'

She made her voice sound excited and some of the children shouted 'Yes!'

'Good,' Chas said. 'Follow me. We're going in a special elevator.' Turning to Martha, she said, 'This way leads back into the hospital. It should be safer.'

'I know,' Martha said. 'How do you have access?'

'Doctor Nelson.' As Chas said her name again the force of her revelation hit her. She had never felt close to the woman she had called mother all these years. And now she knew why.

'Chastity? Are you alright?' Martha said taking her arm. 'You look like you're about to faint. I haven't asked about your injuries but clearly something awful has happened to you.'

Chas extracted her arm from the woman's touch. This wasn't the time for tenderness. 'I'm fine. Come on. Let's go.'

When they got to the elevator, Chas told them that they would have to go down in two groups. 'I'll wait here with the second group,' she said to Martha. 'You take the first. Wait at the bottom. It's a secure corridor. There won't be anyone in there.'

The first children and carers went down. As the second lot waited, they suddenly heard footsteps behind them, and a voice shouted 'Stop! You're not taking those children anywhere!'

Chas was at the front of the group, and they all had their backs to the intruders, but she recognised the voice.

'Stand still and put your hands over your heads where we can see them,' Si ordered.

Some of the children began to cry, but all the adults raised their hands.

'We aren't going to hurt anyone,' said another voice. She recognised that too. Keeping her hands up, she turned towards them.

'Chas!' Si exclaimed. He dropped his gun, as did Mish, and walked quickly towards her.

'It's alright everyone, these are my friends,' Chas said.

'Ye can put your hands down,' Mish said. 'We're here to help ye.'

Chas moved out of the group towards Si. They flung themselves into each other's arms. Despite herself, Chas felt tears trickle down her cheeks. Si was not afraid of tears. He was crying too.

'I thought you were dead!' he whispered into her hair.

'I thought you were.'

They pulled back from each other and despite the audience, Si couldn't help himself. He kissed her, full on the lips and she didn't pull away.

'Come on guys,' Mish said, looking around at the wide-eyed faces of the children and carers. 'We've got a job to do. And these kids are getting a bit too much of a show here.'

'Mish!' Chas said, pulling away from Si and hugging him. 'Thank God you're okay.' She turned to the children and adults. 'I told you help would come. Now we'll be okay. For sure. This is Si Hunter, everyone. And this is Mish. They're our friends.'

The children's faces were a mix of amazement, shock and fear.

'We have to contact Capability, to let him know what's happening. He's organising transport for us,' Si said. 'Mish, can you...'

'I'm on it.' Mish called Capability on his Wearable.

A holo-image popped up and Mish explained that they were going out via the hospital. 'Chas is here!'

I see that,' said Capability. 'Good to have you back, Chas. How many are there?'

'Ten children and four carers, plus us,' she said.

'I'll have transport at the hospital entrance ASAP,' Capability said.

The elevator arrived and they managed to squeeze in.

'Come on everyone,' Martha cajoled. 'We're going on an adventure, remember?'

One little boy began to cry. 'Hey, it's okay,' Chas said, wiping a tear from his cheek. 'We're going to look after you. And you're being really brave, like... an explorer.' The boy gave her a shy smile and took the hand that Chas offered him.

Si had so much he wanted to find out from Chas, and she had much to tell him, but this wasn't the time. Instead, he stood on the other side of her and they made do with entwining their fingers through each other's for a few brief moments.

21

Resolution had been given his Wearable and tried to contact Excellence, but to no avail. From the people around him and from what he was reading in news feeds, it was clear that the Rulers had been captured and the rebels had control. It was over. He needed a plan; to escape without being captured himself. If he waited here, they would surely come for him, especially if Silence or Chastity had anything to do with it.

He began to mull over a few ideas for escaping from the Citadel and making a new life for himself, somewhere abroad.

*

Excellence had given himself up to the rebels and asked to be taken to Capability. He made his way to the meeting room, under guard, where his father was still holding Zephyr. Several calls from Resolution had come up on his Wearable but he had ignored them. The Rulers were defeated. He had watched them being transported to the Bastille and decided it was time to face his father.

Capability was surprised when he entered the meeting room.

'What do you want, Excellence?'

Excellence acknowledged Zephyr's presence. 'Premier.'

Zephyr didn't speak. He had made a statement on video, that would soon be broadcast across the nation, handing over power to the rebels and specifically to Kate Hunter, as their leader. Temp was on alert, wary that Excellence may try something.

'Father,' Excellence said, turning to Capability. 'I have something to say.'

Capability saw defeat in his son's eyes, and despite everything, felt some pity for him. 'Go on.'

Excellence shrugged and looked at the floor. Capability saw the ten-year-old boy in him, on the day when he had finally admitted to stealing his sister's favourite teddy, in a fit of spite, and throwing it in the river to 'drown it'. He told her what he had done to make her cry, but when challenged by his parents, had denied everything. It took him three months of processing the guilt to come around to admitting his crime.

'I became Resolution's second-in-command because he showed faith in me and made me feel honoured. I saw it as a fast-track career move into power and money. I didn't like everything I saw Resolution doing, I admit that. But it didn't stop me from going with it. I gave my allegiance to Resolution. But now, I see I was wrong.' He glanced at his father. Capability showed no emotion, just waited for him to go on. 'I was loyal to the Rulers, but they have been defeated.' He glanced at Zephyr. 'You may see me as a turncoat, but I offer you my allegiance and ask you to accept it.'

Temp spoke first. 'You don't deserve our acceptance. You went against your own father.'

'My own father was a Ruler at the time,' Excellence said. 'I didn't know he was working under-cover for you. You could say that he was the traitor, not me.'

Temp's eyes narrowed. 'You little upstart! Your father was in a difficult position...'

'No Temp,' Capability interrupted. 'I was a coward.'

'And he is being a coward now, switching allegiance.'

'You also switched sides,' Excellence said to Temp. 'It may be a long time ago, but you too were once a Ruler.'

Behind them, Zephyr began to laugh. They all turned to him. 'Of course, the boy is right, Temperance. You were my mentor as they prepared me to be the face of the Party. You were just as hungry as the rest of us for power, back then.'

Temp felt anger surge from his belly, but he held it in check. Zephyr was right, of course.

'I'm sorry, Father,' Excellence said. 'Let me work for you now. Please.'

There was silence. Capability was not really in a position to promise his son any kind of immunity. But his son's apology had touched him. Excellence never apologised unless he meant it. After the incident with the teddy, Excellence had never been unkind to his sister again.

'Prove your loyalty to us,' Temp said.

Excellence nodded. 'Okay. How?'

'Find Resolution and bring him to us.'

'No one knows where he is,' Zephyr said.

'He's been trying to contact me,' Excellence admitted. 'I can find him. I'll do it.'

'We're taking Zephyr to the Bastille. Bring him there,' Capability said.

Temp came up close to Excellence. 'If you fail us, you will be arrested and put in the Bastille with the rest of them.'

'I understand,' Excellence said, looking at Capability.

Capability nodded. His fatherly instinct was to embrace his son and protect him, but he wasn't a little boy anymore and he needed to prove to Temp that he meant what he said.

*

In the hospital, an orderly came back to find that Resolution had disappeared from the trolley he had been lying on. The canula was tossed on the floor and the drip line hung limp. It wasn't difficult to abscond amongst all the chaos, but the orderly knew Resolution was in no fit state to be discharged. He went to alert a doctor.

Resolution found a side ward, where a man lay sleeping, and raided his wardrobe for clothes. The patient stirred and, seeing Resolution, began to protest. But he was soon silenced by Resolution's hand over his mouth and nose until he passed out.

Resolution got into the clothes and put on a cap, hoping that no one would recognise him. Head down, he made his way back to the Fortress. He didn't think he wouldn't be able to get away with being anonymous for long, but he had a plan to ensure his safe passage out of the country. He was in a lot of pain but used to ignoring such things.

He had DNA access to the corridor that led to the Complex, so he intended to let himself into the Fortress that way. There were too many rebels swarming around the entrances. He needed to find a weapon and he knew where to get one, once he was inside the Fortress.

*

Having descended in the elevator, Chas, Si and Mish led the way towards the doors of the secure corridor. The boy still held tightly to Chas's hand. 'Look,' she told him. 'You're being a leader now.'

He grinned up at her and Si noted the softening of her hard persona.

'What do we do when we get these children out of here?' Mish asked.

'I think we should find Capability and Temp,' Si said.

'I want to find Zeph and Grace first and make sure they're okay,' Chas said.

'Maybe we should transport them to the Angel with the children,' Mish suggested.

Si glanced at Chas, wondering if he was about to put his foot in it. 'I think Zeph might have to be treated as a political prisoner for now,' Si said. 'Until we can establish his loyalties.'

Her face clouded. 'I can vouch for him,' she protested. 'He's on our side.'

'I know,' Si agreed. 'But I'm not sure Temp and Capability will have the same confidence in him until they've interviewed him.'

She pulled a face, as they reached the door, but she could understand their caution. 'I'll talk to them.'

Resolution was not far from the door to the secure corridor. No one was taking any notice of him, having so much to deal with, but he kept his head down. He was thinking that he would have liked one last chance to take revenge on Chastity, but he may never get the chance now, and getting away unscathed was more important to him. At least she had not had the courage to kill him when she could have easily done it on the moors.

He could see the doors leading to the corridor now, but just as he was approaching, Doctor Nelson came around a corner. She too was walking towards the same doors, ahead of him. Fearing that she would recognise him, he ducked into a nearby room to wait until she passed.

As she opened the door, Anya was surprised to see Chas leading the children down the corridor.

'What are you doing here?' Chas said.

Si noticed the sharp tone in her voice.

'I was coming to find you to see if I could help with the children. But I see you have it in hand and reinforcements have turned up.' She nodded to Si and Mish.

'Don't you have patients to attend to?' Chas snapped.

'Chas!' Si was puzzled by the tension between the two of them. 'It's good to see you, Anya. There's nothing much for you to do here, though. Everyone is fine and we're taking them to meet transport, to take them to safety.'

'Oh, that's good. I'll escort you to the hospital entrance, so no one tries to stop you.'

'Thank you,' Si said.

Chas said nothing and turned away from Anya, talking to

Martha and reassuring the children.

As they exited the secure corridor, Resolution was able to see them from the room where he was hiding. The temptation to confront Chas was strong, but he knew it would be futile right now. His focus had to be on self-preservation and escape. It riled him, but he had to let her go.

Once they had gone, he entered the corridor and went up to the Complex. At least he knew she would hate what he was about to do next.

*

The children were escorted safely to the hospital entrance. When they got there, they found a minibus waiting for them.

'Will they be safe in this?' Chas asked, looking uncertainly at the vehicle.

There were four rebels with guns guarding it. 'Yes,' one of them said. 'Don't worry. We'll be on board. The windows are bullet-proof.'

'You will take them straight to Kate Hunter, won't you?'

'Those are our instructions. Yes.'

'They'll be looked after, Chas,' Si said. 'You can go with them if you like.'

Chas was tempted. She wanted to make sure they got there safely, but she also wanted to make sure Zephyr and Grace got out safely. She turned to Anya. 'You want to be useful? You go with them.'

Si looked at Anya. 'Can they spare you here?'

'Not really,' Anya said. 'There are lots of injured people

coming in all the time.'

Chas was becoming more and more irritated. 'You'll probably be arrested when they find out what you've been doing with the cloning. This way you can get out and be granted immunity by Si's mum.'

The word mum stuck in her throat and she walked away. Si didn't miss the odd look that had passed between them. He followed her. 'What's going on with you two?'

Chas looked back at Anya, talking to the carers, and shook her head.

'Come on Chas. Tell me. Something has happened.'

Chas grimaced and bit her lip, hesitating. She didn't like or understand all the conflicting emotions that were churning around inside her. Maybe if she told Si she would be able to concentrate more on the task in hand. So, she blurted it out. 'She told me that I'm her daughter.'

'What? How?' Si said, incredulously.

'She had an affair, when she was eighteen, with a married man. A Ruler. She hid the baby – me – with a poor family. My mother... Malina (turns out she's not my mother) worked for her parents. She took me in, for a large payment, and pretended I was hers.'

Si looked across at Anya in shock. He didn't know what to say. He shook his head. 'I can't believe this. It's... I don't know... I see why you're being odd with her now, though.'

'Yeah, it's doing my head in.'

'Yeah, I'm not surprised,' Si said, pulling her into a hug.

She looked up at him. 'I'm glad I told you.'

He hesitated, then decided to ask what was on his mind. 'And your father? Do you know who he is?'

'Yes.'

'Do you want to tell me?'

Chas heaved a huge sigh and blew it out slowly. She pulled away and shook her head, trying to clear the tears that were pricking her eyes. Si mistook this for a 'no.'

'It's okay. You don't have to.'

'It's Ambition,' she said. 'I don't know what's worse; thinking that Res was my brother all these years or finding out that he's not and Ambition is my father.'

'Wow! Ambition! It's a close call. I see why you can't get your head round it. Does he know about you?'

'He thinks she had an abortion, like he told her to. He kept an eye on her when she went to university, then brought her to work at the hospital, making sure she never gave anything away.'

'Wow! That's a lot to handle.'

'Yeah, I know. But I can't think about it now. We need to get these children out of here. Come on.'

She began to walk away, but he caught her arm and she turned back. 'Chas. I'll always be here for you. I... you know...' He felt shy about telling her exactly how he felt. He never knew how she would react.

She smiled. 'I know.'

All the children and carers were aboard now, and Mish was talking to the driver.

Anya was standing beside the bus. 'I can't go with them,' she said. 'I'm needed here. They'll be okay with their carers.'

Chas nodded.

'I'm going back in now. When this is over, Chas, please

say you'll find me. This is my number.' She handed over a scrap of paper, as Chas didn't currently have a Wearable.

There was an awkward pause. Anya longed to hug her, but she was certain Chas wasn't ready for that yet. She didn't want to lose her again, but she had no choice except to walk away. 'What will you do now?' she asked.

'We're making sure Zeph and Grace get out safely, then we're going to meet Temp. See what else we can do to help.'

Anya nodded. 'Goodbye Chas. I hope...' she broke off and smiled, sadly. 'I just hope.' She walked back into the hospital. Chas watched her, feeling a strange sense of loss biting at her.

She shook it off and stepped up into the minibus to speak to Mish. 'Everything alright?'

'Seems to be. Good to go.'

'Maybe you should go with them,' she said.

'No. They're in good hands, Chas. I'm stayin' here wi'ye.'

She didn't argue and turned to speak to Martha, then to all the children. 'You're going on an adventure today. Wait 'til you see the massive Angel of the North. It's amazing!'

'Are you coming with us?' little Zephyr said.

'Not yet,' Chas explained. 'I'll see you soon though and I'll be bringing your big brother with me.'

The boy's eyes lit up. 'When?'

'I don't know. Soon. I promise.'

When the bus had gone, Mish, Si and Chas stood outside the hospital for a while, just listening. The noise of explosions and shooting had stopped. There were no people screaming or running, but still a lot of activity at the front of the hospital. Casualties were coming in, and ambulances arrived every few minutes.

'Is this it?' Mish asked. 'Is it finished?'

'I think it's only just beginning,' Si said.

Chas shook her head. 'What do you mean?'

'Well, firstly, there's all these casualties to deal with and then there'll be a lot to sort out about government,' Si replied.

'Yeah,' Mish replied. 'But if the fighting's already over, it was a short battle.'

'A good thing,' Si said, watching the injured arriving. 'Fewer lives lost.' He turned to Mish. 'Can I borrow your Wearable? I'd like to speak to my mum.'

'Aye. Sure.' Mish took it off and handed it to Si. 'Do ye want us to go somewhere else?'

'No, you're fine. How did she react, when you saw her, about our maverick rescue expedition?'

'Not too bad on the phone, but I didn't get back there in the end. I joined the rebellion, at the walls of the Citadel. I don't think she had time to think about much other than the imminent attack.'

'She'll be fine with you Si,' Chas said, 'Don't be a wuss. Just call her. She'll be desperate to see you. Look, Mish and I are going to find Zeph and Grace. They've got Wearables. We'll contact you and let you know where we are.'

'Okay.' Si was secretly glad of the privacy to ring his mum. He moved to a quieter spot around the side of the building and made the call. A holo-image of Kate appeared in front of him.

'Si!' she exclaimed. 'I was expecting Mish. Thank God you look okay. Are you alright?'

He couldn't help grinning. 'I'm okay. I'm with Chas and Mish. They're okay, but Chas has been in a car accident and did you know she lost the babies?'

Kate nodded. 'Yes. Mish told us. Is she injured?'

'Not badly. She's been treated. She's also had some shocking news about her past. Long story. She can fill you in later.'

'To do with her brother?'

'Sort of, but he's dead. He was also in the car crash.'

'Wow! Poor Chas. She's been through a lot. We can help her when she gets back here. If she'll let us, of course.'

'Yeah, I know she can be difficult,' Si said. 'But she's mellowing. I'm sure of it.' His attention wandered to the times they had kissed since they had been reunited.

'Si? What's up?'

'Oh, nothing,' he said, pulling himself back to the present. 'Are you up to speed with what's happening?'

'Yes. We're keeping in touch with Temp and Capability. The Rulers have been transported to the Bastille. And Zephyr has made a spectacular speech, renouncing his leadership of the Party and handing himself over to us. He spoke of the corruption of the Rulers and admitted that they had failed the country. He said more than we'd given him to say. He told the people to look to us now. He's after immunity, of course.'

'What are you going to do with him?'

'He's going to the Bastille with the others, until we've had time to consider the best course of action for them all.

Peter's there, with some of our people, to take charge of the place for now. Nick and I are treating casualties. We've already had some come in. What are you doing now?'

'The children have just left, in a minibus. They should be with you soon.'

'We're preparing places for them now. Nick and I are going to spend some time assessing their mental health and then we'll need to decide what's to be done with them. They're effectively orphans.'

'Orphans that people won't understand,' Si said.

'We'll have to do some education, to get people to accept them for what they are; children without parents.'

'We have Young Zephyr here,' Si said. 'Mish and Chas have gone to find him. We'll send him on to you too. He's not like the Premier. He seems to want change. Keep him secure, until you've made a decision about him. Chas seems to trust him though. He'll be travelling with a girl called Grace. She's helped Chas a lot, and she's pretty hot on Zephyr.'

'Okay. Thanks for that. I'll keep Peter and Nick in the loop. I'm just heading back to the Ops room now.'

'I'd better go, Mum.'

'Stay safe and I hope to see you really soon. Shalom, Si.'

She didn't say this very often, but he always felt different when she spoke this blessing of peace over him. He made his way back inside the hospital and awaited a call from Chas.

22

The Complex appeared to be deserted, but Resolution kept alert in case he encountered any rebels. He made it out of the doors and down in the elevator. First of all, he needed to find a weapon and he knew there was one locked in a drawer in his office. Keeping his head down, he hoped he would blend in with the rebels in these clothes, but he was on his guard in case he was recognised.

There were lots of rebels milling around inside the Fortress. Law-keepers and guards had been rounded up and were being held in groups. Resolution wondered what they intended to do with them. The rebels looked disorganised and dishevelled and he overheard snippets of conversation giving away that they were uncertain what to do next. It would be so easy to overpower someone and break some of the law- keepers free, but he would blow his cover and he wasn't sure if the guards would jump to his aid or not.

Some of the rebels were acting like tourists, looking around a museum. They peered behind doors that were unlocked, gawped at ornate ceilings and lavish decoration. He overheard various comments about the 'disgusting wealth' and 'the waste of good money.' Someone spoke to him as he hurried past, but he kept his head down and mumbled something about being needed on the next floor.

Eventually, he arrived at his office. It was locked of course, but he had access. Just as he opened the door, someone shouted at him from down the corridor.

'Hey! How did you get in there?'

Resolution looked up to see two men coming towards him with guns.

One of them recognised him. 'It's that Commander.' They began running towards him. 'Stop! Surrender. The Premier has...'

Resolution didn't wait to hear the rest. He bolted into his office and shut the door. They wouldn't be able to get in, but it also meant that he was stuck here. They weren't going to leave until they had him in their custody.

He found his gun where he knew it would be. Being recognised now was inconvenient. If he waited, they would send for reinforcements and he wouldn't stand a chance of getting away. If he went out, he stood a good chance of being shot, or arrested.

At the moment, they were banging on the door, like the fools they were, demanding him to open it. He released the lock and they virtually tumbled in. Not expecting this, they were disconcerted, and Resolution had a couple of seconds of advantage. The door closed behind them.

'Drop your weapons,' Resolution ordered, grabbing one man by the throat and pushing his gun into his temple. The other raised his weapon, but Resolution was too quick for him and shot him in the chest. 'Idiot!' Resolution said.

'You are coming with me,' he said to his hostage. 'We are

going to walk through the corridors together and you are going to make it look like I'm one of you. If you give any hint of who I am to anyone, I'll kill you, just like your friend here. Understood?' The man nodded. Resolution pushed him out of the door, prodding him with the gun. 'Take the frightened rabbit look off your face. If anyone challenges us, tell them we've been sent to set prisoners free from the cells. Is anyone already down there?'

'I don't know,' the man said. 'I don't really know what's going on.'

'No, I don't think you do,' Resolution said. 'How you got control of this building is beyond me. If I'd been here it wouldn't have happened.'

They moved, unchallenged, along the corridor. A couple of people spoke to the man and he answered them with brief replies. Resolution took him to the elevator that led down to the cells. He hoped that the rebels wouldn't have figured out how to get past the security codes to get down here.

He was right. There were only guards down there, who had not surrendered to the rebels because no one had been able to get to them.

'Raise your hands,' he said to his hostage. 'They won't shoot you if they recognise me in time.'

The man did as he was told, and Resolution could see him trembling. As the elevator doors opened, Resolution took off his cap and braced himself, ready to be challenged. Two guards with guns were waiting for them.

'Don't shoot!' The hostage cried, stumbling forward with his hands in the air. 'I'm a prisoner of the Commander.'

The guards immediately recognised Resolution, despite his injuries and dishevelled appearance. 'Commander! What happened to you?'

'Never mind!' Resolution snapped. 'Take this idiot and lock him up. I need to take a couple of prisoners with me. And you can come too. We need to get them out of the Fortress and out of the Citadel. I intend to use them as hostages. If you want a ticket out of here, help me, and I'll make sure you escape.'

The guards nodded. One of them took the man and bundled him into an empty cell.

There were several prisoners being held there, but Resolution was only interested in two. He unlocked the door. 'Get up! You're coming with me!'

They jumped up. 'What's happening?'

'You'll find out soon enough.' The two guards came into the cell and cuffed the prisoners. Resolution held Ben tightly by the arm. 'You're going to get me out of here.'

A guard grabbed Honour and they headed up in the elevator.

Ben and Honour had no idea what had been happening in the Citadel over the last few hours. From their cell underneath the Fortress they had only heard vague rumblings from the explosions going on outside. Honour was trying hard not to cry. She refused to be a coward. If the Commander was going to torture her, she was not going to give him the satisfaction of showing her fear for as long as she could hold out. That didn't mean she wasn't terrified.

Ben kept looking at her and mouthing reassurances, but he knew he couldn't protect her, and he hated that.

As they emerged from the elevator, they were confused by what they saw. There were people everywhere, but they didn't look like guards. They hadn't had time to think about the Commander's strange attire.

Ben plucked up the nerve to speak. 'What's going on?'

'The rebels have taken the Fortress and you're going to be my passage out of here. Shut up, do as you're told, and I might let you live.'

So, they were his hostages. Torture was off the menu. But they still might end up dead. Ben began thinking about how he could get them away from the Commander. Maybe he would see someone he knew among the rebels.

Resolution wanted to find Temp and make his demands for safe passage out of the country. He hoped Ben and Honour were worth something to the rebels. He knew that love for a child had driven Temp away from the Rulers many years ago, and this gave him confidence that he would do everything he could to save them. He also knew that they were important to Si and Chas, which gave him even greater hope of using them to secure a successful escape.

His head was throbbing again, and the chest pain was getting worse, but he had to go on.

'Are you alright, Commander?' one of the guards dared to ask.

'Of course I am,' Resolution snapped. 'Just do your job. Do as I say, and I'll get us all out of here. Understood?'

'Yes, Sir.'

Resolution approached the first rebel he saw. 'Take me to Temperance Alliston. I presume he's here somewhere.'

The man had no time to pull out his own weapon. One

of Resolution's guards had a gun trained on him and he could see the guns pointing at Ben and Honour's heads. Several of the other rebels nearby were about to come to his defence.

'Don't even think about it!' Resolution roared. 'These children die if any of you try anything. Drop all your weapons!'

The rebels laid down their weapons and raised their hands, looking curiously at Ben and Honour.

'Now, take me to Alliston,' Resolution demanded.

'We don't know where he is,' the man replied.

'Someone must be in contact with him.' Resolution snapped. 'Or is this rebellion even more of a shambles than I anticipated?'

'I can take you to my group leader,' the man offered.

'Do it then! Tell everyone ahead of us to drop their weapons, or the children die.'

Ben hated being the means of Resolution's escape. Surely there was something he could do. But what, without endangering Honour? What would Chas do? He had thought about her and Si so many times while he had been in that cell; wishing they would come and rescue him and Honour. He had no idea whether they were dead or alive, right now.

Resolution and the guards followed the man, keeping watch for other rebels who might attempt to take them down. The man called out to others to drop their weapons, until they reached his group leader.

'Call Temperance Alliston, now!' Resolution demanded.

The man looked at Ben and Honour and did as he was

told. A holo-image of Temp appeared. 'What is it?' he asked.

'Sir, we have Commander Resolution here, asking to speak to you.'

Temp and Capability were still in the meeting room, awaiting news of transport for Zephyr. 'You have the Commander? What do you mean? In custody?'

'No Sir, he has hostages. He's demanding to speak to you.'

'Let me see him,' Temp said.

An image of the full scene appeared in the meeting room. Temp muted the line for a moment.

'I thought he was dead!' Zephyr exclaimed.

'Hmmm. Pity you were wrong,' said Temp.

'Is that Ben and Honour?' Capability asked.

Temp sighed. Ben and Honour. Yet again they were in the thick of it. How the Commander had even come to be in the Fortress, let alone have these two as hostages was a discussion for another time. Temp unmuted the call.

'What is it you want, Commander?'

'It's simple, Temperance. You arrange a car to take me to a port and give me safe passage to leave the country. The hostages are coming with me all the way, until I'm out of the country. I want to be in my car within the hour, or I will kill one of these two. I haven't decided which yet, but I suspect it might be the girl first.'

Honour shivered involuntarily, biting her lip to stop herself from whimpering.

'You won't kill her first, because I won't let you,' Ben shouted.

'Cut the heroics, boy. I will kill whomever I like first. You can hardly stop me.'

Ben suddenly took Resolution by surprise, thrusting his cuffed fists into his stomach, whilst kicking out at him, making him double over and cough, because of his injuries. However, the guard quickly knocked him to the floor and pointed his gun at him. 'Shall I kill him now, Commander?'

'Don't even think about it until I give the order!' Resolution snapped, recovering his breath and kicking Ben sharply. 'Get up boy, and stop being an idiot.'

The guard pulled Ben to his feet and put the gun to his head, leaving Resolution free.

He turned his attention back to Temp. 'So, you have one hour. Get a move on, Temperance.'

The holo-image disappeared.

'What are we going to do now?' Capability asked. 'Should we just give him what he wants and let him go?'

'No,' Temp said. 'We don't give in to his demands. And besides, he has many crimes to pay for.'

'What about those children, Temp?' Zephyr said. 'Are you going to sacrifice them?'

'Be quiet, Zephyr,' Temp replied. 'This is no concern of yours.'

'I'll find out how long that transport is going to be for him,' Capability said. 'We could think more clearly without him chipping in!'

Temp leaned both hands on the table and bowed his head. He had to free Ben and Honour and capture Resolution. For him, this was the only option.

'Five minutes,' Capability said. 'They're sending people up to escort Zephyr to the car.'

'Finally!' Zephyr said, sarcastically.

They ignored him. 'We should go down with him,' Temp said.

'We can't now,' Capability replied. 'We've got this to sort out.'

'Oh dear!' Zephyr said. 'I can go by myself if you like.'

Temp gave him a look.

'Get your son on the phone,' Temp said. 'Where is he anyway? I thought he was supposed to be finding Resolution.'

'I think he was genuine,' Capability said, calling Excellence at the same time.

'Let's see, shall we,' Temp said.

Zephyr laughed derisively. 'He's a turncoat. He'll go where the winning side is, and that appears to be you at the moment.'

'Shut up!' both men shouted at Zephyr. Temp took him by the throat. 'I swear, if you utter another word, I'll kill you with my own hands, right now. To hell with any agreement you've made with Kate.'

Capability pulled Temp off Zephyr. 'Hey! Take it easy.'

Zephyr put his hands to his throat, coughing as Temp glared at him.

Capability phoned his son. 'Excellence, where are you?'

A holo-image appeared in the room. 'I've got people out searching the Citadel and making phone calls, looking for any sign of the Commander's whereabouts. We have a report of him in the hospital, but he disappeared about an hour ago.'

'He's in the Fortress. He has hostages and is making demands for safe passage out of the country,' Capability said.

'Where is he?'

Temp spoke to Excellence. 'Not sure at the moment. I'll try to find out. He doesn't know you've defected, does he?'

'No. And he's been trying to contact me.'

'Good,' Temp said. 'You could get close to him. He trusts you. Then take him out without harming the kids.'

'Kids?'

'Yes. The hostages he has are two children. They were prisoners at the Priory.'

'Okay,' Excellence said. 'I'll take some men and sort this.'

Capability noted the sharp u-turn in his son, from following the Commander blindly to being willing to kill him. He wasn't sure if this was a good thing or not. 'Will you be able to do it?'

Excellence nodded. 'I'll have some men waiting with tracking rifles. And maybe I can get close to him. We should be able to take him out without harming the hostages.'

'He has two guards with him,' Temp said.

'I'm on it. Get me his location.'

Temp called his man back. 'Put the Commander on.'

'Have you made a sensible decision, Temperance?' Resolution asked.

Temp nodded. 'You'll have your car in one hour. We've decided to let you leave the country, but you'll never be able to return.'

'It is I who hold all the cards here, Temperance, not you. I make the conditions, not you.'

Temp sighed impatiently. This upstart had always wound him up. 'You get what you want and so do we. As a gesture of goodwill between us, we want you to hand over the girl now.'

Resolution laughed. 'Goodwill? There has never been, nor will there ever be goodwill between us, Temperance. She stays right by my side until I have what I want, and you know I won't hesitate to put a bullet through her head if you don't give it to me. I still have another hostage.'

He pulled Honour closer to him and put his gun to her temple, so that they could see it on the holo-image. Honour whimpered and closed her eyes. They could hear Ben shouting in the background.

'Don't do anything stupid, Resolution,' Temp said. 'I swear that if you hurt them, I will kill you myself.'

'I doubt it,' Resolution said calmly. 'And you don't want the blood of innocents on your hands, do you? Oh, I nearly forgot, you already have it all over you, from the village. They'd all still be alive if it wasn't for you, wouldn't they?'

Temp's mind flashed back to the commune where he had first met Si. Si had always felt the deaths of the villagers sharply, on his conscience. However, Temp knew that it was as much because of him, that they had died. He shook the thought off. No! It was because Resolution was a ruthless psychopath. He wished it could be him that finally pulled the trigger on the man.

'Where are you now?'

'You don't need to know that. Just get me the car. Your time is running out.'

'We're arranging that now,' Temp said. 'I'll alert all the group leaders to let you pass. My men will escort you to the entrance. We'll send someone with you to escort the children back from the port.'

'No!' Resolution said. 'You can come and pick them up after I'm gone. No one follows me. If you do, you will only have bodies to retrieve. You know I'm not bluffing.'

Honour couldn't help herself now. Tears rolled down her cheeks and a sob escaped her tightly pressed lips. She had been in a few scary situations since she had first followed Ben, but this was the most terrifying.

'Call me when you have the car waiting,' Resolution said. Then the line went dead.

Temp swore.

'He always knew how to get what he wanted,' Zephyr said.

Temp didn't even look at Zephyr, knowing that the way he felt right now would mean he might just strangle the man.

'I've just received a message. There's a car ready for him,' Capability said, indicating Zephyr. 'I think it's too risky to have him out there while this is going on with Resolution. Let's tell Resolution the car is for him.'

Temp nodded. 'I'll alert the group leaders to tell everyone to stand down and let them pass. Get Excellence back. I'll make sure that our people know that he and his men are working for us now.'

Capability called his son. 'Resolution won't give us his

location, but you call him and see if he'll tell you. And have your men waiting near the entrance to the Fortress. He's going there with the hostages.'

Excellence nodded. 'Right. I'll try and convince him that I can help him. If I can get close to him, I can possibly get the hostages clear for an easier shot.'

Resolution saw that Excellence was calling him and picked up. His holo-image appeared. 'I've been calling you, why didn't you answer?'

'I'm sorry, Commander. In your absence I've had a lot to organise. Where are you? You look awful, what's happened?'

'No need to go into details now. I see you didn't do a very good job against the rebels.'

Excellence bristled. 'I did my best, Sir.' He resisted the temptation to blame Resolution for not being around when needed. It would only rile him. 'Where are you, Commander? Can I help you?'

'Why haven't you been rounded up with the rest?' Resolution asked.

'I'm in hiding, with a few of my men,' Excellence replied. 'We're in the Fortress. Where are you?'

'Also in the Fortress. I have hostages and I'm getting out.'

'Let me come with you. We can help each other.'

'I don't need your help. You are clearly less competent than I gave you credit for. Find your own way out of this mess.' Resolution ended the call.

Excellence swore. Time was running out.

*

Chas and Mish found Zeph and Grace in the same place she had left them; watching news reports on a holo-screen on the wall. This part of the hospital had escaped much damage. Grace was holding Zeph's hand and he was dozing in and out of sleep.

'How is he?' Chas asked.

'He's doing okay. Pain relief has made him drowsy,' Grace replied.

'And are ye alright?' Mish asked.

'I'm okay. Just bruises and cuts, nothing serious. Look! The rebels have taken the Citadel and the Fortress.' She indicated the screen. 'But I'm guessing you might have had something to do with that.'

'Yeah,' Mish said.

'Where's Si? If you two found each other, wasn't he with you?' Grace directed her question at Mish, but Chas answered.

'We got the children out' Chas said.

'That's great,' Grace replied.

'Si is just calling his mum. We need to get you two out of the Citadel. Do you think Zeph is up to it?' Chas asked.

As she said this, he stirred and opened his eyes, smiling but only half awake.

'Where do you want us to go?' Grace asked. 'Isn't this the best place for him?'

'A hospital? Yes. But maybe not here. Kate and Nick will know what to do with him.' Chas had talked about them in the Complex. 'And we know he'll be safe from anyone who wants to harm him, if he's in the bunker at the Angel of the North. Can I use your phone?' Grace handed it over. 'Thanks.' She phoned Si. 'Hi. Can you get hold of Temp? Explain to him we have Zeph, and we need an ambulance to transport him to the Angel. He needs medical attention there.'

'Sure,' Si said. 'I'll tell Temp. I'll see what I can sort out here. Maybe I could get Anya to go with him.'

'She said she's staying here,' Chas said.

'I know, but I might persuade her, especially if I explain that she would be helping with the sick and wounded that arrive at the Angel.'

Chas hesitated. Her feelings about Anya were so confusing, but her help with Zeph could be valuable. 'Okay, see what you can do. We'll meet you at the entrance. Zeph probably needs a wheelchair.'

'I'll go and find one,' Grace said.

'I'm coming with you,' Mish said.

'I don't really need an escort.'

'Yeah, but I just want to make sure you're okay.'

When they had gone, Chas took Grace's place beside Zeph. She held his hand, as Grace had done, and he opened his eyes again at the change of touch. 'Hey,' he said, sleepily.

Chas smiled at him. 'Hey. How are you feeling?'

'I've been better,' he said. 'She's nice.'

'Who?'

'Grace, you idiot,' Zeph said.

'Oh, yeah, she is,' Chas said, smiling.

'I really like her.'

'Me too,' Chas said.

'No! Really like her, you know.' He had a sleepy, silly smile on his face.

'Oh!' It dawned on Chas what he was saying. 'Well, that's good. I'm sure the feeling's mutual. She's not so daunted by who you are anymore, and she likes looking after people.'

'Yeah, she's been lovely. What's happening now, Chas?'

Chas explained everything to him. 'You know you might be a hate target, so we need to get you to the Angel, where you'll be safe.'

'What will they do with me? Do you think they'll put me in prison? Execute me?'

Chas was shocked. She hadn't realised he was thinking like that. 'No! I think they'll question you and they'll want to see if you're genuinely interested in helping rebuild the country.'

'You know I am.'

'Yeah, I know, but they don't know you. You may have to prove yourself. But that can all wait 'til you've recovered.'

'I feel crap right now,' he said, laughing, then regretting it.

'You look it. Now, shut up and rest. Let us take care of things.' She squeezed his hand. 'I won't let them do anything bad to you. Not that they're likely to.'

He closed his eyes, but then opened them again. 'Did you say the children have got out safely?'

'Yes. They're on their way to the Angel. I told little Zephyr that you'd be joining them soon.'

'Cool,' Zeph said, smiling. 'My little bro. He's all the family I have.'

He closed his eyes again and Chas stroked his hand. She

felt sorry for him, not having parents, but then what she had found out in the last twenty-four hours had made her wish she didn't have parents either.

As if she had conjured her with the thought, Anya walked into the room with Si. 'Hi. I've decided to go with Zephyr. I've arranged an ambulance. It'll be here in a few minutes. Let me have a look at him.'

Chas moved aside as Anya bent down and began to talk to Zeph. He opened his eyes and tried to answer her questions. As she was examining him, Grace and Mish returned with a wheelchair.

'This was hard to find,' Grace said. 'Oh, hello Doctor Nelson.'

'Hello Grace. Do you know what meds he's had? There's no record here.'

'Painkilling injection. Not sure what it was.'

'When?'

'About an hour or so ago.'

'Okay, I'll get some things together and meet you all at the ambulance in fifteen minutes. I'm afraid he needs a trolley really, not a wheelchair. I'll sort it and get it sent here.'

'Thank you,' Grace said, moving in next to him again.

'Yeah, thanks,' Chas added, looking hesitantly at Anya.

Anya nodded and went to get her things.

Si handed Mish his Wearable. 'Thanks for lending me this.'

'No problem.' Mish strapped it back on his wrist.

'We should ring Temp and ask what to do next,' Si said.

'Sure. I'll do it now.'

As soon as they saw Temp's holo-image, they could tell he was agitated about something.

'What's up?' Mish said.

'Who's with you?' Temp asked.

'Si and Chas. We're waiting for the ambulance to take Zeph and Grace to the Angel.'

Temp nodded. 'Good. We have a situation here.'

They all crowded around the Wearable, appearing in the holo-image that Temp and Capability could see.

'What is it?' Si asked.

Temp saw Chas and hesitated.

'Tell us,' she said.

'Resolution is alive.'

'What? I swear he was dying out on the moors!' Chas exclaimed.

'Well, he's here, in the Fortress and he has hostages, to bargain for his safe passage out of here and abroad.'

'No!' Si said. 'How many hostages?'

'Two,' Temp said. 'And he has two guards helping him.'

'Can you rescue the hostages?' Chas asked.

'We're going to try. Excellence is moving in on him now.'

'What? He was Resolution's next protégé.' Chas said.

Capability chipped in. 'He's changed sides. Sadly, his loyalties are to the winning side, whoever that may be.'

'He's a traitor!' Chas said. 'You can't possibly trust him!'

Si spoke up before Chas exploded. 'I know he's your son, Capability, but won't he just defect back and escape with Resolution?'

'We think not,' Temp said. 'A turncoat he may be, but he knows who's winning this.'

Chas grumbled under her breath.

Temp continued. 'But there's more you should know.'

'What?' Si asked.

They saw Capability shake his head. Temp hesitated.

'Tell us,' Chas said. 'You can't hold back now.'

Capability walked away but Temp knew he had to tell them. 'The hostages he's taken are Honour and Ben.'

Chas and Si were speechless for a few moments.

Si looked at Mish. They had intended to go back for them after rescuing Chas, but everything had gone wrong when the miscarriage happened. In the chaos that ensued, they hadn't had the chance.

'Did he bring them here after those killings at the Priory?' Chas asked.

'He must have,' Si said. Again, he looked guiltily at Mish.

'We won't let him harm them, Chas. We're dealing with him,' Temp said.

'We're coming!' she said.

'No!' Capability protested, coming back into view and looking at Temp in annoyance. 'You'll only complicate things. Go with Young Zephyr to the Angel. The best thing you can do is get yourselves to safety.'

'He's right, Chas. We're dealing with this,' Temp said. 'We'll keep them safe. I promise.'

'You can't promise that!' Chas shouted.

'Si,' Temp said. 'Get her out of the Citadel. It'll only complicate things if you get involved.'

'You can't make me leave!' she said.

Si and Mish looked at each other, then at Chas. She had that defiant look on her face that they both knew well.

'We're all coming,' Si said. 'We know Resolution. We can help.'

'No! I'm ordering you...' Si cut the call dead before Temp could finish his sentence.

'When Anya gets back,' Chas said, turning to Grace. 'Go with her. Get Zeph out of here. We'll join you as soon as I've settled things with Resolution once and for all.'

Si grabbed her by the arms and made her face him. 'Chas, this isn't your personal vendetta anymore. Remember that! Ben and Honour are our priority.'

She turned on him, with the fury she had exhibited in the days when they had first met, and shook his hands off her. 'I know it's about Ben and Honour. I'm not stupid! That's why we're going in there. And I'm going to make sure that Resolution pays for what he's done.'

Si shook his head. 'Stop it! You're already doing it! Revenge messes with your head.'

'Yeah? Good!' she said, turning away.

Grace stood up and went to Chas, trying to calm her. 'Chas, maybe you should come with us. There are plenty of capable people here who will rescue your friends.'

Chas shook her off too. 'None of you really get it, so don't try to stop me.'

'You won't think straight,' Grace said.

'I'll think straight enough, just watch me.' She stormed to the door, about to go by herself.

'Okay,' Mish interrupted. 'Stop, Chas! We get it. But,

you're not going alone.'

Just then Anya came back with an orderly, pushing a trolley. 'Everything alright here?'

Chas stormed past her, but Mish grabbed her arm firmly. 'Wait!'

She looked daggers at him, but he had an iron grip and he stared her out, resorting to a grin in the end, which made her give in.

Si shook his head in exasperation. 'Sorry, Anya. Take Grace and Zeph. We have to sort something out before we come to the Angel.'

She saw the scowl on Chas's face and still dared to ask what was wrong. A mistake.

'Just go!' Chas shouted and stormed out of the room, nearly pulling Mish over. He and Si pursued her. She gripped the small surgical knife she had acquired in the operating theatre earlier. A gun would be more useful, and she intended to get one between here and the Fortress.

23

Temp told Resolution that a car was waiting for him outside the main entrance. Excellence had placed men with tracking rifles in strategic places, hidden around the entrance hall. But Resolution was suspicious. There was something not right about the timing of Excellence's call. He decided they were going out a different way. Leaving the rebel leader behind, he put Temp's number into his Wearable and got into the elevator with Ben, Honour and the two guards.

'We're going through the Complex and out through the hospital,' he informed them. 'Then one of you will go back to the Fortress to pick up my car and bring it to me there. I don't trust Temperance or Excellence. In fact, I trust no one.'

The elevator doors opened, they stepped out and Resolution gained access to the Complex. Ben was desperately looking for a way to get himself and Honour away from the Commander. But Resolution held Honour closely in front of him and one of the guards had Ben in an iron grip. Both had guns held against their temples. Resolution and the guards were vigilant for any opposition, but it was deserted in the Complex.

Resolution's Wearable began to vibrate. He saw it was Excellence and ignored it. Excellence was trying to locate him, but the GPS had been turned off on Resolution's Wearable, since he had begun working clandestinely for the Premier.

Temp called Excellence. 'Where is he? He should have appeared at the front entrance by now.'

'I'm sorry,' Excellence said. 'I must have spooked him. He's not coming this way. I'm looking for him. He's not answering my calls.'

'We need to get Zephyr out of here,' Temp said. 'Capability and I are heading down to the front entrance with him now. Let us know when you locate Resolution. Unfortunately, I think Si, Chas and Mish are on their way over here too.'

'What? Why?' Excellence said.

'Chas is stubborn. She has a personal vendetta against Resolution and those kids are important to her. I don't really want her interfering, so hopefully we can intercept them.'

'Shall I get my men to detain her if we see her?' Excellence asked.

'Definitely,' Temp said. 'Just don't let her anywhere near Resolution.'

'Understood.'

*

'We'll go in through the Complex,' Chas said. 'There was no one left up there when we took the children out. And we need weapons. Guns.'

'I've got one,' Mish said, producing his.

'We need more than just one,' Chas said.

'We'll have to see what we can do' Mish said. 'One might be all we can get.'

Chas touched the scalpel in her pocket as they stood in the elevator. It was no match for a gun, but it was something. The doors slid open, and suddenly they stood face to face with Resolution's party. Everyone stepped backwards, in shock.

'Chas!' Ben exclaimed, his eyes lighting up. Mish reached for his gun, but the guard already had his gun trained on Mish.

Resolution grabbed Honour tightly around the throat. She let out a strangulated scream. Ben lurched towards Resolution, only to be restrained by the other guard.

'Don't try anything!' Resolution shouted. 'Put your hands in the air and get out of the elevator. Step away to the left or I will blow her head off.'

Mish, Si and Chas did as they were told, keeping their eyes fixed on Ben and Honour. Honour had her eyes tightly shut and was trying not to cry out.

'Take their weapons.'

A guard took Mish's gun and frisked them, swearing as he put his hand on the scalpel in Chas's pocket. He drew it out, his fingers bleeding from contact with the blade.

'Serves you right,' she spat at him.

'Bitch!' He moved towards her, but Resolution stopped him.

'No! We don't have time for this. Don't be stupid, Chastity, and no one gets hurt. We're going to leave in the elevator and you're not going to follow us.'

'You don't need both of them,' Si said. 'Let Honour go.'

Resolution held her more tightly. 'Neither of them is going anywhere until I'm out of this country.' He pushed her towards the elevator, telling the guards to get in with Ben.

'You won't get far,' Chas said. 'You know they'll come after you. I'll come after you.'

'Just drop it, Chastity. I'm one hundred percent done with all this now and especially with you.'

'I'm not done with you though, Resolution,' she said. 'I'll make a deal with you. Take me instead of them. You can do what you want with me. Just let them go.'

Si was impressed and horrified at the same time. 'No!' He protested. 'You wouldn't want her. She'll kill you the first chance she gets, and you know it.'

'Si!' Chas glared at him.

'No,' Ben said. 'I agree with Si.' He looked at Chas. 'I don't want you to take my place.' Then he turned to Resolution. 'Please, let Honour go. You have me. You don't need both of us.'

Si stepped forward, with his hands raised. 'Take me instead. My life for theirs.'

Resolution stopped. The prospect was tempting. To have Kate Hunter's son back in his grasp was a much better proposition than these two children. He was a much more valuable hostage.

'I'll give you the girl for Hunter,' he said, looking at Chas.

Chas's stomach lurched. She didn't want to sacrifice Si. Not again, but she had little choice.

'Deal!' Si said, before Chas could protest. 'But only in exchange for both of them, not just one.'

Resolution laughed, sardonically. 'I make the rules, Hunter. You for her or no deal.'

'Me and Si, for the kids,' Mish said, stepping forward to stand beside Si.

Resolution looked them both up and down. 'Such gallantry!' He thought for a moment. Silence was valuable, but a child was more valuable than Mish as his back-up hostage. 'No!' He said. 'In a moment, I'm leaving in this elevator, either with Hunter and the boy or with these two. You have ten seconds to decide.'

'Me and Si,' Chas said. 'Swap Ben and Honour for me and Si.'

Mish, Si and Ben gave her the same exasperated look, but time was running out, so they didn't argue.

Resolution couldn't resist taking Chas. This might be his one last chance to get rid of her. He knew that she was dangerous, but she had shown weakness on the moors when she hadn't put a bullet in his head. She wanted to kill him so many times, but now he was convinced that she would never be able to do it.

'Deal.' He turned to the guards. 'Give the boy to me and get in the elevator. You!' He looked at Mish. 'Move away. And don't try anything. I should have got rid of you back at the flat when you first showed up.'

Mish glared at him. 'The feeling's mutual.'

Si and Chas surrendered to the guards. Resolution pushed Ben and Honour towards Mish and stepped into the elevator. As the doors closed, Chas shouted, 'Get them out of the Citadel, Mish. Don't follow us!'

Mish didn't respond for a few moments, trying to decide what to do for the best. Honour slumped on the floor and wept. Ben crouched down to soothe her. 'Hey. It's okay. You're safe now.'

'I'm just relieved,' she said, trying to stifle little hiccupping sobs that escaped intermittently. 'And I... I feel guilty that he has Si and Chas in our place.'

'Hey, it's not your fault,' he said, wanting to hug her, but being prevented by the cuffs. He stood up and spoke to Mish. 'What are we going to do now?'

'I'm gonna call Temp and let him know what's happenin', then we're gonna get ye out of those cuffs. Are ye alright, lassie?' He helped Honour as she tried to stand up without the aid of her arms.

She wiped her face on her sleeve. 'I'm okay.'

'It's the shock,' Mish said. 'I'll call Temp.'

A holo-image of Temp appeared from his Wearable. 'Temp, we're in the Complex. We came across Resolution. He has Chas and Si and is heading for the hospital, through the secure entrance from here.'

Temp swore. 'Great! That's all we need. What's he done with Ben and Honour?'

'They're here with me. He exchanged them for Si and Chas.'

'Okay,' Temp said, 'Well at least they're safe. I'll get Excellence on the phone and send him to the hospital. Bring Ben and Honour to the main entrance of the Fortress. We're putting Zephyr in a car to the Bastille. Resolution's car is here waiting for him.'

Ben spoke up. 'He's sending a guard to pick it up and take it to the hospital.'

'Right. We'll let him come and then intercept.' Temp's phone showed another incoming call. 'I've got to go! Looks like he's calling me.'

Temp ended the call to Mish and answered the call from Resolution.

'Is my car ready?'

'Yes,' Temp said. 'It's waiting at the main entrance.'

'I'm sending someone to pick it up.'

'So, what about the hostages?' Temp asked.

'I told you. Once I'm safely on my way out of the country, you can have them. Except, I've exchanged the previous ones for more valuable hostages. I have Silence and Chastity now.'

'I know,' Temp said. 'I know where you're headed, Resolution.'

'I don't care. Just don't try to stop me, or you will lose your first hostage. And tell your traitorous son, Capability, that I will take pleasure in killing him if I see him.' The line went dead.

Capability had been listening. 'How does he know?'

Temp shook his head. 'Intuition, I guess.'

*

'Come on,' Mish said to Ben and Honour. 'You'll be fine now. The place is in rebel hands. We're gonna get ye safely to the Angel of the North. That's where Kate is. They'll look after ye both.'

'We can't go without knowing Chas and Si are going to be

348

okay,' Ben said.

'Och, ye'll have to. I'll let ye know the minute I know anything. I promise.'

'Are you not coming?' Honour asked.

'No. I'm going with the others to get Si and Chas back.'

'I want to come,' Ben said.

'And me,' Honour said.

Ben looked at her. 'You're not coming! You're going straight to the Angel. Look at the state of you! You don't want to get caught up in all that again, do you?'

Honour shook her head, feeling defeated. She had to admit to herself that the thought of getting out of here to somewhere safe, was appealing. A picture of her mother came into her head. While they had been in the cell, she had thought of her mother and sister often, knowing that they would be beside themselves with worry, because they would have seen what had happened on Lindisfarne. She had also thought of her father, dead from plague. It added fuel to the fire of hatred that she felt towards the Rulers. Now that she was virtually homeward bound, the picture of her mother was of someone seriously angry with her. She smiled. She was happy to face the consequences of her mother's wrath, just knowing it meant that she was going to see her again.

'You're not coming either, Ben,' Mish said. 'Didn't ye hear what Chas said? She wants to know you're safe. She gave herself up so that ye would be safe. Ye need to honour that.'

Reluctantly Ben agreed, realising that he couldn't argue with that.

Mish took them down through the Fortress to Temp and Capability at the front entrance. Zephyr had just been taken away.

'We'll get you into a car soon and send you back to the Angel,' Temp said. 'You do get yourselves into some of the worst situations.'

Ben shrugged. 'We didn't intend to end up here.'

'No' Temp said, smiling at them. 'I've spoken to Kate and she's trying to arrange for your mum to be at the Angel when you arrive, Honour.'

Honour looked worried.

'She'll give you a hard time I imagine,' Capability said.

'Probably,' Honour agreed.

'Aye, but more than anything, she'll be pleased to have ye back safe,' Mish said. He turned to Temp and Capability. 'I'm going to the hospital to help stop Resolution.'

'It's not necessary,' Temp said. 'We have it covered.'

'I canna just hang around here while he has Si and Chas,' Mish protested.

Temp felt the same. He looked at Capability. 'Excellence might need some extra back-up. Will you wait here with these two? I'm going with Mish.'

'Okay. Keep me posted,' Capability said.

*

Resolution and his party made their way through the secure corridor and into the main hospital. There was no rebel presence in the hospital, apart from those being treated, but Resolution and the guards had their weapons out and ready.

'Keep out of our way and no one will get hurt,' he shouted as they passed through the hospital. Medics backed off in fear. No one tried to stop them.

Chas wished she still had the scalpel, so she could find an opportunity to at least be able to rip it across Resolution's face, if not his carotid artery. She imagined the horror, as he watched blood pour down his neck through his probing fingers. He was struggling with pain from his injuries and she could see that he was weaker than usual. Maybe she could still overpower him with Si's help. But first they had to deal with the guards.

Just as she was thinking about this, two rebels appeared from a ward, carrying guns. 'Drop your weapons!' one of them shouted. Two more rebels emerged beside them.

Resolution held his ground and spoke calmly, with arrogant self-assurance. 'No! You drop yours! This is Silence Hunter.' He had Si in an arm lock and his gun pressed painfully into Si's temple. 'He's the reason you're all here. He's your leader. Now back off or he's dead!'

The rebels hesitated, then one fired a shot at the guard who was holding Chas. It missed.

'Idiot!' shouted another of the rebels. But his cry was immediately extinguished as the guard shot him dead. Another shot was fired by the rebels, and this time the guard took it in the shoulder. The other guard fired on them and another rebel went down as everyone ran for cover.

Chas saw an opportunity. One guard wounded, the other having his attention drawn from her by the attack.

'Don't be fools!' shouted Resolution. 'Put your weapons down.'

'Stop!' Si cried. 'Listen to me! Don't fire on us!' The shooting ceased. 'Let us pass. No more bloodshed.' Then he spoke to Resolution. 'We need to call doctors for the injured.'

'There are plenty of doctors here. When we're out of here they can attend to them.' Resolution didn't look at the dead man, lying only a few feet away, as blood oozed thick and fast out of his wound. He squeezed harder on Si's neck to make him be quiet.

'Get out of our way,' Resolution said, 'Or you will all end up one hundred percent dead!'

He spoke to the guard who had been shot but didn't look at him. 'Are you fit to carry on?'

'Yes, Sir. It's nothing.'

Resolution nodded then spoke to Si. 'Tell them we're coming out and to hold fire.'

Without warning, Chas leapt on the injured guard next to her and began grappling for the gun. Si tried to help her, but Resolution had him in a vice-like grip, despite his injuries. The other guard came to help his colleague. They wrestled her to the floor and pinned her there, face-down. A gun was pushed into her hair from behind.

Resolution and Si stood up, cautiously. The two rebels who were still alive had backed off and were nowhere to be seen. He dragged Si over to Chas and kicked her.

Si struggled to push Resolution away from Chas.

'Get up!' Resolution said. 'This is trying my patience. Don't try another foolish move, Chastity. Let's get out of here.'

They stepped around the injured and the dead. People

were cowering in the wards nearby. Resolution and the guards moved cautiously forward, shouting out warnings to keep out of their way. Behind them, medical staff rushed to the aid of the men who had been shot.

When they reached the hospital entrance, Resolution sent the injured guard to pick up his car, then looked for a strategic place to wait.

'Commander!' A voice came out of the bushes at the side of the car park.

They all looked in the direction of the voice. Excellence stood up, pointing his tracking rifle at Resolution. 'We have you covered. Drop your weapons and let them go!'

Resolution shouted back. 'I knew you had defected. I don't make many mistakes, but trusting you was one of them.'

Excellence didn't react. 'Put down your weapons, Commander.'

Resolution pulled Si closer, using his body as a human shield, and having his back to the wall. The guard did the same with Chas. 'You won't shoot! Even with those weapons you can't guarantee you won't hit the hostages. Temperance promised me safe passage and he has reneged on that promise. I should kill one of them now!'

He removed his gun from Si's temple and pointed it at Chas's head.

'Go on then, do it!' she snarled at him, through gritted teeth.

Their eyes locked and, in that moment, she saw the real difference between them. It wasn't a flesh and blood difference. It was a difference of conscience, of driving forces and of humanity.

'Just do it!' she said, closing her eyes.

'No!' Si shouted, twisting free of Resolution, causing him to lower the gun from Chas and slam the butt against his own skull. He reeled from the blow, but Resolution held on to him so that Si was still in front of him.

At that moment, Temp and Mish came around the corner, with their weapons held out in front of them. 'You can't kill either of them,' Temp said, coming slowly towards Resolution, with Mish by his side. 'You need them, or you're a dead man.'

Resolution did not like being backed into a corner. He was adamant that he was not going to lose here. 'Don't come any closer! If you want them back in one piece, your only option is to let us go!'

Mish spoke up. 'Ye won't let them go though, will you?'

Resolution smiled. 'You'll have to take that chance. All I'm interested in is my freedom.'

A message came from Excellence to Temp. 'No chance of taking him out safely without risk to Si and Chas.'

'Resolution,' Temp said. 'Let them go and I will come with you to guarantee you safe passage. Look, I'm putting my weapon down and your car will be here in a few minutes.'

Resolution was running out of options. Kill Chas and Si now and he was definitely a dead man. But what if he shot Chastity, just to prove he was serious? He would still have Silence and they wouldn't want to risk him killing the boy. His plan had been to kill them anyway. More than anything, he didn't want Chastity to get out of this alive.

'Get the car here. I'm not making a different deal here,

Temperance. If the car is not here in 5 minutes, Chastity dies.'

The guard holding her looked at Resolution in confusion. He knew that if she was killed then his human shield was gone. But Resolution was not interested in what happened to him.

Temp swore again under his breath. 'The car is on its way here. Let them go and I'll make sure you get away.'

'No deal,' Resolution said. And you have four minutes.'

Chas looked across at Resolution, from the stranglehold she was in. She struggled with the guard, but he held her firmly, with the gun to her head.

This was not how her life was going to end, at the hands of her ex-brother. She had to get free and time was running out.

Just then, the car arrived, parking right in front of Resolution. The driver was one of the rebels. He got out and moved away.

'Let's go!' Resolution said.

Temp, Mish and Excellence watched silently. 'Keep alert,' Excellence said into his Wearable, to his men, positioned at different angles around the perimeter of the car park. 'Take the first opportunity to safely take out the targets.'

Resolution got into the car first, across the passenger seat, keeping low and dragging Si in behind him. It was painful and Resolution was coughing a lot. Si gagged as Resolution's hold around his neck tightened. The guard opened the back door and pushed Chas into the back seat.

Suddenly, a shot rang out and the guard was dead before he could climb in. Chas looked out of the car, to see the man lying face down beside the car, splattered in blood. Realising she was free of her captor, she jumped at Resolution, before he had the chance to react. Taking him by surprise, she knocked the gun out of his hand. Si jumped on him before he had the chance to get it back. Chas climbed through to the front of the car and they struggled and grappled with Resolution, finally pinning him across the front seat.

At once the car was surrounded by Temp, Mish, Excellence, and some of his men, wielding guns.

'It's over, Resolution,' Temp shouted.

Resolution wasn't struggling anymore. His strength was gone. Adrenalin had been keeping him going, but now he had none left and lay motionless, his chest aching as he struggled to breathe.

'Chastity, Silence; get out of the car,' Excellence ordered.

'The gun is down there, under the seat somewhere,' Si said. 'I can't get it.'

'It's okay,' Excellence replied. 'We have him covered. He's not going to be able to get it. Don't move, Commander, or you will be shot.'

Chas pulled Resolution's head back by the hair. 'Goodbye brother!' she spat. 'I never want to see your hideous face again.' She slammed his head into the seat, making him groan, and got out of the car.

Si climbed out after her, keeping his body weight on top of Resolution for as long as he could.

'Thank God you're safe,' Mish said, as they stood beside him. 'I hated letting ye go back there.'

'You had no choice,' Chas said.

Si rubbed his hands over his neck, glad to be free of Resolution's stranglehold. 'You got this lot here. Thank you.'

'Glad to be of assistance,' Mish said, with a slight grin.

'Both of you, over there,' Excellence said, nodding towards the bushes, but keeping his focus on Resolution in the car. 'Some of my men are there. Get down with them where we know you're safe.'

Si and Chas walked towards the bushes.

'Get out now, Commander, slowly, and put your hands above your head,' Excellence demanded.

Resolution didn't move.

'Commander!'

'Is he dead?' asked Temp.

'I can't lift my right arm that high,' Resolution said. 'I'm injured from a car accident.'

'Just get out and put your hands where we can see you. Now!' Excellence demanded.

Slowly, Resolution lifted his head and saw that he was surrounded, with no hope of escaping. He saw Chas and Si walking away and felt a final pang of regret that he hadn't succeeded in killing Chas. He knew he was finished. He noted the weapons pointing at him and assumed there were more, further afield. Moving slowly, partly due to the pain from his injuries, he made time to think.

'We're waiting Commander,' Excellence said.

Resolution opened the driver's door and began crawling out.

'Slowly!' Excellence said.

His right arm was bent beneath his body as he looked up

at the sea of guns facing him. He wasn't going to spend the rest of his life in prison, or worse, let them execute him in a televised act of public shaming. He knew he was a dead man, but there was one last thing he could do. The next moments happened very quickly. He had been feeling for the gun under the seat and found it. He drew his hand from beneath him. His aim was excellent. He had one chance. But Mish had seen him and, in a split second, realised what he was doing. Guessing who the target would be, and knowing he couldn't kill him from that angle, Mish threw himself into the line of fire and fired his own weapon.

Resolution's gun went off at the same time.

24

Chas and Si dropped to the ground as the shots rang out.

'You okay?' Si said, from face down in the grass.

'Yeah,' she replied.

Several other shots rang out and then silence.

Cautiously, they turned and looked back, keeping low to the ground. Resolution's body was hanging out of the car, covered in blood.

Then Chas saw the other body, motionless on the ground. 'Mish!' she screamed and was on her feet, running back to the car, closely followed by Si.

Temp and Excellence were already at Mish's side. 'Get a doctor out here!' Temp shouted.

'Is he still alive?' Chas asked, crouching over his body.

Blood was oozing from Mish's chest. His eyes were closed. Temp tried to find the artery in his neck. 'He has a faint pulse.' He put his hands over the wound to try and stem the bleeding.

'Mish!' Chas said, urgently. 'Mish stay with us. Help is coming.'

'What happened?' Si asked.

'Resolution found the gun and took a shot, before we

knew what he was doing,' Temp said. 'I think he was aiming for you Chas. Mish must have realised and threw himself in the way.'

Chas was crying and holding Mish's head on her lap. 'Mish. Please hold on. Don't die. Why did you do it, you idiot? Come on. Stay with us.' She looked up and shouted, 'Where are the doctors? This is a hospital!'

'Someone has gone for them. They'll be here any moment,' Excellence said. He turned to his men. 'Get the dead bodies out of here.'

Si put his arm around Chas and held her, as they waited for the medical team, praying beneath his breath. He tried to reassure her but didn't think it was doing much good. 'He's still alive. They'll save him.'

She was rocking over Mish's head, crying. 'I wish Anya was here. She would save him.'

Si held her tightly. 'There are lots of good doctors here, Chas. The best in the country. They'll save him.'

'Where are they?' she screamed.

'Here,' Temp said. 'Let them get through.'

A team of paramedics rushed towards them. 'Make some room please,' one of them ordered.

Everyone moved, except Chas.

'You need to move out of the way please. We'll take care of him, now.'

Reluctantly, Chas laid Mish's head gently on the ground and backed away. Si wrapped his arms around her, protectively, as they stood and watched.

The paramedics worked quickly, Mish's shirt was cut away as they examined his injuries and his breathing. The medic packing Mish's wounds began to bark orders at the others, 'Get an airway in and start bagging please, Abe. Seren, can you get a line in? He's shutting down so try the jugular.'

'Don't let him die. Don't let him die,' Chas chanted, like a mantra, as Si held on to her.

A grey needle pierced Mish's neck and a bag of fluid was attached. Seren asked Excellence to hold the bag up as the fluid ran down a long tube, replacing the blood that Mish was losing. Defibrillator pads were placed on Mish's chest and the three medics turned to look at the screen, 'He's in VT, have we got an output?'

Seren put his fingers to Mish's neck. Chas looked on, holding her breath, as time slowed down. Seconds felt like minutes until Seren silently shook his head. Abe immediately started chest compressions, counting out loud as he rhythmically pushed on Mish's chest.

Chas pushed her face into Si's chest, unable to watch. His lips moved in silent prayer as he held her tightly.

Abe pushed a syringe of adrenaline into the needle in Mish's neck as the lead medic, Ange, hit a button on the defibrillator. A long beep, rising to a shrill crescendo came from the machine.

'Stand clear!' Ange ordered. She pressed the button again and Mish's body shook as the electricity coursed through his heart.

The seconds following seemed to last for hours, as the medics' eyes lit up when a spike appeared on the screen followed by another. Seren put his fingers to Mish's neck. 'There's a pulse!' The relief was apparent in his voice. 'It's not great but it's definitely there, can we get a BP?'

'76 over 38,' Abe replied, 'Can you squeeze that bag a bit harder for us please?' he asked Excellence.

Ange started grabbing the kit they had strewn around, 'Let's get him inside.'

Suddenly the slow, rhythmic pulsing of the machine changed. A frantic, irregular beep led to a flurry of activity amongst the medics. Ange dropped the kit she was holding and started compressing Mish's chest again. Seren pressed the defibrillator button, and they heard the same long, rising beep. 'He's in VF. Stand clear!'

Mish jerked as the defibrillator shocked his heart. Again, there was a long, seemingly interminable pause as the medics stared at the screen, Abe pressing two fingers to Mish's neck, shaking his head. 'Nothing.'

More adrenaline was injected as they began chest compressions again, Abe squeezing the bag to inflate Mish's lungs and fill them with oxygen every time the others paused.

Desperately, Chas pulled away from Si and turned to look at the screen. The green line on the monitor bounced and shook with the compressions but, when they stopped to inflate Mish's lungs, the line flattened. 'Please,' she whispered, 'Please.'

But there was nothing.

A doctor came running towards them, her shirt stained with blood, hair dishevelled, 'I'm Miss Cartwright, A&E consultant, what's happened?'

In staccato, Ange described the events since the three medics arrived. The cold, clinical description tore through

Chas's soul.

The consultant surveyed the scene in front of her; the pool of blood spreading across the tarmac, Mish's soaked clothes. 'There's nothing more that can be done for him, I'm sorry.' She glanced briefly at Chas as she walked away, the pain of her decision clear in her eyes.

Silently, the paramedics gathered their equipment.

As they hurried away, Abe paused, 'I'm so sorry, there's nothing more we can do for him, but we might be able to help others.' He placed a hand on Chas' shoulder, then they were gone.

Chas saw that a sheet had been laid out over Mish. The blood was already soaking through the white linen. She collapsed into Si and they slumped to the ground together, weeping. Mish had been a faithful friend. He had risked much and suffered much. It wasn't fair that he should die now, when it was all over.

Temp knelt in front of them. 'I'm so sorry.'

'We can't leave him here,' Si said.

'He'll have to stay in the hospital morgue for now,' Temp said. 'Chas?' He waited for her to look up. She wiped her face on her sleeves and he touched her arm, gently. 'We need to go. You and Si are going back to the Angel now. I've got some things to sort out here with Capability and Excellence, then we'll follow.'

She nodded.

'Is Resolution dead?' Si asked.

'Yes,' Temp said.

'Are you sure?' Chas asked.

'Definitely,' Temp said. 'Mish shot him, then we all

fired. He's well and truly dead this time, Chas. I'm calling someone to drive you now.'

She nodded and allowed herself to be led away, not daring to glance back at Mish's body.

*

When they arrived at the Angel of the North, Kate and Nick were waiting. There were no words. Kate and Nick just wrapped their arms around them and held them. As they stepped back from the hug, Kate said, 'I'm so sorry about Mish.' She had tears in her eyes, feeling their loss of a good friend. Si nodded, unable to speak as a lump caught in his throat again.

Chas was silent. She hadn't spoken at all on the journey, just sat in the back of the car, her hand in Si's.

'Come into the Ops room and I'll make you a drink,' Kate said. 'You must be shattered.'

They followed Nick and Kate through the shelter. There were people moving around, but the atmosphere was calm and orderly. Kate made them hot drinks and gestured to chairs around the big table. Nick placed a packet of biscuits on the table.

Kate reached across and took a hand of each of them in hers. 'I can't tell you how glad I am to see you both.'

Si smiled at her, but Chas had not met anyone's eye. She stared down into her drink.

'It feels good to be back, Mum,' Si said. 'I'm sorry...'

Kate interrupted, shaking her head. 'No need for any of that. I know what you're sorry for, but it's over now. You did what you thought was needed at the time. And look, it

364

paid off, Chas is here.'

Kate looked across at her, but still she didn't look up. 'Chas, I know you're not okay. You've been to hell and back, but you're safe now.' She squeezed her hand.

'We're going to help you process what you've been through. It's a huge amount to take in,' Nick said.

There was silence for a moment, then Si said, 'I think we both just need some time and rest.'

'Of course,' Nick said. 'We've made up some beds for you in one of the dorms and you can shower. There's a meal in a couple of hours, but we can get you something more substantial now, if you're hungry.' He moved the packet of biscuits towards them.

Si shook his head at the biscuits. 'Thanks Nick. Chas, do you want to go and lie down for a while?'

For the first time, she looked up. 'I want to see Zeph and Grace, the children and Ben and Honour.'

Kate nodded. 'They're all here. All safe. You got them out.' She smiled at Chas, but it didn't make any difference. 'You can see them soon. Honour's mum's here. They're with her now. You can imagine that reunion.'

'Was she very mad?' Si asked.

Kate shook her head. 'About as mad as I was with you... well, just a little bit madder actually, but not for long.'

'How are Zeph's injuries?' Chas asked.

'He's going to be fine. He's being well looked after.'

'I want to see him.'

Kate looked at Nick and Si. 'Well... yes, you can see all of them, but don't you want to rest for a while first? Have a shower? You'll feel better for it.'

Chas looked blankly at her, then down into her cup again. 'I just want to see them.'

'Maybe we could have a quick chat with them,' Si said, 'Before we rest.'

'Okay,' Nick replied. 'I'll take you.'

'And what about Doctor Nelson?' Si asked. 'Is she here?'

'Yes,' Kate replied. 'She stayed with Zephyr for a while until she was certain that he was stable. Then she was checking the children over, until about half an hour ago, when Nick ordered her to take some rest. You can see her too, if you like. She was anxious for any news of you.'

'I don't want to see her,' Chas said.

Si wasn't sure what his mother knew about the situation with Anya and Chas. 'Maybe later, Mum. She must be exhausted too.'

Nick stood up. 'If you've finished your drinks, we'll take you to see Zephyr and Grace first. She hasn't left his side, despite looking like she could do with a few hours' sleep herself.'

'Is it really over?' Si asked. 'Are the Rulers really defeated?'

Kate nodded. 'It looks that way. Peter's at the Bastille. They're all locked up and the Bastille is in rebel hands. Most of the staff are working willingly with us. There've only been a few minor skirmishes.'

'Law-keepers all over the country are surrendering or turning their allegiance to us,' Nick said. 'It's astonishing how many of them seem relieved to be free of the Rulers. There are still a few volatile situations going on in some cities, where we haven't got communication established with anyone, but we're working on it.'

'There's going to be a lot to do, of course, to get things back on the right track,' Kate said. 'But this is the beginning of a new era. We can make this happen. The plague can now be eradicated across the country, without opposition, using the NMBs.'

Si smiled at her. 'That's great. I just can't quite get to grips with it.' He put his hand on Kate's. 'Dad would be so proud of you, Mum.'

She nodded. 'Of all of us. We did this together.' She looked at Chas. 'And many people have sacrificed themselves for the good of others.'

They drained their cups. 'Come on,' Nick said. 'We'll take you to see Zephyr and Grace.'

They got up and followed Nick down a corridor. 'I have to warn you that Zephyr is in a locked room.'

Chas looked sharply at him. 'He's not a criminal. He's a victim.'

'Yes, I'm sure that's true,' Nick said. 'It's for his own safety, really. Until we can establish that, to everyone's satisfaction, we need to keep him safe from anyone who might decide he's a risk.'

Chas nodded, but her reply was surly. 'Fine.'

Kate unlocked the door to a private ward, created way back when the bunker was first built, for VIP patients. Grace was sitting by Zephyr's bed, her hand on his and her head lolling to one side; dozing. As the door opened, she woke with a start. When she saw Chas, her face lit up and she rushed over to hug her.

'You're here. I'm so glad you're safe,' she cried.

Chas didn't return the hug.

'You too,' Grace said, turning to Si and hugging him.

'It's good to see you're okay,' he said.

'Listen, we're going to leave you to it for a while,' Nick said. 'Call us if you need us.' He pointed to the interface on the wall. 'We'll be back shortly.'

'How's Zeph doing?' Chas asked, moving to the other side of the bed.

He opened his eyes as she sat down beside him. Si stood at the end of the bed.

'I'm doing okay,' he said, smiling at her.

She nodded. 'Good.'

'And you? Are you both okay? How long have you been here?'

'Not long,' Si said.

'What's happening in the Citadel now?' Zeph asked.

'Everything's under control,' Si replied. 'The Rulers are under arrest in the Bastille.'

'Good. And what about me? Am I under arrest?'

'No,' Chas said. 'You're not one of them. They know that.'

He nodded.

'Where's Mish?' Grace asked.

Si looked at Chas. She was biting her lip, still fighting back tears. Si answered. 'I'm so sorry to have to tell you this...' He swallowed hard.

'He's dead. He got shot,' Chas said, abruptly.

Grace put her hand to her mouth. 'No!' Tears welled in

her eyes. 'That's awful.'

There was silence for a moment.

'He saved me from Resolution,' Chas said, her voice choking.

Grace came alongside her and put her arm around Chas. 'He was a good guy! He'd be so glad to know that he saved you and you're going to be okay.'

'What happened to the Commander?' Zeph asked.

'Also dead,' Si said.

'Good,' Zeph replied. 'Your friend didn't die in vain, though it's no consolation, I know. When I can get out of this bed, I want to do everything I can to help. I have lots of information that might help rebuild the country. We have to do it to honour people like Mish.'

'I'm sure my mum and the other leaders will be glad of it.'

Zeph reached out for Grace's hand, as she tried to comfort Chas. 'Do you think people will accept me? How much do they know about the clones?'

'I don't think the ordinary people knew much up to this point,' Si said, 'but rumours spread. If we play it right in terms of propaganda, we'll make people feel sympathy towards you and the children. None of this is your fault.'

They talked for a while more, until Chas said she wanted to see the children.

'Give little Zeph a hug from me,' Zeph said. 'They allowed him to come and see me and he was a bit upset, but tell him I'll be better soon, and I'll come and see him.'

They called to be let out and Nick came. He took them to the room where the children were. It was basic, with only a few tables and chairs in it. There were no toys down here in the bunker, apart from one or two that they had brought themselves. But some tablets had been found for them to play games on and an interactive HTV screen. The carers were already organising activities to keep them occupied.

Martha was pleased to see Chas, but the children were wary at first. So much had happened, and this place felt so strange to them. Chas introduced them all to Si, then she and Si played with some of them. Soon the children were telling them about their games and teddies, as well as asking lots of questions about the Angel and the bunker.

'I've seen your brother,' she said to little Zephyr. 'He's doing great. He told me to give you this.' She hugged him. Si was surprised to see her so genuinely affectionate with the boy. 'He said to tell you that he'll come and see you when he's back on his feet again.'

Zephyr seemed pleased with this. 'Can I live with him when we get out of here?' he asked.

Chas looked at Si and shrugged. 'It makes sense to me.' Si gave her a warning look and she back-tracked slightly. 'We'll have to see how things work out. Zeph will have a lot to do when he's better. He's going to help us make things good again.'

'Were things not good before?' the boy asked.

Si was sitting on the other side of Zephyr. He realised that the boy had never really experienced anything but the cosseted life he'd led in the Complex. Being told all sorts of lies. 'No. Things weren't good for a lot of people. But now they'll be better and Zeph is going to help us make that happen.'

The boy smiled. 'He's nice, my brother.'

Si and Chas smiled too. 'We think so too,' Si said.

Another boy wandered up to them. He was about four years old and sucking the edge of a well-worn, well-loved blanket. Chas hadn't taken much notice of him before, but he climbed onto her knee and looked up into her face. She was shocked at the likeness she saw there. This boy had to be Ambition's clone. Her stomach lurched. He was the closest thing she had to a real brother. His DNA and hers would have a match. Tears sprang into her eyes, threatening to overwhelm her. She looked pointedly at Si and indicated that he should look closely at the boy.

'Are we going to live here forever?' the boy asked. 'I don't like it. It's scary.'

'Not for long,' Si said, suddenly recognising the likeness.

Chas took a deep breath, then smiled and cuddled him in. She didn't need to ask his name. 'Can I call you Ambi?' she asked.

He nodded and stuck his thumb in his mouth.

Chas stroked his hair. 'We're going to find you somewhere very very nice to live.'

His body relaxed as she said that, and he snuggled in closer to her. She shrugged at Si and he smiled back. The hard-hearted girl that had threatened to kill him in the woods when they first met, had a soft heart. But he had always known that.

After a while Ambi fell asleep, 'We should go,' Chas whispered. 'But I don't want to disturb him.'

Martha had noticed Chas shifting position. 'He looks

very content on your knee. But I can take him if you need to go.'

Chas gently passed the sleeping child to her. 'Thanks.'

'He's a very sweet little thing, isn't he?' Martha said. 'Come any time for a cuddle. I'm sure he'd love it.'

Chas smiled. 'Maybe I will. Thanks.'

When they had left the room, Chas shook her head. 'That was really weird.'

'What? You cuddling a child? Yes. Never seen that before,' Si said, a grin emerging on his lips.

'No,' she said, pulling a face. 'He's Ambition's clone.'

'Yeah, I guessed that. You can see it in his eyes, hair, shape of his nose.'

'So he's sort of...'

'Your brother?'

'Yeah.'

Si nodded. 'Weird. But nice?'

Chas shook her head. 'Not quite sure what to do with that at the moment.'

'I think what you did was just right,' Si said.

She raised her eyebrows. 'Really?'

'Yes. You were lovely with him.'

'He was kind of cute,' she said, wistfully.

'Yes. And interesting what Martha said about him. We've wondered, haven't we, about whether they'll be exact replicas of their clones.'

'I guess they're proving that, on the inside, they're as individual as those of us born the old-fashioned way,' Chas said.

'Reassuring,' Si agreed. 'We can use that to convince

people that there's no need to be scared of them. There's a lot to think about though, in terms of what'll be done with them now? Where will they live? Who'll look after them?'

'I have the same questions,' Chas said. They walked in silence back to the Ops room. Chas seemed calmer. 'Thinking of little brothers,' she said. 'Let's find Ben and Honour. I want to see how they are after their ordeal with Resolution.'

'Do you think Honour's mum might still be with them?' Si asked, not wanting to face Sarah right now.

'Maybe,' Chas said. 'They might need some back-up by now, if she is.'

Si smiled. They peered into the Ops room, but it was empty. 'Come on, there's no one here, so let's find them ourselves.'

They looked into some of the other smaller rooms where Si thought they might have been taken. As they did so, they noticed a lot more activity around the bunker. People were beginning to come in from the fighting. Those who weren't injured were helping those who were. Other people came to help them and lead them down to the hospital area. They didn't see Kate or Nick and assumed they were already there. Chas kept watch for Anya. She must be around. She couldn't imagine her resting while all this was going on.

'Do you think we should see what we can do to help?' Si asked.

'We will, but let's find Ben and Honour first,' Chas replied.

It didn't take long to find them. Sarah was with them but there were no recriminations.

'Can we come in?' Si asked, peeping into the open doorway.

Ben saw him and his face lit up. 'Si!'

'Yes, come in,' Sarah said.

Chas walked in behind Si. Ben leapt up from the bed he was sitting on and hugged them both hard, as if they might disappear again if he let go.

'Hey, put us down now,' Si laughed.

'You can sit here,' Sarah offered, patting the bed next to her. There weren't any chairs in the room, only beds and bunks. Honour was sitting next to her mother. Her eyes were red and puffy.

'We've just been catching up on all the things these two have been getting up to. They've just about scared the life out of me. I don't think I can hear any more of it. I'm just glad it's in the past and they're here in one piece.' She turned to Chas. 'I'm very grateful for what you did.'

Chas nodded.

'How are you feeling now?' Si said.

'We're okay,' Ben said, his old cheerful spirit burning bright again.

'Yeah, I thought the Commander was bad, but the wrath of Mum is worse!' Honour said, smiling now.

'Where's Mish?' Ben asked.

Chas lowered her eyes.

'Is he injured?' Honour asked.

Si glanced at Chas, but he knew she was already getting upset again. 'I'm so sorry to have to tell you this. He... he didn't make it.'

'What do you mean?' Honour asked. 'You can't mean...

he's... dead?'

Si nodded.

'No!' Honour protested. 'Not Mish!' Tears began rolling down her cheeks.

Si began to explain what had happened. He took Chas's hand in his and held it tightly, as she struggled again with the overwhelming emotion of it all.

'You've all shown such courage,' Sarah said. 'And your friend Mish will always be in your hearts.'

'I can't believe I'll never see him again,' Honour sobbed.

Sarah cuddled her daughter in. 'It's so hard when someone you care about dies,' she said, thinking of Ethan.

'It doesn't seem fair,' Ben said.

Si shook his head. 'It never is. All we can do is remember his sacrifice.'

They sat for a while, processing what had happened. Eventually, Si asked, 'Will you all go back to Seahouses soon?'

Sarah nodded. 'That's the plan. As soon as it's safe to travel, Kate said she would arrange transport back there. Your sister will be pleased to see you,' she said to Honour and Ben. 'She wanted to come, but I thought it safest to leave her with the neighbours.'

'Are you okay with going back, Ben?' Si asked, glancing at Sarah.

'Yes,' he said, looking sheepishly at his adopted mother. 'As long as you promise I'll still see you both.'

Chas looked up for the first time since they'd spoken about Mish. 'Of course you will,' she said. 'We promise, don't we Si?'

'Absolutely,' Si said. 'I don't really know what we're going to do yet. I think we'll be busy for a long while, helping to sort everything out.'

'But we'll keep in touch on our Wearables,' Chas said.

Ben nodded. 'You'd better!'

Si stood up. 'We need to go now. We've been told to rest, but a lot of injured people are arriving. We'd better see what we can do to help. You should try and eat something, even if you're not that hungry. Go up to the canteen. There weren't many people left behind to cook, once the fighting started, but there'll be something.'

'Come on, you two,' Sarah said. 'We might be able to help in the kitchen.'

They went their separate ways, Chas and Si making their way to the medical facility. They were shocked at how over-crowded it was when they got there. Injured people were sitting on the floor in the corridor as they approached. Volunteers and medics were tending them as best they could, assessing the most serious cases and rushing them through. In the melee of it all were Kate, Nick and Anya.

Anya saw them first and beckoned them over. Chas hesitated but Si indicated that they should go. Anya was busy fixing up a drip. 'Good to see you,' she said, without taking her eyes off the task in hand. 'Make yourselves useful and see what you can do to help the volunteers. See that woman over there?' She nodded in the direction of a tall woman with dreadlocks, handing out bandages.

'Yes,' Si said.

'She'll tell you what to do.'

Chas was relieved at the matter-of-fact nature of their

reunion. She and Si busied themselves with whatever task they were given. Their stint in the medical area lasted for several hours, as there were plenty of jobs that needed doing. By the time there was a lull in proceedings, it was gone midnight.

Si was busy giving water to those who needed it, when Kate came to speak to him. 'I think you and Chas should go and have some rest now. You've done a good job here, but we can cope.'

'Everyone needs a rest, but you're not going to get one, are you?' he said.

Chas came over as they were speaking. 'We can stay on. I'm not tired. Couldn't sleep anyway.'

Kate sighed. 'Well, if that's what you want... but I insist you go and see what food you can scrounge. Nick and I won't be far behind you. I'm ravenous!'

When they got to the canteen it was almost deserted apart from one or two others who were similarly seeking nourishment at this late hour. Some sandwiches and snacks had been left out for those who hadn't made mealtime.

Si saw Anya, sitting by herself. 'We should go and sit with her.'

Chas grimaced then shrugged. 'Okay.'

She had her back to them and didn't see them coming. 'Can we sit here?' Si asked.

She looked up and gave them a tired smile. 'Sure.'

They ate in awkward silence for a while. This perhaps wasn't the best time to try to get them to talk about anything significant, but Si thought he might as well try. 'You two need to talk,' he said, thinking, at the same time, that this was obvious.

Anya didn't look at either of them. 'When Chas is ready.'

Chas looked down at her sandwich, not saying anything.

Si was not feeling at his most patient. 'Chas!'

She didn't respond except for a shrug.

'She hasn't done anything wrong, Chas. What she did was to try to protect you. You need to get your head round that.'

Anya shook her head. 'Not now, Si. We're all tired. I'm going back to the Citadel early in the morning. They need me at the hospital. We've managed to get them to keep a lot of the wounded there. They have better facilities for treating them. I'm taking some of the worst cases from here back with me. Even with the bombing, the hospital is still in decent shape. It was only hit directly once.' She looked at Chas. 'Nearly took us out.'

Chas still wouldn't look at her.

Anya got up to leave, gathering her rubbish to place in the bin. 'I would like the chance for us to talk, Chas, but I'm not going to force it. When you're ready, you know where to find me.'

When she had gone, Chas looked up. Her face was blank, but Si knew there was more going on inside. He wanted to shout at her, but instead he asked, 'Want to talk to me about it?'

She sighed. 'I don't know. It's late. Maybe we should just go and find a couple of bunks somewhere. Get some sleep.'

Si nodded. 'Okay. But you know you can tell me what

you're thinking, and I won't judge. All I'm saying, is give her a chance.'

Chas got up. 'Are you coming?'

It was now the early hours of the morning. They'd had a hell of a day and they were exhausted, all that was true. But she did frustrate him intensely, at times like this. He followed her out of the room, wishing he knew what to do to sort this out.

25

Chas tossed and turned on the top bunk that she had found empty. Her mind would not let her rest, despite being exhausted. Every time she closed her eyes, she saw Mish's body with a gaping red hole through the chest. And when she did fall into a fitful sleep, she dreamed horrible things: Mish shooting Ambition to save Anya from him. Resolution crawling out of a wrecked car and trying to strangle Grace, as Zeph shouted helplessly from where he lay, with his legs severed. Little Ambi cuddling into her as she looked down to find his blood smeared all over her shirt. At that point she woke with a start, gasping for air, and knowing it was time to give up on sleep.

Si had gone to another dormitory to find a spare bunk, so she couldn't even talk to him. By 5.30 she was in the canteen, with a mug of hot chocolate between her hands. There were a few others around, and breakfast was already on the go.

Her mind thrashed the subject of Anya back and forth. She was leaving this morning. What should she do with the revelation that she was her mother? It was all too much to take in. They would never have to see each other again. Anya could go back to the Citadel and Chas could go back to life in a commune, pretending she hadn't found out that she had a whole different family now. But could she? Nothing was going to be the same now. The country was going to go through big changes. Would she even be able to live in a commune again? And what about Si? She wanted to be with him, but where would he want to go?

She got up and headed for the doors. She needed some fresh air. It was cold outside, and the sun was just rising, so she walked up the hill towards the Angel. The great being towered above her, plane-like steel wings outstretched in a strangely welcoming gesture. She sat in front of its huge ribbed feet and clasped her knees up to her chest. The cold didn't bother her. She was used to it. She didn't know how long she had been sitting there, when she saw people moving from the bunker towards the car park. She hadn't noticed several ambulances waiting there. Among the people, she saw Anya, carrying some equipment and talking to a couple of volunteers, who were pushing a patient on a trolley. Anya hadn't noticed Chas watching, as they loaded everything into the ambulances. Just as the doors were closing, Chas leapt up and began running towards them.

'Wait! Anya. Wait!'

Anya saw her and got out of the ambulance. Chas stood panting in front of her, suddenly not knowing what to say.

'I've got to go,' Anya said, gently. 'We must get these people to the Citadel as soon as we can.'

'I know,' Chas said, her breathing slowing. 'I just wanted to say...' she paused then swore. 'I don't know what I want to say. It's all jumbled up in my head.'

Anya touched her arm. 'You came. That's all that matters to me. Let's leave it open so that in time we might have a conversation.' She got back into the ambulance.

'I... I don't blame you,' Chas said. 'I just want you to know that.'

'Thank you,' Anya said, smiling. Then the ambulances pulled away and she was gone.

Chas wandered back to the bunker and found Si in the canteen. He was stuffing his face with toast and cereal.

'I was wondering when you'd surface,' he said. 'You must have slept well.'

She gave him a sarcastic smile and sat down, taking a slurp of his coffee. 'I hardly slept at all. I've been up since 5.30. Went outside and sat by the Angel.'

'Did it give you any inspiration?' Si asked, half in jest.

'I saw Anya leaving,' Chas said.

'Oh? And?'

Chas told him about their brief exchange.

'Well that's good,' he said.

She shrugged and changed the subject. 'What's happening today? Has anyone heard from Temp?'

'Mum's called a meeting in the Ops room at 08.00 hours. I'm sure she'll tell us of any updates.'

She stood up and yawned, looking at the clock. 'I'm going to get a coffee first. Do you want another?'

He nodded. 'Mmm. Thanks.'

At eight, they found Kate and a few other key people assembled in the Ops room.

'Thanks for being so prompt,' Kate said. 'I just want to make sure everyone is up to speed with what's going on. You're probably keeping up with the news on your Wearables. We have control of the Citadel. Temp and Capability are talking to various organisations within the Citadel, to determine what's to be done next. There's going to be a live broadcast from there, telling the people what's happening. We need to form a temporary government, to begin to put things right and establish law and order under a new regime. We'll be putting that in place as soon as possible, made up of people who've been instrumental in bringing about the revolution. As you can see from the news, this kind of disruption always provokes a certain level of opportunist crime. We have to stamp on that. But people need to know that we intend to introduce democracy back into the governance process. There'll be elections, once there's been a chance for things to calm down. I'm also arranging for the NMBs to be rolled out across the country to hospitals and plague camps. I think we need to leave the bunker behind and head to the Citadel so that people see we're not hiding.'

Someone raised their hand. 'Do you think the Citadel is the best place? After all, it has so many connotations of corruption from the old system.'

'It may not remain as the capital city,' Kate said, 'But let's use it for now. There are a lot of things to change and it can't all happen quickly. They have the infrastructure there to get us going. We need to start where the seat of power has been. If we show that we've taken the stronghold, people will hopefully be eager to support us.'

'What are we going to do with the Rulers and Zephyr?' asked Si.

'Another decision that we'll have to think carefully about,' Kate said. 'They'll each receive a fair trial. There will be no mass condemnation of anyone, without a proper hearing. We have to be different.'

'A lot of people want them dead,' Chas said.

'I know,' Kate agreed. 'But we must show that we're different. God teaches us to act justly, love mercy and walk humbly. That's our aim and that's something that hasn't been seen for a long time.'

'What about Excellence?' Si said. 'We know he helped in the end, but can you trust him?'

'Shouldn't he still be disciplined?' another person asked.

Nick nodded. 'He went to Capability, after the shooting and volunteered to do time in the Bastille for his crimes. Capability agreed that he should give himself up and await trial, so he was taken to the Bastille.'

'That's tough on Capability,' Si said.

'Yes,' Kate agreed. 'But Capability agreed that it was the right course of action, and he'll get a fair trial. His acts on behalf of the rebellion and capturing the Commander will be taken into account.'

'And what's going to happen to young Zeph and the children?' Chas asked.

Nick replied this time. 'We're going to talk with Zeph today and see how he feels about getting involved with the re-establishment of a democratic government. We need to do a lot of work with the people, for them to accept that he's not going to be the same as the old Premier. He looks so like him. It might be difficult.'

'But possible,' Si added.

'Definitely,' Nick said. 'And the children will be moved, as soon as possible, to more suitable accommodation, where we can protect them, until we're sure they'll be safe in the outside world. They may even need new identities.'

'How are you going to do that when they look exactly like the Rulers they're cloned from?' Chas said.

'Remember,' Kate said, 'The public have had very little exposure to what the Rulers look like. The only person they saw a lot of was Zephyr. That was deliberate.'

Chas shrugged. 'The Press are bound to post pictures of them when you give them their fair trial.'

'At this stage it's all conjecture,' Kate said. 'We have a lot to work out. But one thing's for sure, things are going to get better for the people from this moment on.' There were nods and enthusiastic affirmations from everyone in the gathering. It was exciting and daunting at the same time.

Over the next few days, they prepared to move to the Citadel, taking with them those who were injured, so that they could receive treatment in the hospital. Anya had been in touch with Kate, to let her know that the hospital was ready to receive them, due to the hard work of the staff.

'There's a different atmosphere since the Rulers went,' she told Kate. 'People are exhausted, yet more buoyant.'

Some of the others, who had been in the bunker, were going back to their own communities to help reshape things from within. Some pockets of rebellion had sprung up from businessmen and officials who had benefited from corrupt deals and bribes under the Rulers. Kate promised them, that if they cooperated with the new government, they would be treated fairly. Those who didn't want a fairer society would have to deal with the intervention of the law-keepers under new guidelines.

Ben and Honour were leaving for Seahouses. Chas and Si came to see them off.

'Keep in touch,' Ben said. 'Promise?'

They both smiled. 'Of course,' Si said. 'You're not getting rid of us that easily.'

Chas hugged him. 'You know you're my adopted little brother Ben, don't you?'

'That means you have to be part of our family then,' Honour said.

'I don't know about that,' Chas said, glancing at Sarah. She was never quite sure if Sarah liked her or not.

But Sarah smiled at her. 'You're always welcome at our house. Both of you.'

'Thank you,' Si said.

They hugged each other and then they were gone.

Zeph was no longer being held in a locked room. Having talked to him at length, Kate and Nick were satisfied that he was not a threat to anyone, but in fact a great asset. They were also sure that no one in the bunker intended him any harm, now that they had been given assurances about where his loyalties lay. Grace had been with him the whole time and Chas and Si could see quite a bond forming between them.

The four of them were going to travel back together, to the Citadel, with an armed guard, just in case of any attempt on Zeph's life.

Before they left, Kate held a ceremony, in the shadow

of the Angel, to give thanks for their newly forming, yet fragile freedom from tyranny. Lots of followers of The Way attended, along with many others. Zeph and Grace stood across the hill from Si and Chas. They were holding hands. Si nudged Chas to look across. She smiled and nodded in approval.

Kate began by thanking everyone for their dedication and courage. She led an act of remembrance for those who had given their lives for the freedom of others, promising to mark the day annually with two minutes silence. She mentioned some by name, including Mish.

Then, she led prayers of thanks and read a passage from the Psalms:

The Lord is my light and my salvation—
*   whom shall I fear?*
The Lord is the stronghold of my life—
*   of whom shall I be afraid?*
When the wicked advance against me
*   to devour me,*
it is my enemies and my foes
*   who will stumble and fall.*
Though an army besiege me,
*   my heart will not fear;*
though war break out against me,
*   even then I will be confident.*

The words flowed over Si. They were familiar to him, from time spent among the followers of The Way as a child, but now they felt meaningful. Through the whole struggle and culminating battle, he had felt the presence of God more and more strongly. He couldn't explain it or prove it, but he knew it like a child knows the love and security of a good parent.

He glanced at Chas. She was standing next to him, her eyes closed, as if trying to take it all in.

As people dispersed after the service, he took her hand. 'You okay?'

'Yeah, I'm fine.' They walked back to the bunker. 'That was nice. I mean, what your mum said and that reading from the Psalm. I don't really get the God thing entirely, but I can see that you all have something special.'

'You see it in me then?'

She stopped and turned to him as if he was being stupid. 'Yes of course, you idiot! It's been there from the start.'

He laughed. 'No, it hasn't. Definitely not all the time.'

She looked at him curiously and shook her head. 'Yes, it has, whatever 'it' is. Just because you couldn't see it, doesn't mean it wasn't there.'

They kept walking. Si shrugged. 'I've struggled with the idea of God. You know I have.'

'I do. But he, she, it... whatever God is... that presence was kind of unexplainably... hanging out with you.'

He raised his eyebrows. 'Fair enough. Hanging out with me... hmm. Maybe. I'm glad of it now, anyway.'

They went inside the bunker and gathered the few belongings they had. Zeph and Grace were meeting them at the entrance, in fifteen minutes. Kate and Nick were following on later.

'I want to go and see Mish,' Chas said, as they stood at the door.

'I'm sure we'll be able to,' Si said.

'I want to take him back to the commune, to his family and friends. That seems the most appropriate place for him to be buried or cremated or whatever.'

'We can do that,' Si said. 'I'll tell Mum and she'll organise it.'

'No. I want it to be just you and me who take him,' Chas said.

Si put his arm around her and pulled her towards him. 'Okay. We'll do it.'

Zeph and Grace came to join them. Grace was grinning from ear to ear, and her hand was firmly planted in Zeph's. Despite her melancholy thoughts about Mish, this made Chas smile.

'You two look happy,' Si said.

'We are,' Grace said, swinging Zeph's arm.

Zeph laughed. 'Speak for yourself!'

'Hey!' She shoved him playfully.

'Ow! Mind the other arm!'

Grace looked horrified. 'Oh, oh I'm sorry.' She began rubbing it.

'Joking!' Zeph said. 'Stop! That feels worse!'

'She'll be bossing you around Zeph, watch out,' Chas said. 'She was always bossing me around.'

'She already is,' he laughed. 'But I know it's for my own good.'

'Are you ready to face the Fortress again?' Si asked.

'Yes,' Zeph replied. 'It'll be strange, but I know we can rebuild what the Rulers destroyed. I just hope I can shake off the image of my predecessor; in more ways than one.'

Chas and Si were well aware of what he meant. Even though they knew him, it was hard not to see the previous Premier in his identical features.

'You'll do it,' Chas said, reassuringly.

Kate and Nick came to say goodbye, accompanied by two people, carrying guns, who were going to act as bodyguards. 'The car is waiting. We'll see you later.'

There were hugs all round. 'I love you, son,' Kate whispered as she hugged Si. 'I'm grateful to still have you with me.'

'I love you too, Mum,' he said. 'You've done amazing things. Wish dad was here to see it.'

She nodded and smiled sadly.

26

One Year later

The weather was perfect for a wedding. The sky was a clear, pure blue with only a few wispy clouds straggling overhead. The sun was warm, but not too hot. They were by the River Tyne. Along to their left was the striking steel arch of Tyne Bridge, spanning the river between its two towers. To their right was the 'winking eye' of the Millennium Bridge, opening like an eyelid between the two shores.

The ceremony had been held in the Baltic; an old flour mill that had been converted into a contemporary art museum at the beginning of the 21st century. It had recently reopened, and this was the first wedding that had been held there.

Guests spilled out onto the South Bank of the Tyne where a marquee had been erected in the Arts Quarter. It was the first time so many of them had been together in a relaxed setting, since the defeat of the Rulers and the storming of the Citadel.

Life had been tough and very busy since then and no one had had any time for leisure. Kate and Nick had been travelling around the country, setting up clinics and teaching doctors how to use the NMBs to cure the plague and numerous other illnesses.

Anya had taken over the management of the hospital in the Citadel and kept closely in touch with Kate. An overwhelming weight had been lifted off her shoulders since Ambition had been arrested. The fear of condemnation was gone. There had been no contact from Chas, even though she wasn't very far away. Anya hadn't given up hope, but at the same time had resigned herself to the fact that Chas had her own life and that it might never include her.

Si had barely seen his mother. He and Chas had travelled with Mish's body to Northumberland, where they had stayed with the commune for a week, before returning to help with all that was happening in the Citadel.

A new government had been formed, called The Stewards. Kate had made it clear to the people that they were there to look after the needs and welfare of the people and the land. Hence the title: Stewards. Capability, Peter, Si, Chas and Kate were part of the inner council, supported by many other people. It had taken some persuading to keep Chas in the Citadel. But with the promise that it would only be until a democratic election was held, she agreed. She found herself enjoying being part of the decision-making process.

Temp became the leader of the temporary government, with the title of Chief Steward, because Kate wanted to move back into a medical development role. And most surprisingly of all, the people had accepted Zeph as part of the new council.

Ben and Honour had been allowed to travel to the

Citadel, six months ago, to see Si and Chas and enjoy the sights of the city in a way they had not been able to before. These days, many tourists travelled to the Citadel, curious about what was there. Gradually, trust was being fostered between the people of the Citadel and the outside world.

It was a blessing to be here today, on the banks of the Tyne, relaxing in the sunshine as they waited for the bride and groom to leave the building.

'It's so exciting,' Grace said. 'I just love weddings!' She squeezed Zeph's hand.

'You love all things pretty and girlie,' he teased.

'And what's wrong with that?' she said, holding up her left hand, where a diamond engagement ring caught the light.

Ben was leaning over the railings alongside the river, feeling uncomfortable in his suit. 'Get down, you idiot!' Honour laughed. 'That shirt will be filthy. Wish I could join you, but wouldn't dare. Mum would kill me if I got this dress dirty.'

'When did you ever do what Mum told you?' Ben laughed.

She shrugged and climbed up beside him.

Temp, Peter, Anya and Capability were waiting by the entrance to the Baltic, with drinks in hand. 'I'm glad they finally got round to organising this,' Temp said.

'Hey, I had a lot to do with it,' Peter laughed.

'I gather you pulled a few strings to get this venue,' Capability said.

'Of course,' Peter smiled.

'She looks beautiful,' Anya said, sipping prosecco. 'So

happy.'

Temp took a sip of his beer. 'Well, they deserve happiness. They're well suited. I just hope they take a proper break after today.'

'Here they come!' someone shouted.

There was a wave of cheering, and confetti flew up into the air, like upwards falling snow, swirling around in the breeze.

Kate and Nick stepped out of the entrance, big grins on their faces. Si and Chas were behind them, having witnessed the signing of the register. The Press had been allowed to take some photographs, but now stepped into the background so that the official photographer, friends and family could take theirs. After many photos with the River Tyne and the bridges in the background, they made their way to the marquee and sat at the top table, with Si and Chas on one side and Nick's parents on the other side. Food was enjoyed, speeches were made and dancing was done. The party continued late into the night.

'I need some air,' Si said. 'It's so hot in here.'

Chas followed him out of the marquee. They leant over the railings and watched the black water, studded with reflected lights, rippling and dancing. The arc of the Millennium Bridge rippled with changing colours.

'Peaceful' Si said.

'Mmm,' Chas nodded, deep in thought.

Si put his arm around her and kissed the back of her neck. It didn't feel awkward anymore. They were comfortable to express how they felt about each other now.

'I want to leave the Citadel, Si,' she said.

He leant his cheek on the top of her head. 'I know.'

'Oh.'

'You've stuck it out for a whole year. I'm impressed. I didn't think you'd last a month, to be honest.'

'Cheers for the vote of confidence,' she said.

He grinned. 'What do you want to do?'

'Go back to the countryside. I want to build a village somewhere. Invite like-minded people to join us. Live simply. Could you be up for that?'

He moved away slightly so that he could look at her. 'Where you go is where I want to be.'

She pulled a face. 'Don't go all soppy on me just because your mum got married today.'

'It's not soppy. You need me to protect you from strange idiots who might come wandering in the woods late at night.'

She laughed. 'Hmm, true. Okay. You're in.'

They looked out over the river for a while.

'I had this recurring dream,' she said. 'When I was...' she looked down at her flat stomach. 'When I was pregnant. I was running, but not running from anyone or anything. It was more a feeling of running towards something. There was a wooded path, meandering through silver birches. It was a bit overgrown with nettles and ferns. Sometimes I could feel the ferns brushing against my legs in the dream. And I swear I could smell damp earth, like when it's just rained.'

Si was listening intently. 'Sounds lovely.'

She chewed her bottom lip. 'Yeah. I think that when I find that path, I'll know that's where we should set up the village.'

He raised his eyebrows. 'Sounds visionary. Maybe prophetic.'

'Not sure about that,' she said, 'But... who knows.'

'Do you want to take anyone with us at the start?'

She shook her head. 'No. I think just you and me at first. See if we can build a home, make it work. Then maybe invite some people...'

'Anyone in mind?

She nodded. 'I'd like to ask if Ambi would be allowed to come. If he wants to. He's my brother, isn't he? He's my true family.'

'He might be a bit lonely without other children,' Si said.

She narrowed her eyes, giving him an odd, enquiring look.

'No!' he said quickly. 'I didn't mean that. Not yet anyway. I meant we could invite other people with children.'

She agreed. 'And maybe some of the clone children.'

So far, they had been housed back in the Complex, but without the boundaries and restrictions that were in place before.

'We can ask,' Si said. 'Come on, we should get back. I can hear that song you like. You definitely should dance to that.'

He took her hand to lead her back to the marquee.

'Si,' she said, pulling back a little. 'I've also decided something else.'

'What?'

She hesitated, looking out over the river, and Si wondered

if the water was whispering to her.

'I want to get to know my mother. I've decided to talk to Anya.'

He smiled. 'I'm really glad.' He tightened his grip on her hand. 'Come on. I need to see you do some crazy dancing.'

'Well, if I'm doing it, you're doing it with me.' She laughed, pulling him forward.

But this time, he held her back and kissed her. 'I'm doing it all with you, from now on, Chas. Together. United. Agreed?'

She smiled. 'One hundred percent!' Then she pushed him playfully away. 'Race you back!'

Also by Karen Langtree:

Breaking Silence
Breaking Lies

Knights of the Wobbly Table
My Wicked Stepmother
Fairy Rescuers
Return to Elysia
Angel Small
Angel Small Follows the Star

Musicals by Karen Langtree:

Angel Small
The Rainboat
Go Grace Darling
School for Angels

For more information go to:

www.monkeyislandpublishing.com

About Karen...

Karen Langtree is the author of ten books for children, teenagers and adults, as well as four musicals for schools. She used to be a primary school teacher and still teaches piano and singing. Her two creative passions are words and music. She lives near York with her husband, who is her greatest supporter and works tirelessly to promote Monkey Island Publishing.

In her spare time (which is scarce) she loves walking in the spectacular landscapes of Yorkshire and Northumberland, running, reading and being with family.

If you have enjoyed this trilogy and want to buy more books by Karen, visit our website shop where there is *free postage* within mainland UK. Karen loves to hear from readers and always replies to emails. Find us at:

www.monkeyislandpublishing.com

Please review this trilogy on social media, book review websites and Amazon. In this way you will help to spread the word so that others can enjoy the books too. You can also visit the Breaking Silence Facebook page and leave a message. In doing so, you will encourage this author to keep on writing!

Thank you.

Big Thanks...

My thanks go to a huge team of people who have encouraged me to persevere to the end of this trilogy for the last few years, and helped me to make it the best it could be. Without them there would be more typos, fewer commas, and more 'bloopers' for you to laugh at.

So, here goes:

Gill McLean: thank you for the fantastic book covers and interior layouts. You always give me a superb look.

The editorial team: Hayleigh McLean, Ian Smith, Olive Overton and Karen Bruin. Thank you for eagle eyes, perfect pickiness and great comments to help me shape and refine these novels. My favourite blooper was the 'blood-steaked face'!

Antony Stones: ex-paramedic, spoken-word poet and Advanced Clinical Practitioner, thank you for medical input and a great rewrite of the death scene. Together we made everyone cry!

Jane Hibbert: ex-nurse and midwife, thank you for reading through the pregnancy and miscarriage scenes, for authenticity.

Lizzie Linklater: thank you for being my tutor on the YA fiction writing module at York University, all those years ago. Your comments on my assignment, which included the first chapters of Breaking Silence, encouraged me to finish the book. And look where it led!

Family: thank you for not minding too much that I'm always sitting in the corner typing, instead of cleaning, cooking or doing other boring things. Thanks for doing some of those.

And finally... to my readers. Thank you for reading these books and emailing to encourage me to keep going. You inspire me, and without you I may have given up long ago. Please keep spreading the word and writing online reviews of my books. It really helps me to reach more people.

Karen